Ignazio Silone was born Secondo Tranquilli on May 1, 1900, at Pescina, a small town in the primitive mountain region of central Italy. He adopted the pseudonym when his political activities brought the threat of government reprisal on his family. Silone early turned from his Jesuit schooling to active participation in attempts to alleviate the suffering of the local peasantry, a path that led him to clandestine resistance after the Fascist takeover of Italy and finally into exile in Switzerland in 1930. In 1931 he severed his connection with the Communist Party, for reasons later set down in an essay published in *The God That Failed,* but he never ceased his struggle against the forces of oppression, writing in exile the books that made his name famous and brought to world attention the plight of his native land. *Fontamara* appeared in English in 1934, to be followed by *Bread and Wine* (1936), *The School for Dictators* (1938), and *The Seed Beneath the Snow* (1942). After the liberation, he returned to Italy, where he became a member of the Italian National Assembly. In recent years, Ignazio Silone has returned to literature with *A Handful of Blackberries* (1953) and *The Fox and the Camellias* (1961). A new version of *Fontamara* and this, the new version of *Bread and Wine,* were revised and freshly translated to conform more closely with the author's matured sense of both life and art. At present, Mr. Silone resides in Rome.

*Ignazio Silone*

# BREAD
## and WINE
(1936)

A new version,
translated from the Italian
by HARVEY FERGUSSON II

With an Afterword
by MARC SLONIM

A SIGNET CLASSIC

Published by THE NEW AMERICAN LIBRARY,
New York and Toronto

# A Note on the Revision of Bread and Wine

It is not exceptional for a writer to observe a stranger intent on the reading of one of his books. But a case of this kind that happened to me many years ago made an impression which I still remember, perhaps because of a combination of circumstances of which I was not then aware.

I was in an empty compartment on a train between Zurich and Lugano. An elderly, modestly dressed woman got on at an intermediate station, and after having greeted me with a brief nod of her head, took a seat in front of me, next to a window. As soon as she had sat down, she took a book out of her traveling bag and opened it at a page marked with a narrow little ribbon. For my part, I still had some newspapers and magazines to read and I at first paid her no attention. But after a while my eye was caught by the colored cover of the book the woman was reading, and I realized that it was the German edition of a novel of mine which had come out a couple of years before, *Bread and Wine*. At that point, I put aside my newspapers and magazines and began to observe the woman seated in front of me.

She was dressed with great simplicity and she wore her hair in the same way. She had no personal ornamentation of any kind, as is still the custom in the country there, especially in the Protestant cantons. In spite of her age, her cheeks were still rosy and her features had remained regular and sharp. Her facial expression was open, cordial and pleasant. She had certainly been beautiful in her youth, and I imagined that she might be a retired schoolteacher or a doctor's wife. Very probably she was a strong and well-balanced woman, but not untouched by sorrow.

On the pretext of putting a couple of magazines on the luggage rack, I got up to see what point in the novel she had come to. It was a chapter I remembered well because it had cost me no little trouble. From that moment, though pretending to continue my reading of a newspaper, I set myself to follow in my mind this unknown woman's reading, page by page, and, I might almost say, line by line. Her face was impassive. Only once or twice did I see her close her eyes for an instant, to take up her reading again thereafter. I had a curious feeling. I was faced with an unknown person to whom I was secretly telling a long story. Fortunately that edition of my novel did not have a photograph of the author; if she had recognized me I would certainly have been very embarrassed. In fact, an unusual discomfort was forcing itself into my mind. The page that the woman was reading did not satisfy me at all. On the contrary, at that moment it even seemed stupid to me. Why had I written it? If I could have foreseen that people like this would read my book, I thought to myself, I certainly would have omitted that page. I would have left others out too; and I would have thought more about certain expressions. I asked myself why most writers, in writing a book, think more often of their colleagues and the critics, who read a hundred books a year, and not of the strangers to whom the book can have some personal importance.

Never before, perhaps, had I felt the privilege and responsibility of the writer's trade in so precise and direct a fashion. I remembered the state of anguish that a letter from an Italian worker had caused me a year before. This letter had been written in the name of a group of his companions, who, like him, had emigrated to Switzerland. They had been arguing about a certain phrase in my book, and not agreeing on its meaning, they had decided to turn to the author. But I had written that phrase in a state of complete distraction. . . .

The woman got off the train before I did, and for the rest of the trip I continued to reflect on the great dignity and power of literature and on the unworthiness of most writers, myself included. In any event, my intention to re-read *Bread and Wine* with a critical eye dates from that meeting.

I had written it out of the fullness of my heart just after the Fascist occupation of Ethiopia and during the Purge

Trials in Moscow, which had been set up by Stalin to destroy the last remnants of the opposition. It was hard to imagine a sorrier state of affairs. The inhuman behavior of General Graziani to Ethiopian combatants and civilians, the enthusiasm of many Italians for the conquest of the Empire, the passivity of most of the population, and the impotence of the anti-Fascists all filled the soul with a deep sense of shame. To this was added my horror and disgust at having served a revolutionary ideal in my youth that, in its Stalinist form, was turning out to be nothing but "red Fascism," as I defined it at the time. But my state of mind was more prone to exaggeration, sarcasm and melodrama than to calm narration. I must add that the exceptional, and for me entirely unforeseen, success of the book deluded me only a little, since I knew that sometimes a writer's defects, more than his merits, contribute to his success. But had I the right to return to it and correct it? Although examples in my favor were not lacking, even illustrious ones, I was inclined to think that a book, once published, no longer belongs to the author, but to the public.

However, the problem rose again later in another light, when, after the fall of Fascism, my books could be printed for the first time in Italy. How could I fail to make the most of this reversal of a situation which for so long had been prejudicial and painful to me? It was therefore with a good conscience that I took advantage of this circumstance to modify the books I had published while in exile: *Fontamara, Bread and Wine* and *The Seed Beneath the Snow.*

As the critics have been able to establish, the structure of these books and the idea behind them have remained unchanged; and the roles of the characters as well as the style are largely the same. But secondary elements and affairs of only contemporary concern have been removed and their fundamental theme has been given more attention. No vanity could keep me from admitting that I lived through an experience which confirms the similarity between the art of writing and that of swimming, in the sense that writing, too, is learned and perfected only through practice. On this matter, I have already had occasion to confess that if it were for me alone to decide,

I would willingly pass my life writing and rewriting the same book—that one book that every writer carries within him, the image of his own soul, and of which his published works are only more or less approximate fragments.

Now I must explain what I seem to have learned: primarily that the writer moved by a strong sense of social responsibility is exposed more than anyone else to the temptation to exaggeration, the theatrical, the romantic and the purely external description of things, while the events in the inner life of the characters are what count in literary works. Even the countryside and the other objects among which the character moves deserve to be mentioned only inasmuch as they are a part of his spiritual life. And since the pathetic cannot be expelled from human life, it seems to me that, to make it bearable, it is useful to accompany it with a bit of irony.

With the passage of years, I have developed a repugnance for every form of propaganda. After all this talk about the artist's "commitment" what remains? The only "commitment" worthy of respect is that which corresponds with a personal vocation. Furthermore, one cannot sacrifice art's integrity to an effect without sacrificing the effect as well. As for style, I think the supreme wisdom in storytelling is to try to be simple.

If I have not made the least concession to the new literary fashions that grew up in the interval, and which are already on their way out, I did not do so just to be different. I consider it foolish to measure a writer's modernity by the technical tricks he uses. To think one can renew literature with formal devices is an ancient illusion of the phrasemakers. I regard with even greater repugnance the current fashion for erotic descriptions, to which even talented writers dedicate themselves, together with many tradesmen who pander to the public's bad taste. In my view, there is nothing more false than to justify the literary commercialization of eroticism in the name of liberty, though I am persuaded that it cannot be fought effectively by censorship or other bureaucratic means.

Having said all this, I do not think it is still necessary to justify the fact that the revised texts are issued in countries where the pre-war editions also had a wide sale.

It is enough to consider that in the meantime many years have passed and there is a new generation of readers. What is most important, then, is the validity of the texts; but the last judgment on them belongs to the readers themselves. However, the inversion of the title in the new Italian edition of *Bread and Wine*—from *Pane e Vino* to *Vino e Pane*—serves the purpose of distinguishing the two, and also of indicating a greater difference between them. I have the impression that in the new version wine plays a larger role than bread.

*Ignazio Silone*

Rome, 1962

# 1

Seated on the garden's low wall in the shade of the cypress tree, old Don Benedetto was reading his breviary. On this wall, which served as his bench, the black of his priestly garments absorbed the shade of the tree and extended it. Behind him, his sister Martha was weaving at a loom set up between a box hedge and a bed of rosemary. The shuttle jumped back and forth in the warp of black and red wool, from left to right and from right to left, accompanied by the rhythm of the treadle raising the warp cords and of the lamb pushing back the woof.

At a certain moment the priest's sister interrupted her work to observe with ill-concealed anxiety a vehicle which had stopped at the foot of the hill. Disappointed, she went back to her weaving. It was a farmer's cart, drawn by oxen.

"Just wait. They'll be here any minute," she said to her brother.

He shrugged his shoulders, pretending unconcern.

On the right were the railway and the Via Valeria which ran through fields of wheat, potatoes, beets, beans, and corn to Avezzano, climbed to Colli di Monte Bove, descended to Tivoli, and finally, just as every river widens its mouth at the sea, led to Rome. To the left, among vineyards, the peas and the onions, was the provincial road which clambered steeply up the mountains and penetrated into the heart of the Abruzzi, into the region of the beech and holly trees and the few remaining gardens and from there led to Pescasseroli, Opi and Castel di Sangro.

The priest's sister pushed the shuttle to the right and to the left, without losing sight of the road in the valley. But she saw only the people and the things which came by there every day, not what she was waiting for.

Along the little provincial road, which was as stony
and as hard to travel as the bed of a dried-up stream,
there came a young farm girl mounted on a small donkey,
with a child in her arms. In a tiny field behind the cemetery, an old bare-headed peasant was tracing brown
lines with a wooden plow behind two oxen. Life as seen
from the priest's garden resembled a monotonous old
pantomime.

Don Benedetto had turned seventy-five that day. It
was a warm afternoon late in April, the first real spring
day after a very hard winter. Seated on the garden wall,
he too raised his eyes from his breviary every once in
a while to look down into the valley. He was expecting
a group of his former students. One by one, the young
men were supposed to come, from the right and the left,
from the city and from the mountain villages, from
wherever life had scattered them after they left school.
But would they come?

Below Don Benedetto's garden, at that time of day,
the few houses in Rocca dei Marsi seemed deserted. In
the midst of these poor houses, huddling against one
another, was a narrow square, paved with pebbles and
grass. In the back of this square could be seen the low
porch of an ancient church, topped with a great stucco
filigree rose. The houses, the streets, the square, all seemed
abandoned. A beggar in rags crossed the square and went
on his way without stopping. A young girl appeared on
the threshold of one of the houses and stopped to stare.
Then she hid behind a hedge among some clumps of
bushes and continued to stare.

"Maybe you should have bought some beer," said the
sister. "And you could at least have shaved. Today's your
birthday!"

"My birthday? What a frightful time for birthdays!
As for the boys, fig juice will do for them; that is, if they
come," said Don Benedetto.

Fig juice came from the city, in bottles, while straw-
berries, mushrooms and eggs were brought from the
mountains by Matalena Ricotta.

Don Benedetto put his breviary down on the wall and
began to watch his sister weave. What a disappointment
for Martha if the young men did not come. She had sent

out the invitations in secret, but that morning she had
had to tell her brother everything to make sure that he
would stay home all afternoon. But suppose they did not
come? Each tried to avoid the other's glance, hoping
to hide his anxiety.

"Did you know that Sciancalla has gone back to bar-
tering?" said Martha. "Now he'll take nothing but onions
and beans for coal."

"For some time I've been having an upset stomach
after dinner," said Don Benedetto, "and bicarbonate
costs three times as much as it used to."

Bicarbonate came from the city, like insecticides and
safety-razor blades.

"But what safety? If you shave with those blades, you
scratch yourself worse than with those old strop razors,"
said his sister.

"Safety is always relative," said Don Benedetto. "The
so-called Office of Public Safety would do better to call
itself the Office of Public Peril. Now that I think of it,
my former pupils will prefer wine. After all, they are no
longer children."

In fact, the young men for whom Don Benedetto was
waiting had left the *liceo* just after World War I and
were now a little over thirty years old.

Martha got up from her loom and took from the kitchen
the refreshments for the young men they were awaiting
and placed them on the granite table in the garden, between the tomatoes and the sage. Perhaps this was a
propitiary rite to make the young men hurry.

"Nunzio at least will come," she said. "At least he
won't fail to come."

"He is a doctor," said Don Benedetto, "and he has
many things to attend to."

Martha went back to her loom and sent the shuttle
with the spool of red wool among the threads of the warp.

"Did you know that we have a new commissioner in
town?" she said. "Naturally he's another stranger. It seems
they're planning other changes because of that new war
coming in Africa."

"War time is promotion time," said Don Benedetto.

The transfers, promotions, and changes always came
from the city. The commissioners, inspectors, bishops,

prison directors, speakers for government agencies and preachers for spiritual exercises had all been sent from the city, with the latest up-to-date directives. The newspapers, such songs as "Tripoli, Fair Land of Love," "Valencia," "Giovinezza" and "Dark Little Face," the gramophones, radios, novels, and picture postcards also all came from the city. From the mountains there came the poor friar Gioacchino, a Capuchin, with a knapsack for the alms, every Tuesday; and Sciatàp came for the market. Every Saturday Magascià came for salt and tobacco. Sometimes Cassarola, the wise woman, came by with her herbs, and the skins of badgers and snakes, which were supposed to ward off the evil eye. Late in November, the bagpipers came by to celebrate the Advent: *O suffering and afflicted ones, lift up your hearts unto hope. A savior will be born.*

"Did you hear that Clarice is engaged to a mechanic in the sugar works?" said Martha. "Marrying in wartime is like sowing among thorns."

A knot formed in the warp cord and Martha had to get up to undo it.

"Some women are lucky enough to be born with a talent for playing the war widows," said Don Benedetto. "Poets are made, but war widows—and bishops—are born. I don't mean Clarice specifically. She seems a bit innocent to me."

"Clarice has a good dowry, a dowry in hemp land," said Martha.

"Does the mechanic want to leave the factory to cultivate hemp?"

"On the contrary," said Martha, "Clarice wants to sell the land. Hemp isn't doing well any more."

Hemp used to do well, but no one bought it now. It was too expensive. And besides, it was rough and primitive.

"Hand-woven wool isn't doing well either," said Don Benedetto. "Nor are we."

"Hand-made shoes and solid wood furniture aren't doing well either. The tradesmen are closing up their shops one after another."

"We aren't doing well either," said Don Benedetto. Factory-made things were more elegant and cost less.

Anyone who could, closed his shop and went to the city; the old stayed in the country and waited for death.

Martha had to get up to turn the warp beam at the rear of the loom. ("Rough and primitive" was just what Monsignor had said: "Your brother, dear lady, is too rough and primitive to be a teacher in a *liceo* where the richest—that is, the best—families of the diocese send their sons.") One had to admit that Monsignor was neither rough nor primitive. Knowing that Don Benedetto was timid and resigned in all things concerning his career, he had fired him on the pretext of ill health.

From that time on, Don Benedetto had lived with his sister in retirement, in his house above Rocca dei Marsi, among his old books and his garden. Since he was a quiet and taciturn man by nature, it did not take much to give him a reputation as an eccentric, a misanthrope, and something of an idiot. But those few people in whom he sometimes confided knew that beneath his peasantlike timidity was concealed an independence and vitality of spirit which was audacious for one in his position. In short, it was somewhat compromising to be his friend.

Just think of his brothers, cousins and all his other relatives. Was it worth all those sacrifices to support him in the seminary if he was going to end up like this? They actually hated him for not having had the influence with the authorities they could have expected from a priest if he had not been forced to live like a hermit—at a time when honest hard work was worth nothing without it. The last meeting he had had with his relatives, in the notary's office at Fossa, had ended in a very painful scene for this reason.

At one point, an old aunt of his had yelled at him, "You're a disgrace! Why do you suppose we sacrificed so much to have a priest in the family?"

"Surely," said Don Benedetto, "you did it to bring God's favor on you."

He should never have said it. In the eyes of these good Christians his innocent answer sounded like irony, and only the intervention of the notary saved the old priest from their legitimate wrath. After that they never saw him again. Deprived in this fashion of all companionship but his sister's, Don Benedetto turned his affections to some young men who had been his pupils, attempting to follow the contradictory events of their careers. He had nothing else in the world.

Some of them, those who lived nearest and who liked him most, had been invited by Martha to come to Rocca dei Marsi to their old teacher's hermitage to help celebrate his seventy-fifth birthday. Martha had begged them to bring others whom she could not find, and she was very much afraid that the refreshments might not be enough and that the dozen unmatched glasses, lined up on the granite table, might be too few. But she was more afraid of the opposite possibility—that no one at all would come. Martha continued to weave, and between one trip of the shuttle and another she examined the valley road and all the routes by which the guests might come.

"At least Nunzio should come," said Martha.

"But if the boys are late, it's because the trains and the buses don't arrive on time," said Don Benedetto. "Since strangers don't come here, what good is a time schedule?"

From Rocca dei Marsi, one descended gradually to the vast hollow which used to be the lake of Fucino but which had now been drained and taken over by a prince. Around the hollow, an immense green chessboard of fresh grain, furrowed with long rows of poplars and ranks of canals, rose a great circular crown of diminishing hills, and on almost every hill was a small village that looked like a crèche, a little smoke-blackened town with towers, some clustered together like grapes and others in the form of a very high wall; some of the houses were hollowed out of the slopes like caves. They were villages with ancient names and old histories, but a good part of them had been destroyed and badly reconstructed after the last earthquake. Behind the crown of hills rose the mountains, furrowed by the floods and torrents and still covered with snow at that time of year.

Martha stopped weaving and went into the house.

"Where are you going?" said Don Benedetto.

"I have something to do," she answered.

She went up to the second floor and sat next to the window facing the valley. The confused noise which rose up from there at dusk only strengthened her feeling of isolation from the village. Some women in black appeared in the dark doors of the houses. They were dirty women, old before their time. Other women carrying copper pots on their heads and with handkerchiefs fastened under their chins slowly returned from the fountain. A peasant woman in black crossed the square and entered the church, almost dragging a little girl dressed in yellow. An old peasant seated on a donkey passed by, kicking the beast in the flanks. But soon the little streets were empty once more and Rocca dei Marsi again seemed deserted.

"They're coming!" cried Martha from the window. "Nunzio's coming."

Don Benedetto got up quickly, attracted by the loud cries that were coming from the road. But it was hard to know what all the fuss was about. All he saw at first was a long cloud of dust which overflowed from the road onto the vineyards and nearby gardens. Within the cloud a dirty-yellow river of sheep was coming slowly forward, and behind that, Don Benedetto caught sight of a donkey carrying a shepherd's utensils: the straw canopy, a sack of cooking pots, pails for milk, and cheese molds. The shepherd marched behind the donkey, surrounded by great white dogs. A small open convertible brought up the rear with two young men inside yelling at the shepherd: "Make room! Make room to the left!" but with no apparent result. The shepherd made no reply. He was gesturing, perhaps to indicate that he couldn't hear, that he was deaf and dumb, and that they should leave him alone. But since even a deaf-mute should be able to understand that a car can't go along forever behind a herd of sheep, the young men were yelling louder and louder at the shepherd. The whole thing would have come to blows if the shepherd had not had three fierce dogs with nail-studded iron collars by his side. One of the young men, in the uniform of a militia officer, standing up by the driver's seat, couldn't stop threatening the deaf-mute and telling him with yells and gestures to let the car pass by moving the herd to the right.

The shepherd, in the company of his dogs, remained unperturbed and indicated with gestures that he didn't understand. This had been going on for a good stretch of the road when Don Benedetto came up to the herd and crossed the cloud of dust, cordially greeting the shepherd and at the same time his two former pupils, whom he recognized in the car.

"Welcome, welcome!" said the old priest. Turning to the shepherd, he added cordially, "They're some friends of mine, coming to visit me."

All of a sudden the shepherd recovered the power of speech and peevishly cried to the men in the car, "Why didn't you tell me you were coming to see Don Benedetto?" Then he gave an order to the dogs, and in the twinkling of an eye the herd lengthened out on the right bank of the road, leaving plenty of room for the car.

The two men in the car could not recover from their surprise at the false deaf-mute.

"What's that rascal's name?" asked the officer of Don Benedetto. "I'll fix him! I'll fix him for the rest of his life!"

Meanwhile Martha, too, had come up.

"This man in the uniform," said Don Benedetto to his sister, "this man is not a coal seller but just Concettino Ragù. This other man, as you know, is a real doctor, Doctor Nunzio Sacca; two fine fellows."

"What's that rascal's name?" said Concettino, turning to Don Benedetto and his sister.

"I've reached the age of seventy-five without ever having been a spy," laughed the priest; "it would be too late to start now." He took his two former pupils by the arm and led them to the garden.

But the shepherd seemed to think he was right, since he continued to shout from the middle of the road, "Why didn't you tell me you were coming to see Don Benedetto?"

"Please be seated," said Martha to distract them from the shepherd. "The others won't be long in coming."

Concettino still couldn't get over the insult. He was so suprised that he could not even get angry.

"What's his name?" he kept asking.

"Forgive him," said Martha. "He's not a bad man. He's a poor man with many children. As a matter of fact, he's one of the most honest shepherds around here."

"My dear boy," said Don Benedetto, who had probably

wanted to avoid this explanation, "there is no reason for me, who abstains from politics, to explain to you what your uniform means to these poor people. The day when the tongues of the false deaf-mutes are loosened will be an atrocious one, from which I would have you spared."

Concettino looked at Nunzio as if to say, was it worth it, coming up here? We're right back at it again.

Nunzio tried to change the subject.

# 2

"We have come to your hermitage, sir," said Nunzio, "so that you would not feel entirely alone, that the men whom you have educated . . ."

" 'I owe this leisure to God,' " quoted Don Benedetto, smiling. From his voice one could feel his intention of observing the amenities. "Sit down now and be at ease," he added. "Not on the ground there, that clump is not grass, but thyme; and this is basil, *acimum suave*; over there is parsley, *apium petroseleum*, as you no doubt know; and along the side we have mint. These are all ancient and honorable things. Be seated here."

The three men sat on a wooden bench, at the foot of a graceful and silvery olive tree. The old man sat between them and Martha asked permission to resume her weaving.

"I have just a few minutes' more weaving to do," she said. "In the meantime perhaps more of the boys will come."

For a little while nothing was heard in the peaceful garden but the rhythm of Martha's loom; the rhythm of the treadle, the shuttle and the card. The air was wrapped in a tender green light; the trees were surrounded by a golden dust; and the subtle odors from the aromatic herbs seemed to come from the light.

"How peaceful it is," said Nunzio.

The old man asked, "Tell me the news, please. Here I never see anyone. What happened to Luigi Candeloro? I haven't heard anything about him."

"He died of typhus in Libya two years ago," said Nunzio. "Didn't you know? After he got his engineering degree, he was unemployed for three years. He accepted a job in Libya, with the Civil Service, as he would have accepted a job anywhere, even in hell, as he told me,

20

just so he could exist. He died two weeks before sailing back home, to marry a cousin of mine."

The old man sadly shook his head and was silent. After a while he said, "What is Battista Lo Patto doing? Does he still paint?"

"He plays cards," said Concettino. "At scientific scopone he is unbeatable."

"Does he ever do anything else?" asked the old man.

"On Sundays."

"Does he work on Sundays?"

"On Sundays he shoots pool."

"And Antonio Speranza? How is his shop going?"

"For ten years," said Nunzio, "he has fought against bills and complaints about rotten sardines, rancid oil, moldy pasta and unlicensed scales. Finally, to make his fortune, he contracted some important debts and declared himself bankrupt. He can't go out at night because his creditors would jump at the chance of beating him up. But he's even more afraid of the police."

"And poor Carlo Caione? Is he still ill?"

"He died of tuberculosis, leaving a wife and two children," said Nunzio.

"Does the wife have some means of her own?"

"No, but she's pretty," said Concettino.

The old man stopped talking, tired and depressed already. Martha's loom stopped also. The first shadows of dusk gathered around Fucino. Don Benedetto said, almost in a whisper, "Please excuse these questions. I assure you that it is not curiosity. I am very much alone and I think of you often. I never see anyone here." Then he added, "Where is Di Pretoro? Does he still work for the railroad?"

"They fired him a long time ago," said Concettino. "I don't deny that Di Pretoro was best in Latin; but I always thought he was a confused, half-baked Socialist. Just imagine, to be a good socialist you have to be a millionaire. In his home town, he had a casual affair with a poor seamstress, who had nothing of her own but her sewing machine. I'm not condemning him for that. How does it go, '. . . cast the first stone,' and so forth. But the seamstress knew the sort of man she was dealing

with and very intelligently got herself pregnant straight
off. Like a fool, he married her. Punctually every year
the seamstress has presented him with another child.
Four years of marriage; five children, including the poor
kid in advance. In the meantime he's been fired from
the railways for his unpatriotic ideas. In fact, the imbecile
has allowed himself that luxury. Now it's obvious that
anyone who's been fired from the national railways can't
get a job anywhere else in the government. But since
even private companies have to hire people from the
government employment office, and they have to disregard
anyone who's politically suspect, there's no doubt at all
about that idiot's future. On the other hand he's too proud
to do any manual work. What's the use of studying for
ten years if you're going to end up a carpenter? For her
part, the wife is always either pregnant or nursing her
latest, so she can't practice her trade. Di Pretoro can
find nothing better to do than to go to a bar and drink—
on credit. And when he comes home drunk he beats up
his wife and kids until the neighbors come to make peace.
You know what they're saying? They're saying, 'That's
how students in priests' schools end up!' "

Don Benedetto looked at first one and then the other
of his young guests, obviously struck by the near-indif-
ference with which they related such painful events.

"Couldn't you help him?" he said, turning to them
both.

"I saved him from prison," said Concettino. "But maybe I did wrong. At Ponza, or somewhere else, they would
at least have supported him. And the wife could marry
again."

Don Benedetto got up with difficulty. His lean, pale
face showed great exhaustion. He took a few steps in
the garden and went into the house without saying a word.

Meanwhile Martha had finished weaving. But she
stayed where she was, bent over the loom as if her back
hurt her. After a while she said to the two young men,
pointing to the work on the roller, "This rug is my birthday present to Don Benedetto."

She always said "Don Benedetto" respectfully and
distantly.

"Dear lady," said Nunzio, "every day you give Don

Benedetto a far greater gift. You have given him your life."

Martha blushed to the roots of her hair and shook her head energetically.

"On the contrary," she said. "Where would I be without him?"

She was taller, a bit more delicate, and somewhat more bent than her brother. She even looked older than he, although she was ten years younger. Her forehead, eyes and mouth still bore traces of bygone beauty. Martha got up from her loom and went to sit on the bench, between the two guests.

"Don't think we're unhappy because we're alone," she said in a low voice so her brother couldn't hear her. "It's the hostility and suspicion around us that make life bitter."

"You know well enough that this is, unfortunately, all Don Benedetto's doing," said Concettino. "Is there any hope that he will recognize his mistakes?"

"I really don't know," said Martha. "Don Benedetto does not confide his disappointments to me. What little I hear comes from other people. But what have we done to deserve all this?"

"The past is past," said Nunzio. Turning to Concettino he added, "Can't anything be done about it?"

"It's up to him, to his own good will," said Concettino.

"Talk to him," implored Martha.

Don Benedetto reappeared on the threshold of the door, carrying a bundle of yellowed papers in his hand.

"Did you get my proposal to bless the flag?" asked Concettino. "It would be a fitting occasion to remedy past misunderstandings."

"Yes," said Don Benedetto. "I received it."

"Will you bless the flag?"

"Of course not."

"Why? Why do you want to ruin yourself? Why don't you take advantage of the occasion to redeem yourself?"

"Redeem myself?" said Don Benedetto, surprised. "Why do you talk to me as if I were a common criminal?"

Concettino muttered something under his breath which no one understood.

"You must understand," said Don Benedetto. "I am

a poor old priest full of fears and faults. But I am still an old-fashioned Christian and I cannot act against my conscience. Believe me."

"Is the blessing of the national flag, the flag of the governing party, a sin against your conscience?"

"Yes, one of the worst. It is idolatry."

"But other men . . ." Concettino began to say.

"I already know what you want to say," said Don Benedetto. "But idolatry is a sin against the spirit, who- ever commits it."

"Excuse me," said Martha with her eyes full of tears, "I just don't understand you. Is this a friendly meeting? Is this how you celebrate Don Benedetto's birthday?"

The clear eyes moist with tears gave the old woman's face a piteous expression. Her heartbroken voice touched everyone just a little.

"Signorina Martha is right," said Nunzio, who was the most embarrassed. "We haven't come to argue, but to record our affection for our former teacher."

"Whatever I have said has been said in the name of friendship," said Concettino in an apologetic tone.

"I do not doubt it," said Don Benedetto, smiling and clapping him on the shoulder. "Why do we have to argue? You know, I think of you often. It is not difficult. I have no one else."

"What are those old papers?" said Nunzio, hoping to calm the situation with friendly memories.

Don Benedetto was still carrying in his hands the bun- dle of yellow papers he had taken from his study shortly before.

"They concern you," he said. "This morning I came across an old photograph we had made, fifteen years ago, when we separated. Do you remember? I even found the last Italian compositions I assigned you: 'Say sincerely what you would like to become and what you would like to do with your life.' I reread your papers, and Caione's, Di Pretoro's, Candeloro's, Lo Patto's and others whose fortunes—and misfortunes—you have just been telling me about. Now I must confess in all humility that I am beginning to feel that I do not understand anything. I have even begun to doubt that it is worth the trouble to seek an explanation. The truth, perhaps, is sad, as a Frenchman of the last century remarked. Like you, he was educated in religious schools."

Don Benedetto's voice had become lower and more serious. He hesitated a great deal in speaking, as if listening to something, as if he had some internal censor, or as if he were a blind man among unknown objects and were afraid of hurting, not himself, but the objects. Don Benedetto unfolded some of the yellowed papers he had in his hand.

"With compositions like these," he said, "after so many years, one must, of course, make many allowances. They are full of literary ornamentation imitated from Carducci, Pascoli and d'Annunzio. There is also the peculiar ingenuous quality of pupils in a priests' school, and the illusions common to the period when they were written. There are the echoes of the great armistice which had just been concluded. But beneath all that, beneath the literary frills and the plagiarisms, I thought there would be something essential in some of them, something personal which coincided with the observations which I had been able to make on each one of you during the years of gymnasium and *liceo*, something more than mere banalities. Whatever it is, this something had not developed later when you entered society. I refer to the news you have just given me about some of your schoolmates. But— excuse me, I do not wish to offend you—I am thinking of you two as well. If I am not mistaken, you are both about thirty-two or -three years old, and you already seem like bored and worn-out old skeptics. I ask myself seriously what use teaching has been. You understand that for me this is more than a fatuous question. A poor man who has lived with the idea of making decent use of his own life, having arrived at a birthday like this one, cannot avoid asking himself, 'Well, what have you accomplished? What use has your teaching been?' "

"Dear Don Benedetto," said Concettino. "School is not life. You can dream in school but you have to adapt yourself to life. You never accomplish what you want to."

"What?" said Nunzio in an ironic tone to his friend. "Is this how a party activist talks? This from one of Nietzsche's fans?"

"Leave literature out of this," said Concettino. "This is a serious conversation."

Martha was on pins and needles. She got up quickly and went to the table where the refreshments and the dozen glasses were ready.

"Do you think the others will still come?" she asked. The poor woman was trembling as if in fever.

"They certainly intended to, but perhaps they were held up," said Concettino evasively.

Martha was about to take the extra glasses back to the kitchen.

"Leave one more," said Don Benedetto, "for Don Piccirilli."

"We didn't invite him," said his sister. "I excluded him from the invitations on purpose, as you well know."

"Just for that reason, he will not fail to come." said Don Benedetto. Then, turning to the two young men, he added, "Do you remember Di Piccirilli? He was the only one in your class who chose an ecclesiastical career. But his family, who were small landowners, could not afford to educate him any longer. So he had himself taken in for nothing by the Silesians; studied theology, and took holy orders. But no sooner had he been ordained than he abandoned the Silesians and went back to his family. This was certainly not a proper way to act toward his benefactors. Now he is the curate of a nearby parish. But that is not enough for him. Perhaps he wants to be a professor in a seminary, or a canon. To curry favor with the bishop, he acts as his secret informer. Secret, that is, in a manner of speaking; we all know what he is up to. He always appears where something worth reporting to the bishop might be said. As you can well imagine, he pays me the honor of frequent and cordial visits."

In the meantime the garden had grown dark and Martha was having trouble filling the glasses. And a brisk breeze had come from the mountain, causing Don Benedetto to have a fit of coughing.

"We'd better go in," said Martha.

The two young men helped her bring in the bottles and glasses. On the ground floor was one single room which served as kitchen, work room and living room, as with the peasants. Martha lit a large lamp with a yellow

lampshade and some candles and placed them in a corner
of the room. A pleasant odor of quinces and nuts filled
the room.

"It's pleasant here," said Nunzio. "Nothing is changed."

A fishing rod was leaning on the doorpost. The reel
hung from a nail on the door. Flowered majolica crockery
was set out on the bookshelves. A great variety of pots
and pans was hanging from the mantelpiece. Peppers,
sorb-apples, onions and garlic hung from the hood over
the fireplace. In a corner of the room, probably Martha's
work corner, was a small niche decorated with lace,
with a colored chalk Madonna, surrounded by cardboard
lilies.

"Sit down and help yourselves," said Martha.

Someone knocked on the door. It was Don Piccirilli.
Don Benedetto got up and greeted him at the threshold.
Don Piccirilli embraced him and wished him all sorts of
wonderful things. Don Benedetto returned the embrace
and invited him to join the others.

"Sit down and have something to drink," he said.
"There's a glass for you."

Don Piccirilli was pinkish and well fed, with a jovial
and expansive air. He said he was late because he had
had to finish an article for the diocesan bulletin.

"The title of the article is 'The Scourge of Our Times,' "
he said. "It has come out well, even if I do say so myself."

"Have you written about war or unemployment?"
asked Don Benedetto. "Congratulations."

"Those are political questions," answered Don Piccirilli
stiffly. "In the diocesan bulletin we deal only with religious
questions. From a purely spiritual point of view, the
scourge of our times, in my opinion, is an immodest way
of dressing. Don't you agree?"

"The scourge of our times," said Don Benedetto calmly,
looking him straight in the eye, "—must I tell you?—is
insincerity among men. It is the spirit of Judas Iscariot
which poisons men's relationships. Excuse me if I fail
my duties as host by speaking in this way."

Don Piccirilli attempted a smile, which came out like
a scowl.

"In my parish in these last years, enormous spiritual
progress has been made, thanks be to God," he said.

"Enormous!" he repeated with emphasis. "The number of confessions has gone up by forty per cent and the communions by thirty. Even if I do say so myself, I don't know what parish can beat that."

"Why do you talk of spiritual progress and then express yourself in percentages like a shopkeeper?" said Don Benedetto in an ironic, mocking tone.

Concettino made a desperate gesture, as if to say, "Here we go again!" Nunzio was seized with a violent fit of coughing, which did not look the least bit natural. Poor Martha was the most unhappy victim of the situation. She was watching all her hopes for her brother's reconciliation with the authorities being dashed to pieces; the poor woman could hardly keep back her tears. Thinking to bring some conventional cordiality into the company, she took from her brother's hands the old photograph in which he appeared surrounded by his pupils and opened it out on the mantelpiece.

"Do you see yourselves in the photograph?" she asked everyone, trying to give a noncommittal tone to her voice. "I bet it won't be easy."

They gathered around the fireplace, each one looking in the picture for himself first of all, then expressing surprise that he did not recognize this one or that one. Don Benedetto was enthroned in the midst of his pupils, like a hen surrounded by chicks. The brood seemed quite a mixed lot. The only common trait, one might say, was the style of haircut. The smallest boys sat cross-legged in the first row, the others were lined up standing in three rows. Among the smallest ones in the first row was Concettino. Like the rest, he had his hair cut short, and he had a dark-gray expression, like a cat's. After so many years only his eyes had remained the same. His present haircut and his little goatee made him look as if he were made up as a musketeer in a provincial theater company, nothing of which had been at all foreseeable fifteen years previously. On the other hand, Nunzio Sacca had changed little, apart from his forehead, which had been heightened by the loss of some hair. In the photograph he was behind Don Benedetto and was discernible by his slender neck, slightly narrow shoulders, deep-set eyes and the timid, absent-minded air which he had retained.

"Who were your favorite pupils?" Concettino suddenly asked Don Benedetto.

"The ones who most needed me, of course," he said without hesitation.

"Who were they?" all three former pupils asked at once.

Don Benedetto seemed perplexed. All at once he asked, "Where is Pietro Spina now? What has happened to him?"

In the photograph, Pietro Spina was seated next to Don Benedetto, who had put a hand on his shoulder. Spina had a lean, earthy look and a surly air. His necktie was crooked. After a pause, since no one answered, Don Benedetto asked again, "Doesn't anyone have any news about Pietro Spina? Where does he live now? In what country?"

The three young men looked at one another, embarrassed. Perhaps, in the bottom of her heart, Martha had still harbored some illusions, but now she sat wearily down on a bench with the defeated air of one who had been finally convinced that there was nothing further to hope for. Nunzio drew closer to her and gave her a smile of fraternal commiseration, while Don Benedetto did not seem to be aware of anything. He turned directly to Concettino.

"If I remember correctly, Pietro Spina was your best friend in school," he said. "You liked him so much one could almost say you were in love with him. Where is he now? What news do you have of him? What is he doing now?"

"How should I know? Am I my brother's keeper?" answered Concettino, avoiding Don Benedetto's glance.

The old man, who was standing near the fireplace, turned pale at this answer and, almost staggering, came slowly up to Concettino, put one hand on his shoulder and, looking him straight in the eye, almost with tears in his own, said in a low voice, "You poor man! How reduced you are! You do not know what terrible words you have uttered!"

In the ensuing silence which was painful for everyone present, Don Benedetto went away from the young officer to sit in the far corner of the room, in an armchair, beneath the niche where the image of the Madonna stood.

"Yes, it is true," he said. "Pietro Spina was in a sense my favorite pupil. Do you remember him? He was not satisfied with what he found in the textbooks. He was insatiable, unquiet and often lacking in discipline. He worried me. I was afraid of what might happen to him. And was I wrong? I do not know if you remember that the most severe punishments he received in school were almost always provoked by his protests against chastisements meted out to his schoolmates which he thought were unjust. This was one side of his character. He loved his friends a great deal, perhaps too much. If his superiors committed a mistake, he protested. When he knew that he was right, there was no kind of opportunistic argument that could silence him. Isn't that so, Concettino? Was he not like that?"

Don Benedetto sought among the yellowed papers of their last essays in school for Pietro Spina's paper.

"This is Spina," he said. "Listen: 'If it were not a frightful bother to be put on the altars after death, to be prayed to and adored by a great number of strangers, most of whom would be ugly old women, in my life I would wish to be a saint. I do not wish to live according to circumstances, places and material conveniences; but, without taking heed of the consequences, I would wish to fight for what seemed in my eyes to be just and true.' When I read this confession fifteen years ago," continued Don Benedetto, "without doubting the boy's sincerity, I had no idea of the extent to which rhetoric had led him in developing the theme. At this period he was devouring lives of the saints. Just a few years before he had become an orphan, and the family misfortunes had reinforced his tendencies to meditation."

Don Piccirilli impatiently waited for the old man to pause. Then he got a word in edgewise. "In 1920 Spina wanted to be a saint," he said. "That was all very well, but in 1921 he joined the atheistic, materialistic socialist youth group."

"Politics is no concern of mine either," said Don Benedetto in a stiff fashion.

"Atheism, the battle against God, is no concern of yours?" asked the young curate, intrigued.

Don Benedetto smiled lightly and ironically.

"Dear Piccirilli," he said slowly, pronouncing his words almost syllable by syllable, "no doubt you can teach me many things, for example the art of building a career; but I have been your master in philology, your master in the use of words; and take note that I am not afraid of words."

After a pause he added with a newly serene voice, in an imploring tone, "Can any of you give me any news about Pietro Spina? Where is he now?"

Finally Nunzio decided to tell what he knew.

"He was arrested early in 1927," he said, "and we found out that he was exiled to Lipari Island. The following year he escaped and took refuge in France."

"I knew that already," said Don Benedetto. "His grandmother, Donna Maria Vincenza, told me."

"He was deported from France after about a year," said Nunzio, "and then he went to Switzerland. It seems that the same thing happened to him there, and he went to Luxembourg. He was deported from there, too, and moved to Belgium. If they haven't thrown him out of Belgium, he must be there still. I don't know how he manages to exist, but he's probably often hungry. I heard from an uncle of his that something's wrong with his lungs."

"What a sad fate," said Martha. "Do you think he chose it voluntarily? Do you think he's mad?"

"He's an enigma for me too," said Nunzio. "It's too bad, since he was really the best of us all."

"Couldn't his relatives help him?" asked Martha again. "They are rich, after all. Who knows how much his grandmother, Donna Maria Vincenza, suffers for him?"

Don Benedetto was looking fixedly at the floor.

"I do not believe that this story is entirely new," he said. "On the contrary, it is a sad old story. The wolves have their dens and the birds their nests, but the son of man has no place to lay his head."

Trembling and pleading, Martha looked at her brother. The three young men got up to take their leave.

"It's late," they said. "We must be going."

The parting was brief, almost laconic. Martha sought in vain to have a word in private with Concettino.

"It's late," he excused himself.

Don Benedetto and his sister went with their guests to the crossroads. Don Piccirilli took the path which led to the left, toward the mountain. Concettino and Nunzio, with their car, took the Via Valeria.

The old man and his sister watched them depart in silence.

As they were leaving Rocca, Concettino murmured to Nunzio without looking at him, "Pietro Spina is in Italy. He sneaked in from Belgium. The police have spotted him and they're on his tracks right now. Maybe he's already been arrested. But what can I do if he's crazy?"

"Couldn't you help him? After all, he's one of us."

"If he's crazy, what could I do? He was lucky enough to get abroad. He should have stayed there."

"Couldn't you help him?"

"How? That's the trouble. I have to watch out, too. You're wrong if you think I'm completely safe."

## 3

One morning at dawn, Doctor Nunzio Sacca was called to the bedside of a dying man. A youth from Acquafredda had come to take him in a cart. The doctor appeared on the threshold of the house, still very sleepy, with his emergency bag in one hand, and after having looked closely at the youth he said, "We've met before, I believe."

"I'm Cardile Mulazzi, of the Acquafredda Mulazzis," said the other. "We do know each other. I'm sorry to come for you at this hour, but I'll explain. My grandfather had the old mill and the lands from Monsignor the Bishop. They were good lands and expensive. For three years my father rented a vineyard from your family. Do you remember? Then came all the misfortunes, the lawsuits and the illnesses. Two of my brothers are in Brazil. And they don't write."

"Yes, yes, we know each other," said the doctor. "But who is ill?"

The narrow sunken roads in the countryside were still in darkness. Dawn's livid light was barely touching the roofs of the houses. Some farmers in front of their doors were loading up their donkeys to go to the fields. The cartwheels creaked on the freshly surfaced road. The horse was walking against the wind, a wind which brought rain with it. The doctor lowered his hat on his forehead and raised the collar of his coat to his chin. It was cold for him since he had just gotten out of bed.

"Rain is good at the end of April," said Cardile. "You gave a speech on the square at Acquafredda, for the church and the people, when I was a boy. Do you remember? On the banner was written *Liberty*. Our family belonged to that party. It was right after the war, when they allowed liberty. The Church wasn't for the govern-

ment then. It was for the people. We were in the same
party. But now the wind has changed."

The doctor observed the youth with curiosity.

"What a strange thing to say," he said. But he did not
seem displeased.

"There's a reason," said Cardile. "You'll see."

"What reason?" asked the doctor.

Four policemen were at the corner near the station.
Why so early in the morning? One of them recognized
Doctor Sacca and greeted him. The cart came out of
the village, proceeding against the rain. The road went
slightly downhill and the horse started to trot.

"Now," continued Cardile, "the women and old men
have stayed on the Church's side; and we, you understand,
mind our own business. My father is sixty years old and
he is the prior of the Confraternity of the Sacrament.
You can check up on that if you like. Every Sunday he
sings the office; on Good Friday and Corpus Domini he
joins the procession with his red vestments and answers
when the priest says *oremus*. Every year we give two
barrels of wine to the parish of Acquafredda for the
Masses. All our dead are buried in the Chapel of the
Sacrament, in the cemetery of Acquafredda, on the right
as you enter. This doesn't make us any better than the
others; I just happened to remember all these things. In
other words, I wanted to tell you that we belong to the
same party."

"We know each other," said the doctor. "We know
each other. Who is ill? Someone in your family?"

The cart left the highway and took a little road full
of puddles, among fields planted with beans and peas.
The road climbed up a hill in a zigzag course. A light,
whitish mist was suspended on the skeletal arms of the
apple trees. The horse slowed to a walk with no need of
orders from his master.

"But there are many ways of knowing each other,"
said Cardile. "We peasants know people by the amount
of land they own or by papers. But is this a way of knowing
each other? You work, buy, sell, rent, and you always
need papers and certificates. If you go abroad to find
work, you have to deal with all kinds of offices, you have

to get references. But is this any way of knowing anyone?"

"I understand," said the doctor. "But now tell me where you're taking me. You certainly didn't get me up before dawn to make me these speeches."

"We'll be there soon," said Cardile. "Just a little while longer. What I've been telling you isn't just chatter."

The cart came to the top of a hill, along with the first rays of a delicate sun. The horse was sweating, but he took up his trot again of his own accord. The road had degenerated into a country path, from which the whole village could be seen. On the black and gray mass of the houses, the smoke from the chimneys was gathering into a bluish pall.

"I left home at sixteen," said Cardile. "I could have found work with my father, but it bored me. I went to France with some other peasants. I worked at L'Estaque, near Marseilles, where they were digging an underground drain. One day someone said to me, 'There's someone from your home town, an educated man.' This will be someone who wants to gyp me, I thought to myself. All my papers are in order; I've paid all I was supposed to pay. What can he want? The man came to the restaurant where we ate, sat down and said that for some years he had been gone from Marsica, and started talking about Acquafredda, about the land, the people, their life, his village and Fucino. The following evenings he did the same thing all over again. We went to the breakwater of l'Estaque, sat on the ground and talked until late at night. This became a habit. We used to go to the movies or to a dance hall. I liked his company. I had never had a friend like that. I don't know if you understand what I mean.

"During the day I worked in the tunnel. The day was eight hours long, but everyone did two or three hours of overtime, to make more money. But from the time I knew that that man was waiting for me at the surface, I stopped after eight hours. What did we talk about? We talked about men, land and life. We talked, but we made jokes and laughed, too. I thought to myself, here's someone I don't have to deal with for work, papers or for anything else. He doesn't come to me as a priest or a schoolteacher,

nor as a propagandist—the sort of people who know
everything and who are paid to convince other people.
Here's someone who comes to me just as a man. One
sad day he left and I didn't hear anything more of him.
I felt that something was missing right away. Then I
found out that he had been deported from France on the
report of the Italian consulate."

"I can already imagine who it was," said the doctor.
"But why are you talking about him?"

"I want you to understand me," said Cardile. "I am
talking about myself. It's obvious that I'm nothing special.
I was born a peasant and stayed that way. A peasant
lives according to custom, but there's more than the
custom of carrying a knife in your pocket. There are
other customs."

Two policemen coming down from the mountain met
the cart. They recognized the doctor and greeted him.
At that point it started to rain again.

"Two years ago," said Cardile, "coming back in my
cart from the Feast of San Bartolomeo, on the Magliano
road, I came across a dog that had been run over by a
car and had broken its leg. It was whining on the side
of the road so you couldn't bear it. I put the dog in the
cart, bound up his leg with my handkerchief and took
him home. After a couple of months a carter from Scur-
cola came by and picked him up because it was his dog.
I tell you this just to let you know what the customs are.
Last summer I found a sheep limping on the road. I put
him in the stall, between the cow and the donkey. Afterwards his master came by and took him back. That's how
the customs are. That's what I'd do and that's what anyone else would do. Well, that man I'd known at l'Estaque
knocked at my door last night. At first I didn't recognize
him."

"Pietro Spina is here? Are you taking me to Pietro
Spina?" asked Doctor Sacca in a state of panic.

Cardile stopped the cart and drew it up to the side of
the road. The two men got out. Cardile tied the horse to
a tree and covered him with a wool blanket. The preoc-
cupied doctor looked around. The rain had let up and
was headed over to Tagliacozzo. But more clouds were
coming from the direction of Avezzano. The countryside

seemed deserted. The two men continued to talk by the side of the cart.

"This man knocked at my door, as I said," explained Cardile. "But he didn't want to come in, even though he was pretty sick and had a fever. We walked a bit outside. Leaving the village, we took a country road until we sat down under a tree. After some memories of l'Estaque, he began telling me how he came back into Italy and got to Rome, miraculously escaping the police. Since he had lost contact with his friends in the party, he couldn't risk looking them up, at least for a while, for fear of being arrested. He told me he'd been wandering over the mountains for several days, but he had to stop because of his fever. After much hesitation, he decided to come to me, so that I could hide him while he caught his breath. He said to me, 'You're a worker. And I've come back to Italy for the workers' party. Don't betray me.' Last night I hid him in a stall, and now I'd like to know what we can do for this man. Can we leave him to die like this?"

"All he had to do was to stay abroad where he was," said the doctor in a tone of annoyance.

"But now he's here. You find him at your door, like an injured sheep or dog, like some dying beast. Can we leave him to die like this?"

"He has nothing to lose. He's alone. I have a wife and children. Our political ideas are not the same," said the doctor.

"Excuse me, this isn't a question of politics," said Cardile. "There's a dying man in there. In the catechism, which they made me learn when I was a boy, it is written: The works of mercy are to give drink to the thirsty, to clothe the naked, to give shelter to pilgrims, to cure the sick. . . . There's nothing about curing the sick whose political ideas are the same as yours. It's just cure the sick, nothing else. I wonder if I'm doing the right thing."

"Did he send you to me? Did he tell you he knew me?" asked the doctor.

"He told me he went to school with you. But he told me not to send for you on any account," said Cardile. "That's the truth."

The men continued talking beside the cart. A peasant passed with a donkey loaded with wood, who looked suspiciously at them. After a while an old woman came by with a goat. Cardile was not sure he should tell everything. Finally he decided.

"On my honor! Listen! He didn't want me to. As a matter of fact, he told me last night, 'I came back to my country for the workers' party and if I ask you to help it's because you're an honest worker. But Doctor Sacca is an intellectual who has his career to make. What's more,' he added, 'Doctor Sacca frequents the bishop's circle, and to curry favor with the authorities, he would be capable of reporting me to the police.' I'm telling you this, but I don't believe it. He was very much against my going to tell someone in his family. He told me he was dead to his family, as if he had gone into a monastery. In his opinion, only one man would not be afraid to help him, a priest who had been his teacher in school. But the man is too old, and he would prefer to save him the risk. That's how we left it last night. As you can imagine, I couldn't sleep for worrying about him. I dozed off about three and had a nightmare—that he was dead. I came straight down and found him worse. Then I came for you without asking his opinion. Even if he were just a sheep, for the love of God, we'd have to help him."

The doctor was leaning on the cart and was looking around him as if he were sick at his stomach. Finally he got up his nerve.

"We have to get him to leave the country right away," he said. "I'll try to persuade him. If he needs medicine, I'll give you a prescription in the name of someone in your family. May God help us!"

"He's down there," said Cardile, "in the stall behind the nut tree. It's a stall my father uses in the summer. You go alone, while I stand guard here."

Behind the nut tree, all curled up on the threshold of the stall, the doctor found an aged man who looked something like a stable boy. This irritated him, because Cardile had not told him that anyone else would be around.

"Where's the sick man?" he asked angrily.

"Nunzio, what are you doing here?" said the man. "Whom are you looking for?"

"Cardile told me someone here is sick," said the doctor,

all the more irritated at hearing the man call him by his first name.

"I'm sorry," said the man getting up. "But I did forbid him categorically to call you here."

Only now did the doctor recognize his former schoolmate Pietro Spina. But he was breathless with surprise.

"It is you?" he managed to stammer. "What a state you're in!"

Spina's great eyes starting forth from his deep eye sockets and his large, spacious forehead were the only traits which reminded the doctor of his classmate.

"You're my age," said the doctor, "and you look sixty. What kind of disease do you have, anyway?"

Pietro smiled. No, his premature aging was not the result of a loathsome disease. Must he reveal his secret? To change his appearance and to avoid recognition by the police, he had covered his face for some weeks before coming back to Italy with a mixture based on iodine, gaining in this fashion the wrinkles of premature age.

"It's a recipe I found in the biography of an old Russian revolutionary," said Pietro. "And it can be used for other purposes, too. When the ideal of the average young Italian ceases to be the lover of a Swiss or American tourist and turns to more serious things, then perhaps it will be necessary to open for the more fragile fops some Institute for Artificial Uglification, in contrast to the present Beauty Institutes."

Nunzio looked in compassion and wonder at the head of his contemporary. Pietro had never been what was called a handsome lad, but his face had often been illuminated by vitality and frankness, which had made him attractive to women. How could political dogmatism have led him to make himself so ugly in such a barbarous fashion?

"They've recognized you in spite of your disguise," said the doctor. "The police and the militia are combing the countryside for you."

"They haven't recognized me at all," said Pietro. "I've been reported to the police; if I succeed in escaping anyway it will be because they've circulated a copy of an old photograph of me. Furthermore, I have no intention of settling in Rome, but in some southern province."

All these spy-story intrigues made the doctor realize that he had let himself get caught in a dangerous and childish situation. The far-off noise of a truck on the highway made him jump up suddenly.

"Don't be afraid," said Pietro smiling. "Sit down. How are things going with you? I've heard something: wife, children, professional success, and the respect of the authorities. Congratulations. Are you a Commendatore already? . . . No? But what an injustice!"

"I'm going," said Nunzio abruptly. "Why should I sit down? Do you think I want to compromise myself with you? Argue with you? Or listen to your silly ideas?"

Spina motioned him to calm down.

"I know you've always been like a rabbit," he said. "Go right away. Your fearful trembling is annoying. If they haven't made you a Commendatore yet—and you're certainly dying to become one—I suggest to you an excellent way of getting the title. Report me to the police."

"Don't be insolent," said Nunzio. "Only a madman would confuse good sense with cowardice. What's more, I've been called here as a doctor; not to argue, but to see what you need."

" 'Physician, heal thyself,' " said Pietro. "I assure you that I'm better off than you. You may not believe me, but it wasn't I who called you."

Nunzio seemed suddenly moved to compassion and sat next to him.

"Weren't you safe abroad?" he said. "Why did you come back straight into the lion's mouth? If you love freedom, why didn't you stay in a free country?"

"I came back for air," said Pietro, taking a deep breath. "You see, even when I was far away, the reality I lived in was my native air. But with the distance it slowly became an abstraction for me and an incubus. I really needed to feel my feet on the ground once more."

"The greatest revolutionaries," said Nunzio, "your masters, Mazzini, Lenin, Trotsky, the ones who fought whole decades for their ideas, passed their lives in exile, and you can't?"

"Maybe you're right," said Spina, "I'm a pretty poor

revolutionary. To hell with politics, tactics and strategy. I mean, I don't know how to preserve myself in the expectation of some great role. At any rate, I'm not going back abroad. You see, Nunzio, I'm like the wines of our vineyards. They aren't bad. But when they're taken into another climate, they're awful. Other wines and other men seem made just for export."

"What if they arrest you?" asked Nunzio.

"I must admit that prison would be rather uncomfortable," said Spina. "I can assure you that I won't go there of my own free will. But what can I do if they take me there against my will?"

"In other words, you're not going back abroad."

"No."

"In that case," said the doctor, "the affair is no concern of mine. I wash my hands of the whole business."

"I like hearing you express yourself in Biblical metaphors," said Pietro ironically. "I see that some of that priestly education has stayed with you."

"But fanaticism has stayed with you," said Nunzio. "You don't believe in God any more, but in the proletariat, with the same absolutism as before."

Pietro made a gesture to indicate that he shouldn't talk about things he couldn't begin to understand.

"Last night," he said, "to escape the police and the militia, I walked the entire length of the path that goes around Monte Croce. I saw from a distance the school where we lived together for eight years. The flower beds we cultivated must still be in the garden. Do you remember our geraniums? That dormitory must still be there on the third floor, with the beds so close together that we could talk late into the night without the prefect knowing about it. Do you remember the fantastic plans we made then?"

"It seems to me as if you were calling up the prehistoric past," said Nunzio.

"When we left school," continued Pietro, "we found a society like nothing we had ever dreamed of and every one of us had to make his choice, to submit or to risk everything. It seems that at one time there were alternatives, but after that war they were closed to our generation. How many years have passed since then? Barely fifteen, and if someone were to see the two of us now he would never believe that up to the age of twenty our lives were parallel and that we cherished the same hopes for the future."

Nunzio appeared both annoyed and nervous.

"It's true," he said. "Now we belong to different parties."

"To two different humanities," corrected Pietro. "To two different races. I can't find any other words for what I mean. In the situation I find myself in, almost at your mercy, pretending esteem for you and others like you would cost me an effort of which I'm not capable. But it's still too soon to settle accounts. You can go!"

"There are a lot of other things you're not capable of," said Nunzio. "You're not capable of understanding that man ordinarily makes no choices whatever. He finds the conditions of his existence laid out for him. If they contrast with what he prefers, the best he can do is to wait for them to change."

"And if they don't change by themselves?" asked Pietro. "Who is to change them? How miserable is intelligence if it's good for nothing but making alibis to keep the conscience quiet! Get out of here! At least do me that favor."

Pietro went back into the stall and sat down, exhausted, on a donkey saddle. The doctor remained a bit uncertain, then he went up to him and said, "Let me at least examine you. I can get some medicine for you through Cardile."

With ill will, Pietro took off his shirt. His prematurely old head, with its burnished color, contrasted grotesquely with his clean, thin, slightly arched chest, which was white and graceful like an adolescent's. The doctor bent over Pietro's sick chest, tapped every rib and listened carefully for the desperate beating of his heart. He tried to examine the tired panting of the lungs from every side. The examination exhausted Pietro's last ounce of resistance and he slid off the saddle and stretched out on the straw-covered floor, half closing his eyes. All of a sudden a sense of fraternity and goodwill came over Nunzio.

"Listen, Pietro," he said, "let's get this clear. You're not going to die."

He sat down next to him in the straw and began to

talk openly. He told him of the illusions, disillusions, miseries, lies, intrigues and annoyances of his professional life.

"We all live temporary lives," he said. "We think that just for now things are going badly, that we have to adapt just for now, and even humiliate ourselves, but that all this is temporary. Real life will start someday. We prepare to die with the complaint that we've never really lived. Sometimes I'm obsessed with this idea. You live only once, and for this one time you live a temporary life, in the vain hope that one day real life will begin. That's how we exist. Of those I know, I assure you, no one lives in the present. No one thinks that what he does every day is anything but temporary. No one is in a position to say, 'From now on, from whatever day this is, my life has really started.' Even the ones who have power and take advantage of it, believe me, live on intrigues and fear. And they're full of disgust with the prevailing stupidity. They live temporary lives too. They're waiting just like everyone else."

"You mustn't wait," said Pietro. "Even in exile you're waiting. That's the trouble. You should act. You have to say, 'As of now, I've had enough.' "

"But if there's no freedom?" said Nunzio.

"Freedom is not something you get as a present," said Pietro. "You can live in a dictatorship and be free—on one condition: that you fight the dictatorship. The man who thinks with his own mind and keeps it uncorrupted is free. The man who fights for what he thinks is right is free. But you can live in the most democratic country on earth, and if you're lazy, obtuse or servile within yourself, you're not free. Even without any violent coercion, you're a slave. You can't beg your freedom from someone. You have to seize it—everyone as much as he can."

Nunzio was thoughtful and embarrassed.

"You're our revenge," he said. "You're the best part of all of us. Pietro, try to be strong. Try to live, to survive. Really take care of yourself."

"Nunzio," said Pietro with difficulty, "if all I accomplished by coming back to Italy was to bring out that part of you, it was worth it. That's the way you used to talk at school, when everybody else was asleep."

Cardile came to the door, dripping from the rain.

"It's still raining," he said. "There's not a living soul to be seen anywhere."

Cardile and the doctor talked a little longer.

"You'll stay here in hiding," said Nunzio to Pietro. "Stay here all day and Cardile will bring you what you need. Meanwhile we'll find you a better place."

"I'm not going back abroad," said Pietro.

"I'm afraid you couldn't even if you wanted to," said the doctor. "You're in no condition to take a long trip. We'll have to find a nice quiet safe place to hide you for a couple of months. After that, you can do what you want."

After the doctor and Cardile left, Pietro climbed up the ladder to the loft above the stall. This was his sanatorium.

## 4

Finally he could relax, comforted by the heat of his fever. This was his first calm moment since he had come back to Italy.

"I feel as if I were in a crèche," he told Cardile.

But for the comparison with the crèche to be complete, he needed a cow on one side and a donkey on another. In his case they weren't lacking, but they were down in the stall. However this was only at night, because during the day they had to earn their living. The beasts came home tired when the outlaw was already asleep. He could sleep on the straw. There was no noise to bother him. A stream ran behind the haystack, and during the night it sang him a lullaby. In the darkness the country nymphs came forth from the stream and reminded him of the fairy tales he had forgotten since childhood. Pietro opened his eyes when Cardile came with food and medicine. He ate, took pills, and went back to sleep on the straw. Cardile came twice a day. He came on the donkey or the horse, got off, unloaded the animal and tied him by the halter to a nail in the wall. He looked around, then went up to the loft. Pietro recognized his every movement. The visit took no longer than was absolutely necessary.

"Any news?"

"No. Be patient."

He was not in a hurry. The loft had a great opening without a door, through which the straw was taken after the threshing. Through this opening he could see a wide expanse of fields without himself being seen. There were fields of tender green grain, fields of beans—little black dots in leaves of silver. And there were vineyards, apple orchards and almond trees. Way in the back he could see a small piece of the highway. One night a long procession of carts went by, with a line of lights dangling

45

from between the wheels, going to some fair. Pietro closed his eyes to go with them to the fair.

"Aren't you bored?" asked Cardile.

No, he wasn't bored. It was hard for him to explain his state of mind. He was struck by the naturalness of all the things around him, everything in its proper place, no longer in the fictitious country he had inhabited in his imagination when in exile; and by the naturalness of his own body, along with all the other natural things, an object among other objects, a bundle of indolent bones. It wasn't even a central or an important object in comparison with the others, but concrete and limited. It was a product of the earth. His body was stretched out on the straw between a loaf of bread and a jug of wine. This was the food which Cardile usually gave him. The straw was yellow, the bread brown and the wine red.

"Bring me some colored pencils," he told Cardile. "I'll draw you a picture."

But one evening Cardile came in completely exhausted.

"What? You're still here! Can I believe my eyes?" he said to Pietro.

"Where did you think you'd find me?"

"Doctor Sacca heard just now that you'd been arrested in a hotel in Avezzano."

"Well, that depends on who told him."

"An officer in the militia, a friend of his."

"In that case," said Pietro seriously, "we might have expected such news."

"Are we going to celebrate?" asked Cardile. "This is important news."

"To the glory of the militia!" exclaimed Pietro, raising the bottle of wine.

"The militia is always right," said Cardile. "Have another drink."

The bottle was drained in no time.

"Couldn't you bring me some newspapers?" said Pietro.

"I'm sorry. I never buy them," said Cardile. "You can count the newspaper readers in Acquafredda on the fingers of one hand. I wouldn't want to raise any suspicion."

Pietro did not dare insist. He had kept with him some notes on the agrarian revolution. In spite of the fact that they could incriminate him if found in a routine search by the police, <u>he had not wanted to get rid of them,</u> thinking that they would be useful for a wider study of the southern question, especially if he had to be absent for some weeks from active party affairs. But when he went through his notes at leisure in the loft, he found that he simply could not read them. It was as if they were written in Chinese. Actually, theory had always bored him.

One day Doctor Sacca gave Cardile a lecture on vitamins, and he ended up by saying that Pietro needed more substantial nourishment. From that day on, Pietro regularly got two rolls and twice as much wine for lunch. Every once in a while Cardile was able to steal some cheese and salami from home. When he did, it was a sumptuous banquet for Spina.

Cardile came by the stall at dawn and at dusk to take care of the animals and bring them to and from work. Pietro came to recognize everything he did by the sound: when he piled up the manure, when he spread the litter, when he half closed the door because he was coming right back and when he really shut it. <u>The beasts' watering trough </u>was just a short distance away. It consisted of a large wooden vessel which took the water from a small tube of iron fixed in a dry stone parapet. Behind the stone was a spring. <u>The water continued through an opening in</u> the vessel on its way down the hill, <u>forming the stream Pietro heard during the night</u>.

One morning, after Cardile's usual visit, Pietro couldn't resist the temptation to take a bath. It was a bright day, the sun had just risen. The apple and cherry trees were shining with dew. On the plain, troops of peasants were intent on weeding the new grain and on the spring planting, but on the hill there wasn't a soul to be seen. Following the cattle tracks, Pietro had no trouble in finding their watering place. The water in the vessel was cold, transparent and slightly greenish. But Pietro had hardly taken off his shirt and was getting out of his shoes when a young peasant girl came by with a pail in her hand. There had been no footsteps because she was barefoot. Evidently she had come to fetch water. Pietro hurriedly put his shirt back on.

"Excuse me," he said, trying to smile.

"Haven't you any springs where you live?" said the

girl in an arrogant tone. "Why do you come to other people's land to bathe?"

"I'm a pilgrim," said the man, confused. "I'm just passing through here."

He tried to appease the strange girl with courtesy.

"May I help you fill your pail?" he asked.

"Nobody ever went on a pilgrimage in the spring," said the girl. "In Christian countries, you go on a pilgrimage in August or September. In the spring you work."

"I made a vow," said the man. "Surely you know what a vow is. This is a case of conscience."

She was a strong, self-confident girl, and it wasn't easy to intimidate her. She had very thick eyebrows and her shoulders, neck and hips were a little thick, indicating that she was a working woman. But her nose was graceful and her eyes alert and ironic. The slimness of her calves showed she was a cut above the ordinary.

"Can't I help you?" asked the man. "I'm in no hurry, you know."

The girl observed him attentively and returned his gaze without embarrassment.

"Are you from around here?" asked the man. "It'd be nice to know that you're not in a hurry either."

Without answering him, the girl plunged the bucket into the water with a practiced gesture and brought it out full. Before going away, she turned to the man, trying to think of something to say.

"Good luck," she finally said, in an affable tone which left a profound impression on the man. Why did she say that and what did that change in her voice mean?

He tried to follow her with his eyes as far as he could. When he got back to the loft, he placed himself behind the opening with his eyes fixed on the last trace of the path on which he had seen her disappear. The path advanced into an orchard beyond which, above the trees, rose the roof of a farmhouse. Was that her house? Pietro stayed all day at his post. The hours went by without his being aware of the passage of time. For him time had stopped. But wasn't it an illusion when he saw her come back that afternoon, just as in the morning, with the pail in her hand? In any case, he ran down the ladder after her. But he instinctively came up to the watering place as if he had come from the top of the hill.

"Are you still here?" said the girl, pretending she was surprised. "Have you forgotten your vow?"

"I was waiting for you to come back," said the man loyally.

"How did you know I would come back?" said the girl. "You flatter yourself."

"No, really. I was afraid you wouldn't," said the man. "But I was hoping you would. I haven't thought about anything else all day."

"Where were you, if I'm not too bold?" asked the girl.

"Up there, on the haystack," said the man. "I've watched your house all day, that one beyond the orchard."

"Did you sleep on the haystack last night too?" asked the girl. "It's not comfortable this time of year. What do you do if it rains?"

"I was waiting for you to offer me a better place," said the man. By this time they both had their cards on the table. The girl did not answer. She was waiting for the man to continue.

"Do you have any family at home?" said the man. His voice trembled and he smiled courteously to mitigate the crudeness of his question.

"Yes. There's my sister-in-law," said the girl.

"Sisters-in-law go to bed some time," said the man.

For the moment, the girl defended herself with irony. "Really," she said laughing, "you're not bad for a pilgrim." After a while she added, "There's a dog too. He sleeps all day and takes turns with my sister-in-law."

"Well, I'll wait for you here," said the man. "It's warm outside. But don't keep me waiting too long."

"Are you in such a hurry?" said the girl in a provocative tone.

"It's boring to be alone," said the man.

The girl forgot all prudence and laughed out loud.

"You could say your rosary," she said.

"I'll wait for you as soon as it's dark," said the man. "Don't keep me waiting."

That evening Cardile was later than usual in coming. A peasant's day is regulated by the weather. It would

be foolish not to take advantage of a sunny day in April.
But Pietro was impatient.

"You look much better," said Cardile. "I'm glad the
air in my stall has done you good."

"I feel like a new man," said Pietro. "But last night
I couldn't sleep because of a dog. Who's in the house
beyond the orchard?"

"A cousin of mine and her sister-in-law," said Cardile.
"The girl's husband is working in the sugar works right
now."

"What sort of people are they?" asked Pietro.

"Not to be trusted," said Cardile. "We hardly speak
to them."

"Excuse me, I'm sleepy," said Pietro. "I hope the dog
will leave me in peace tonight."

As soon as Cardile had gone, he came down from the
loft and went straight to the watering place so as not
to be late, without taking the trouble to conceal the direction he came from. The girl was already there.

"You're playing hard to get," she said.

"I was held up because I saw a man near the stall,"
he said.

"He's my cousin," said the girl. "It was a good idea
to avoid him."

"What sort of person is he?" said the man.

"Not to be trusted," said the girl.

"At least you're different," he said.

"How do you know? Are you sure something won't
go wrong?" she said.

"Did your sister-in-law let you go out?" he said.

"I asked permission to go into the village for an errand," she said. "I can't come back late. I have to say
goodnight to her when I come in."

On the ground next to the trough was a bottle.

"I brought you something to drink," she said.

"Thanks," said the man. "We can drink later. I'm not
thirsty for wine right now."

"Has it been a long time since you've had a woman?"
she asked. "Be gentle, like a good boy. . . . No, not on
the ground, can't you see it's wet? . . . Let's go there,
under the tree where it isn't so dirty."

"What's your name?" Pietro asked her.

"Margherita," said the girl. "And yours? . . . No, please don't answer. You'd just tell me more lies."

"Do you think I've already lied to you? Do you think I'm a liar?" he said.

"You're not a pilgrim," said the woman, smiling.

"You're right," said the man. "But that wasn't a lie. That was just a manner of speaking."

They were stretched out on the grass. The air still had some of the heat of the day. The village at the foot of the hill was a mass of feeble lights.

"It's nice here," said the man.

"Want to bet I can guess your name?" said the woman.

"Why?" said the man. "If you guess it right, it wouldn't have been worth it in the first place, because I know my name already. And if you're wrong, it's a stupid waste of time. Do you like to waste time?"

"A few days ago," said the woman, "the police visited all the houses around here. There's a fugitive around, they warned us. If he asks for food or lodging, pretend to give it to him and report him to the police right away."

"Have you reported me already?" asked Pietro.

" 'He's an enemy of the government,' they explained, 'and whoever reports him will get a reward,' " added the woman. "They're saying around here that your real name is Pietro."

"Aren't you attracted by the reward?" said Pietro. "Or would you rather have another one, from me?"

Margherita's reaction was immediate; she took away her arm on which Pietro was resting his head, put her clothes in order and sat up.

"Excuse me," said Pietro. "That was idiotic."

"Did you think a poor Christian woman wouldn't betray a man only because she wanted to lie down with him?" said Margherita.

"You're right," said Pietro. "I beg your pardon."

"You may not believe me," said Margherita, "but if the fugitive were a woman instead of you, I wouldn't have acted any differently."

"I believe you, Margherita. Excuse me," said Pietro.

"Want to know who brought me up like that?" said

Margherita. "In my father's house, when I was a little girl, we hid an escaped convict for several months. He was a stranger, but he'd had a lot of bad luck. My father told us that for honorable people the first work of mercy is to help those who are persecuted."

After a while she added, "It must seem funny that I'm talking about honor right now."

"You were talking about it in the sense that I respect most," said Pietro. "You might say that every part of the body has its own honor. But for too long people have believed that the most important honor was between the legs."

"Pietro, let's be sincere with each other," said Margherita. "What's the good of arguing? It's better not to talk."

The two faces slowly came together.

"Your lips smell like a child's," said Margherita. "Is it true that you're from around here, from Fucino? I heard people saying you were."

"What else have you heard?" said Pietro.

"That you came from a rich family, that you lost your parents in the earthquake—and that you're a little crazy," said Margherita. "Why do you live like that?"

"For what you were talking about a while ago," said Pietro. "I have a certain sense of honor."

"Do you want to send a message to your grandmother?" said Margherita. "I could go to call on her. They say she's a great lady."

"I renounced all my blood relations several years ago," said Pietro. "It's not easy, but that's where I think you have to begin."

"How can you?" said Margherita. "What a funny idea! You weren't a foundling, by any chance?"

"The only relationships I have any respect for are those between soul and soul," said Pietro, "like what has just sprung up between us."

"Pietro, let me think a minute about what you said," said Margherita. "Yes, I have a warm feeling for you. Pietro, listen, I want to ask you something."

The girl got up and tidied her hair. Then she gave Pietro a hand to help him get up.

"Let's say good-bye without lying together," said Margherita. "After what we've just said, it seems the best thing to do. Do you agree? I'd like it that way.

"But wait a minute," she added. "You still haven't tasted my wine."

Pietro raised the bottle and drank for a long time.

"It's strong," he said. "Have some yourself."

Margherita took just as much as Pietro did. The gurgling in their throats mixed with the murmuring of the stream. This duet continued until the wine was all gone.

"How much was it?" said Pietro.

"Three liters," said Margherita. "Now it's time for me to go."

"I'l go with you as far as the orchard," said Pietro.

"That wouldn't be a good idea," said Margherita. "Our dog is unleashed at night and he might chase you."

They parted without a word. But when he saw her disappear at the end of the path, Pietro was overcome with despair. He sat on the ground and started to weep. His trip back to the loft was hard for other reasons. Some imbecile had entirely changed the layout while he was away. The door, for example, had grown larger; and someone had misplaced it. The ladder was hopeless. The next morning even dawn came earlier than usual, when Pietro had not yet slept off the effects of the wine. Cardile found him crumpled up in the manger.

"What are you doing down here?" he said. "Why didn't you sleep up in the loft?"

"There was a great big mouse," said Pietro, rubbing his eyes. "I wasn't afraid of him, but I didn't want to waste time arguing."

"The bottle I brought you last night has gone to your head!" said Cardile, laughing.

Cardile rapidly rubbed down the cattle and then climbed up to the loft to fetch their daily feed. Pietro meanwhile was trying to decipher an enigmatic letter from Nunzio, but his reading was interrupted by exclamations of surprise from the floor above.

"How can it be?" said Cardile. "I can't believe my eyes!"

He ran down the ladder with the bottle he had brought the night before. It was full.

"What did you get drunk on last night," said Cardile, "if the bottle is still full?"

Pietro was no less surprised. But it did not last as long with him because of his innate tendency to remain impassive before whatever strange things nature might bring up.

"How can you explain it?" Cardile was asking.

"Well," said Pietro, "this seems to be proof that the proverb about not being able to have a full bottle *and* a drunken wife or friend is wrong. All we can do is to take note of it."

"I don't understand," said Cardile.

"I'm not surprised that you're alarmed," said Pietro. "You're a peasant, and a peasant's life runs on proverbs. But, fortunately, truth is greater than proverbs."

This was enough to close the conversation, but not to prevent Cardile from looking suspiciously at the bottle and shaking his head every once in a while. While he was thus occupied, Pietro could get back to decoding Nunzio's letter. In it, he spoke in Sibylline terms of some expedient for hiding Pietro securely in a mountain village for two or three months, which was the minimum time needed for his recovery. What did Pietro think of this? The details of the plan were either not mentioned or not clearly explained, but it seemed important to Pietro to have a change of scene and to take the burden from Cardile. Therefore he said he accepted. Among other things, he had not understood that he was to leave immediately.

That same night, when he had just lain down on the straw, he heard someone calling him from the stall.

"Pietro, Pietro," said a voice. "Come on down!"

Groping in the dark, Pietro was able to raise the trap door and look down into the stall. It was Nunzio calling him, standing between the cow and the donkey with a lantern in his hand.

"Bring everything you'll need with you," said Nunzio. "You're leaving right away."

When Pietro came down, Nunzio showed him a package of ecclesiastical clothes by the weak light of the lantern.

"It's a complicated farce," said Nunzio. "And, to tell you the truth, it's not all my doing."

Pietro was astonished. He had not understood at all from the letter that he would have to masquerade as a priest.

"I hate carnival time," said Pietro. "Even when I was a boy, I never put on a costume."

"Given the situation," said Nunzio, "we couldn't find better protection for you."

Pietro continued to shake his head.

"I left the Church a long time ago," he added, "but dressing up like a priest just goes against my grain."

Nunzio liked his scruples.

"If we didn't know you," he said, "if we had any idea that you might misuse this habit, we wouldn't have offered it to you."

Pietro was quickly clothed in his vestments, by the dim light of the oil lamp. The horse was sleeping. The cow did not seem to care. She just huddled up in the straw and closed her eyes. But the donkey stood up and watched. This attention annoyed the doctor, who took the beast by the halter and turned him around. The donkey let himself be turned around, but then he turned his head and looked fixedly at the strange man who had come down from the loft and was putting on a long black soutane with a long row of little buttons in front.

"Don't forget that the habit doesn't make the monk," said Nunzio.

But Pietro had lost all desire to joke and kept muttering incomprehensible things. To distract him, Nunzio improvised a little speech of consecration, in a semi-serious tone.

"These vestments," he said, "come from the primitive-mystery religions, from the priests of Isis and Serapidis, as you well know. They were adopted by the Catholic Church in the first monastic communities which tried to save Christian values from worldly contamination and to assure the essential charismatic virtues to a minority living outside of and in opposition to the society. Thus the rites date back to a time in which people were passing from one religion to another and from one society to another. Now you, who are initiated into the new revolutionary mysteries, into the mysteries of matter in revolt,

vest yourself with the black garments which for thousands
of years have been the symbol of sacrifice and super-
natural inspiration."

Pietro had to smile in spite of himself. "Don't be ri-
diculous!" he said.

"I don't understand," said Nunzio in the same vein,
"why Lenin didn't introduce vestments like these, or at
least the tonsure, among the personnel of the Kremlin,
to distinguish the functionary, the guardian and interpreter
of the sacred texts, from the simple proletarian who
carries his card and pays his dues."

Time was short. Cardile was waiting on the road with
his cart.

"We'll stop at my clinic," said Nunzio. "You'll get
a bath and a haircut, and I'll take an x-ray."

"Promise to visit me," said Pietro.

"All right," said Nunzio. "What will you call yourself?"

Pietro thought a minute. Then he suggested, "Spada."

"All right," said Nunzio. "We'll call you Don Paolo
Spada."

"Why Don Paolo?"

"Pietro Spada would sound too much like your real
name. So, Reverend Don Paolo Spada, let's be off. Have
you forgotten anything? Is everything in your bag? Hat?
Breviary? Rosary? Scapular? And the special instructions
for your holy mission?"

"Let's go!" said Don Paolo Spada. *"Procedamus in
pace."*

# 5

"The horse doesn't like to travel at night," said the coachman. "I don't blame him."

"I don't either," said Don Paolo, "but I've missed my train. I was delayed in the bishop's office."

"The bishop should buy himself a clock," said the coachman. "Why does he send his priests around at night time, in this awful weather?"

It had just stopped raining, but there was a sharp, wintry wind.

"Are you cold? Shall I put the hood up?" said the coachman.

"As long as it doesn't rain it's all right," said Don Paolo.

The road was dark and lonely. The noise of the carriage woke up the dogs along the way and set them to barking. Curious faces appeared in some of the lighted windows. The coachman sat up front, smoking his pipe. To keep the horse at a trot, all he had to do was to shake the reins once in a while. The coachman turned to Don Paolo to ask him, "How much do you get for a funeral service? I just wanted to know."

"Do you plan on dying soon?" said Don Paolo.

"Not just now," said the coachman, and he touched a part of his body. "I'd just like to know, just for a comparison."

"Leave it," said Don Paolo. "Comparisons are bad."

"Are you familiar with these places?" said the coachman.

Don Paolo did not answer. This was his native heath, from which he had been expelled ten years before. His heart was beating rapidly, and in spite of the nocturnal cold he felt himself bathed in sweat. Mount Velino was fading away to the rear, with its two summits still covered with snow; and in front, the mountainous barrier sur-

rounding the hollow of Fucino arched all the way across
the horizon, looking like the gloomy walls of a shut-in
world against the dark and cloudy sky. The carriage came
across a settled area where the recently constructed palaces and villas contrasted with clusters of barracks and
piles of ruins. There was not much light, and the darkest
places coincided with the parts of the road where the
puddles were widest and deepest. At one point the carriage was brusquely halted by two policemen who let
it continue immediately, as soon as they saw that its
only passenger was a priest.

"Good evening, Father," they said.

*"Pax vobiscum,"* said Don Paolo.

Outside the settled area the road was being repaired
and the horse slowed to a walk. Don Paolo was reeling
in the carriage. He held on tight so as not to fall out.
It was hard, but at least it kept him busy. When they
came to a normal stretch of road, the coachman turned
to him and said, "Do you believe in the new African
war?"

"A priest, if he believes, believes in God," said Don
Paolo. "That's already a great deal."

"I wanted to know," said the coachman, "if you thought
the new war would be profitable."

"Not to the ones who leave their bones there," said
Don Paolo.

The coachman took this as a joke and laughed for a
while. But he was really asking something else, and he
explained himself with different words, "Do you think
there'll be a lot of loot?" he asked. "Do you think there'll
be gold, lots of gold?"

"Do you think wars are just for loot?" said Don Paolo.

"That's what they're all saying," said the coachman.
"Should those boys die for nothing? Are the English the
only ones with a right to some loot?"

"I'm sleepy," said Don Paolo. "Leave me alone."

Gravel had just been spread on the road. Don Paolo's
native village was just around the corner. The carriage
was reeling in space and time. This was a region where
Don Paolo knew every bridge, vineyard, stream and tree.
At the crossroads before Orta was an old tavern. Acquasanta, the manager, was closing up and some girl

was helping her. Could Acquasanta's daughter be that big already? The wheels of the carriage got stuck in the gravel and could hardly turn. Suddenly the first houses of Orta came into view. There was the electric light on the carriagemaker's shop at the entrance to the village. Don Paolo closed his eyes. He did not want to look. The first one to note the carriage's arrival was the carriagemaker's dog. He barked two or three times, as he usually did, then he stood behind the door and listened, snarling to himself in puzzlement. The carriage passed by the shop and almost bumped into the door. At that the dog let out a long, shrill howl. He was answered by the dog who guarded the garden behind the church. Don Paolo kept his eyes closed, but he knew from the sound of the wheels that the carriage was on the pavement of the square in Orta. The dog in the church garden started barking hysterically, waking up her litter asleep in the kennel, and jumped against the garden gate. One by one, the other dogs in the village took up the cry. Even the ones by the mill were awakened, and the city-hall dogs, and the dogs in the carter's stall.

"What the hell's going on?" yelled the coachman. "What have we come to?"

Don Paolo did not answer him. There must have been thirty of forty dogs yelping, barking, snarling and howling from every alley and courtyard. The carriage drew away from the last houses in Orta and the dogs were still barking. Then, one by one, they stopped. When Don Paolo opened his eyes again, the carriage had stopped at a fountain with a large place for the cattle to drink. There was a bronze plaque which said: "Built by the Spina family." Don Paolo said to the coachman, "Wait a minute, I'm getting out, too."

He got out of the carriage, took some of the water in his hands and drank, then he bathed his face. The road was no longer graveled, and the horse could go at a trot. Don Paolo sat with his back to the coachman, so he could look at the last houses of the village. He could see a dozen or so lighted windows. One on the hill went out, then another one lower down by the mill, and then a third by the river, and finally one more on the hill. Don Paolo could recognize every house, road, window and garden. What was his old grandmother, Donna Maria Vincenza, doing? Was she still alive? Was she thinking about him? Had the authorities bothered her? What was <u>Faustina</u> doing? Did she remember him? Had she gotten married? It seemed like a trip beyond the grave. The carriage passed by an old lime quarry that had belonged to Don Paolo's father. As a child, he had played hide and seek with the workers' sons there. Half way up the hill, he recognized "<u>his</u>" <u>vineyard</u>, the last of his inheritance. The fig trees were still in their places, but where were the cherries? And the nut trees? His uncle who managed the vineyard must have had them taken down. Don Paolo's eyes filled with tears.

Then the wind rose and turned to the east, rustling the trees. Don Paolo bent his head and fell asleep.

The coachman woke him up at Fossa dei Marsi, in front of the Girasole Inn. He was expected. A woman took the priest's bag.

Before taking his leave, the coachman asked a favor of Don Paolo.

"Could you write me a reference?"

"A reference? But for what and to whom?"

The coachman thought a bit and said, "I don't know just now, but I'm sure I'll need one sometime. Couldn't you write me a general reference?"

"But I don't know you," said the priest.

"I didn't know you," said the coachman, "but I brought you up here."

"I paid you for that," said the priest. "Good night."

Don Paolo did not remember anything else about his arrival. He must have been bewildered with his new role—and dead tired.

## 6

The next morning Don Paolo woke up early but stayed in bed for a long time.

From Nunzio he had received some typewritten sheets on the theme, "How a priest is to comport himself outside his own diocese." Don Paolo was of the Frascati diocese and was traveling to the diocese of Marsi to regain his health in the mountain village of Pietrasecca. The greatest difficulties he could encounter were foreseen in his instructions, and they also explained how to overcome them. Don Paolo read and reread them.

The carter who was to take him to Pietrasecca would not come until the afternoon, so he dressed at his leisure and spent the morning in his room. He was delighted to find that the room had a basin with running water. After camping out in the loft, a wash basin seemed a great luxury. Furthermore, it showed him what progress had been made in the countryside. On the basin was a handwritten sign, in beautiful calligraphy: "The honorable guests of the establishment are requested not to urinate in the basin. If they do, it stinks." In fact, it did stink.

Don Paolo looked at himself in the mirror. At Nunzio's clinic his hair had been cut very short. With his black cassock and shorn head he looked positively grotesque. He almost wept. His cassock had twenty-eight buttons down the front. What a nuisance it was going to be to button and unbutton twenty-eight buttons! He wouldn't have time for anything else. Luckily he discovered that all he had to do was to unbutton the cassock from the neck to the waist and take it off, either by raising it over his head or by letting it fall to the floor. These feminine gestures amused him.

But other difficulties arose. Don Paolo was annoyed at the idea of having to raise the gown every time he wanted to get into the pockets of his trousers. Wouldn't it look funny for him to lift up the gown when he was in public? But later he found an opening in the gown which led directly to his pockets. This discovery made him very happy. Well, it wasn't so hard to be a priest after all!

As soon as he came down, Don Paolo met the manager of the inn, the widow Berenice Girasole. The old woman's greeting was somewhat alarming to him. She must have been in the midst of some trouble, because her eyes were filled with tears and her voice with sighs, all of which boded no good for Don Paolo.

"You were sent here by Providence!" she said, kissing his hand.

"No. The doctor sent me," said Don Paolo.

And he fled. There was a shop next to the inn. To make it look natural, he pretended to look in the shop window. But the howling laughter of some young men drew his attention to what was in there: brassieres and feminine underwear. He left there in a hurry and stopped in front of a hat shop. In the window there was a large mirror, in which he saw himself by an even more brutal light than in his room. Horrible! He went back to the inn, tired and depressed.

It was lunch time.

"Do you eat spaghetti, Father?" asked Berenice.

"God save me from that!" said Don Paolo. "Anything but spaghetti."

Luckily, Berenice had other people to serve.

The walls of the dining room were for the most part decorated with colored pages from a famous illustrated weekly, showing all kinds of human-interest events: the station-master's daughter saving a train from certain catastrophe, an airplane being attacked by an eagle and the cages in a city zoo broken open with the wild beasts in hot pursuit of the terrified passersby. There were about a dozen other guests in the dining room, all of whom seemed to Don Paolo to be staring at him and talking about him. He forced himself not to take his eyes from his plate. When she served the coffee, Berenice sat down at the table with the priest to tell him about her troubles. She wore no corset and her vast bosom floated free, and she was sweating copiously from the work of serving the guests. As soon as Berenice started talking about Providence again, Don Paolo interrupted her rudely.

"I'm sorry," he said, "but I'm not from this diocese. I came here *just* for a rest!"

The woman was offended, but she stopped talking, despairing of getting him to listen. Don Paolo took advantage of her agitation to sun himself in front of the inn. Five or six young sports were sitting around a table, snoozing with their hats over their faces, spent cigarettes in their mouths. At a further table some other young men were playing cards. They were also distributing great blobs of spit of a butterfly-yellow hue in the dust around them. They were wearing the emblem of the party in power in their buttonholes. With them was an older man with a broad-brimmed hat whose face reminded one of a retired actor. He was playing cards too, and he drank his coffee with loud gulps. At the sight of the strange priest he gave the usual signal against the evil eye.

"Iron! Iron!" he cried.

The sleeping boys woke up at once and took emergency precautions. Don Paolo recognized the rite and was about to answer in kind, but he did not, because the way they behaved was one indication that he could pass for a priest. He stayed where he was. The flag-bedecked headquarters of the party in power was just ahead of the inn. The city hall had a portrait of King Umberto with his usual gigantic mustaches. A slim usher was seated at the door, and he had gigantic mustaches too. He was surrounded by flies, and every once in a while he roared and spat, with a wide, ample trajectory which came as far as the center of the square. The presence of the strange priest brought a crowd of beggars to the inn, each of them with his own crowd of flies. A cripple hobbled along on his crutches, asking for alms in the name of them all. Don Paolo fled inside the inn. But Berenice was waiting for him there. The woman took him by the arm with a vicelike grip and began the story of her troubles all over again, with the same tearful voice.

"Listen, for the love of Mary! My only daughter is dying!" she said in a painful tone. "Don't be cruel!"

"I'm sorry," said Don Paolo, who was about to get angry. "I've already explained it to you and now I'm telling you again. I'm not from this diocese and I'm not authorized to care for souls around here."

"Not even in urgent cases?"

"In no cases whatsoever!"

Berenice could not hold back her sobs.

"All right," she said, "but at least let me tell you what it's all about. You might at least give me some advice. This is how it is. The girl is dying and doesn't want to confess to the priest here because he's a relative. Can't you understand? She was overjoyed when I told her there was a strange priest here. She said Jesus Christ must have sent him."

"I'm sorry," said Don Paolo. "If it's an urgent case, why don't you call the priest from a nearby parish?"

"Because there isn't time," said Berenice. "And besides, there'd still be a scandal. People would ask, 'Why didn't they call the priest in the family?' "

"I'm sorry," said Don Paolo.

Berenice could hold back her tears no longer.

"What can I do?" she said. "How can I leave my daughter to die without a priest or a doctor?"

"Why not a doctor?" said Don Paolo. "What's this all about?"

Berenice was afraid of having said too much and she looked around her in alarm.

"May I talk to you as in the confessional?" she asked.

Don Paolo nodded. Still weeping, Berenice told him what it was all about, in a low voice.

"The girl is not married and she got pregnant. To save herself and her family from dishonor, she tried to get rid of it alone, you understand. This is against the law, as you know. If a doctor, or a midwife, or anyone else, helps a woman to get rid of it, they go to jail. There're lots of cases like this—you just have to read the newspapers. Some are even worse. The daughter of the notary in Fossa drank seaweed poison with a child of four months in her belly. A girl from around here who was a maid in the mayor's house went to Tivoli and jumped into the falls. But my poor little girl tried to get rid of it herself. She had only two choices—to risk death, or to risk dishonor. She risked death, and now she's dying. Can you imagine a poor mother's sorrow? I can't call a doctor because he'd report it. There'd be an investigation and then a trial, and everything would come out. And she doesn't want to call the priest around here, like I told you, because he's a relative. Sure she's sinned, but there's forgiveness for us all. Didn't Christ die on the cross for us all?"

Don Paolo was stupefied. This sort of thing wasn't foreseen in Nunzio's instructions.

"My dear lady," he said, "I'm awfully sorry, but I just don't know how to advise you."

The poor priest's eyes were full of tears. Berenice saw this and motioned the priest to come with her, as if she wanted to tell him something more. Don Paolo followed her up the stairs to the second floor. Berenice opened the door of a little room without making any noise. The room was almost dark and smelled of medicines. There was a small iron bed in one corner, under a great black crucifix.

"Bianchina," said Berenice softly, "look who's here."

Something moved on the bed. A livid little face was to be seen amid a large mane of black hair spread out on the covers. It was the face of a child, but it was deformed with pain. When Don Paolo realized that Berenice had already gone, it was too late. He remained standing right by the door. Several minutes had already gone by. He was about to go, but the great wide-open eyes of the dying girl held him. How could he explain to this dying girl that he wasn't a priest like the rest of them? Don Paolo was paralyzed. He didn't know what to do. The dying girl continued to stare at him with her great feverish eyes.

"Courage," he said. He even tried to smile.

He came up to the girl slowly, on tiptoe, bent over her and kissed her hand. Her big eyes filled with tears. The light covers outlined her slender tormented body. Her breasts were like lemons, her legs like sticks.

"I know the whole story," said the priest. "I beg you not to tell me anything, not to humiliate yourself, not to renew your sufferings. You don't need to be confessed. You've already confessed."

The girl said, "Do you absolve me?"

"You have been pardoned," said the priest. "Who couldn't forgive you? You have already done your penance, and it's been too hard."

"If I die," asked the girl, "where will I go?"

"To the cemetery like the rest of us," said the priest.

"Will I be saved?"

"Of course you will, but don't be in such a hurry; try and postpone your departure," he said, forcing himself to joke about it.

Don Paolo held one of the girl's hands in his. His hands were on fire.

"You've got a fever too, are you sick?" said the girl.

Don Paolo nodded.

"I'm doing penance too," he said, smiling.

At this point a voice cried out from the street, "Where's that priest who's going to Pietrasecca?"

Don Paolo wanted to go, but the girl held him by the hand.

"Don't leave me right now," she said. "When will I see you again?"

"I'll be thinking of you," said Don Paolo.

"I can't believe that," said the girl. "You must have so much else to think about."

"Don't you believe me? Why don't you believe me?" said Don Paolo.

He bent over her face and looked at her closely. They looked each other in the eye in silence for some minutes. Don Paolo was overcome with pity.

"Why don't you believe me?" he said.

"Yes, I believe you," said the girl. "I've never believed anything as I believe this. You have weird eyes that don't lie. I've never seen anyone with eyes like yours."

"I'll be thinking of you," said Don Paolo.

An angry voice came in through the window. "Is that priest coming or isn't he?"

"I have to go now," said Don Paolo. "Don't be afraid, you've been forgiven. What won't be forgiven is this corrupt society which has forced you to choose between death and dishonor."

Old Magascià was sitting on the threshold of the inn. He had already had his soup and was dunking his bread in the wine. He was a tall, barrel-chested man with a beard. His left sleeve hung empty from his mutilated shoulder.

"Let's go!" said Magascià to Don Paolo. "We have a long way."

He had the priest sit next to him. The two-wheeled cart went very slowly, drawn by a donkey at a walk. Magascià was bringing to Pietrasecca its weekly provisions of salt and tobacco.

"It's not a cart for a priest to ride in," said the man. "Least of all a sick priest."

"That's all right," said Don Paolo. "Has it been a long time since you lost your arm?"

"Two years ago last Candlemas," said Magascià. "There's no use complaining. God will send flies to an old donkey. Did you know Berenice before?" Magascià added. "Did you know her daughter too? There's a lot of talk about her."

The priest did not answer.

Magascià tied the reins to the brake and lit his pipe.

"I don't have to hold the reins," he said. "This donkey's been on this trip every Saturday for ten years, and she doesn't make mistakes. She knows where to stop to drink, where to answer nature's call and how long every hill and slope is."

Magascià had bought a new hat at Fossa and was wearing it on top of his head, right over the old one.

"The donkey's name is Bersagliera," said Magascià, pointing to the poor beast which was dragging the cart. "It should mean that she goes like lightning, but now she's old."

"We all get old," said the priest.

"The donkey's lucky," said Magascià. "A donkey usually works until it's twenty-four years old, a mule to twenty-two and a horse to fifteen. But poor man has to work till he's seventy and then some. Why did God take pity on the animals and not on man? But after all, He can do as He likes."

As soon as the road left the village, it began to climb. The priest looked at the mountains, the valleys, hills and streams as if they were old friends. The villages still bore traces of the earthquake. They looked like beehives that had been split apart and only partially repaired.

Along the road Magascià's cart came on a peasant family
—the man, his wife, and a child—all riding the same
donkey. The woman's breasts were bared and she was
nursing the child.

"How are crops?" asked Magascià of the man on the
donkey.

"Bad," said he.

Magascià whispered in the priest's ear, "He's expecting
a good harvest."

"Then why did he tell you the contrary?"

"To save himself from envy," said Magascià.

"And how are your crops?" said the priest.

Magascià crossed himself.

"Disastrous," he said.

"Are you afraid I'll envy you?" said Don Paolo.

"Envy is in the air," said Magascià.

Every so often by the side of the road they came on
roadmenders who were sitting on the ground next to
piles of gravel, hammering at the larger stones. Magascià's cart crossed the village of Lama dei Marsi. Ox horns
were to be seen fastened to all the huts, a precaution
against the evil eye. On the thresholds were groups of
silent old men and swarms of half-naked children. Outside
of Lama dei Marsi was a chapel to the Madonna. Magascià crossed himself and explained to Don Paolo, "This
is the chapel of the Madonna of the Roses. It commem-
orates an old miracle. That year, in the month of January,
the roses bloomed, the cherry trees ripened and the sheep
foaled. Instead of being happy about this, people were
of course afraid. Didn't all these wonderful things mean
that some disaster was coming? They did. The cholera
came that summer."

"Why did they build the chapel?" said Don Paolo.

"You know better than I do," said Magascià. "To keep
the Madonna quiet." Then he added, "Crops are good
this year too—not for me, you understand. I mean generally the crops are good. Who knows what disasters
are coming?"

After it passed the chapel, the road wormed its way
across two hills, crossed a bridge and came into the Pietrasecca ravine, which was wide at one end but at the
other so strangled by great rocky gray cliffs as to form

a sort of prison. Among the rocks and in the little valleys worn by the torrents were little cultivated fields, tiny farms measured in rods and hands, not acres. More of these minute holdings were to be seen further up the mountain, strung together like wax plasters. The cart advanced slowly. The road had two ruts, worn by carriage wheels, like railroad tracks, and it passed by the stony bed of a stream. The sides of the valley appeared more and more split, cracked and bereft of vegetation. Among the rocks, a herd of goats, stripping the last grass from the cliff, lifted their beards at the strange priest who was coming on the salt-and-tobacco cart. When the road got steeper, Magascià got off the cart to lighten the load.

A small villa constructed in Renaissance style came into view after a bend in the road. It lay on a space dug out of the rock, and all its doors and windows were barred.

"It belonged to Don Simone Scaraffa, a peasant who got rich," said Magascià. "Have you ever heard about him? After having spent thirty years in Brazil making money in coffee, he wanted to come back here to enjoy our envy, and so he had the villa built. But our envy won out. The first week he lived there, he went stark raving mad and they had to lock him up at the asylum of Aquila, at Santa Maria di Collemaggio, where he still is. Was it worth it?"

Further on, a cross was planted in a pile of rocks, with a date on it.

"This is where they killed and robbed Don Giulio, the notary from Lama," said Magascià. "They counted seven knife wounds in him at the autopsy, and they never found out who did it. Don Giulio lent money at interest, thirty per cent, with security. There wasn't any more loaning money like that after he was gone."

The first houses of Pietrasecca came into view.

"It looks like the end of the world," said the priest, shivering.

"It's a very unlucky village," said Magascià. "It's been destroyed twice by floods and once by earthquake."

"How many people are left here?" said the priest.

"About forty hearths. Whoever can, goes down to the plain," said Magascià. "Anybody who can escape escapes."

They came on a new wooden cross planted in a pile of stones with a date by the side of the road.

"It was here . . ." Magascià started to say.

"I don't care about what happened here," said Don Paolo, "I'm sure it was something awful."

"How did you know?"

"You've told me nothing but horrors. Do you want to frighten me away?"

Magascià laughed.

"Not even the devil in person could frighten a priest away," he said. "Isn't it you people who dispense death?"

The cart came to Pietrasecca about sunset. Don Paolo saw about sixty run-down little houses, some of whose windows and doors were closed. They were probably deserted. The village was built in the shape of a funnel, hollowed out into the enclosed valley. There were only two civilized-looking houses. One, just after the bridge, was the inn run by Matalena Ricotta, where the priest was going to stay, and the other, which was older and larger at the other end of the village on a wide space and surrounded by walls, was the Colamartini family mansion, the only house in Pietrasecca to have survived all the floods and earthquakes. Beyond was a little church with a small bell tower and a door which faced the valley.

"Is Mass said in the church?" asked Don Paolo.

"For thirty years, the church has had no priest," said Magascià. "They don't come often. The village is poor. How could we support a priest?"

Even around the village the little land remaining between the rocks looked as if it had been crumbled into several tiny fields. There were so many of them and so many high stone walls dividing them that the whole looked like the foundations of a long-destroyed city. Just beyond the village the ravine was closed up like a barricaded street. No road led beyond. Two brooks came down the side of the mountain and came together in the valley to form a stream which divided the village in two parts, joined by a wooden bridge. Don Paolo looked around him and did not conceal his anxiety.

"Don't you like it?" said Magascià.

"I don't understand why they build villages in such stupid places," said the priest. "If someone wanted to escape from here, what road could he take? <u>This isn't a</u> <u>village. It's a trap.</u>"

"There are no conveniences," said Magascià. "The only advantage is that the authorities don't bother us very much."

There was a little fountain in front of the inn. A boy with a nosebleed was washing his face in the water, which was bloody. Under the bridge a group of women and girls, kneeling on the bank of the brook, were doing the washing, beating the clothes over and over again. When they caught sight of the priest, they stopped as if they were bewitched.

Magascià brought the cart up to the inn, where the old woman who ran the place was waiting. She was a short, sturdy woman, bundled up in many petticoats. A distinguished-looking old man came up, a hunting rifle over his shoulder. He welcomed the priest to his poor village. Magascià introduced him.

"This is Don Pasquale Colamartini," he said.

Don Paolo excused himself; he was dead tired.

The woman led him to his room.

"What do you want for supper?" she asked.

"Nothing," said Don Paolo. "I just want to sleep."

In the darkness of his room he heard the voice of a woman calling her boy who had stayed out late playing with the other boys.

"I'm coming, Mother. Right away!"

# 7

In the space between the bridge and the inn, under Don Paolo's window, there was a baptism of a donkey, bought at the last fair, on Sunday morning. A boy held him by the halter and an old peasant was beating him with a piece of wood. After every blow the two of them yelled in the beast's ears, "Garibaldi!"

Garibaldi was the name they had chosen for the donkey. In the peasant's mind this meant force and courage. The baptism took a long time, because naturally it took a long time to persuade the donkey that he was Garibaldi. The man was beating the donkey on the rump with neither anger, impatience nor resentment, but hard, just as if he were beating a mattress, and after every blow the two of them yelled in the beast's ears, "Garibaldi!"

The donkey was looking at them, and every now and then he shook his head. The man was beating the donkey on the side, one blow for each rib. When he had beaten all the ribs, he started all over again. The heroic name of Garibaldi sounded again and again in the square of Pietrasecca, alternating with blows of the wood on the donkey—until the man got tired and said to the boy, "That's enough. He must be convinced by now."

The boy made an experiment. He took a handful of straw, went over to the bridge and called the donkey from there, showing the straw.

"Garibaldi."

The donkey trotted over to the bridge.

"He's convinced," said the boy.

Don Paolo was in bed, burning with fever. The trip had exhausted him. The repeated invocation of Garibaldi which came through the window surprised him and made him wonder. Could the party of the republic still be so strong in such an out-of-the-way village?

72

"What's happening?" the priest asked the woman in charge of the inn.

"Nothing unusual," said Matalena. "Sciatàp is baptizing his new donkey."

Old Sciatàp was known by this name throughout the valley. He had been baptized with a stick of wood in the same way. As a young man he had worked in America as a helper for a man from his home town, a certain Carlo Campanella, who sold coal in the winter and ice in the summer on Mulberry street in New York. Actually the man, who was Carlo Campanella in Pietrasecca, had become in New York Mr. Charles Little-Bell, *Ice & Coal*. He treated his helper like a beast of burden. Every time the poor beast complained, Mr. Little-Bell yelled at him, "Sciatàp!" *shut up used in 1961 vers.*

It seems that this means *be quiet* in English. When Sciatàp came back to Pietrasecca, after several years in America, the only English word he knew was *sciatàp*, and he repeated it on every possible occasion. His wife could not open her mouth, because when she did he put his finger on her mouth to indicate, "Sciatàp."

In this way the word came into the valley's dialect. It was the only English expression known at Pietrasecca, the only element of modern, foreign culture in that ancient and humble peasant tradition.

Don Paolo got out of bed and went to the window, curious to see the man. Sciatàp and the donkey were going down toward the stream by a narrow path, near the bridge. At the beginning of the path was an old sign reading: "It is prohibited to throw garbage and trash into this place." But this very place was full of garbage, kitchen scraps and other refuse. Don Paolo smiled. He liked any kind of nonconformism; and there was more to it than printing clandestine pamphlets.

Matalena had given up her room to the priest. It was on the second floor of the inn and had an immense bed which took up about three quarters of the space, barely leaving room for a little table, a chair and an iron washstand. A crucifix, with livid, skinny, tortuous arms and legs and the face of a starving peasant hung from the wall at the head of the bed. A small statue of The

Immaculate Virgin in the act of crushing the snake's head
was on the table.

Don Paolo's health stayed about the same. The mountain climate did not bring the rapid recovery he had hoped
for. He stayed in bed almost all day without getting any
real rest. The days and nights just never finished. The
air was hot and inert, and the smell of cabbage and fish
from the kitchen made him sick.

To complete his costume as a priest, Don Paolo had
received from Nunzio some devotional books, the breviary, the *Massime Eterne* of Saint Alfonso Maria dei
Liguori, the *Filotea*, a *Life of Saint Camillo de Lellis,*
a seventeenth-century saint from the Abruzzi, a life of
San Giovanni Bosco, a Piedmontese saint of the last
century, and a liturgical manual. Don Paolo began to
leaf through some of these books to pass the time, just
as he would have done with any other reading matter,
such as a detective story or the catalogue of some chemical
company. He had seen some of these books before, at
home or at school, and many of these pages and illus-
trations brought up forgotten memories. The symbols
of childish terror rose from the darkest corner of his
mind. In this way there came a day when he found himself
more and more attracted to these books and ended up
reading them every night as long as his eyes held out.
In this state of mind he wrote his first letter to Nunzio.
This was the one chance he had to communicate without
lying, even if he had to sign himself Paolo Spada. "I thank
you particularly for the books," he wrote. "What strange
impressions! I seem to have found a treasure under a
rock." More than the books, the extreme weakness to
which his illness had reduced him brought back the years
of his adolescence, when he had been sick for a couple
of days and, on account of his generally weak health
and his status as an only child, he was always helped and
comforted by his mother, his grandmother, his aunts
and all the servant girls in the house, wrapped in an
atmosphere of affection and female tenderness. Though
chance had forced him to take refuge in a circle socially
somewhat inferior to the one he had grown up in, even
at Pietrasecca all the signs of life visible to him were
women and children, since the men spent the day at work

in the mountains. Don Paolo had to use what little strength he had to defend himself from Matalena's energetic affection.

"With all due respect," she said, "I could be your mother. Let me treat you as a son."

"If you don't stop, I'll leave," he said. "I have no intention of being treated like a child."

Matalena considered <u>the presence of the priest in her inn as a blessing above all,</u> and she was always near him on one pretext or another. She thought she would be free from misfortune as long as the priest stayed in her house. Fear of earthquakes kept her in a state of perpetual anxiety. A cow's skull with two huge horns was firmly mounted on the roof of the inn.

"What are those two horns for?" said Don Paolo.

"Against the evil eye," said Matalena, and she crossed herself. "Just against the evil eye. It's no good against other calamities, I'm afraid."

In fact, in spite of the cow's horns, Matalena's house, along with several others, had been destroyed in the earthquake of 1915.

"It was the biggest one around here," said Matalena. "My husband, God rest his soul, had suffered six years in Argentina to build it. All the money I had left went to the builders and carpenters. When the house was destroyed, it had been finished for three months. I was buried in the cellar for a week. I really didn't know there'd been an earthquake. I thought it was only the evil eye and that it was just my house. You can imagine how I felt. After a week, when they'd cleared out the rubble enough so I could get out, I was scared to. 'Let me die here,' I told them, 'I haven't anything more to live for.' I really didn't want to live. But they reassured me. 'Almost the whole village is gone,' they said. 'Almost all Marsica has been destroyed; thirty towns have been razed to the ground and fifty thousand dead have been counted so far.' It was true. It wasn't a private evil eye, but a chastisement from God. How does it go? 'If it's everybody's misfortune, it's nobody's misfortune!' My husband, God rest his soul, had to come back to Italy for the war, and with God's help he got out of it alive. After the war he went back to Argentina and worked another five years to save enough money to build another house. As soon as he'd done that and was about to come back to enjoy it, he stopped writing. After six months, I got a message from town. I thought it was a new tax. I went, and a clerk told me, 'Your husband died in an accident. He was run over by a car.' I started to cry and said, 'It was envy, because he was going to come back and enjoy the new house.' "

Telling the story brought on a flood of tears.

"An automobile accident can happen to anyone," said Don Paolo.

"Excuse me, did it happen to you?"

"No."

"And why not?" said Matalena. "And if you don't believe in the evil eye since you're a priest, why do you wear black? With all due respect, why do you hide your legs?"

But Matalena's funny ideas couldn't get Don Paolo out of his bad mood. Nunzio was not answering his letters, but every two or three days he sent him clippings of the most important political news in a sealed envelope. It was too little to calm his anxiety. For how long was he condemned to exile in this Siberia? Matalena's uninterrupted chatter soon became as natural to him as the wind or the babbling of the brook. Apart from that, Matalena was a pious woman who boasted that she respected Wednesdays and Fridays and dedicated the month of March to St. Joseph, May to the Madonna, June to the Sacred Heart and November to the dead. She was well past the forty years of age required in a priest's housekeeper, and as she talked she went around the house always undone, uncombed and bursting out of her clothes. She took a lot of trouble to keep the priest well fed. After every meal, she waited for compliments which never came. Don Paolo had never been a glutton, and at Pietrasecca there was little choice of food. What he liked best was bread soaked in wine. But every morning Matalena came to his room to ask what he wanted to eat that day. Even if there was not much to choose from, the daily question continued. One day the priest got tired of this and told Matalena to serve him what every inhabitant of Pietrasecca usually ate. Matalena was offended and agreed, just to take revenge. In the morning she gave him a piece of black bread with an onion and at noon she served him another piece of black bread and some raw peppers, with oil and salt. In the evening he got a bowl of bean-and-potato soup. This diet lasted only two days because all Don Paolo could eat was the soup in the evening. The peasants heard of this and laughed. Living like the poor is easier said than done. Matalena took advantage of her victory and returned to her morning question. She had fixed ideas about what to do for diseases of the lungs.

"Fresh eggs are the best medicine," she said.

She kept about a dozen chickens in the garden in back of the inn. As soon as an egg was laid, she took it to the priest. If a hen was late in laying, she pursued it, and when it was caught she felt it to see if there was an egg inside. After that, she would call to the priest from the garden, "A little patience. It won't be long."

Staying in bed did not prevent Don Paolo from following the life in the village. It was rudimentary. In the morning a certain Chiarina came by the inn with a goat. Matalena took a bowl and milked the goat herself, to the last drop. By that time the men had already gone and the women were shaking the bugs out of their hair. Filomena Sapone came to the inn about noon with a baby on her arm and some lettuce from her garden. She sat on the threshold, opened her dress and took out her breasts. The little brat did not have to be persuaded. Filomena was the first to ask Don Paolo to hear her confession, but the priest answered that he had no permission. Word of this got around, to the great disappointment of everyone. It was often discussed, at the communal oven and in the cobbler's, carpenter's and barber's shops. Matalena went to ask Don Pasquale's opinion, which put her to silence.

"If you annoy him, he'll go away," he said.

On the square between the inn and the bridge the boys played military games. One day they had an argument about who the enemy should be. Everyone complained that it changed too often. Three boys came to Don Paolo's room and asked him, "Who's the enemy now?"

"What enemy?" asked the surprised priest.

"The hereditary enemy," said one of the boys.

The priest did not understand, or at least he pretended not to.

"We always have two sides in our games," explained the boy. "The Italians are on one side and the hereditary enemy on the other. For a long time the schoolteacher told us that this was France or Yugoslavia. Then she told us Germany, then Japan. This morning, she said, 'Boys, the new hereditary enemy is England.' But in the schoolbooks there's a chapter with the title, 'Italy's centuries-old friendship with England.' Now we don't understand anything at all. Who's wrong, the schoolteacher or the book?"

"The book," said Don Paolo. "It was printed last year, so it's out of date."

"Good," said the boys, "we'll beat the hereditary English enemy."

"The English fight on the sea, not on the land," said the priest.

The boys decided to fight in the brook. Don Paolo followed their game from the window. The new hereditary enemy was rapidly beaten, but the defenders of the national honor came out of it soaking wet.

The boys in the village, in a sense, made up their own community with their own laws, rites and dialect. Among them were champion stone throwers, brook jumpers, lizard hunters and long-distance pissers against the wind. Mothers called for their sons from morning to night. The air was often full of the most terrible curses, which did not mean anything to anyone since they were repeated so often.

In the afternoons, if the weather were good, the women attended to their housework in the street. Some hung up the wash, others cleaned potatoes, others attended to their mending and still others picked the lice from their children. The few who hadn't anything to do came to sit in front of the inn. These women were barefoot and dressed in rags. They had oily hair and the facial expressions of dumb goats. Among these was a certain Cesira, an old woman exhausted by hunger and childbirth, who was always complaining of the same pains. Mostly the women talked about bearing children. Annunziata had just borne her fourteenth child. Lidovina had had eighteen. It was hardest to get the first one out, the others found the way prepared. There was also one Annina, who was pregnant. She touched her belly and said, "Here's the head, here's a foot, and here's the other foot. It must be a boy, because sometimes he kicks me."

"That's in the hands of God," said Cesira. "God decides things according to our sins. Every sorrow is a chastisement."

When the noise of their chatter was lowered, it was evident that they were talking about the priest. What could Matalena be making up to assuage their curiosity? It was hard to imagine. A low murmur was all the priest could hear. The only changes in the routine were made by the weather. The suffocating heat was interrupted every once in a while by brief and violent showers.

Don Paolo took out his ill humor in the notes he wrote to Nunzio. "I feel like a carcass surrounded by clouds of flies," he wrote. "I can't possibly stay here for long." He couldn't rest nor stay seated nor remain on his feet. Nor could he read or write.

From morning to night a troop of semi-nude children, covered with mud, played around a puddle formed from the fountain's overflow. They went away only when the schoolteacher, Signorina Patrignani, came up.

When the weather was good, most of the women cooked the soup in the street, setting up a tripod over a fire on some stones and a copper pot over the tripod. The whole valley smelled of cooking beans.

At dusk Signorina Cristina Colamartini came to the inn. The deep silence which immediately followed her appearance showed how respected she was. In the silence Don Paolo recognized the girl's voice asking after his health and giving advice to Matalena on how to treat him. Then she went rapidly away. Don Paolo had not yet seen Signorina Cristina, but he had heard from Matalena that she had studied music for many years in a convent and was about to take the veil herself.

"Donna Cristina is no woman, she's an angel," Matalena said about her; however, Matalena had poisoned arrows for the rest of her family. At home Cristina had to help her ninety-year-old grandmother, her parents and an aunt, who was also very old. Her good-for-nothing brother was always away. "If you're interested," said Matalena, "you can ask Magascià. He knows all about them."

"I'm not interested," answered the priest.

Cassarola the wise woman, on the other hand, was a positive nuisance. After having worried that the arrival of the priest would reduce her power, she had been reassured on hearing that Don Paolo had no permission to administer the sacraments. One day she went to him to offer her magic herbs against coughs. The sick man refused. She was a horrible old hag with a turned-up nose and huge prominent lips like a Negress. To show the priest how religious she was she started to mutter prayers, magic works and responses in barbarous Latin; she unbuttoned her blouse and revealed the medals, scapulars and rosaries she wore on her bosom and showed her arms covered with sacred tattoos.

"God rules over good, but not over evil," she said with self-assurance. "Otherwise, why wouldn't he cure his priests when they get sick? Why don't you pray to God and get cured?"

Don Paolo, not to be outdone, offered her some advice.

"Go to hell," he told her.

Fortunately the old woman had other customers. Antonia the seamstress' daughter was sick. Cassarola prescribed a glass of wine for her every morning.

"She's only three years old," said the mother.

"She's already three?" said Cassarola. "Well then, you can give her a glass of wine at night, too."

Matalena's principal occupation in her capacity as nurse and custodian of the consecrated man was to explain to everyone over and over again why Don Paolo could not administer the sacraments.

"Not even paying twice as much?"

"Not even then."

"Not even if you pay three times as much?"

"Not even then."

"Not even whatever he asks for—on credit?"

"Nothing on credit."

The curate of Lama, Don Cipriano, should have been

able to provide for the small religious needs of the population of Pietrasecca—the baptisms, weddings and funerals —but as he slowly advanced into old age, his visits became rarer and rarer. For this reason an unwritten agreement had grown up between nature's blind laws and the peasants' instincts whereby these ceremonies were always grouped together at Pietrasecca. Weddings were celebrated between October and November, so the children were expected between May and July. It was a sort of conscription from which few were exempt. Many children died in their first months of life. It was a periodic slaughter of the innocents.

On Sunday mornings various women would go as far as Lama to hear Mass. They wore black shawls on their shoulders, handkerchiefs over their heads (because it wouldn't have been decent to show their hair), black shoes and stockings. From his window Don Paolo saw them coming and going. The oldest of them walked with their rosaries in hand, moving them slowly between their thumb and index finger. They kneeled very respectfully when the carriage bringing Don Pasquale and Signorina Cristina to Mass passed by. But there were some circumstances in which the absence of a parish priest made itself felt, so that not even Matalena's careful protection was enough to save Don Paolo from some unpleasant incidents.

A peasant woman, Teresa Scaraffa, was expecting a child, and one night she dreamed that it would be born blind. Early the next morning the poor woman came to Don Paolo, kneeled at the foot of his bed and said, "Last night I dreamed that my child would be born blind. Only you can save him."

"My poor woman, I'm sorry, but there's nothing I can do," said the priest.

The woman started to weep and beg.

"I don't want my child to be blind. Why should the other children see, and not him?"

Her yellow round face somewhat resembled an old sheep.

Don Paolo tried to calm her down, but it was no use.

"I dreamed it," said the woman, "I saw it with my own eyes. If you don't help me, he'll be blind!"

The woman did not want to go. But Don Paolo knew

quite well that if he were to pretend to recite some prayers
or carry out an exorcism in just one case, the whole inn
would be full of people waiting for their turn.
He would not be able to refuse anyone. They would all say
to him, "You helped Teresa Scaraffa. Now help us." The
rumors would spread down the plain. Aside from con-
ducting a farce, he would attract the attention of the
authorities to himself.

He therefore called Matalena and told her, "Get
that woman out of my room, however you do it. I don't
care about her dreams."

But Teresa got up in a rage and yelled, "Why does
my child have to be blind? Why can the other children
see the light, and not mine?"

Teresa waited for him to answer; instead, Don Paolo
repeated brusquely that it was out of his jurisdiction.
The woman got on her knees again, slamming her head
on the floor and tearing her hair out by the roots, and
saying all sorts of senseless things. "Why should he be
blind? Why? Tell me why! I just want to know why! The
other children will see and he won't. The other children
will go to school and he won't. Everybody will steal from
him and he won't know! They'll all make fun of him
and he won't see them! No woman will want to have
anything to do with him when he grows up!"

Then she got on her feet and was calm.

"Now I know what I'll do," she said. "I'll jump out the
window. He'll die with me."

The woman went to the window. Don Paolo had no
doubt that in her hysterical state she really would jump
out of the window. She was on the window sill when the
priest called her.

"I'll do what you want," he said. "What do I have to
do?"

Matalena went to fetch the church keys, which were
kept in the Colamartini house, and brought a glass of
holy water from the church. Don Paolo was frightened
and did not have anything to say.

Teresa brought her swollen belly up to the priest.

"Here," she said. "The head must be here, and the
eyes over here."

The priest made two crosses where Teresa pointed,

one for each eye, moving his lips as if he were praying.

"Now he's all right," said the woman. "The trouble is over. Thank you."

The woman went off, and after a while she came back with a dead chicken,

"Are you still here?" cried the priest angrily.

The woman showed him the chicken.

"I can't accept," answered Don Paolo. "Priests can't take gifts."

The woman protested.

"It's no good," she said. "If you won't take the chicken the grace isn't any good and the child will be born blind."

"Grace costs nothing," said Don Paolo.

"There's no such thing as free grace," said the woman. To conclude the discussion, she abandoned the sacrificial victim on the table and escaped.

This happened one Saturday. It was the day Magascià came down to Fossa with his cart for the weekly supply of salt and tobacco. Don Paolo sent for him at once and gave him a letter for Nunzio. "I've had enough," he wrote his friend. "As soon as I'm well, I'm leaving for Rome."

## 8

He was seated on a bench under the apple tree, and on his knees he was holding the three-legged stool Matalena used to keep her skirts dry when she did the wash by the river. He was writing a letter.

"I'm writing to you even if you don't answer me," he said in his letter to Nunzio, "to avoid talking to myself and being taken for mad wherever I go. If it continues like this, I'll cure my lungs at the expense of my sanity. This is not just a masquerade I play for amusement. . . ."

A <u>procession of ants</u> was climbing down the tree trunk and spreading out over the ground. Every ant was carrying a load. He watched the ants for a moment and continued.

"If I could just go to sleep and wake up tomorrow morning to load up the donkey and go to the vineyard. If I could just go to sleep and wake up again not only with my lungs all well, but also with the mind of a normal man, with my head freed from all abstractions. If I could just go back to conventional life, hoeing, planting and harvesting, being able to earn a living and talk with the other men on Sundays. To fulfill the law which says '<u>In the sweat of thy face shalt thou eat bread</u>.' Perhaps my anguish comes from the infraction of this ancient law, from my habit of living among the cafés, the libraries and the hotels, of having broken the centuries-old chain which bound my ancestors to the earth. <u>Perhaps</u> I feel myself an outlaw not so much for having disobeyed the arbitrary decrees of the party in power as for <u>having been outside that ancient law which had established that in the sweat of thy face shalt</u> thou eat bread. I'm not a farmer anymore, but I have not yet become a city man. It is impossible to go back to the land and it is much harder to forget it."

He was still in the garden when a girl came from Fossa dei Marsi in Magasscià's cart.

"There's the inn, to the right after you cross the bridge," the carter said to her.

The girl ran up and asked Matalena, "Does Don Paolo Spada live here?"

Matalena was jealous of her priest, and before answering the strange girl she wanted to know, "Why?"

"He saved me when I was dying and I wanted to thank him."

"The Don Paolo who lives here isn't a doctor but a priest," said Matalena.

"Maybe he's neither a priest nor a doctor but a saint," said the girl. "I was dying, he arrived, touched my hand; and I was well."

Matalena was proud of having a priest in her inn, but the idea of having a saint who performed miracles while he was still alive was very disturbing to her.

"If he's a real saint," said Matalena, so as not to look as if she could not recognize a saint, "he's living here in penance, like a real man of God. I don't know if he'll want to receive you; you see, he's not from this diocese."

"Maybe he's more than a saint," said the girl from Fossa dei Marsi. "I think he might be Jesus in person."

Matalena was thunderstruck. She sat on a bench and murmured, "Are you crazy? How can you think he's Jesus himself? Why would Jesus come to my inn? Isn't He in heaven, at the right hand of the Father?"

Matalena was talking in a low tone, so that the one who lived at her inn, if it were really He, could not hear her doubting words.

"It wouldn't be the first time Jesus came to earth to see how the poor people are getting along," answered the girl. Then she added in a very soft voice, "Have you seen His pierced hands and feet? That's the surest way to tell. He can dress himself up as He likes, but if it's really Him, He can't hide the stigmata."

Matalena was in unspeakable rapture. She was not prepared for such an eventuality. O Lord, what should she do? Supper was already laid on the table: two eggs and a lettuce salad. She blushed at the thought. It would be shameful to offer two eggs and a salad to the Son of God. At least she should slaughter a lamb. But what if it were not He after all?

"How do you know it's Him? Where did you get that

idea? Tell me, if you're not crazy," said Matalena, wracked with doubt.

The girl answered, "I recognized Him by his voice. When He appeared, He took my hand, and before I could open my mouth He told me: 'Courage. I know the whole story.' All of a sudden, I felt this wasn't a human voice. I know men. They don't talk like that. I have an uncle who's a priest at Fossa, and he sure doesn't talk like that."

"Tell me," asked Matalena, "what do we do if he really is Jesus? Should we tell Don Cipriano? Should we call the police?"

The police rules were displayed on the door of the inn. But the arrival of Jesus was not covered there.

The two women tiptoed to the second floor, not even daring to breathe. They knocked on the door. No one answered. Slowly they opened the door. The room was empty. Matalena was about to faint.

"He's gone," she said.

The two women looked at each other in alarm. At this point they heard someone cough in the garden. They ran down. Don Paolo was seated on a bench at the foot of the apple tree, with an open book on his knees.

"Is someone looking for me?" he said.

The women came up trembling.

"It's me, Bianchina," said the girl. "Bianchina Girasole from Fossa dei Marsi, Berenice's daughter. Do you remember me?"

"I'm glad to see you're still alive," said Don Paolo smiling. "You know, I've thought of you often."

"Did you keep your promise?" said Bianchina, radiant.

"Don't you believe me?"

"I believe you," said Bianchina. "I was just about dying, everyone had given me up, you touched my hand and saved me."

Don Paolo had a fit of coughing. The sun had gone down. The cold shadows of the night were coming up from the bottom of the valley. He got up and the two women followed him to his room. Don Paolo was tired and he sat down on the foot of the bed. Bianchina stayed by the door. After getting up her nerve, she said in a trembling voice, "Show me your hands—please!"

Don Paolo smiled. "Are you going to tell my fortune?"

Bianchina took a close look at his hands. There was no trace of the stigmata. No sign of the crucifixion. He was not Jesus. He was a saint, but not Jesus.

"It's better that way," said Bianchina, satisfied. "I'd rather have you a man."

"Did you think I was a ghost?" said Don Paolo laughing.

Matalena was also relieved, and she went back to the kitchen. The two of them were silent for a while.

"Can't I do anything for you?" said Bianchina. "I see that you're sick."

"Thanks," said Don Paolo.

The girl's face seemed all the more delicate in contrast to the door's dark rectangle. Her neck was slender, her mouth red and a bit wide (a bit too wide when she was laughing), but the vitality in her eyes and gestures and the frankness of her questions gave her an ingenuous, almost childish expression.

"My mother wanted to throw me out of the house," said Bianchina with a scowl.

"Why?"

Bianchina sought for the words. "My mother thinks I'm the dishonor of the family. Maybe she's right. If I like a man, I don't know how to resist him. I suppose you agree with my mother."

"I don't know," said Don Paolo. "I've never been a mother yet."

Bianchina burst into laughter. But she went right back to melancholy.

"Even if my mother could stand me," she said, "I couldn't live at home any more. It smells of mold. Have you ever smelled mold?"

"What are you going to do?" asked the priest.

"Can't I do anything for you?"

"It seems to me you should think of yourself first," said the priest. "What'll you do if your mother throws you out?"

"I don't know," said Bianchina. "I can't do anything. When I knit, I always drop a stitch; when I sew, I prick my finger; if I hoe the garden, I always hit my foot with the hoe. The sisters taught me to make pastry, to embroider and to sing the Gregorian chant. Maybe I could sing the Magnificat or Salve Regina in a nightclub?"

"But if you can't do anything," said the priest, "what would you do for me?"

"Anything, just so I could be with you."

"By the way," said the priest, "where are you staying tonight?"

It was a thorny problem. Don Paolo sighed and Bianchina's eyes filled with tears.

"At Pietrasecca," she said, "there's an old schoolmate of mine, Cristina Colamartini. She's a little saint too; maybe she'll help me. Do you know her?"

It was time for Cristina's daily visit to the inn. Matalena told her Bianchina had arrived and Cristina appeared on the threshold of the invalid's room. Bianchina ran to her and embraced her.

"How beautiful you are," she said and repeated it.

Matalena brought up another chair so Cristina could sit down and fix her disheveled hair. Don Paolo knew her only by her voice, which, he discovered, corresponded perfectly with what he saw. She was a very graceful creature with a thin but perfectly formed face and tall, slim figure. She was wearing a black dress closed at the neck and the wrists like a schoolgirl's. The way she wore her jet-black hair strengthened the impression. It was parted in the middle, lightly waved at the temples and gathered at the back in a knot.

Cristina said good evening to the priest and excused herself for disturbing him.

"You mean you don't know each other yet?" asked Bianchina. "This is Cristina and she was my first love. We were together three years at the same sisters' school. She was first in the class, and of course I was last; and we liked each other for that too."

Then she added, "There always comes a time in life when you return to your first love. And he," said Bianchina to her friend, pointing to Don Paolo, "is a saint to whom I owe my life."

Don Paolo paid no attention to what Bianchina was saying because he was enchanted with her friend. Could there be such a girl at Pietrasecca? Her face, neck and hands had the pallor of white roses; but there was nothing in nature to compare with the light in her eyes and the charm of her smile.

"We're tiring Don Paolo with our useless chatter," said Cristina, blushing, as she got up to leave.

"I'm coming with you," said Bianchina. "You wouldn't want to leave me alone with a priest. I'll be back tomorrow morning," she added to Don Paolo. "You still haven't answered my question."

Matalena was aware that her guest's mood had changed, but in spite of all her attempts, she could not find out what had changed him.

"Magascià has told me all kinds of stories about that girl," said the woman. She did not go on because he was not listening.

"I feel better," said Don Paolo. "It's strange, but I almost feel settled here."

But that night he could not sleep a wink. In the morning, Matalena chided him as she served the coffee.

"You look like a drowned rat," she said. "People will think I treat you badly."

The priest stared out the window.

"I'm surprised that Donna Cristina took in that girl," added the woman, "after all the stories about her and Cristina's brother."

Through the open window, the priest saw Cristina leaving the house. He hurriedly got dressed and came down the stairs.

"Hello," he said, smiling. "You're up early!"

"I'm glad to see you a moment before Bianchina gets here," said Cristina. "You don't know what power you've acquired over my friend."

"She's a bit too imaginative," said Don Paolo.

"Yes, but she's been through some terrible things," said Cristina. "Last night she told me about them. I couldn't even close my eyes all night. Believe me, you're the only person who can save her now."

"Will Bianchina accept being saved—and in what sense?" said Don Paolo.

"You can show her the right way."

Don Paolo did not hide his doubts.

"Will Bianchina go along the right way without anyone with her? I certainly can't go with her," he said.

"Your thoughts can go with her," said Cristina. "Maybe that will be enough. You don't know how influential your promise to Bianchina was—to think of her from time to time. She assures me that from that time on your thoughts were with her."

"As a matter of fact, I have thought about her," said the priest. "But may I continue? You may not be aware, Cristina, that I am too inclined to obsessions."

This confidence was visibly embarrassing to Cristina.

"I meant you should remember her in your prayers," she said, blushing.

"What sort of plot are you hatching against me?" cried Bianchina, running up with her hair in the wind.

"I must make coffee for the rest of the family," said Cristina suddenly. "Until we meet again."

Don Paolo invited Bianchina to keep him company for a while in the garden of the inn.

"Come, sit here," he said.

"I hope you've thought about my question," said the girl. "Can't I do something for you?" Then she added, "I wouldn't want to go back to the life I've been leading. I'd like to see you at least once in a while. But I don't want to be a parasite."

"Yes, I do need you," said Don Paolo.

"Really?" said Bianchina, jumping up. "Will you take me with you when you go back to your diocese?"

"Right now," he said.

"Aren't you afraid of a scandal? In a small town like this everything will get out."

"I'm not asking you what you think I am."

"I'm afraid I haven't anything else to give," said Bianchina.

"You have many other things," said Don Paolo.

"Are you sure? What, for example?"

"I'm serious," said Don Paolo. "I have to send someone to Rome to a friend of mine, on a very delicate personal errand. Only you can do this."

"Why just me?"

"I don't trust anyone else but you."

"You're not making fun of me? Excuse me, I didn't mean to doubt your word. But no one's ever told me that before. I never thought anyone would trust me."

"But I trust you."

"Is this trip to Rome on important business?"

"Very important," said Don Paolo. "But I'm afraid I can't tell you what it's all about. There are some secrets priests can't talk about. Don't you trust me?"

"I'd jump in the fire for you," said Bianchina. Then she added, "Are they secrets of the confessional?"

Don Paolo nodded. "Listen, Bianchina," he said. "You mustn't tell anyone you're going to Rome for me, not even Cristina or your mother. You can think up any excuse you want."

"Thinking up excuses is one of my few specialties," said Bianchina. "But this is the first time I'm doing it for a priest. Are these sacred lies?"

"They're not really lies," said Don Paolo. "Just white lies."

"When I'm away, will you think of me?"

"I promise," said Don Paolo.

"You won't two-time me with Cristina?"

"Don't talk nonsense!"

# 9

Don Paolo's anxiety shifted between thoughts of Bianchina, who had left for Rome unaware that she was involved in a risky attempt to set up once again his contact with the clandestine organization, and the ardent desire to see Cristina again, whose beauty had entirely fascinated him. As if to worsen his desperation, Cristina was not seen at Matalena's inn in those days. Was she perhaps aware that she had stirred up a dangerous fire in Don Paolo? Was she resisting temptation? He sent Matalena on some excuse to explore the situation. No, Cristina's thoughts were elsewhere, because the day of her departure for the convent was approaching. Her family was resigned; her outfit was prepared; the abbess had been informed; but the day before she was supposed to leave, Cristina's old grandmother, who had always been against the idea, succeeded in persuading Don Pasquale. The conversation between father and daughter had been very painful.

"Your grandmother is right," he had said. "You know to what a point we've been reduced. Your brother's no good any more. He's extravagant; he can't hold a job; and he never does a thing. We don't even know where he is. If you leave, too, I'll be alone with your grandmother, your mother and your aunt—three completely useless old women. That's how we'll end up in the care of some maid who'll rob us of what little we have left."

After a long, tearful crisis, Cristina ended by giving in to her father.

"I'll do nothing against your will," she said.

But her father loved his daughter, and didn't dare to forbid her vocation entirely. All he asked for was a postponement.

"If God wants you, He'll provide," he said.

For once the people of Pietrasecca were unanimously

on the old woman's side. "A daughter belongs to her family first and then to the Church," was the common opinion. Don Paolo had already heard a lot of strange things about Cristina's grandmother, the tyrant of the Colamartini family. Her grandmother wanted Cristina to marry. The family fortune was on the rocks. Only a good marriage could save it. But this was something Don Pasquale couldn't talk about with his daughter. Sad and silent, Cristina continued to run the house without complaints. She attended to the hens, made the beds, swept out the rooms and swept up and down the stairs, helped her mother and aunt in the kitchen, ironed and cared for the bees in the garden. She came out of the house rarely and for only a few moments. But one morning, while Don Paolo was in Matalena's garden, Cristina came up suddenly with some onions to transplant. Don Paolo was in ecstasy. The morning light seemed to wrap the girl in a golden veil. Some bees were flying around her head as if it were a flower, and this resemblance to a flower seemed beautiful to the priest, though it was a pale flower. He screwed up his courage and asked her, "Excuse the indiscretion, but are you perhaps disappointed at not having left for the novitiate?"

Cristina smiled.

"I hope you won't find it discourteous," she said, "if I answer you with three great words which they taught me as a child and which I've never forgotten: *Jesus autem tacebat*. These are the gospel words which have perhaps made the greatest impression on me. Jesus has taught us to be silent when we are under torture."

"Does secular life torture you?" asked Don Paolo. "Isn't the abandonment of your family a form of flight?"

Cristina looked at the priest with uncertainty. Was he perhaps playing the part of the devil's advocate to test her?

"Real flight is to flee from God," she said. "Whoever is far from God is also far from his neighbor."

"Can't you be pious within your own family? Can't you pray and meditate at home?" he asked.

"One mustn't be bold, but docile. One must let oneself be helped," she said. "Just this morning I read in a book by a French nun: 'Does a newborn babe get up by himself to take his mother's breast? Or is it not the mother who takes her little one and gently bends over him to nourish him and still his cries?' We are all like newborn babes, and the Church is like our mother."

These were conventional subjects. Don Paolo and Cristina hardly knew each other. The priest's answer was conventional too.

"I didn't mean to discuss theology with you," he said. "But here's an area in great economic misery, and even greater spiritual misery. If ever a peasant succeeds in mastering his animal instincts, he joins the Franciscans; if a girl frees herself from slavery to the body, she enters a convent. Don't you think this is the source of many ills? Don't you think every creature should live and struggle among other creatures, rather than locking himself up in an ivory tower?"

"The believer absorbed in his prayers is never far from his neighbor," said Cristina. "Only the soul which does not feel God is a leaf torn loose from the tree, an isolated leaf, which falls to the earth, dries up and rots. But the soul united to God is like a leaf united to the tree. By the sap which feeds it, it communicates with the branches, the trunk, the roots and the earth. Isn't that right?"

Don Paolo smiled. He was in an inferior position, since he had, in addition to the rest, to express himself in language compatible with his ecclesiastical clothes.

"But you know more about this than I do," added Cristina with a smile. "Is the examination over?"

"I assure you, I had no intention of examining you," said Don Paolo. "At first, this forced solitude irritated me, but now I'm getting used to it. Now I must think of certain things which are not easily considered in the active life. I would like to discuss them with you."

"You must let yourself be carried away by the silence," said Cristina, smiling, "as a drowning man is carried by a deep current of water. Only then does God talk to us."

Cristina shook hands with Don Paolo and said cordially to him, "I hope to see you soon again. I like to talk to you, too."

When he got back to his room, Don Paolo sat at the table, took a notebook and wrote on the cover: "Dialogues with Cristina." After a moment of thought, he began to write: "Lying has never been so repugnant to me as now. As long as it is a question of subterfuges to deceive the police, I do not mind. I even enjoy it. But what torture it is to carry on this farce with Cristina and not to tell her what I would like to if I could speak frankly. Dear Cristina, I will talk to you in this notebook. At least here there will be no need of pretense."

The dialogue with Cristina was also a conversation with himself. "I seem to have a certain number of strong entanglements. I can't go on like this. Perhaps that is why I am ill."

He stopped writing, got up and went to the window. The Colamartini house seemed deserted, a great gray rock nestling against the black mountain. It looked like a fortress. Which was Cristina's room? Don Paolo went back to the table and began writing again.

"Being in this little village in contact with these primitive people and then meeting this girl has all reduced me to what I was fifteen years ago. I find many traits of my adolescence in Cristina, almost a portrait of myself, certainly a touched-up and idealized, feminine version, but substantially a mirror of what I felt and thought: the same infatuation with the absolute, the same repudiation of compromise and of the white lies of everyday life, even the same readiness for sacrifice. Going through my native village at night, I saw the ghosts of that egotism and hypocrisy from which I am fleeing. I felt like a dead man going back through his past life. I heard nothing but the barking of dogs, but they seemed a faithful recording of the thoughts of most of the people who were sleeping there. No, I am not at all sorry to be separated from them. But the question is this: have I been faithful to my own promise?"

He remembered his first entry into a Socialist group. He had left the Church not because he no longer believed in the dogmas or the efficacy of the sacraments but because it had seemed to him that the Church was identified with the corrupt, wicked and cruel society which it should have been fighting. When he became a socialist, that was all that drove him. He was not yet a Marxist. He was to come to know Marxism later in the group, but for the present he accepted it "as the rule of the new community." Meanwhile, had not that community also become a synagogue? "I am saddened by all enterprises that intend to save the world. They seem the surest possible way to lose one's self."

At the time it had seemed to Don Paolo that his return to Italy had been, basically, an attempt to get away from that professionalism, to go back to the ranks in order to find the key to the difficulty.

These thoughts were to give him no peace. At dinner he was silent and more than usually distracted. Matalena spoke to him in vain: it was as if he were deaf. To the innkeeper's great regret and offense, he did not even pay attention to what he put in his mouth. He went into the garden as soon as he had his coffee. Seated on the bench, and with the notebook on his knees, he began to write.

"Is it possible to take part in politics, to serve one party, and to remain sincere? Hasn't truth become for me the party's truth? and justice, party justice? Has not the organization ended up by extinguishing in me all moral values, which are held in contempt as petit bourgeois prejudices, and has not the organization itself become the supreme value? Have I then not fled the opportunism of a decadent church to fall into the Machiavellianism of a sect? If these are dangerous thoughts to be banished from my revolutionary consciousness, how, in good faith, can I face the risks of clandestine struggle?"

Don Paolo read over what he had written and realized that he had only asked questions. A flock of sparrows and some wild doves came up and fluttered about him as in a bird house. It seemed to some women, observing the scene from a distance, that he was talking with the birds. In fact, not having anyone else to talk to, the poor priest was talking to himself. The women immediately ran to the inn to announce the miracle.

"Your priest talks to the birds like St. Francis," they said to Matalena.

"Yes, he's a saint, a real saint," she replied.

## 10

"We should see each other more often," said Don Paolo to Cristina, mastering his shyness. "Believe me, it does me good to talk with you."

"My father sends the same invitation," said the girl, laughing. "He thinks we haven't been hospitable enough to you. But you would excuse us if you knew of our family afflictions."

"Up to now, I've had to keep to my bed," said Don Paolo. "But for the rest of my time in Pietrasecca I would like nothing better than to let myself be spoiled, if not by your family, by you."

The air in Pietrasecca had restored to the priest's face some of its lost freshness. His face had a dark and muddy hue, but he had gotten rid of the wrinkles.

"You look twenty years younger after staying in my house, even if I do say so myself," said Matalena.

Cristina agreed with Matalena on some improvements to be made in the treatment of the guest. The girl was a genius at creating beauty out of nothing; and it was wonderful to see Don Paolo's room freshened with flowers at her hands. As their meetings became more frequent, Don Paolo and Cristina became more open and sincere with one another. At first, Don Paolo was still embarrassed at his concern not to arouse suspicions about his real identity, but as he became more acquainted with Cristina's innocence, these preoccupations died out. He allowed himself to talk of his adolescence, his village, his first studies, his first religious experiences, and his first steps in real life—taking care only to situate all these memories not in his own but in the Marsi diocese. Without being aware of it, he began to live his fictitious role, feeding it with living memories from his youth. There was so much

97

spontaneity, sincerity and warmth in what he said that Cristina was enchanted.

At one point she observed, "If you were to write all this down and if someone were to read it without knowing who you were, I bet they'd think it was written by a boy of eighteen."

Their mutual sympathy made the arguments which sometimes sprang up between them less painful. What Don Paolo did not dare to tell her he confessed to his diary with a lover's tender expressions. He often was absorbed in his diary until late at night, writing a line or two, then crossing it out, rewriting it and crossing it out once again.

One morning when he opened the window, he saw Cristina on the balcony on the third floor of her house. She smiled, nodded her head in greeting and went in. It seemed to him that the girl had been waiting for him. It was the first time that Don Paolo had seen someone on that balcony, the door to which had always been closed. It was right across the square from his window. A new life began for the balcony. That morning Cristina had put two vases of geraniums there. This novelty did not escape Matalena, who discussed the affair openly. "I don't see why Cristina has put the geraniums on that balcony. The sun never shines there."

"Maybe she's experimenting," said the priest. "You shouldn't discourage her."

"Cristina never seemed to me to be the sort of girl to try any experiments," said Matalena.

She became all the more concerned at the many times Cristina watered the geraniums.

"What can Cristina be up to?" she said. "The geraniums will die with all that water and no sun."

She also discovered that Don Paolo's work table had been moved to the window. She was almost breathless with surprise.

"You always complained about drafts," she said. She realized what was happening, but she did not dare call it by its right name. All she said was, "I never thought a priest would encourage such foolishness."

Matalena was not jealous; she was offended and alarmed. She regarded her priest with old-fashioned respect and would not even have dreamed of allowing the slightest impropriety in her relationship with him. Since she was old, she had accepted old age. But Don Paolo was "her" priest and "her" protector, and no one else's, not even the Colamartinis'. Matalena began to fear that his friendship with Cristina might induce the priest to accept the Colamartinis' hospitality. Aware of this threat, she was no longer restrained from defending herself with all possible means. That same day she refused a hare Cristina had given her to cook for Don Paolo. This was Matalena's way of warning her that she had been found out.

"Thanks," she said drily, pushing the gift away. "He doesn't like game."

Cristina seemed thunderstruck. "Couldn't you ask him?" she said. "Perhaps you've been misinformed."

"I don't have to," said Matalena. "And he's my guest. If he needs something, I'll get it for him."

"He's only your boarder," said Cristina, angrily, "and my father can give presents to anyone he likes."

But she probably thought it was indecorous to continue the conversation and went off before Don Paolo, who had heard the discussion on the stairs, came down to the bar.

Even though she did not mean it, Cristina was in the wrong. It was not true that Don Paolo was just any old boarder at Matalena's. Without his being aware of it, he became more important by the day. It did not mean anything to Matalena that he did not exercise his priestly functions at Pietrasecca, since this took nothing from the sacred character of his person. On the contrary, because he did not administer the sacraments, his divine investiture remained inaccessible to the inhabitants of Pietrasecca and was concentrated, as it were, in his person alone. Its exorcising power could only be strengthened.

Matalena felt differently toward him from day to day; sometimes she felt like his nurse, then like an orphan, or like a widow. And as the days passed, she felt herself an orphan, in a strange way, rather than a widow or a nurse. Don Paolo had prudently pretended not to understand all this.

"I couldn't imagine what this house would be like without you," she began repeating more and more often.

"I couldn't live without your protection. I'm sure the evil eye and envy would fall on my house, while they stay away from me now, out of respect for your consecrated person."

Matalena was not so naïve as to imagine that Don Paolo would stay inactive in that poor mountain village for long. But in the meantime she was hatching a foolish plot in her primitive mind—to keep "her" priest at Pietrasecca and through him to dominate all the valley.

"Why don't you have the Pope transfer you here?" she said the evening after her altercation with Cristina. "Do you know the Pope personally?"

"Why should he transfer me here?" asked Don Paolo.

"The climate is good here. If you leave, you'll get sick again," said Matalena. "So it's worth it to get transferred here. You could administer the sacraments, hear confessions, baptize, and conduct funerals. It doesn't matter that the valley is poor. I'll take care of your expenses if you come to live here."

"If you say another word on the subject," said Don Paolo icily, "I'll leave tomorrow morning at dawn."

"You don't understand," said Matalena. "I'm only thinking of your health. We can talk about this later. There's plenty of time."

"Less than you think," said the priest.

The woman remained open-mouthed, with the rapid breathing and facial expression of a beaten dog.

The next day the whole village was interested in the arrival of a gentleman's carriage on the square in front of the inn. Was it someone to see Don Paolo? No, it was an unknown prelate. He was tall and thin and he carried himself almost elegantly. As soon as he got down from the carriage, he went to the Colamartini house. A coachman in uniform stayed to watch the carriage. A group surrounded him and began asking him questions, and it developed that the prelate had been Cristina's confessor and spiritual director while she was in the convent school. So Miss Cristina was going to win the argument? The coachman did not know. After a couple of hours the prelate reappeared with Don Pasquale, and before he left he wanted to say hello to Don Paolo. Their conversation was carried out almost at the door of the inn. Don

Paolo was respectful, silent and a little bit distant.

"Signorina Colamartini has spoken very highly of you," he said to Don Paolo. "I was coming through Marsica, and I decided on an excursion to Pietrasecca, on the prayers and insistence of the Mother Superior and the nuns in the convent who love her and who are very sad that she is not there with them."

Don Paolo seemed very embarrassed; he stood there with his shoulders to the wall, holding his breviary to his chest. All he said was, "I have not taken part in any of the discussions the Colamartini family may have had."

"That is proper," said the spiritual director. "Not even I have desired to bring any pressure to bear on the young woman with my visit. However, I considered it my duty to ascertain what reasons have led her to postpone her answering a vocation to which, without any doubt, she is called."

"She could also be very useful here in Pietrasecca," said Don Paolo.

"Certainly," said the spiritual director, "if one considers her ordinary human qualities. But since she has an extraordinary intelligence and sensibility, I do not see how such gifts can be used in so primitive a village. But haven't you noticed that there is even more? She seems to me to be among that number of predestined beings who, even on earth, according to the Biblical expression, bear the sign of the Lamb on their forehead."

"She has made a profound impression on me also," said Don Paolo. "But I don't know that it would be so bad for her to stay among people who need her so much. Even here, nothing would prevent her from devoting part of the day to prayer and meditation. A religious vocation doesn't always mean you have to live in a convent."

The spiritual director was stung to the quick and was about to reply when the coachman respectfully informed him that it was getting late.

After the prelate had gone, Don Pasquale went to the inn to thank Don Paolo for his sensible words, and he was imprudent enough to say this in Matalena's presence. And in a sincerely regretful tone he apologized for not having invited him home. "But if you knew our family's situation . . ." he said. Until Don Paolo felt obliged to interrupt.

"You don't need to apologize at all," he said. "I haven't come here to visit, but on doctor's orders."

But Don Pasquale insisted on apologizing.

"You don't know our tradition," he said. "According to the custom of the Abruzzi, especially in small villages, the inns are only for tradesmen. The other travelers, even if they're strangers, are usually put up in private houses."

"I appreciate your tradition," said Don Paolo, "but it's really no concern of mine. I've only come here for a night or two."

"I assure you, there's no trouble about how long you stay," answered Don Pasquale. "In the old days we used to have guests in our house for months at a time. But now we have three sick old women, and no servants."

The conversation went on like this for quite a while and finished with an invitation for Don Paolo to visit the Colamartini house the following day. The priest accepted with pleasure.

But as soon as Don Pasquale had gone, the priest had to face Matalena. He had never seen her so wrought.

"I hope you didn't believe a word of the old man's nonsense," she said with emotion.

"He seemed a perfect gentleman to me," said Don Paolo.

"That's only his looks," said Matalena. "Want to know what's behind all that?"

Although the priest had never encouraged petty gossip, it made a spicy addition to his supper that night. Of the three old women in the Colamartini house, Matalena told him, the oldest, Cristina's grandmother, was an unscrupulous tyrant. Matalena said, "She's not a woman, but a female devil." She had been the terror of the valley from the time she was a young girl, Matalena explained. And this was not the first time that Don Paolo had heard someone talk about her like that. Her daughter-in-law, Cristina's stepmother, according to Matalena, wasn't sick at all; she was just an idiot. She was no more intelligent than a five-year-old girl. Don Pasquale had married her just for her dowry, after his first wife's death. The whole family lived on that dowry. Perhaps Don Pasquale was right when he said that the other old woman, his sister, was sick. As a matter of fact, no one had known anything about her for several years; it was as if she had been buried alive. The poor woman was a contemporary of Matalena, who remembered well that as a young girl she had been very bold and beautiful. There was no lack of young men of good family from the nearby villages who wanted to marry her. But her mother, that devil incarnate, made one condition: no dowry. She had no intention of dividing up the family lands, which had been reserved for Don Pasquale as the firstborn. Some of these young men would have married her even without a dowry. But the girl was too proud to marry under those conditions. And so forth and so on. Matalena unloaded all the resentment of the poor at the Colamartini family. The priest listened with disgust, but he did not dare to interrupt.

"Does Cristina know all these stories?" he said at one time.

"I don't know if she knows all of it," said Matalena. "But the little saint breathes that air. At least she'll know the stories about her good-for-nothing brother Alberto."

Young Colamartini, Cristina's brother, was reputed to be a vagabond who had learned no kind of trade. He never showed his face in Pietrasecca after his father refused to recognize his signature which Alberto had forged on some checks. But amid all this petty gossip, nothing could have interested Don Paolo more than the name of Bianchina, which he heard mentioned at one point. When Bianchina had come to the inn asking for Don Paolo, Matalena did not know who she was. It was only a few hours later that Magascià had told her that the girl had been Alberto's mistress. Magascià knew many secrets. No wonder, what with his travels with the cart between Pietrasecca and Fossa and the Girasole inn, that this surly and apathetic old man heard all sorts of stories. For some time, according to Magascià, young Colamartini had had free use of the inn, the food, and Berenice Girasole's daughter. He was set up like a sheik. Berenice had talked him into marrying Bianchina, but the Colamartinis were against it. Later there was a lot of gossip about Bianchina's being very sick. After she had been in bed for a while, the girl had reappeared, considerably thinner.

"I have a headache from all your chatter," said Don Paolo, getting up from the table. "Good night."

The next day, at the agreed time, he went through the Colamartini gate with uncertain steps. Don Pasquale and Cristina received him in a large semi-darkened room on the second floor. Three small, thin, old women, dressed in old-fashioned clothes, were seated around a heavy walnut table. They were put there to receive him. The air smelled of honey, and of the tomb. Don Paolo was seized with a cold sweat, in spite of the fact that Cristina smiled at him. She performed the introductions. "My grandmother, my aunt, my mother," she said.

Then, without delay, she helped her aunt and her mother to move into the next room. Her grandmother remained. Under her little white cap, her head looked like a vulture's. Her face was dry and immobile, like a mummy's.

"Where are you from?" she asked the priest in an infirm and shrill voice.

"From Frascati," said Don Paolo, shivering.

"Have you any brothers or sisters?"

"No, I was an only child."

"Then it wasn't right for you to be a priest," said the old woman at once. "It wasn't right at all."

"My vocation . . ." Don Paolo apologized.

"The Church can't want families to be destroyed," she said. "Without families, there wouldn't be the Church or anything else."

The old woman lifted her head toward him.

"Why don't you say Mass?" she asked. "Have you been suspended by the Church? That's what they did to Don Benedetto."

Don Paolo was very embarrassed. Cristina smiled at him in sympathy and pity. But he did not take advantage of this help.

"What did you say?" the old woman asked the priest.

"Nothing," he said.

The old woman made a sign to her granddaughter, who came forward at once to help her into the next room.

"Excuse me," said Don Pasquale to his guest and

pointed out an armchair for him to sit in. Then he sat next to Don Paolo.

"Since we lost all our servants," said Don Pasquale, "this room has been living room, kitchen and dining room for us."

An entire wall was covered with all kinds of copper pots and pans. A garden was visible through a window protected by bars, and beyond that stood some bee hives.

Cristina brought a tray with a bottle of Marsala and a couple of glasses. At one end of the table she took up what she had been doing when Don Paolo had arrived. She was ironing tablecloths, folding them and putting them away in wicker baskets.

Don Pasquale served the Marsala.

"Last Sunday, at Rocca dei Marsi, Cristina and I met Don Benedetto," said Don Pasquale. "He asked after you several times."

"He asked after me?" said Don Paolo. "That's strange."

"Why is it strange?" asked Cristina. "Wasn't it Don Benedetto who sent you to Pietrasecca for your health?"

"Of course," said Don Paolo. After some thought he added in an embarrassed tone, "I'm only surprised, in a certain sense, that he does me the honor of remembering me."

"Quite the contrary," said Cristina. "I got the impression that you are what concerns him most."

"Unfortunately not the only thing," said Don Pasquale. "He had other people with him, and the conversation turned to a former pupil of his, a certain fugitive named Pietro Spina. Well, Don Benedetto dared to defend him. But you wouldn't be able to appreciate this, since you don't know the man."

"He not only defended him," said Cristina, "he delivered an exaggerated eulogy."

"He was scandalous," added Don Pasquale. "It was all the sadder for me since Don Benedetto is an old friend of the family and, as far as his private life goes, a saint."

Cristina had finished ironing and was trying to light the fire. On her knees, bent over the fireplace, she was blowing with all her might on the fire, which wouldn't catch. The wood was damp, and all she got was smoke.

Don Pasquale tried to lead the conversation to Cristina's

future. Of course the family's point of view was an interested one. But what sort of objective view could Don Paolo give?

"I'm certainly not objective," Don Paolo hastened to say. "I would like Cristina to stay in Pietrasecca, too."

Cristina laughed. And since the wood had just then caught fire, the reflection of the flames served to hide her blush.

"Even the wolves reject me," said Cristina jokingly.

"Real or figurative wolves?" asked Don Paolo.

Then Don Pasquale related a curious episode from his daughter's infancy.

"She wasn't out of the cradle yet, and since she liked lambs and it was warm in the sheepfold, we left her there alone in the evening, in her carriage. When we were gone, a wolf got into the sheepfold. I heard the whole herd bleating, ran up with my rifle and the dogs, but the wolf got away."

"Was Cristina asleep?" asked Don Paolo.

"She wasn't asleep. She was sitting up in the carriage calling for her mother. She probably wasn't scared of the wolf, thinking it was a wild dog come to eat the sheep."

"Maybe the wolf thought she was too small and planned to come back when she got bigger," said Don Paolo.

"If you go on like that, you won't be able to keep me here," said Cristina laughing. "The windows in the convents all have solid bars."

The reference to the convent suddenly put Don Pasquale into a bad mood.

"That's how the Colamartinis end up," he said bitterly. "A good-for-nothing son and a daughter in a convent."

The three of them were silent for a moment in the darkened kitchen. Cristina went upstairs to put away the tablecloths she had been ironing.

"It's sad to see the end of one's own family," said Don Pasquale.

What else could anyone talk or think about in that room?

"It doesn't seem to me that the family's fate depends on Cristina's decision," said Don Paolo.

"You're perfectly right," said Don Pasquale. "We're so badly off now that nothing can save us."

"You can at least end up with dignity."

"You just don't know how badly off we are ending up."

"Perhaps it's not good to talk of good and evil as if nothing could be done about them."

"But that's the way it is in our case. Believe me, there's nothing more I can do about the family's reputation."

"In some desperate cases it's better to forget about the family's apparent reputation."

"If I were alone, I would forget about it, by God!" said Don Pasquale, raising his voice. "But I can't exactly send the three old women you just met to eat grass on the mountain."

With this his eyes filled with tears.

"Excuse me," said Don Paolo.

"I have four pieces of land left; two vineyards and two fields," said Don Pasquale. "Up to a few years ago I used to get about seven thousand lire a year from the wine. Now, after the phyloxera and other diseases, all I get is a few hundred. If I were to buy the wine at the market instead of growing it, it would cost a third as much."

The old man got up and took out his ledger, a greasy old book stuffed with receipts and checks.

"Look at this," he said. "The fields I've planted are just enough to pay for the labor, even though that's gone down to four or five lire a day, which isn't much. But I have to pay taxes. For several years I've been asking myself why I bother to farm the land. I can't even grow enough to eat. Every year I have to spend two hundred lire on vegetables, three hundred on cheese, fish, meat and flour; and I have to buy eight quintals of wheat. And then the cloth and shoes! All in all it adds up to five thousand lire I have to take from what the family has saved up in the last fifty years."

"Everyone's talking about the crisis," said Don Paolo to change the subject.

"Failure!" said Don Pasquale. "If it weren't for family pride, which keeps me from selling that land that has belonged to the Colamartinis for centuries, I should have sold it several years ago, in my own interest. The land doesn't pay any more. Near Lama I have an old house, which is used as a stable now, and I have rented it. Do you want to know how much it's cost to legalize the lease? Exactly six times the miserable rent I get from it! Do you think I'm exaggerating? There are sixteen different fees for that rent: legal paper, drawing it up, inventory, honorarium, archivist's fee, registration tax, transfer copy, copy for transmission, notary fees, copy for the holder, transcription fees, postal fees, income taxes, copies to both parties and the legal paper for the receipt for having paid all the above!"

"What you've told me confirms my belief that private property is finished," said Don Paolo. "Don't you think so? Otherwise what can we do?"

"I don't know," said Don Pasquale. "Before coming to this conclusion, I've resorted to all sorts of things, some of which aren't exactly dignified, and I've thought about it day and night. Well, Father, I still don't know what to do."

"How are the small landowners doing?"

"As well as I am. With the difference that they and their families sweat blood on their little bit of land for the whole year. Now every peasant aspires to be a small landowner, even though the few that make it live worse than the others. You really need unlimited money to farm the land."

"If the land doesn't make any money," said Don Paolo, "why were the Socialist peasants, who wanted some, arrested and shot?"

Don Pasquale's expression changed for a moment.

"Those were sacred executions," he hastened to say. "But that doesn't mean that they were inspired by good sense or that they solved anything. The landowners who continue to invest money to farm their land are simply insane fanatics. But what else can they do? A farm hand can get a laborer's job in industry, but a landowner can't do anything."

"Are the farm hands better off?"

"It's true they're not well off, and if they stay here to scratch the earth, it's just because the emigration has been cut off," said Don Pasquale. "But they're better off than I am. They're used to suffering."

"I have the impression," said Don Paolo, "that times are getting harder and harder and only men like that can survive, for just the reason you gave—they're used to suffering."

Meanwhile Cristina had finished putting her ironing away and came back to keep the two men company. It was Don Pasquale's turn to get up. At the back of the house he had a stall with two cows, a heifer and a horse. He excused himself for a few minutes to take care of the animals.

"Would you like some more wine?" asked Cristina.

"Thank you," said Don Paolo. "It's very good."

"You probably heard the landowners' lamentations from my father," said Cristina.

"Cristina," said Don Paolo, "I can't tell you how dismayed I am that your life is so hard."

"Did you think that was why I decided to take the veil?"

Don Paolo did not answer.

"No," said Cristina. "I can assure you that my vocation is authentic. But in all fairness I should add that it undoubtedly comes at an opportune time. What would have become of me without this special call of Christ, if I had stayed here?"

"You would have the chances that life offers to other women," said Don Paolo. "You could be a good wife and mother."

"When I see what's become of the good families," said Cristina, "I'd much rather die on the rack."

"You don't think much of the good families."

"I meant that it's an especially hard time to reconcile one's duties to one's rank with those to one's soul."

"A good Christian shouldn't put the duties of his rank on the same plane as those to his soul."

"Certainly, if one abandons the life of this world. But everyone who stays in the world has a rank which imposes duties on him."

"But when the duties of the rank, as you know, become irreconcilable with those of the soul, there's no alternative but to abandon the former."

"Following the example of Pietro Spina, I suppose,"

exclaimed Cristina. "Did you know that you're using the same arguments that I heard from Don Benedetto last Sunday?"

"You may be surprised, Cristina," said Don Paolo in an ironic tone, "but I don't consider your comparison with Pietro Spina as insulting."

"But it seems to me that the official teaching of the Church is different," said Cristina. "Social inequalities were created by God and we must humbly respect them. . . . But I wonder why all our conversations end up in an argument. It must be my fault because I'm headstrong and presumptuous. Let's change the subject."

The truce did not last for long.

"Any news of Bianchina?" asked Cristina.

"I heard something strange," said Don Paolo. "I heard of an amorous relationship between your brother Alberto and that girl."

"Again!" said Cristina angrily. "Hadn't that ended a long time ago? It's a scandal!"

The argument started up again. Don Paolo's blind anger had a new excuse to come out.

"There's a very simple way of stopping the scandal," he said. "Let them get married. That would solve everything."

Cristina's face wrinkled and became hard.

"Impossible!" she said drily.

The priest pretended not to understand. "Impossible? Why?"

"My grandmother and my father would consider it a dishonor, not only for him, but for our ancestors," said Cristina, who had decided to cut short the argument. "Please, let's change the subject."

"Your ancestors have nothing to do with it. It concerns only Alberto and Bianchina," said Don Paolo obstinately. "If they're in love, that's the only honest thing to do."

"I won't argue about my family's honor," said Cristina, exasperated.

"Even you have these silly medieval notions?" said the priest with pretended astonishment. "Even you?"

"Of course even me," said the girl, accepting the challenge. "Who are the Girasoles? Where are they from?

As for Bianchina, I would only have you remember the rather special circumstances in which you met her."

"I haven't forgotten them at all," said Don Paolo. "But what would you think if Master Alberto were not unconnected with the girl's illness?"

"How dare you!" cried Cristina and jumped to her feet, as if to counter a personal insult.

"Sorry," said Don Paolo.

Without hesitating, he bowed lightly in greeting and went off toward the door. Pale and trembling, Cristina saw him go and did not make the slightest sign to keep him.

## 11

During the priest's absence Matalena had secretly called in Cassarola, the wise woman. The old wise woman came, dragging her feet and complaining of mysterious pains in various parts of her body.

"I need you very much," said Matalena. "Envy is taking away my priest."

"I don't understand," said Cassarola. "Do you have your own priest?"

Matalena whispered her troubles in her ear.

"I still don't understand," said the wise woman. "Maybe it's because I'm still fasting."

Matalena gave her some bread and cheese and a glass of wine. She waited a moment, then asked, "Isn't there some good way of keeping Don Paolo here?"

"Your cheese is strong and smelly!" said the wise woman, spitting on the ground.

Matalena hastened to offer her some more wine.

"Hurry up and talk," she said, "because Don Paolo might come back any minute."

"Let's see . . ." Cassarola began. "Have you been sleeping with him?"

The innkeeper showed herself sincerely shocked.

"What!" she exclaimed. "At my age? And with a consecrated man?"

"I would have thought so too," said the wise woman. "And if you had, he probably would have left long ago. So why do you want to keep him tied to your apron strings? Are you making money off him?"

"No. I want his protection. How else could I keep the house going?"

"Take it easy. Just let me think."

Matalena filled the empty glass and urged her to think quickly.

"I can't live without him," she insisted. "I'm as scared as a little girl."

"What are you scared of?"

"I'm scared of everything!"

Cassarola closed her eyes. She had a hard time breathing, and she kept complaining about her mysterious pains.

"I want something to drink," she murmured. "I'm burning up."

"Do you want some nice cool water?"

"What do you think I am—a cow?"

Matalena brought her a jug of wine and put it next to the glass. But the wise woman drank right out of the bottle. There were some noisy gulps.

"We'll tie him up like a sausage," she said with a leer after her drink.

"No, just make him stay here."

"He'll obey the both of us, <u>like an animal</u>. With him, we'll run the whole valley, we'll give orders to the souls in Purgatory and we'll say exorcisms."

"We'll control the cataclysms," added Matalena, "and all the subterranean forces."

"To start off," said Cassarola, "<u>put seven of your hairs in every plate of soup you give him</u>. That's just to start. Of course your hairs have to be black, not dyed."

"I don't think he'd enjoy them."

"All you have to do is cook them in the soup. He doesn't have to eat them."

"Are there any magic words to go with the cooking?"

"I'll say them. Do you have any kind of a woman's picture?"

"No—just one of the Madonna of the Rosary."

Cassarola snorted in disgust and began complaining about her pains again. She took the jug and drank deeply.

"Well, take a piece of paper and make a woman's picture yourself. You don't have to do it all, just draw the holes. Listen and don't interrupt! Make nine holes on the piece of paper, for the nine holes of the body. Then put the picture under his pillow."

"He'll find out and he'll ask what it's all about."

"Well, put it under his mattress. Couldn't you get me some of his hair?"

"I'll look in his comb tomorrow," said Matalena.

As soon as Cassarola had gone, just to be on the safe side the innkeeper lit a lamp in front of the Madonna of the Rosary. Standing on the chair, she was trembling with anxiety. She brought her lips up to the Virgin's ear.

"Holy Mother," she said, "watch over my poor priest. Keep him here. If you keep him here, I'll light a lamp for you every day in the year."

These precautions calmed her down. She took a chair out in front of the inn, and she sat there, waiting for Don Paolo's return. The heat of the day began to abate. A pleasant breeze came down from the mountain, bringing the smell of elder trees and new-mown hay. Fortunately, she did not have to wait as long as she thought she would.

"How did it go?" Matalena asked. Her tone of voice was as fearful as if she had been begging.

The priest did not answer. His expression was strange; he seemed both irritated and satisfied. Fra Gioacchino came up behind him, all covered with dust and mud. The bag, which the mendicant friar carried on his back, was almost empty.

"Not many alms?" asked Don Paolo.

"Not even enough to make up for the shoeleather I've worn out," said the Capuchin.

He stood humbly by the door. His feet, in worn-out sandals, seemed deformed and black because of the scars and the swelling. Matalena offered him a glass of wine, but he refused. The presence of the priest awed him; and he did not know whether to stay or to go, or what to say. Some of the curates had reported him several times to the Provincial for his excessive familiarity with the peasants and for his love of wine.

"Drink up! Don't be ashamed!" said Matalena. But her insistence only made the Capuchin more embarrassed.

"We all serve the Lord as best we can," he said, "some with words, some with charity and some with holiness. It has fallen to my lot to walk. I'm the Lord's donkey, as my confessor told me."

Don Paolo smiled. The Capuchin barely dared look at

the priest with a peasant's submissive glance.

"Why do the people give fewer alms? Is there less religion?" asked the priest.

"Now in the valley they have insurance—an invention of the devil," said the friar. "If I ask for something for Saint Francis for him to protect the harvest from hail, they tell me the harvest is already insured. Well, it'll protect you against fire, I tell 'em. They tell me they have insurance against fire too. But why is it that with all that insurance they're still scared? What are they scared of?"

"Poor people are always scared," said Matalena. "You build a house and along comes an earthquake. You're healthy and you get sick. You get some land and along comes a flood. Envy's in the air."

"At one time there was a patron saint for every trade," said the friar. "The shoemakers had San Crispino, the tailors Sant'Omobono, the carpenters San Giuseppe. Now they all have their unions. But they're not a bit more secure. There's still fear."

"Are you any better off in a monastery?" asked Matalena.

"I'm not at all well off, but I'm secure," said the Capuchin. "I have no family, so I'm not scared. And I have hope."

"What hope?" asked Don Paolo.

The friar pointed to heaven.

"That's not for everyone," said Matalena. "We can't all become monks or nuns."

"You know what's holding you back?" asked the friar. "Greed for property. It's like a chain on a dog. The devil used to take the form of a woman. Now it's property."

"Not the form of a woman any more?" asked Matalena. "Maybe you're misinformed, Brother."

"Woman has been unthroned," repeated the friar. "Perdition is in property now."

"Will the poor be saved?" asked Matalena. "I don't think the poor will be saved."

"You won't be saved if you're greedy for property," said the friar. "There are the false poor. Let me tell you; I know from personal experience. After a bad year, when we lost all the harvest, my father had to sell a vineyard he had behind the castle. He ruined the rest of his life to get it back; he became avaricious, wicked and cantankerous; but he died without getting it back. My brother wanted to buy the same vineyard; he murdered someone for it and ended up in jail. My other brother went to Brazil with the idea of saving enough to buy it back. But he could barely earn enough down there to keep alive. Meanwhile the vineyard passed from hand to hand. Every three or four years someone else bought it. How many people are making money off it?"

"What kind of a vineyard is it?" asked Matalena. "Is it bewitched?"

"It's just an ordinary vineyard," said the friar. "It's a vineyard just like the rest of them."

"But is it more fruitful than others? Why did your family want that particular vineyard?"

"It had been in the family for generations. In every other way it was like all the others."

"Every woman is also just like all the rest, after all," said Matalena, "But if we bring the devil into it . . ."

"Now, when the necessities of my collection bring me around here," said the friar, "and I see that vineyard from a distance, I make the sign of the cross, as if the devil were there."

"Do you come by here often?" said Don Paolo.

The friar nodded. "I know I shouldn't," he said. "When you take up religious life and leave this world, you should go far from home. Changing your name isn't enough if the water, the stones, the grass, the plants and the dust on the road are all from the village where you were born. You should go far away."

"I was far away," the priest confided in a low voice. "But I couldn't take it any more, and I came back."

"Maybe you should go somewhere you can't come back from."

The friar said this in such a gloomy voice that Don Paolo had to keep himself from embracing him.

"Drink," he said and gave him a glass of wine. This time the friar accepted. He drank slowly, after having passed the back of his hand over his cracked lips.

"This wine must be from Fossa," he said to Matalena.

"It is from Fossa," she said.

"Yes."

"Is he afraid?"

Berenice brought Don Paolo something to drink and went back to the kitchen.

"The doctor's in a difficult situation," said Cardile. "There's rough competition between him and the other doctors for the job of hospital director. Try to understand. He's not a bad man, but his future depends on it. The least suspicion could ruin him."

Bianchina showed up at the door of the inn. She looked luminous in her white clothes.

"Don Paolo!" she cried joyously.

The priest went up to her.

"How are you?" he said. "How did your trip go?"

"Just exactly as planned," said Bianchina.

Her mother, who was setting the tables, looked at her with pleasure.

"You can tell me about it later," said Don Paolo, indicating her mother, who could have overheard them.

He did not know what excuse the girl had given for her trip to Rome. From every point of view she looked better, without that ragamuffin air he had seen about her when she came to Pietrasecca. With a certain emphasis, so her mother could hear, she began telling the priest about the churches and museums of Rome. But as soon as her mother disappeared into the kitchen, she said softly, "I've brought some papers for you, they're hidden in my room."

"What are they about?" asked Don Paolo.

"I don't know; they're sealed," said Bianchina. "Since you trusted me, I respected your secret, for once. I'll put them in your room."

"Good!" said Don Paolo. Turning to Cardile, he added, "Order me something to eat. But don't order any spaghetti. I'll be right back."

On the staircase Bianchina gave him a large yellow envelope.

"Thanks," he said. "We'll get together later." He went into the room which had been reserved for him and closed the door. His hands trembled as he opened the envelope. It was the first message from the "Center

"It must be from halfway up, above the lime cave," he added.

"Since you like it, drink some more," said the priest, smiling and filling his glass.

"Thanks," said the friar. "It's a wine you can trust."

Don Paolo was happy. The poor friar moved him.

"Come on in; don't stand at the door," he said. "Come sit at my table. Matalena, bring us a bottle."

"A whole bottle?" said the friar, taken by surprise.

"Why not? And if we feel like it, we'll have a second one after the first," said the priest. "I'll take care of it."

"To your health," said the friar, raising the chalice. "Couldn't you bring me a piece of bread?" he said to Matalena. "It helps me to drink," he said to the priest.

The friar broke the bread and gave some to Don Paolo.

"There's nothing better than black bread soaked in red wine," said the friar. "But you must have a pure heart," he added smiling.

Don Paolo became cheerful. Matalena had never seen him like that.

"Why are you laughing?" the friar asked him.

"One day we'll beat the devil," Don Paolo confided in his ear. "Yes, the devil, that filthy enemy of mankind."

"How?"

"With the abolition of private ownership of land."

"You mean give the land to everyone? Even the vineyards?"

"The fields, the vineyards, the woods, the sand caves and the canals."

"You mean you believe in the revolution?"

Don Paolo whispered in his ear, "I don't believe in anything else. Meanwhile drink and be happy."

"Do you believe in the Kingdom? On this earth?"

"On earth as it is in heaven. Amen."

"Who do you think will make the revolution? The Church?"

"No. As usual, the Church will bless the revolution, but only after somebody else has made it."

"Then who will make the revolution? God himself?"

"No. You know the old rule—God helps those who help themselves."

"Who, then?"

"The poor will make it," said the priest with a solemn voice. "That is, the poor who aren't contaminated with greed for property."

The friar looked around him, then he said in the priest's ear, "Did you ever know one Pietro Spina?"

"Why do you ask?"

"He thinks the way you do," said the friar. "At least that's what they tell me."

"Have you met anyone else on your rounds who thinks like that?" asked the priest.

"Yes," said the friar. "But in secret."

"To your health," said Don Paolo laughing. "Drink, friar, and be happy. We'll make a revolution which will beat the devil, that dirty old bastard."

Matalena was listening open-mouthed. What strange things for people of the Church to say! She was waiting for them to be finished speaking so that she could ask a question; she wanted to know from the friar if a cataclysm was to be feared.

"My husband is dead," she said, "and if a flood were to take away my house, who would make me another?" Her voice was like that of a helpless orphan.

"We'll have worse!" said the friar.

He hid his face and said no more. Matalena made the sign of the cross and murmured in terror, "Worse?"

"What's going to happen?" asked Don Paolo in a friendly voice to induce confidence.

"One night when I was praying in my cell," the friar said without daring to look the priest in the face, "I saw a red shape from the direction of Rome, on a horizon as black as pitch. It was looking among the clouds."

"It's possible," said Don Paolo with a smile.

Matalena was reassured; the threat from heaven was not against Pietrasecca, but against Rome. Meanwhile the bottle was empty. The friar wanted to leave because it was getting dark and he was hoping for a place to sleep in the Colamartinis' stall as usual.

"Good-bye," he said to Don Paolo. "If we don't see each other again, we'll meet above."

"Above? Where? On the mountain?" asked the priest. "In secret?"

"In heaven," said the friar smiling.

"In case of need," said the priest, "I'll look for you before that."

"You can find me on the road," said the friar.

Don Paolo watched him go. He walked rapidly, with a light, dancelike step. The Colamartini gate was open. The friar went up the three steps which led to the door and pulled the bell cord. Then, since there was no sign of an answer, he sat down patiently on the threshold. A little mouse peeped from a clump of rose bushes. It was brown like the friar's habit. The two looked at each other in a friendly way, but they were interrupted by the creaking of the door.

"Sorry," said Don Pasquale, "my daughter just caught a light cold."

## 12

The arrival of a letter from Bianchina in Rome put Don Paolo in a state of unusual anxiety. Not that it contained sensational news; on the contrary, the message was almost banal. The trip had gone well, Bianchina wrote. She had easily found the person to whom she had been sent. She had seen no one else all the time she had been there, thus leaving her time to visit the city. She would return soon. She was certainly going to bring him a lot of papers to read. This brief message had an almost miraculous effect on Don Paolo. He felt suddenly invigorated. The end of his enforced isolation was in sight.

From that moment he tried to flee the languorous feminine atmosphere around him; he forgot Cristina and sought the company of men. He wanted to get to know them better before he left Pietrasecca. But they worked in the fields all day and came back only toward dusk in little groups behind their laden donkeys. From the garden at the inn Don Paolo would watch their tired progress up the valley. They were ragged and hungry, and as they walked they bent forward, as a result of their hoeing, of bending over the earth to scratch it, and by force of habit from long servitude. Now that Don Paolo was better, he would go out of doors, to get away from the complaints of Matalena who was afraid he was going to leave, and the other complaints from women who were knitting stockings and picking off their lice, in front of the inn, and from his breviary, the eternal maxims, and the ghosts of his adolescence, which he thought were gone but which had taken advantage of his solitude and his physical weakness to surround him once again.

One afternoon he crossed the wooden bridge and took the path down to the valley. He was like a car that had been repaired and starts up again by itself along its usual path. He was driven anew by his natural instinct—the instinct of the social man, the man of revolution. In his solitude he had been a being out of his vital element, a fish out of water. He sat on a stone by the road and waited. Waiting was natural for him. As a boy, in Orta's main square he used to wait for the other boys to join him in the evening after catechism. Almost all of them were the sons of poor men and they were going to play *campana, sbirri* or French war. Later, in Rome, when he was a member of the Socialist student group, he would wait for some worker at the gate to the Tabanelli offices, outside St. John's gate, or at the gas meter, by Porta San Paolo, to spend the evening with him. At L'Estaque he would wait for Cardile. He knew how to wait.

That evening the first one to come by was old Sciatàp with his son, behind the donkey loaded with wine branches. Sciatàp stopped at the sight of the priest.

"I've been wanting to talk with you for a long time," he said, "but they told me you had a cold and I didn't want to disturb you."

"The cold's all better now," said Don Paolo.

"It's like this," said the old man. "My son wanted to join the carabinieri or the militia, but he hasn't been able to. Couldn't you write him a recommendation?"

"Do you really want to be a carabiniere?" the priest asked the boy.

"Sure," he said. "People say bad things about it because they're envious. You get a lot of money for just a little work."

"But that's not the trouble, you see," said the priest. "You're a worker. If you get into the carabinieri your superiors could order you to fire on dissatisfied peasants. This has already happened, as you probably know, not far from here, at Sulmona, Pratola and Prezza." Sciatàp agreed with the priest.

"Don Paolo's right," he said. "You have to sell your soul to live well; there's no other way."

His son was amused at the way the priest spoke.

"Is there no other way?" asked Don Paolo. "Can't you live well and stay honest?"

"Do you know the story about the devil and the cat?"

said Sciatàp. "Once there was a big devil in a cave. He
dressed in black and a top hat, with rings on his fingers,
like a banker. Three peasants came to him and asked,
'What do you need to do to live well without working?'
The devil answered, 'Bring me a soul, an innocent soul.'
The peasants went off, took a cat and brought it to the
devil, all wrapped up like a young baby. 'Here's a soul,
a really innocent one,' they said. For that they got the
book of commands from the devil, where it's written what
you have to do to live well without working; but, while
they were going, the cat started to meow. The devil found
out. The magic book went up in flames right in their
hands. A cat won't do. You need a soul, a real soul."

"All right," said the boy. "I'd do like everyone else.
But they rejected my application. There are too many
applications."

"That's the trouble, there are too many souls," said
Sciatàp. "The earthquakes, epidemics and wars haven't
been enough. There are still too many souls."

"What's left when a man sells his soul?" said the priest.

The two peasants looked at him in surprise. What a
funny thing for a priest to ask about. Was it right for
him to ask it?

"As long as you're alive, there's always a way of fixing
things up," said Sciatàp. "What's the Church for anyway?
Did the Church forbid the carabinieri to fire? At Fossa,
in the *corpus domini* procession, there are always four
carabinieri in uniform right behind the sacrament, in a
place of honor. You said that the carabinieri fired on the
poor at Pratola. That means that they confessed themselves afterwards. But the peasants who died! Who confessed them? They shared the cold in this life and in the
next they'll suffer the fires."

"I'm sorry," said Don Paolo. "I wouldn't know whom
to recommend you to. I don't know any commandant in
the carabinieri."

Meanwhile the donkey had gone off.

"Garibaldi!" cried the old man in a rage.

But the donkey did not pay any attention, and kept
on walking.

"He doesn't hear me," said Sciatàp to the priest, "because he's hungry and he knows the stall isn't far off. When he's hungry he even forgets his name."

Sciatàp and his son said good night to the priest and hastened to catch their donkey. Don Paolo sat down again.

After them there came a drunken peasant astride his donkey. The man was falling first from one side and then from the other. He straightened himself and kicked and hit the beast.

"Are you going to walk straight or not?" said the man.

A group of peasants around Magascià's cart came up right after.

"We've been to the market," said Magascià, stopping the cart.

"Did you sell well?" said the priest.

"The prices went down," said Magascià. "They've put on a ceiling. We didn't want to sell, but otherwise they would have confiscated our stuff."

"They put a ceiling price on things from the country, but not on things from the city, and they went up," said a man near the cart.

"The carabinieri arrested Giacinto!" said Magascià. "For rebellion. As soon as he heard about the ceiling price he wanted to go back to Pietrasecca without selling anything."

The cart started moving and Don Paolo joined the others. A certain Daniele was walking next to Magascià, a tall man with a horrid old hat at a racy angle on his head.

"Daniele had a sick donkey, which surely won't live another month," Magascià confided to the priest. "He brought it to the market and sold it to a woman from Fossa, who thought it was fine."

"I'll confess next Easter," said Daniele. "God will forgive me."

The whole group laughed in enjoyment of Daniele's cleverness. A young man named Banduccia was walking behind the cart. He seemed drunk and was holding onto the cart to stay on his feet.

"Banduccia went to a bar in Fossa," Magascià told the priest. "He ate, drank and offered everyone there drink. Then he went into the garden on the excuse that he had a certain need. He jumped over the wall and went off without paying."

"I'll confess next Easter, too," said Banduccia. "God will forgive me."

And everyone laughed again. Don Paolo shuddered.

"The owner of the bar, Berenice Girasole, when she found out I'd left," said Banduccia, "tried to make Biagio pay, since he was from Pietrasecca too. Poor Berenice made a bad choice. If there hadn't been people between them, Biagio would have ruined everything. He picked up a log of wood and threw it at her. There would have been hell to pay if he'd hit her."

Biagio was the strongest and most brutal peasant in the valley, and Don Paolo had already heard people talking of him with great admiration.

"Biagio's been arrested three times for violence already," said someone with enthusiasm. "He's a man you have to respect."

"It's all right to dish it out," said Banduccia, "but it's shameful to take it."

"The first time Biagio went to prison, it was because he'd broken his father's arm with a hatchet," said Magascià. "The old man told me, 'He's broken my arm, but I'm glad my son's so strong. At least poor people like him will be respected in life.' "

Some of the others were telling some of the other things Biagio had done, but Don Paolo was not listening any more. There was a young man with a strange look among the peasants around Magascià's cart. He was barefooted, badly dressed, tall and thin. A great lock of hair on his forehead gave him a savage look, in contrast to his soft eyes like a pet dog's. He took no part in his friends' jibes. Don Paolo smiled at him. The young man smiled too and came closer to Don Paolo. When the group passed the wooden bridge and broke up, Don Paolo took the young man by the arm and held him.

"I'd like to talk with you," he said in a low voice. "I want to know what you think about certain things."

The young man smiled at the priest and led him to his hovel. This was in the village's most remote corner, among

some stalls and pigsties. The path which led there was a
sewage ditch. Don Paolo followed the young peasant.
Every once in a while he turned around and looked at
the priest without saying anything but with a moving
expression on his face.

"I wanted to have a man-to-man talk with you," said
Don Paolo. "Please forget for a moment that I wear a
priest's habit and that you're just a peasant."

The boy's place was like a pigsty. One had to bend over
to go in; the door served also as a chimney. It was all
darkness and stink inside, one could barely see a straw
mattress laid out on the floor of pebbles, and there was
a goat chewing his cud on the dirty straw. Don Paolo
was overcome by the smell of filthy rags and excrement
which filled the small place; and he sat near the opening
while the young man prepared something to eat.

"There is a country," Don Paolo started saying, "a
large country in Eastern Europe, a great plain planted
with wheat, a great plain populated with millions of peasants. In that country in 1917 . . ."

The young peasant cut off some pieces of black bread,
tore up two tomatoes and an onion, and offered the priest
a piece of bread with these vegetables. His swollen and
scarred hands still had dirt on them. The knife with which
he had cut the bread must have been used for all kinds
of things. Don Paolo closed his eyes and tried to get the
food down so as not to offend his host.

"There is a country," he started up again, "a great
country, where the peasants in the fields made an agreement with the workers in the factories."

Meanwhile Matalena had been making the rounds of
the houses looking for her guest. "Have you seen him?"
she would ask. At last she found him.

"Supper's been ready for an hour," she said. "I was
afraid something had happened to you."

"I'm not hungry," said Don Paolo. "Go back to the
inn, because I still have some things to discuss with my
friend here."

"Discuss?" said Matalena. "But don't you realize that
he's a deaf-mute and understands nothing but some signs?"

There was the deaf-mute, seated on the threshold of

his hut, next to the priest. Don Paolo looked him in the face and saw how his eyes slowly realized the misunderstanding he had caused.

The priest said to the woman, "That's all right. Go back to the inn anyway. I'm not hungry."

The two men stayed there on the threshold of the hut, and he who had the gift of speech was silent. Every once in a while they smiled at one another. The evening's gray air had given way to the black of night. With the arrival of darkness the village instantly fell into a lethargy. If it had not been for the smell of the huts and the stalls, one would have thought it deserted. After a while Don Paolo got up, shook hands with the deaf-mute and said good night. He had to feel his way in the darkness, like a blind man.

The only open door with a light was the one to the inn. Someone always came there at night to drink or play cards and stayed late. There was nowhere else to go. Some dirty tables, some bottomless chairs and a wooden bench near the fireplace was all the furniture there was. The whole year's provisions were piled up in a corner by the stairs—some bags of potatoes, beans and lentils. There was usually a plate of salted chick peas on the table, to make the customers thirsty. The Madonna of the Rosary had hung from the wall for many years and by this time was part of the surroundings. The customers ate the chick peas, drank, chewed on their tobacco and drank some more. They were constantly spitting on the floor, so that Don Paolo had to be careful not to slip when he came in.

One old man was always there, crumpled up in a corner by the fireplace. His name was Fava. Tired and stupefied, he stared at the floor, chewed his cud and spoke to no one. He was the first to come and the last to go, and when he did he was so drunk he could hardly stand. His daughters came to call him, as did his sons and his wife. He pretended that he didn't understand.

"We have wine at home. Why don't you drink our wine?" asked his wife.

"I don't like it," said Fava with a snort of disgust.

Matalena had to exchange some of her wine for some of Fava's.

"Now we have the wine you like at home," said his wife. "Stay home!"

"I don't like it," he said.

He came back to the inn every night. He spent the few coppers he had earned. His wife ended up by accusing Matalena.

"You shouldn't give him anything to drink," said the woman. "If he wants to drink, he can drink at home."

But there was nothing anybody could do about it. Fava was at the inn every night, always in the same place.

When Don Paolo arrived that night, after his conversation with the deaf-mute, there were only two peasants playing cards.

"Seeing you talking with the deaf-mute," said one of them, "I thought it was a miracle. But it was just a mistake."

Don Paolo joined them at their table.

"It wasn't a miracle; and it wasn't a mistake," he said.

"The deaf-mute," said the other peasant, "is very intelligent. Maybe God made him that way as a chastisement."

The two of them went back to their game.

That night Don Paolo was not sleepy. His restlessness made him feel like talking.

"The peasants have been complaining ever since the world began," he said. "But they're resigned. Will it always be like that?"

"If you could die of hunger," said one of the players, "we'd have been dead a long time ago."

"Don't you think things could be changed some time?" said Don Paolo.

"Yes, when the sick man has already died, the doctor comes," said the other.

Don Paolo became imprudent.

"Haven't you ever heard," he said, "that there are countries where things are different?"

Matalena was the one who answered that.

"Sure there are countries different from ours," she said. "God puts grass where there are no sheep and sheep where there's no grass."

"I understand," said Don Paolo. "Good night."

The two peasants went back to their game. After a

while one of them said to Matalena, "Your priest seems like a good man, but he's a little crazy."

"You wouldn't understand him," said Matalena. "He's too smart for you."

"Yes, he's smart," insisted the other one. "But he's still a little crazy. Why doesn't he say Mass?"

"He's not from this diocese."

"So what? The Mass is the same all over. I still think he's a little crazy."

# 13

The next day was a holiday, and the inn filled up with drinkers and card players, as on all big days. Many were on their feet for the lack of chairs, others were playing childish games outside. Don Paolo stayed in his room at his work table, bent over some notes with the title "On the Peasants' Lack of Political Capacity." But with the noise from the inn, he couldn't concentrate. He heard people coming and going, the chairs scraping, the calls from the games, the springing up of arguments followed by yells and curses and overturning furniture.

"Quiet!" Matalena was imploring. "Don Paolo upstairs is trying to rest."

It was in vain. How can you have fun without making noise? Three or four young men were playing *sette-mezzo*, and an argument arose about one of the cards. In that game the king of diamonds is the most important. Matalena had just two decks of cards and in both of them the king of diamonds was so worn that anyone could recognize it. Daniele had made a proposal for the purpose of the game. "Let's substitute another card, like the three of hearts, for the king of diamonds, which we can recognize. All right? The king of diamonds, which we can recognize, will change places with the three of hearts, and the three of hearts, which we can't recognize will have the value of the king of diamonds."

"That's impossible!" somebody else said, a certain Michele. "Even if we all could agree, it would still be impossible."

"Why?"

"But it's natural," said one Mascolo. "The king of diamonds is always the king of diamonds. It could be dirty or marked or it could have a hole in it. But it's still what it is."

"All we have to do is agree on it," said Daniele. "The game will be better if no one can see who has the king of diamonds in his hand."

"But our agreement wouldn't be enough," said Michele. "There's the law."

"You say the game would go better?" said Matalena. "That may be, but it would be a false game."

Sciatàp, who was at the other table, the old men's table, and who had been listening to the argument, said, "Why don't you call Don Paolo? A priest knows a hell of a lot."

"You can't," said Matalena. "He's resting."

But Don Paolo, who had heard his name mentioned, appeared at the head of the stairs.

"Did someone ask for me?" he said.

All the talking stopped at once and everyone offered the priest something to drink. He thanked them and tried to excuse himself, but he finally had to go around and touch his lips to each glass, according to the custom.

"Who called me?" he said after the ceremony.

Sciatàp explained what it was all about and concluded, "Now tell us who's right."

"This isn't a case of sacred images," said the priest with a laugh.

But Sciatàp blocked his every escape. "A priest knows a hell of a lot," he said.

Don Paolo took the king of diamonds in his hand and asked Michele, "Do you think this has value for itself, or do you think someone gave it a value?"

Michele answered, "It's worth more than the others because it's the king of diamonds."

"Is its value fixed or variable?" said the priest. "Is this card the same in *tresche* or in *briscola* or *scopa*? Or is it different?"

"It varies according to the games," said Michele.

"Who thought up the games?" asked the priest.

No one answered.

"Don't you think the players thought up the games?" suggested the priest.

Several agreed. There was every reason to believe that the players had thought up the games.

The priest concluded, "If this card varies according to the players' whim, it seems to me you can do with it what you want."

"Bravo! bravissimo!" several of them yelled.

Don Paolo was flattered at his success. He turned to Sciatàp.

"Once there was a man here in Pietrasecca," he said, "a man called Carlo Campanella, and in New York there's a man called Mr. Charles Little-Bell, Ice and Coal. Is this one person or two?"

"It's the same person!" several answered.

"Sciatàp!" shouted the one who had been questioned. "I'm the one to answer that." He answered, "It's the same one. He changed his name."

"If a man can change his name, why can't he change a playing card?" asked the priest.

"A king's always a king," said Michele.

"A king is a king as long as he rules," said Don Paolo. "A king who doesn't rule is an ex-king, he isn't a king any more. There's a great country, in the direction of the rising sun, which had a king, let's say the king of clubs, who commanded millions of peasants. From the moment when the peasants refused to obey him he wasn't a king any more. Not far from us, in the direction of the setting sun, there's a country where another king ruled. Let's call him the king of hearts or diamonds. As soon as his subjects stopped obeying him, he stopped ruling, stopped being a king, and became an ex-king. Now he's an emigrant, something all of you can become. So play *settemezzo* however you like and good night."

Don Paolo gave the king of diamonds to Daniele, said good night to everyone and went back to his room, followed by everyone's drunken cheers.

In the following days the demotion of the king of diamonds was the subject of all kinds of discussions among the peasants of Pietrasecca.

The village schoolteacher, Signorina Patrignani, complained about it personally to the priest.

"In the advanced class," she said, "I couldn't teach. The boys talked of nothing but that story of the king of diamonds and the three of hearts. And they repeated what you said to them last night at the inn, without having understood it."

On her bosom the teacher wore the emblem of the party in power, right over her heart. Between one phrase and the next she sighed deeply, and the three-colored emblem bounced up and down like a rowboat in a storm at sea.

"These people are very ignorant," she said. "If they listen to educated people like ourselves, they almost always understand the opposite of what we say."

The schoolteacher had received the latest copy of the news sheet *News from Rome*, which was to be posted on the school door. Before she put it up, she would read the most important news to the peasants in Matalena's bar and comment on it. The rumor that the priest would be there spread among the peasants, and the inn was more than usually filled. Some people came whom the priest had not yet seen. In a short time a crowd of thirty gathered, cowering together in their rags. Don Paolo was seated at the foot of the stairs which led to the second floor, and he could look almost all of them in the face. From the mob there arose an odor of filthy clothes and manure which almost made Don Paolo vomit. They were submissive and diffident people, with deformed heads on deformed bodies, heads deformed by hunger and illness. There were some wild young men among them. The oldest of them—the notables like Sciatàp, Magascià and Grascia—stayed on their feet near the door.

In the presence of the strange priest, the schoolteacher was unusually nervous and talkative. She told them to pay attention and not to be afraid to ask questions about the hard words. Then she began to read the *News from Rome* in a high, strident voice.

"We have a leader," she read, "for whom all the peoples of the earth envy us, and who knows what they would be willing to pay to have him in their country . . ."

Magascià interrupted. Since he did not like generalities, he asked exactly how much the other people would be willing to pay to have the leader.

"It's just a figure of speech," said the schoolteacher.

"In business, there aren't any figures of speech," protested Magascià. "Do they want to pay or don't they? And if they want to pay, how much are they offering?"

The schoolteacher replied angrily that it was just a figure of speech.

"Then they don't want to buy him," said Magascià. "And if it's not true, why do they write that they want to buy him?"

Sciatàp had some points to clear up too. "Would the people who want to buy him pay in cash or by check?"

The schoolteacher turned to the priest as if to say, "Do you see what sort of people I have to deal with in this village?"

The next item was about rural people.

"Who are the rural people?" asked one of the mob who was sitting on the floor.

"You're the rural people," answered the schoolteacher, losing patience. "I've told you that again and again a hundred times."

Some of them burst out laughing.

"We were rural people and we didn't even know it," they said.

The schoolteacher read: "The rural revolution has achieved its purpose along every line . . ."

"Which line?" someone asked. "The railway line?"

"Are we the rural people?" asked Sciatàp. "Is the rural revolution the revolution we're supposed to make?"

"Exactly," said the schoolteacher. "May I congratulate you on your intelligence?"

"What revolution have we made?"

"The word must be understood in its spiritual sense," said the schoolteacher.

Sciatàp did not want to seem ignorant and he pretended to understand, but Magascià was not satisfied.

"That's a piece of paper the government sends us," he said. "It's written that the rural people—that is, according to you, the peasants—have made a revolution and that this revolution has achieved its purposes. What purposes have we achieved?"

"Spiritual purposes," said the schoolteacher.

"What spiritual purposes?"

The schoolteacher turned red and became flustered. No one understood anything. Finally she had an inspiration, called them all to silence and said, "The rural revolution has saved the country from the Communist danger."

"Who are the Communists?" asked Grascia.

The schoolteacher was saved. She did not have to think any more.

"I've explained it to you before, but I can repeat it again," she said. "The Communists are rogues. They prefer to meet at night—in the sewers of the city. To be a Communist, you have to trample on the holy crucifix, spit in Christ's face and promise to eat meat on Good Friday."

"That meat—who gives it to them?" asked Sciatàp. "Do they get it free or do they have to pay for it?"

"I do not have that information," said the schoolteacher.

"You never know what's most important!" said old Grascia.

The schoolteacher turned to Don Paolo, as if to give him the floor and get out of her difficulties. But the priest seemed absorbed in his examination of the cobwebs on the ceiling.

"I don't agree and I'm going," said Grascia.

The schoolteacher invited him to explain what he did not agree with, but the old man went off without answering.

Don Paolo joined him on the square in front of the inn.

"Congratulations," the priest said to him.

"I just said it to get the schoolteacher mad," said Grascia.

He found it intolerable that a woman wanted to teach the men anything.

"When women teach men, the children are born hunchbacks," he said.

The night was warm and the tepid, slightly sickening breeze which was blowing along the path of the invisible brook made one slightly ill. The group which had come to hear the schoolteacher dispersed rapidly. Near the wooden bridge, not far from where Don Paolo and Grascia stood, Sciatàp, Magascià and Daniele had come together.

"Let's have a nightcap before we go to bed," said the priest.

"If it's a question of obeying one of the Church's rules, we can all agree to that," said Magascià.

Don Paolo gave Sciatàp some money for him to buy a bottle of wine from Matalena. Grascia had started again on the schoolteacher.

"There's nothing worse than a hen that wants to change places with a rooster," he was saying.

"Drink," said Sciatàp.

He had brought a glass for Don Paolo, but the priest refused. "It's better to drink it right from the bottle," he said.

Grascia could not get over his annoyance at the schoolteacher. "One of us should do her the favor of making her pregnant," he said. "We could even draw lots for it."

"Who are you talking about?" Magascià asked him.

"The schoolteacher."

"Leave the poor woman alone," said Magascià. "We all have to make a living some way."

"Drink—and pass the bottle," said Daniele. "We can draw for it some other night. You're not in a hurry, are you?"

"All right, I'll wait," said Grascia.

"I'll probably leave in three days," said Don Paolo. "I feel much better. But before I go I'd like to have a better idea of what you think about things."

"We're farmers," said Daniele. "There's not much to think about."

"Even a peasant thinks sometimes," said the priest. "Daniele, just to get things started, couldn't you tell me what you think of the situation?"

"What situation do you mean?" said Daniele.

"Of the situation in the country in general."

"What do you mean by the country? Do you mean Pietrasecca? Do you want to know whether I think Pietrasecca would be better off somewhere else? I'll have to admit that I've never given it a thought. It's always been here."

"You don't understand," said the priest. "I meant the

conditions of life in general here and elsewhere in Italy. What do you think of those?"

"Nothing," said Daniele. "You know, everyone has his own problems."

"Everyone has his own fleas," said Sciatàp. "According to you, should we worry about someone else's fleas?"

"Everyone has his own little plot of land," said Grascia. "Everyone thinks day and night of this piece of land, whether it rains too much, whether it hails, or whether it doesn't rain at all. But Italy has lots of land—mountains, hills, plains, woods, lakes, swamps and beaches. You'd go mad if you had to worry about all that. A man's head's too small. All our little head can think about is a little piece of land."

"Sometimes our head isn't even enough for our piece of land. And what good's thinking? The hail will still fall."

"You didn't understand me," said the priest. "I wanted to know what you think of the present government."

"Nothing," said Daniele.

The others agreed. "Nothing."

"Why is that?" said the priest. "You're always complaining."

"Everyone has his problems," said Magascià. "We don't care about other people's. We're interested in what's around us. We look at our neighbor's lands and vineyards. If his door or window is open, we look through and watch him eating his soup."

"Everyone has his fleas," said Sciatàp. "Probably even the government has them. And it does just what we do—it scratches. What else can we say?"

"You didn't understand me," said the priest. "I wanted to know what you thought of taxes, prices, the draft and other laws."

"Drink," said Magascià. "We've got time to kill. No offense. I mean, these are useless questions. Everyone knows what we think of certain things."

"We all agree on taxes, the draft and the rents," said Daniele. "Even the most frightened and submissive and even the stubbornest. It's no secret. It's not hidden. It would only be strange if we didn't."

"Drink, and pass the bottle," said Grascia.

"It's empty," said Daniele.

Don Paolo wanted to offer another one, but the others were against it. "It's our turn," they said. "We know the rules of courtesy." They collected the money and Daniele went to the inn and came back with a full bottle.

"You drink first," he said to the priest. "That'll be the blessing."

"Yes, you complain," said Don Paolo, returning to the subject. "But you're bowed down and resigned."

"We're born and raised with the same thought," said Sciatàp. "Our earliest memories? They were of the old people complaining. What will our children remember of their childhood? Our complaining. We thought it could never be worse, but it got worse. Even the blind and the deaf-mutes know it. I've never met anyone who thought differently."

"The authorities know it too," said Magascià. "Do you know what the mayor of Fossa said in his last speech? 'I don't pretend that you don't complain,' he said. 'But at least do it at home, not on the street or in the city hall. Just be polite about it.' And he was right, after all. You have to be polite. What good does it do to complain?"

"I don't think so," said Grascia. "It keeps you from bursting if nothing else."

"Drink and pass the bottle," said Daniele.

"But don't you think your troubles could ever be over?" asked the priest.

"You mean in the world to come, after death," said Grascia. "Are you talking about heaven?"

"No, I'm talking about this world," said Don Paolo. "Don't you think that the big estates can be confiscated one day and given to the poor? That the country can be administered by men like you? That your children and grandchildren can be born free men?"

"We know that dream," said Grascia. "Every once in a while they talk about it again. It's a beautiful dream —there's nothing more beautiful."

"But it's just a dream," said Magascià.

"A beautiful dream," said Sciatàp. "The wolves and the lambs will graze together in the same pasture. The big fish won't eat the little fish any more. A fine fable. Every once in a while they talk about it again."

"Do you believe there's eternal damnation on earth?" asked the priest. "Don't you think that one day the laws can be made by you, for everyone?"

"No," said Magascià. "We have no illusions about that."

"If it were up to me," said Grascia, "I'd abolish all the laws. That's where all the trouble starts."

"It's a dream," said Sciatàp. "A beautiful dream."

"Instead of abolishing all the laws, if it were up to me, I'd just have one," said Grascia. "To stop everybody from complaining, believe me, it would be enough to have just one law: every Italian has the right to leave Italy."

"Impossible," said Daniele. "Who'd stay here?"

"It's a dream," said Sciatàp. "A beautiful dream. It'd be like taking the doors off the stables."

"Drink, and pass the bottle," said Magascià.

"There's no more," said Sciatàp. "Shall I go for another?"

"No, it's a little late," said Don Paolo. "And I'm tired."

When he got back to his room, he took from his suitcase the papers entitled "On the Peasants' Lack of Political Capacity" and sat at the table. He remained for long with his head between his hands, thinking. Finally he began to write: "Perhaps they are right."

## 14

Matalena received the news that Don Paolo was to depart on the following day as the prelude to a catastrophe.

"When are you coming back?" was all she could say.

"I don't know," he replied with exaggerated indifference. "Perhaps I'll come back just to pick up the things I'm not taking with me now."

Just then Teresa Scaraffa passed by the inn on her way to fill a pot with water.

"Teresa," Matalena called, "please watch the house a minute! I'll be right back!"

"What's happened?" yelled Teresa, alarmed. But Matalena did not answer.

Just as she was, with her hair not combed and nothing but slippers on her feet, the innkeeper started to run, hobbling along the lane which led from the stables up the steps to the cave of Cassarola the wise woman. She found her stretched out on a sack of chaff, complaining of her pains and breaking some bread for a goat.

"What's happened?" she asked Matalena. "Is your house burning down?"

With what little breath she had left, Matalena was just able to say, "He's leaving."

"It's your fault," answered the wise woman immediately. "I started the fire and you put it out. Why did you stir up trouble between him and Cristina?"

"You know why. It certainly wasn't jealousy."

"Only someone as dumb as you would have ever thought Don Pasquale wanted to have the priest as a guest. You should know who runs things in that house."

Matalena was easily persuaded of her guilt and began to cry like a child. "What can we do now?"

"If there's time, you can make up for it. You can't

139

go against nature when you're trying to hold someone back. Even a priest is made of flesh and blood."

Matalena ran back to the inn to comb her hair, change her apron and put her shoes on.

"Do me a favor," she said to Teresa in a begging tone. "Stay here just a little while longer. I have to call on Donna Cristina."

It was especially annoying for her to have to go to the Colamartini house in such a rush. To her concern at the departure of the priest was added a special reason for timidity. At her last meeting with Cristina, the innkeeper had been very rude and they had not seen each other since then. Fortunately the father opened the door. Did he know anything about why the priest had wanted to hasten his departure from Pietrasecca? Don Pasquale did not know anything about it. Cristina came; and she knew even less, because she had had to keep to her bed for the last few days.

"I'm going to Fossa tomorrow, too," said Don Pasquale. "You can tell Don Paolo that I'd be delighted to give him a lift."

Cristina accompanied Matalena as far as the gate.

"Maybe we've both made mistakes," said Matalena with humility. "Maybe we could have gotten together to keep Don Paolo with us."

"What could we have done?" said Cristina.

"Maybe, without meaning to, you offended him," said Matalena. "He liked you and he still does."

"How is he now?" asked Cristina. "Is he going away without being fully recovered?"

"In the last few days," said Matalena, "he's lost what recovery he's made up to now."

"I'm very sorry to hear that," said Cristina.

Don Paolo was punctual for his appointment the next morning.

It was a bright, clear day and the smell of new-mown hay was coming down from the mountain. There had not been such a morning for quite a while. While old Colamartini fastened the mare to the bars of the cart and slowly adjusted the traces, the bit and the blinders, Cristina came to greet the priest.

"Are you leaving so soon?" she said. "For good?"

"I don't know," said Don Paolo with embarrassment. "I'm leaving some personal things here. Maybe I'll be back to pick them up, or perhaps I'll send someone for them."

Don Paolo was no longer irritated with the girl. But he still felt some rancor and disillusion. However, his mind was really elsewhere. He did not feel ill any longer.

But the girl appeared wasted away.

"Donna Cristina's been sick," Matalena had said to the priest that morning while the priest was drinking his coffee. "She's suffered a lot."

"I didn't know that," the priest had said.

"She spent a week in bed," Matalena had added. "I hope it wasn't your fault."

"My fault?"

"She is a very sensitive girl and she liked you a lot. Didn't you notice that the geraniums on the balcony have withered?"

These words had somewhat irritated Don Paolo.

"The cart's ready," said Don Pasquale.

"Bon voyage," said Cristina. "I hope I'll see you again."

"Good-bye," said Don Paolo.

Cristina was going to add something, but the cart started moving. The two men were silent and a little embarrassed.

"The horse's name is Diana," said Don Pasquale. "I bought her fifteen years ago to go hunting with. We'll never see those fine days any more."

The form of the cart, with its high seats and its four wheels, the back ones big and the front ones little, the ornaments on the horse, the embroidered cushions the men were sitting on, and the way both of them were dressed were also things of bygone times.

A man was coming toward them, riding on a donkey, behind a line of other donkeys. The donkey he rode was small and the man's feet almost touched the earth. The man kept his eyes on the brook and did not seem aware of the cart.

"He rents a small bit of land from me and he hasn't paid me in three years," said Don Pasquale to the priest. "Every time he meets me he turns the other way."

The cart passed a wagon on its way to the valley,

loaded with sacks of grain. The carter was behind the
wagon, adding his weight to the brake.

"How are crops?" asked Don Pasquale.

"Everything I raised is right here," said the carter.
"And I have to take it all to the landlord before the
bailiff comes and confiscates it."

The reddish make-up of the valley became ashen as
they came closer to the plain of Fucino. The hay stubble
stained the sloping fields with yellow. Cones of straw were
visible in the distance, with antlike men around them.
Some women passed by with children in their arms, like
the madonnas in the churches, cantankerous madonnas
dressed in black taking food to their men intent on the
harvest. The heat of the day began to make itself felt.
The horse's head was wrapped in a cloud of flies.

The road was difficult because the paving stones were
not yet beaten down. A group of soldiers in a meadow
cowered in front of a tent with rifles between their legs.
A donkey stood still in the middle of the burning road
and looked as if he were concentrating all the sun's rays
on himself. "He's going to collapse," said Don Paolo.
Some other donkeys laden with sacks of flour were coming
from the mill at Fossa. A group of peasants with wood
under their arms was going toward the station. Even
though the summer heat was at its worst, the people
carried everything they owned on their backs, as if they
meant never to return, as if they were refugees in flight.

Don Pasquale recognized a friend of his in front of a
shop, stopped the cart and invited him to ride with them.
He was a clerk in the tax office, Don Genesio.

"Your profession is not popularly held in esteem," said
Don Paolo.

"That's true," said Don Genesio. "Especially for the
peasants who are more behind than anyone else in the
valley, every clerk is a great parasite."

"They're not all wrong," said Don Pasquale. "What
does Rome do for our problems? Why, it makes more
offices! And these offices proliferate with capitalist out-
siders who run them!"

"Even the priests," said Don Genesio. "Even the priests
are more or less thought of as parasites, like the clerks.
But with all that, people can't do without either."

"How are they considered parasites?" asked Don Paolo. "Like flies and fleas? In that case, they might do very well without us."

"I don't know exactly," said Don Genesio. "Maybe like the cows' horns they put on their houses against the evil eye, or something like that. But there's no use worrying about it. They think they can't do without them."

After that, Don Pasquale and Don Genesio had an animated conversation on familiar topics, on transfers of property and on mortgages, while Don Paolo seemed absorbed in other thoughts. Every once in a while a liturgical song could be heard from a nearby hill. Groups of pilgrims were coming down the footpaths to the national highway.

"They're going to the Holy Martyrs of Celano," said Don Genesio. "They'll be walking all day."

When the cart came to Fossa, Don Pasquale left the priest in the square in front of the Girasole inn and departed immediately, perhaps to avoid seeing Berenice Girasole. The latter ran up to the priest and kissed his hand with great respect.

"Someone's already waiting for you in the dining room," she said.

"Where's your daughter?" asked Don Paolo.

"I'll send for her right away," said Berenice. "She got back from Rome yesterday and, thanks be to the Lord, she's found a good job."

"I'm glad to hear that," said Don Paolo.

He found Cardile in the dining room, seated at a table with half a liter of wine in front of him. Their meeting was very friendly.

"I expected to see the doctor too," said Don Paolo.

"I'm sorry," said Cardile, "he couldn't come."

"Is he coming tonight? Tomorrow morning?"

"I don't think so," said Cardile.

"If he can't move, I'll go to him," said Don Paolo. "I need his help to find somewhere else to stay. I would have died of boredom at Pietrasecca. I have some plans to discuss with him."

"Listen," said Cardile with embarrassment, "we can't count on the doctor any more."

"Why? Did he tell you that last night?"

Abroad" which had gotten to him since his return to Italy. The envelope contained very worn copies of three voluminous essays and a laconic note inviting him to give his opinion of them at once. He just read the titles: "The Crisis in the Direction of the Russian Communist Party and the Duties of the Affiliated Parties"; "The Criminal Complicity with Imperialist Fascism of the Opposition of Both Right and Left"; "The Solidarity of All Parties of the International with the Majority of the Russian Communist Party." He put all the papers in his suitcase and went down to the dining room.

There were few words spoken at dinner.

"Bad news?" said Cardile.

"Very bad," said Don Paolo. "Special delivery from Byzantium," he added after a while with a grimace.

"I don't understand," said Cardile.

"I don't either," said Don Paolo. "But I'm surprised to see that you've ordered spaghetti."

"Does spaghetti disgust you so?" said Cardile. "I don't understand why."

The rest of the meal went by in silence. Toward the end Don Paolo said, "Maybe I'll go back to Rome tomorrow."

"All in all, the time you've spent here has been good for something," said Cardile.

"Yes. I seem to have assembled a fine troop of flies," said Don Paolo. "Where did you leave the cart?"

"Right here," said Cardile. "I'll have to go right away, so my family won't get suspicious. When will I see you again?"

Don Paolo went with him to the cart. Just before they parted, Cardile embraced him.

"You know where I live," he said. "And you know where my loft is."

In front of the inn door there was the usual crowd of loafers, since it was coffee time. There were grown men with a week's beard, in shirt sleeves and slippers, their collars unbuttoned; and some young men with oil all over their copious hair. Some of the latter surrounded an old man who was gesturing, with the facial expressions one might have expected of an actor in some provincial troupe.

"Who's that man?" Don Paolo asked Berenice.

"He's our greatest lawyer," said Berenice, "Marco Tuglio Zabaglia. We call him Zabaglione."

The name was not new to the priest. He asked, "Wasn't he once the Socialist leader around here?"

"Yes, he's the one; but he's a wonderful man."

Zabaglione caught sight of the priest at the door and introduced himself. "My name is Zabaglia; I'm most honored to meet you. Signora Girasole has already told me everything about you. Excuse me, are you from the court?"

"What court?" asked Don Paolo.

"The episcopal court. I asked because I wanted to know if the time had been fixed for the sermons for the departure of the soldiers and who is going to preach the sermon here."

"It will be scheduled any day now," said Don Paolo. "Who'll preach the sermon? Ah, holy Virgin, the usual ones!"

Don Paolo found himself in the company of a man about whom, from the time of his childhood, he had heard the landlords speak with hate and the poor people with love. Zabaglione's reputation in the province came from his speeches. When cases were being tried, and when it was known that Zabaglione was to speak the shoemakers', carpenters' and all the other shops were emptied and everyone who could went to hear him. Some of his most famous speeches had become part of the local lore. In the first years of the dictatorship, Zabaglione had had a lot of trouble getting his past forgotten. The Mazzini-style beard he had worn in his youth had been transformed into a goatee à la Italo Balbo. In the same way he had his hair cut shorter, changed the knot on his tie and tried, though in vain, to get thinner. But if these had been the heaviest and most visible sacrifices to which the old lawyer had been obliged to submit himself, who could possibly describe all the daily mortifications, such as the renunciation of his own ideas, watching how he spoke about the government and breaking off with friends who were under suspicion? No one could deny that Zabaglione had devoted every effort to the project, but, nevertheless, he had never succeeded in completely rehabilitating himself. He was always on the fringes of all the new institutions.

What had pained him most in the last years was having to remain silent when there were so many occasions to speak and move the people in the crowd "to bring them to the level of the events," as he would have put it. In this fashion historical events had been entirely wasted, and this is the worst disaster that could happen to the body politic.

"Would you do me the infinite honor of coming to my house for coffee?" said Zabaglione to the priest. "Some of my friends would be most delighted to make your acquaintance."

"Thank you, but I cannot," said Don Paolo. He went back into the inn, but suddenly he came back. "It's earlier than I had feared," he said to Zabaglione. "I would be delighted to come with you."

## 15

To reach the home of Zabaglia, one had first of all to go through the older part of town, through dark and ancient byways bearing the names of local saints and benefactors. There were silent little squares, hemmed in by stone houses and worn down by time. After the old town there came the newer quarter, which had been built after the earthquake of 1915 to look like a garden in the city. The streets and avenues, which were too wide for local purposes, bore names glorifying the recent patronage of the governing party. The faces of the houses, the fountains, the trees and the garden gates, all wore the heroic mottoes of the day, written in coal, lime or pitch, in various colors; and also in relief, sculptured in wood, and stone, and even fused in bronze.

"Here we are," said the lawyer.

A group of bricklayers, with a little bread, a knife, and some red peppers, sat eating in front of the house. They greeted the lawyer cordially. The house was protected by a wall surmounted with glass splinters. A man on his knees in the garden was weeding a flower bed planted in a pattern whose colors represented the Italian flag. A pretty, delicate lady came to the door. Her hair was in curlers. She was Zabaglia's wife.

"Kiss the priest's hand and make us some coffee," said her husband.

The woman kissed his hand and went into the kitchen. Three very thin little girls, as pale as plants grown out of the sun, appeared in dark clothes. They were the lawyer's daughters.

"Kiss the priest's hand and leave us alone," said their father.

The girls kissed the priest's hand, curtsied and disappeared.

148

"Every Sunday," said Zabaglione, "I send my daughters to Mass. If you don't believe it, you can ask Don Angelo, the curate in Fossa. What would happen to the women without religion's curb? Of course their mother goes with them."

The living room smelled strongly of cat urine. Badly torn blue curtains hung from the windows. The walls were almost covered with dusty book shelves. On the desk reigned the bust of some unknown, perhaps an ancestor, surrounded by numerous yellowed photographs.

"Sit down," said the lawyer cordially. "I feel I know you already because I've heard so many good things about you."

Without many preliminaries, the priest brought the conversation around to the subject closest to his heart.

"About fifteen years ago," he said, "I was engaged in organizing some Catholic peasants. Later, like the Socialist ones, our organizations were dissolved. Thus, in some respects, our situations are the same. How is morale in the old Socialist leagues now?"

Zabaglione became suddenly reserved and busied himself with putting the papers on his desk in order. The silence became oppressive.

To encourage Zabaglione to speak, Don Paolo invented something about his own diocese. He spoke of a crisis in the wine industry and of growing popular discontent. The government's corporations were farces and no one believed in them.

"And here?" asked the priest. "What do the members of the old red leagues think? Are they still Socialists?"

"They never were," said the lawyer.

"But most of the communes were won by your red leagues," said the priest. "Or do I remember rightly?"

"Your memory is perfect," said the lawyer. "But the point is that it wasn't a question of political leagues. The poor farmers, the ones we call peasants, joined the leagues for the sake of company and protection. To them, Socialism just meant being together. To work and to eat as much as they could hold was their most radical idea—to work and sleep in peace, without catastrophe the next day.

At our league in Fossa, there was a picture of Christ in red, the redeemer of the poor, next to the bearded Karl Marx. On Saturday nights, the peasants came to the league to sing 'Onward, brothers and comrades' and on Sundays they went to Mass to respond 'Amen.' The principal occupation of a Socialist leader was to write letters of recommendation. Other people write them now; mine aren't worth anything, so the peasants aren't interested in me any more. That's what a change of government means to a peasant."

"But weren't there any Socialists?" the priest wanted to know.

"In a manner of speaking, the only Socialist around here was me," said Zabaglione. "Of course there was some revival of the leagues among the peasants, but it was severely punished. The ones who are left have to avoid seeing each other."

"But nothing awful happened here as it did elsewhere," said Don Paolo. "Why are people so afraid?"

Zabaglione was silent for a moment.

"Even here," he said softly. "There were atrocities even here. On the nineteenth of January, nineteen twenty-three (it's a date I can't seem to forget) a squad of reformers broke into the home of the head of the league in Rivisondoli, and twenty-two of them raped his wife. This went on from eleven o'clock at night to two in the morning. An episode. At that time some of our peasants fled to France or America. As you know, the ones who stayed aren't peasants any more, but rural people."

"But there are still some elements of opposition," said Don Paolo. "There must be someone who looks back nostalgically at freedom of assembly."

"I hope they stay with us," said Zabaglione, "but I liked Socialism too. As long as you're a priest, may I confess my weakness to you? It's like this, the theories of Socialism always left me cold. But I liked the women. I made the best speeches of my life about Socialism . . ."

To the great annoyance of the priest, the other guests arrived just as the conversation was getting most confidential. They were Don Genesio, whom the priest already knew, the head of the municipal guards, and Don Luigi, the pharmacist. The head of the municipal guard had the magnificent uniform of a prewar general.

"How many guards do you command?" Don Paolo asked him.

"Just one, for the present," he answered. "You must understand, the town is poor and it's expanding only slowly."

Don Luigi was a handsome man, with his hair and mustaches in the style of King Umberto and a patch on his cheek. He said, "Father, I assure you that I send my wife to Mass every Sunday. If you don't believe me, you can ask the curate here. I think religion does for women what salt does for pork. It keeps up the freshness and savor."

Don Genesio had cleaned himself up; his hair, too, seemed neatly combed and oiled. As was to be expected, he too sent his wife to Mass every Sunday.

"Any news?" asked Zabaglione.

"The news of the bank's closing has begun to filter up to its customers in the valley," said Don Luigi. "I ran into Don Pasquale Colamartini from Pietrasecca just a while ago and he seemed out of his mind. Everything he had left from his idiot wife's dowry was in that bank, and he didn't know it was on the rocks."

Zabaglione sighed.

"In other times," he said, "the failure of a bank would have meant a wonderful trial."

"Have you ever heard anything about the notorious Pietro Spina?" asked the head of the guards.

Don Paolo started to leaf through an album of picture postcards.

"He's from the Rocca dei Marsi Spinas," said the head of the guards. "He's a crazy revolutionary. It seems he fled, and now he's back in Italy to cause some trouble. The police have been looking for him for three months. They think he's around here because it seems he wanted to burn up the grain on the threshing floor. Today we got word he'd been arrested in Rome."

"There goes another wonderful trial," said Zabaglione.

"What's that?" asked the head of the guards.

"It'll do him good to be locked up," said Zabaglione.

"Did you say Spina of Rocca dei Marsi?" asked Don Luigi. "I went to the University with Don Ignazio Spina,

that boy's father. The father was a good man. He died
in the earthquake. There's another fine old family de-
generating."

"How was it known that he wanted to burn up the
grain?" asked Don Paolo. "Was he seen around here
at harvest time?"

"No one saw him around here—neither now nor in
past years," said the head of the guards. "He's always
spread his propaganda in the city. But for the first time,
during the harvest, there was some writing in red on the
walls: 'Viva Pietro Spina.' So he must have been around
here."

"Do you think he came back from abroad to write his
own name on the walls?" asked the priest.

"No, not him. His accomplices."

"Ah, his accomplices," Don Paolo couldn't help saying.
"Then are some of the peasants in rebellion?"

He almost lost all prudence.

One of the lawyer's daughters served coffee.

"No sugar for me," said Don Paolo.

"Not among the peasants, but among the young people
there's a lot of unrest," said the head of the guards. "They
say a lot of things to make your hair stand on end, osten-
sibly about corporatism."

"The new generation is a dangerous one," said Don
Luigi. "How would you say it? It's the generation which
presents the bill. The new generation has taken corporatism literally and wants to destroy capitalism."

"That's where the trouble starts," said Zabaglione,
"taking theories literally. No regime should be taken
literally. Otherwise, where would we end up? Did you see
today's paper? In Russia they've brought back capital
punishment for adolescents. Why? Probably because
some of them have taken the Soviet constitution literally.
We should make a rule that a country's constitution is
something only for the lawyers and the more trustworthy
mature citizens—and that the boys should know nothing
of it."

The head of the guards agreed.

"As you know, I've been given the job of watching
over the town library," he said. "I really don't know what
good a library was in the first place. I always said if

someone wanted to read books, he should go buy them. But I had my orders and the library was opened. The books came from Rome, as you can imagine, appropriately censored. But what happened? The boys came and asked for a collection of the first writings of the head of the government. Then they started yelling: 'Look, it says here that we have to destroy the Church, the dynasty and capitalism!' I tried to tell them that books were written for grown-ups and not for boys, and that at their age they'd be better off reading fables. But there was no way to distract them. Finally, with the permission of the higher authorities, I took the books from the library and locked them up."

"You were too late," said Don Luigi. "I found out from my son that extracts which someone copied from those books are circulating among the boys. Some of the boys meet at the Villa delle Stagioni, beyond the river, to read them and talk about them. 'There'll be a second revolution,' my son tells me, 'to carry out what's in those books . . .'"

"Are these young peasants?" said Don Paolo.

"Three or four young students," said the head of the guards. "The authorities know about it and they'll stop it when the time is right."

Zabaglione shook his head. "The worst possible evil," he said, "is when the boys take what they read seriously."

Don Paolo and the pharmacist left Zabaglione's house together.

"You said you knew Pietro Spina's father when he was a student," said the priest. "Was he as 'crazy' as his future son?"

"We knew each other in Naples," said Don Luigi. "Like most of the students then, we were Republicans. Guiseppe Mazzini was our God and Alberto Mario his living prophet. Then we came back to Marsica. He married almost at once. He looked me up some years later. He was already unrecognizable, and I'll never forget what he said: 'Poetry is over. It's time for prose now.' I really am sorry about his son."

"Did you know Don Ignazio's wife?" asked the priest.

"I met her a couple of times with her husband," said Don Luigi. "A wonderful person."

The priest did not conceal his surprise.

"What was your friend complaining about, then?"

"Certainly not about his wife," said Don Luigi, "but about all the petty rivalries, jealousies and sordid interests that are part of provincial life."

"You seem to be justifying his son's rebellion," said the priest with a laugh. "What's his name again . . . I mean young Spina."

"No," said Don Luigi. "His revolt is an illusion and hence contemptible. All the poor boy inspires in me is pity. Now the authorities are complaining that my son Pompeo is stirring up his companions and prattles of a second revolution. I certainly can't approve of it, but I wouldn't want them to take it too seriously and mistreat him. Now he's in the poetry stage, I tell myself, then he'll have some profession, marry, have some children and get on to the prose."

"What would happen if men remained faithful to the ideals of their youth?" said Don Paolo.

Don Luigi raised his arms to heaven, as if to say, "It would be the end of the world!"

"There always comes a time of life" he said, "when the young men get bored by the bread and wine at home. They look for food elsewhere. The bread and wine in the inns at the crossroads can calm their hunger and thirst for a while. But a man can't spend all his life at the inns."

## 16

The priest saw an old gentleman from a distance, leaning on a lamp post as if he were ill, and recognized Don Pasquale Colamartini. He immediately took leave of the pharmacist and ran up to him. The old man was about to faint and did not recognize the priest until he fell into his arms.

"Buck up," Don Paolo said to him. "Buck up."

The old man breathed with difficulty. The pallor of death was on him already and he could not speak. With great difficulty the priest accompanied him to the cart. It was even harder to help him into the seat and put the reins into his trembling hands.

The old man's eyes were full of tears. Finally he was able to say, "It's the end. It's all over."

"Couldn't anyone here go with you as far as Pietrasecca?" said Don Paolo. "Isn't there a friend of yours who could take you home?"

He shook his head. "There's nobody—nobody at all!" he said, whimpering.

Don Paolo kept the cart in sight until it got to the bend in the road. He found a group of people in front of the Girasole inn, talking about the failure of the bank.

"As far as Don Pasquale's concerned," said Berenice, "it's a richly deserved chastisement of God. His second wife was an old idiot whom he married for her money, without having any children by her. Now he's lost the money, his children by the first marriage are going to leave home, and he's stuck with that silly old woman."

Don Paolo was about to protest when he felt someone take him by the arm. It was Bianchina.

"Come along!" she said. "Don't get all hot and bothered."

"How can your mother be so wicked?" said the priest.

"Maybe she thinks she should for my sake," said Bianchina, "like a good mother. At least the poor woman thinks she's a good mother."

"A good mother—what a gloomy institution!" said the priest. Then he added, "I'm sorry I didn't go with Don Pasquale. I think something awful is going to happen."

"Poor old man," said Bianchina. "I'd go to him and help him, for Cristina's sake, if he wouldn't take it in the wrong way. But here you can't lift a finger without it being taken in the wrong way. Don Paolo, listen, please! Take me away from here! I can't stand it!"

"Let's talk about that later," said Don Paolo. "Do you know Don Luigi's son?"

"Pompeo?" said Bianchina. "He's a friend of mine. I'm delighted that he interests you. I've already told him about you. If you want to come with me to the Villa delle Stagioni, I'll introduce you."

The Villa delle Stagioni was a former nobleman's residence which had decayed into a farmhouse. It had once been a baron's summer residence; but he had died later in Rome, riddled with debts.

On the way, Bianchina said, "You'll probably meet Cristina's brother there—Alberto Colamartini."

"I heard something about you and him at Pietrasecca," said Don Paolo.

"From Cristina?"

"No. You know how reserved she is."

"I would have preferred that Cristina had told you about it," said the girl. "She at least wouldn't have indulged in petty gossip."

"But Cristina wouldn't want you to marry him," said Don Paolo.

"I wouldn't want to marry him either," said Bianchina. "Alberto made the mistake of talking about it to his father, without my knowing about it. You know what I wrote to Don Pasquale then? I didn't tell you about that? I have no desire to get married, I wrote him, but if, in a moment of exhaustion, I were to resign myself to such a fate, I would put your son Alberto last on my list of men to make so unhappy."

"Are you that much in love with him?" said the priest.

"It wasn't for that," said Bianchina. "He's too much like me."

They had come to the walls of the villa. The large coach gates through which Bianchina conducted Don Paolo to the grounds were off their hinges and leaned against the walls. Nettles and poppies grew freely along the main road to the villa. An ivy-covered pavilion had become a hay loft, and the peacock cage served as a chicken coop. The villa consisted of two buildings joined at right angles. One wing on the first floor was a stall and another housed the peasants. The upper floors, whose windows had no shutters, gave the impression of being abandoned or of having been converted into granaries. On the façade, between balconies, were four empty niches. Large letters in red varnish could be seen on the cracked and streaked walls: "Long live the corporations without bosses!" "Long live the second revolution." A young man was alone in a corner, playing with a leather ball.

"Alberto!" called Bianchina. "That's the famous Alberto," she said to the priest.

"Did you come down from Pietrasecca today?" said Alberto to the priest. "How's Cristina?"

He had a slight figure and the look and voice of a boy. His face was open and mischievous.

"I'm concerned about your father," Don Paolo said to him in a serious tone. "You know about the failure of the bank where he'd kept all his money. The news was so hard on him it could kill him. Just a while ago I had to help him into his cart. I'm afraid something awful's going to happen."

"The man you call my father threw me out of his house," said Alberto. "He doesn't consider me his son any more."

"If you'd seen him just now," said Don Paolo, "I'm sure you would have forgotten all your past squabbles. He was an old man who could hardly stand on his feet, an old man with hardly anything to live for."

"Aren't you going to Pietrasecca right away?" said Bianchina. "I could get hold of a horse for you."

"If I found him alive," said Alberto, "my arrival alone

would be enough to kill him. If I came too late, my grand-mother would kick me out. Did you ever meet that old witch? . . . But I am sorry for Cristina."

Another young man of about Alberto's age came up, but he was stronger and more vigorous. He was dressed in a sweat shirt and shorts.

"This is Pompeo," said Bianchina.

"Bianchina has already told us about you," said Pompeo.

"It seems you were made for each other," said Bianchina.

"We probably agree on the important points," said Don Paolo. "I don't mean political theories as much as I mean what we should do with our lives. But it would be hard to describe how we agree."

"Why is that?" said Pompeo.

"There are a few superficial things that divide us," said Don Paolo. "We shouldn't be afraid of stripping ourselves of conventional etiquette, for the sake of understanding."

"We're not afraid," said Pompeo.

"We've come to a point," said Don Paolo, "where a sincere Fascist shouldn't be afraid of talking with a Communist or an anarchist; or an intellectual with a peasant."

"Do you mean perhaps that all the divisions among men are artificial?" asked Pompeo. "And that it's useless to struggle?"

"Certainly not," said Don Paolo. "But some divisions are artificial and were set up just for the sake of hiding very important areas of difference. Some forces are divided which should be united, and others, which are united artificially, should be split. Many of the present divisions are just verbal misunderstandings."

"Let's sit down," said Bianchina. "We can think better that way."

Two wooden benches were taken from the ground floor and set against the wall. Just then a young peasant came up and opened the stall door. The cows came out two by two with measured step and went to drink in a tub in a corner of the courtyard. They were thin cows, used to work, black and white ones, with great arched horns, who drank slowly, looking obliquely at the people on the benches. The cowherd closed the stable door and sat next to the others on the bench.

Pompeo was saying, "There was a man who'd saved the country from ruin and showed the way to reform. When he came to power, we were surprised that his acts were in opposition to his words. We asked ourselves, 'Can he have betrayed us?' A few weeks ago someone came through here and revealed the truth to us. 'He's a prisoner of the bank,' he said. Nothing else! But what did he mean? Is he really in chains in the cellar of the bank? Or was that just a manner of speaking?"

"What do you think?" the cowherd asked the priest.

"I couldn't say for sure whether the man you're talking about is really chained up in a bank," said Don Paolo. "Some people think he is. But it's not a question of just one man. But what you can be sure of as long as you keep your eyes open is that the whole country is the prisoner of the financiers."

"So what should we do?" said Bianchina.

"I'm also convinced that we'll have to prepare a second revolution," said Don Paolo. "We'll have to free our country from the bank's clutches. It'll be long, hard and tricky; but it's worth it."

Don Paolo had spoken calmly and with no sort of emphasis, but with a certain kind of firmness which left no room for doubt. Bianchina threw her arms around him and embraced him.

"Who'd have ever imagined that there'd be a priest with us, for the second revolution?" said Alberto with a laugh.

"Don Paolo's not a priest but a saint," said Bianchina. "Didn't I tell you?"

"In all the revolutions," said Pompeo, "there have always been priests who've taken up the people's cause."

"I must tell you," said Don Paolo, "that I can't take these vestments too seriously."

"It would be more prudent if you'd stay a priest," said Pompeo.

"Let's respect prudence," said the priest, laughing.

"But what can we do right now?" said the cowherd.

"With your permission," said Don Paolo, "I'd rather talk about that alone with Pompeo."

The priest and the pharmacist's son went off. They left the grounds of the villa, jumped over a stream and took a path flanked by tall pines and hawthorns.

"We belong to two different gererations," said Don Paolo, "but we're the same kind of men, the kind of men who take seriously the ideals given them by their fathers, their teachers and the priests. These ideals are proclaimed as the fundamentals of society. But it's easy to see that the way society operates contradicts them—or ignores them. Most of us, the skeptics, adapt to the situation; the others become revolutionaries."

"The skeptics tell you that the split between ideal and fact is inevitable. How do you answer that?" said Pompeo.

"Revolutions are facts, too," said Don Paolo. "Everyone chooses as best he can."

"You're right," said Pompeo. "It's a question of what you want to do with your life."

The path was flanked with a row of almond trees now, amid fields of burnt stubble. It was very hot. There were some isolated clumps of mulberries and they stopped to pick some of the berries. Further on, the path joined the national highway, which at that hour was crowded with donkeys, carts and peasants returning from the fields.

"What can we do?" asked Pompeo.

"Let's both think about it," said Don Paolo. "We'll talk about it later."

"I'm awfully glad I met a priest like you," said Pompeo. "I have friends in most of the villages around here. I'll introduce them to you."

"It seems to me," said Don Paolo, "that only now am I getting any benefit from that bothersome illness which forced me to leave my diocese and come here."

Before coming back to Fossa, the two separated so as not to be seen together.

A movie's guttural voice had invaded Fossa's main street, which was crowded with boys, and followed the priest up to his room. Don Paolo was tired but happy. Before undressing, he wanted to pack for his departure the following morning. Without hesitation he burned the papers he had received from Rome. He had barely gotten out of his shoes when he heard a rustling outside his door.

"Can I come in?"

It was Bianchina. She was happy and smelled of perfume.

"Did you know that Pompeo is enthusiastic about you?" she said.

"I very much hope that we'll become friends," said Don Paolo with a smile. "I'm glad you introduced us. It was a great event for me."

"Really?" said Bianchina. "Like a bolt of lightning?"

Bianchina looked at him with a smile.

"The more I see you, the more I like you and the stranger you seem," she said.

"Don't see me too much," said Don Paolo. "You'll make me nervous and make me pretend more than I have to."

"Can I confess one doubt?" said Bianchina. "I'm not at all sure you're a real priest."

"What do you mean by a real priest?"

"A stuffy fellow who has the Eternal Maxims instead of a brain. In other words, someone like my uncle, the curate of Fossa, and lots of others."

"You're right, I'm not at all like that sort of priest," said Don Paolo. "The biggest difference is probably that they believe in a domesticated God, above the clouds, on a golden throne—a very old man. But I think He's a very able young man Who's always in circulation."

"I like your God better," said Bianchina, laughing. "But will you promise me that yours won't grow old like the others?"

"Oh, come now," he said. "How can we be guaranteed against something like that? Every race tends to grow old."

"Well, I won't be sorry about that," said Bianchina. "We can hope that the youth of the gods will last longer than ours. . . . But when are we going to take that trip to Rome you promised me?"

"This time I'm going," said Don Paolo. "I'm taking the first train tomorrow morning. I've already told your mother."

"Are you going to leave me here?" asked Bianchina.

The girl's eyes were full of tears.

"You stay here and help Pompeo," said Don Paolo. "We have to establish communications with the neighboring villages. Maybe we'll have to act earlier than we think right now. I'll leave you expense money."

"Are you coming back soon?" said Bianchina. "You won't forget about me?"

"Stop these foolish questions," said Don Paolo. "You know I think about you a lot."

"I'll set the alarm so I'll get up, and I'll come with you to the station," said Bianchina.

"Please get that idea out of your head," said the priest.

"Are you ashamed of me?"

"That's something a wife would do; and it wouldn't be proper for a priest."

## 17

On the train Don Paolo learned at once how unpleasant it was to travel in disguise, seated among strangers who seemed to be scrutinizing him and who used every pretext to start a conversation. He was under the illusion that he had found a good refuge in the corridor, with his face against the window; but he left that place at the first stop, seeing the faces of some peasants he knew on the platform. He ended up in a corner of the compartment, bent over, with his hat down over his face. He began to read his breviary, holding it close to his eyes as if he were nearsighted. He read at random psalms, litanies and lessons of martyrs and saints, checking on the situation in the compartment after every stop. Fortunately the trip was not a long one.

His priestly clothes permitted him to escape unharmed from the careful police surveillance at the Termini Station in Rome. As an extra precaution, he joined a group of foreign priests who had just gotten off a train. As soon as he was out of the station, he went to a public bath.

"I'd like a bath," he said to the cashier.

The girl gave him his change without really noticing him, since she was called to the telephone.

The corridor where the baths were located was long, low and moist. The old woman who prepared his bath looked at him curiously and said something which Don Paolo did not understand. She received a conspicuously generous tip. In his suitcase Don Paolo had a jacket, a beret and a tie, the absolute minumum of civilian clothes to transform him back into a layman. But he really did take a bath; he needed one. He indulged in the hot water for a long time. He listened to the voices in the corridor for a while before he came out. As soon as he was sure the old woman was cleaning one of the baths, he came out, unobserved. He was Pietro Spina again. He went back to the station to check his bag; but how funny it was to walk without that gown! He felt as if everyone were looking at his legs. He started walking rapidly, almost running; and more than once he made sure his trousers were buttoned. Finally he boarded a trolley which took him to the Lateran Quarter. The large Lateran square was spread out between the basilica of San Giovanni and the Scala Santa and was encumbered with the sheds of a carnival in the process of being taken down. They had already been deprived of their noctural attractions; the carpenters were taking down the skeletal beams, while the tents, the posters and the chandeliers, together with the wooden horses and the tin swords, were being packed into trucks. Plaster-of-Paris statues, a phantom boat painted in a stormy sea and the skin of a Bengal tiger were lying on the ground.

Don Paolo crossed the disorderly square and went to the cool shade of the Scala Santa Church. Some little women in black were climbing the stairs on their knees. They stopped at every stair, on their knees, rested a bit, sighed and recited an interminable quantity of prayers. Pietro stopped by a marble group representing Pilate showing Christ newly whipped: ". . . but this is your hour, and the power of darkness." He did not have to wait long. A man came up to him who looked like an unemployed construction worker and looked at him especially curiously.

"Excuse me," he said, "are you the pilgrim from Assisi?"

"I am," said Pietro. "And who are you?"

"I'm a friend of the chauffeur's."

"I have a message for him," said Pietro, giving the man a letter.

"Do you know where to go tonight?"

"Yes," said Pietro. "I'll try to arrange it."

He went out the Porta San Giovanni and onto the Appian Way. He took a cross-street through a neighborhood centered around some movie houses and a new church. Beyond that was a broad meadow, the realm of cats, wild dogs and vagrants. This meadow was crisscrossed with ditches and trenches and was also the depository for old lumber, bricks, corrugated iron and miscellaneous rubbish.

Some months before, when Pietro had had to flee the police, he had found refuge in an old shack which was the residence of a man from his home town, Mannaggia Lamorra. When Lamorra had been a boy, he had served in the Spina household at Orta, after which he had emigrated to seek his fortune. He had sold soda water in Buenos Aires, laid bricks at St. André, near Marseilles, and after several years he had come back as poor as when he had left. For this reason he was ashamed to go back to his native village. At the present time he was a digger in a sand pit near Rome. Pietro easily found his wooden hut with the iron-plate roof. Lamorra ran up to him in a festive mood, but still the old servant.

"Are you back here again, sir?" he said.

"Just for a couple of days," said Pietro. "Why aren't you at the pit?"

"The company failed," said Lamorra. "I'll have to find another job."

"Good," said Pietro. "You'll work for me for a couple of days." He gave him an address and said, "Go to this address and find out if a bricklayer named Romeo still lives there. Find out if he has a job and where he works if he has one. But act naturally and don't attract anyone's suspicions."

Lamorra went off and Spina went into the hut, which was as hot as a stove. While he was waiting, he fell asleep.

Lamorra came back late; he was drunk, but he had the right information. Meanwhile Pietro had prepared two pallets inside the hut; but Lamorra, seized with sudden respect, would not go in.

"The hut is small," he said. "How could I sleep next to you, sir?"

"Nonsense!" said Pietro. "This is your place; I'm just your guest."

"All the more," said Lamorra. "If fate has made you my guest, how could I sleep next to you?"

He had fond memories of his days with the Spinas.

"Your father was a good man," he said. "When he got

of the bricklayers' chests and a scaffold would soon have to be constructed. Romeo gave some instructions to the bricklayers. When Pietro came up, Romeo asked him in a loud voice, "Are you the owner of the terrace we're supposed to fix?"

"That's right," said Pietro. "I'd like to discuss the costs with you."

The two went into the shed to talk. Pietro designed a terrace on a piece of paper, then said, "I'm to meet Battipaglia this afternoon. But for the practical work around Fucino, I need someone I can trust among our people in Rome, preferably a worker who comes from there and is still in touch with his village. He should go back there and work with me. It's hard for me to build anything permanent without some worker element."

"You're asking for too much," said Romeo.

"We still have to look," said Pietro. "The chances of acting in Fucino are very good; but the people I have to work with are young and inexperienced. I can't do anything without someone I can rely on. But he's no good unless he knows the area."

The foreman thought a moment. "You're asking for too much," he repeated. Then he explained the situation. "The persecution against the Pugliesi, the Abruzzesi and the Sardinians among us has been fierce. As you know, the police come from the country for the most part; and I can't tell you how mad they get when they get hold of a 'subversive' who isn't from the city but from the country like them. If a city man is for freedom, it's certainly a serious offense; but if a worker, formerly a peasant, is against the government, it's a real sacrilege. These types are almost always killed. If they manage to escape alive, they leave the prison cut to ribbons and their old comrades avoid them like the plague."

"That happened to Chelucci?" asked Pietro.

"They picked him up again about a month back, after we put up an antiwar poster. He's in the Regina Coeli Prison now—and he's almost blind."

"What's Pozzi up to?"

"There are suspicions against him," said Romeo. "Nobody knows why Chelucci was arrested and not him, since the police found them together. But the police might have done it just for that reason, to discredit and isolate him. How do you ever really find out what happened? There are several cases like that, the saddest of them."

"Aren't there any more people from Abruzzi in the groups?"

"We used to have Diproia, before he got married. As soon as he did, he didn't want to know anything about it. Now he goes to Mass every Sunday with his wife. We also used to have someone named Luigi Murica, a student; but he's disappeared without a trace. I've sent people to look for him several times, because he was good. But I never did find him."

"What's Anna the seamstress doing?"

"She was Murica's girl."

"I know that. That's why I asked."

"Maybe she went with him. You could look for her where she used to live. Even if she's moved, she may have left a forwarding address. But what good would it do? She's not from the Abruzzi."

"To find Murica."

"Come back tomorrow night when we get off work," said Romeo. "I'll do a little looking of my own."

Pietro took the Via della Navicella and Via Claudia, intending to go into the center of the city to look at it again; but its beauty was already faded. There was nothing to be seen on the street but men in uniform, clerks in the ministries, priests and nuns. It was already another city. But somewhere between ten and eleven the biggest parasites began to show up, the hierarchs, the chief clerks in the ministries, the monsignors with their purple stockings; and now Rome positively made him ill. He turned on the Via Labicana and, after having bought some insect powder, he went out of the city again.

"What's that for?" Lamorra asked.

Pietro told him about it.

"But if the bugs are so important to you," said Lamorra, "it'll go to their heads and they'll never go away."

"Would you like to go back to Orta?" Pietro asked him. "I'd like to give you a secret mission."

"Anywhere else but Orta," answered Lamorra. "I'll

go back there only if I've gotten rich and could buy a house and some land, but now . . ."

"But look, you're no good anywhere else," said Pietro. "Naturally, if you went to Orta, I'd pay your expenses. Think about it."

"I won't go back to Orta," said Lamorra drily.

That afternoon Pietro was to meet Battipaglia, the party's regional secretary. The meeting place was a little church on the Aventine Hill.

When Pietro got there, his friend was already at the church and was pretending to read a notice posted on the wall. Pietro had not seen him for many years. He was somewhat bent, and his hair had turned gray. Prison had aged him. Pietro stopped by him for a moment, going close up to the notice as if he were nearsighted, so Battipaglia could see him, and then entered the building. He did not know the church. A double file of arches divided it into three parts. The arches were supported by antique columns which grew out of the floor without bases and with variously decorated capitals. The stone floor was almost entirely covered with headstones. At the back of the church the main altar looked like a simple stone tomb, with a wooden crucifix in back and four candelabra. The church was dark and almost deserted. There were only two women on their knees in front of the sacrament altar, under a burning lamp. Pietro stood near the door, by the fount of holy water. When Battipaglia came up, he walked slowly around the church. Finally Battipaglia came up to Pietro.

"I've had some money for you the last month," said Battipaglia in a low voice. "I also have a new passport so you can go abroad. How's your health?"

"I don't need the passport just now," said Pietro. "I'm not going back abroad."

"That's your business," said Battipaglia. "It's not my affair, as you know. All that comes from the 'Center Abroad.' I'll send you the passport by Fenicottero. You can do with it what you want. Who's the one you sent from Fossa the last time with your news?"

"Her name's Bianchina. She's the innkeeper's daughter."

"Is she a comrade? When did she join the movement?"

"She's not really a comrade; but she can be trusted all the same. She doesn't know who I am or why she came here."

"Isn't that a risk?"

"She wouldn't betray me even if she found out who I was."

"That's your business. It's not my job to teach you anything. Have you been shacking up with her?"

"No."

"That's your business, and not mine, as you know. The girl talked of a certain Don Paolo, a revolutionary priest who's supposed to be in the mountains. Do you know him?"

"No," said Pietro.

"You should recruit him. He could be useful to you."

A sacristan had come in by the sacristy door and had lit two candles on the main altar. A priest in his sacred costume appeared, having been announced by the ringing of the bell. He stopped for a prayer on the first step of the main altar. Some footsteps outside the church door announced the arrival of some more worshipers. They were nuns. They dipped the tips of their fingers in the holy water, crossed themselves, and went quickly to the altar.

"Have you found work?" asked Battipaglia.

"It's hard among the peasants," said Pietro. "They're more attuned to Gioacchino da Fiore than to Gramsci. All this fashionable concern with the south is a bourgeois utopia."

"Since there's no courier to where you are," said Battipaglia, "the 'Center Abroad' has asked me to get an immediate answer from you on the last political resolution. As you know, it's a formality more than anything else."

"I have no use for formalities," said Pietro. "You can understand that."

"We know that no one could attribute to you the least uncertainty in declaring your solidarity with the majority of the Russian Communist party," said Battipaglia. "You're an old comrade and everyone holds you in high esteem."

"To tell you the truth," said Pietro, "I don't know what it's all about. If it's so hard for me to know my village, let alone my region, how can I have any useful ideas on Russian agricultural policy, disagree with some opinions and approve of others? It wouldn't be serious. You can understand that."

"Did Bianchina bring you the three reports?"

"Yes, but I haven't read them yet."

"When will you? The 'Center Abroad' insists on your opinion at the earliest moment."

"I don't know when I could grind through it all," said Pietro. "I don't even know whether I could understand it and have any worthwhile opinion. I'm much more concerned with the situation right here."

Then, with a great effort he added, "I wouldn't want to lie to you. I burned the papers. It would have been a useless risk to bring them here. And frankly, I wasn't interested."

"That's serious," said Battipaglia. "Don't you know that?"

"In other words," said Pietro, "I just don't feel able to judge things I don't know anything about. I won't submit to any kind of conformism and I won't approve or condemn with my eyes closed."

"How can you dare call our condemnation of Bukharin and the other traitors conformism? Are you mad?"

"It's conformism to always be with the majority," said Pietro. "Don't you think so? You were with Bukharin as long as the majority was with him; and you'd still be with him if he had a majority now. But how can we fight Fascist conformism if we're going to give up our critical faculties? Try and answer me that?"

"Don't you think Bukharin was a traitor?"

"To tell you the truth, I don't know," said Pietro. "I only know that right now he's in the minority. And I know that you dare to oppose him only because of that. Answer me this if you can: Would you be against him if he had a majority?"

"Your cynicism is getting to be just a bit too much!" said Battipaglia, trying to keep his temper.

"You haven't answered my question. Answer it truthfully if you can."

"If it were up to me, I'd have you thrown out of the party right now!"

Battipaglia was shaking with emotion. But their meeting

place kept both of them in check. After a long silence Battipaglia went off without a word. Pietro remained where he was, leaning with his back against the fount of holy water. The services continued. The candles' weak light flashed the gold of the vessel to the altar, creating a crown of illumination around the priest's white head. The ceremony came to an end and the few worshipers in the church moved to the door. One of the nuns was struck by the sight of Pietro as she stopped at the holy water to cross herself. She paused to take a look at him.

"Don't despair," she murmured with a smile.

"What do you want?" said Pietro.

"Courage," she repeated. "Don't give in to despair."

"Who are you?" said Pietro. "What do you want with me?"

"Take heart," said the nun. "God never tries anyone beyond his capacity. Do you know how to pray?"

"No."

"I'll pray for you. Do you believe in God?"

"No."

"I'll pray for you. He's the Father of us all, even the ones who don't believe in Him."

The nun hurried to rejoin her group. After a while Pietro left the church.

Evening had fallen. He had planned to go to a movie; but he gave up the idea. Lamorra was waiting for him outside the hut and he had prepared something to eat. Pietro's appearance made him thoughtful.

"What happened to you?" he asked him. "Did something go wrong?"

"Yes," said Pietro in a tone which discouraged further questions.

"Don't you want something to eat?"

"No."

Pietro did not sleep a wink that night, and Lamorra saw it.

"What did happen to you?" he asked. "Did some woman ditch you?"

"Yes," said Pietro. "Leave me alone."

"Some woman gave you the air?"

"Yes."

"You should never love too hard," said Lamorra. "Your father was a man of passion, too."

The next day Pietro was late for his meeting with Romeo. He had the face of an old man and his eyes were swollen. The site was already deserted. The foreman was waiting for him with a boy, behind the tool shed.

"This is Fenicottero," said Romeo.

"A month ago," the boy said to Pietro, "a Czechoslovak passport and some money arrived for you from the 'Center Abroad.' "

"How do you know the passport is Czechoslovakian?"

"I opened the envelope."

"That was bad," said Pietro.

"Yesterday we put up the posters against the war at San Lorenzo," added the boy, as if to rehabilitate himself.

"What's on the poster?"

"I didn't have time to read it," said the boy.

"You mean you put up posters, too?" asked Romeo.

"Yes. There aren't many of us left, and we all have to do a little of everything."

Romeo got very angry. "What! You're in courier work and you do propaganda too! Don't you know that every time this has happened the whole operation's been sabotaged?"

The boy was embarrassed and confused.

"What's your trade?" Romeo asked him.

"I do a little of everything. I don't really have a trade."

"That's the trouble," said the foreman. "You can't understand clandestine work if you don't have a trade. A bricklayer building a scaffold first puts up the beams, then joins them with horizontal rafters and then fixes the whole to the wall with thigh beams. A bricklayer knows a beam can't serve as a rafter. And that's the way it is in any art. There are even rules for the art of conspiracy. If you don't know them or if you don't respect them, you pay for it with years in jail, or with your life."

Romeo's indignation was sincere. He had his own vested interests.

"I don't want to go back to jail through your doing," he told the boy. "From now on you don't do any more courier work. Understand? Don't show your face around here! If we meet, we'll pretend we don't know each other."

The boy left in great embarrassment.

Romeo gave Pietro the addresses of some people from the Abruzzi who had left the group some years ago.

"You'd be the best one to try and bring them back," he said. "But is it prudent? Judge for yourself."

## 18

Following Romeo's directions, Pietro managed to discover the dwelling of an old friend of his, <u>Uliva the violinist</u>. They had not seen each other for several years, having last met in the Communist student groups. All Pietro knew was that Uliva had been obliged to spend several months in jail. Like so many others, after that he had become separated from the group. He lived with his wife on the third floor of a house on the Via Panisperna, in the Viminale quarter.

A young woman in an obviously advanced state of pregnancy brought Pietro into Uliva's room. Her eyes were swollen and red, as if she had been crying all morning. Uliva greeted his old friend with indifference, with neither pleasure nor surprise. He was an emaciated hunchback in glasses, with dirty clothes which gave him a neglected, melancholy aspect. Even after Pietro's arrival he remained stretched out on the couch, smoking and spitting in the air. He aimed in the general direction of a basin, but he must have fallen short of his target most of the time because yellow stains were to be seen everywhere, on the fringes of the blanket, on the desk and on the walls. The room was dark, disordered and smelly.

"We haven't seen each other for a long time," said Pietro. "I didn't think you'd have come to this."

Uliva answered with a cold laugh.

"Did you think I'd be a clerk in the bureaucracy? An officer of the militia? A Commendatore?"

"Can't you do anything else?"

"It doesn't look that way."

"You should look around," said Pietro. "You're probably too isolated. Some people are still resisting."

"It's an illusion," said Uliva. "You remember our student group? The ones who haven't died of starvation or been put in jail are worse off yet."

"It's worse to give in. You can accept the challenge and fight it.'

"For how long?"

"For ten years, for twenty, for two hundred, for ever! Life's no good without some struggle."

"Do you think ventriloquism is a struggle?" said Uliva. "Why are you so full of phrases? Listen, I've lost my taste for that sort of things. After suffering ten months in jail for having shouted 'Long live liberty!' in Piazza Venezia, I slept in the public dormitories in the winter for a while, and in the summer under the bridges over the Tiber, or under the Esedra Gates or on the church steps, with my jacket rolled up under my head as a pillow. Every once in a while the patrol would come by and ask us, 'Who are you? What's your trade? What do you live on?' You should have seen how they laughed when, for the lack of anything else, I showed them my scholastic certificates, my diploma from the Santa Cecilia Music School. I even tried to establish myself in my home village in Chieti Province. I had to sneak out at night. My relatives said they'd forbid me the house. 'You're our ruin,' they told me. 'You've dishonored the family.' "

"You still shouldn't give up," said Pietro. "All the workers' groups must stay united."

"Don't tell me that," said Uliva. "I know some printers. They're all set up. The working masses have been governmentalized or they've turned cowards. Even hunger has been bureaucratized. Official hunger gives you the right to a hand-out and to the government's soup. Private hunger only lets you throw yourself in the Tiber."

"Don't be fooled by appearances," said Pietro. "The strength of a dictatorship is muscular, not spiritual."

"You're right," said Uliva. "There's something cadaverous about it. It hasn't been a movement for a long time, not even a Vendée-type movement, but just a bureaucracy. But what sort of opposition is there? What are you? A future bureaucracy. You aspire to totalitarian power, too, but in the name of different ideas, which means just different words, and for different interests. If you people win, and probably you'll be unlucky enough to win, we'll just go from one tyranny to another."

"You live on hallucinations," said Pietro. "How can you condemn the future?"

"Our future is other countries' pasts," said Uliva. "Yes, I don't deny that there'll be technical and economic changes. Just as now we have the state railways and the state quinine, salt, matches and tobacco, so then we'll have state bread, state peas and potatoes. Will that be technical progress? Let's admit that it would be. But this technical progress will be an opening wedge for a compulsory official doctrine, for a totalitarian orthodoxy which will use all means, from the movies to terrorism, to stamp out any heresy and tyrannize individual thought. The present black inquisition will be followed by a red inquisition. There'll be red censorship instead of the present one, and red deportations will take the place of the ones we have now—and the most favored victims will be dissident revolutionaries. In the same way, just as the present bureaucracy identifies itself with the fatherland and exterminates every opponent, denouncing him as a hireling of the foreigners, your future bureaucracy will identify itself with labor and Socialism and will persecute anyone who continues to think with his own head as a prized agent of the big landowners and the industrialists."

"Uliva, you're talking nonsense!" cried Pietro. "You've been with us, you know us, you know that's not our ideal!"

"It's not your ideal," said Uliva, "but it is your fate. There'll be no escaping it."

"Fate is the invention of resigned and lazy people," said Pietro.

Uliva made a gesture as if to say that it was not worth arguing any further. But he did add, "You're very intelligent, but you're a coward. You don't understand why and you don't want to. You're afraid of the truth."

Pietro got up to leave. From the door he said to Uliva, who was still on the couch, "You have no right to insult me like that!"

"Get out of here and don't come back!" said Uliva. "I don't want to have anything to do with a party hack."

Pietro was going to go, he had already opened the door.

But he closed it and went to sit at Uliva's feet on the couch.

"I won't go before I've understood why you've become like this," he said. "What's happened to you? Jail? Being out of work? Hunger?"

"In my misery I've tried to find some promise of liberation in books," said Uliva. "I haven't found it. For a long time I've been bothered about this: Why have all revolutions, every single one of them, begun as movements of liberation and ended as tyrannies? Why hasn't even one revolution escaped from this?"

"Even if that were true," said Pietro, "you'd have to come to another conclusion. I'll have to admit that all the revolutions have degenerated, but we want to make one which will remain faithful to itself."

"Illusions! Illusions!" said Uliva. "You haven't won yet; you're still a clandestine movement, but you're rotten already. The passion for reform which used to drive us when we were together in the student group has itself become an ideology, a spiderweb of fixed ideas. That's why there's no excuse, even for you. Mind, you're just at the start of a downward parabola.

"Maybe it's not your fault," added Uliva, "but the fault of the machinery which confuses you. Every idea is crystallized into formulas for the purpose of propagation; it is entrusted to a body of interpreters for its preservation. They are carefully chosen, sometimes appropriately paid, and in any case put under a superior authority, which has the job of resolving doubts and repressing deviations. And thus every new idea always ends up as an obsession, immobile and regressive. When this idea becomes the state's official doctrine, there's no escape. Maybe a carpenter or a plowman could get along even in an orthodox totalitarian regime and eat, digest, procreate and generally mind his own business. But, especially for an intellectual, there's no escape. He has to bow down and enter the dominant clergy, or resign himself to being hungry, and to being eliminated at the first opportunity."

Pietro got angry, took Uliva by his lapels and screamed in his face, "But why does that have to be our fate? Why isn't there any escape? Are we hens locked up in a chicken coop? Why do you condemn a regime which doesn't even exist yet and which we want to create in the image of man?"

"Don't scream," said Uliva calmly. "Don't be a propagandist, here in my house. You understood perfectly well what I said; but you pretend you don't understand because you're afraid of the consequences."

"Nonsense!" said Pietro.

"You know, I watched you a lot when we were together in the group," said Uliva. "Then I realized that fear had made you a revolutionary. You forced yourself to believe in progress, you forced yourself to be optimistic! You worked hard to believe in free will, only because you were terrified by the contrary. And you're still that way."

Pietro made one small concession to Uliva.

"It's true," he said. "If I didn't believe in liberty for men, or at least the possibility that men could be free, I would be afraid of life."

"I've stopped believing in progress—and I'm not afraid of life," said Uliva.

"How have you resigned yourself? It's awful!" said Pietro.

"I'm not resigned at all," said Uliva. "I'm not afraid of life, but I'm not afraid of death either. Against this pseudolife, weighed down by pitiless laws, the only weapon left to man's free will is antilife, the destruction of life itself."

"I'm afraid I understand," said Pietro. He had understood, because a great veil of sadness was spread over his face. There was no use arguing further.

The young woman who had opened the door for Pietro came into the room to pick up some things. Uliva waited for her to leave before saying, "In spite of everything, I have a certain esteem for you. I've seen you in a sort of romantic dispute with life for several years, or, if you prefer, with the Creator; the creature's struggle to surpass its own limits. All this is noble—and I'm not being sarcastic; but it requires an ingenuousness I lack."

"Man doesn't really exist unless he's fighting against his own limits," said Pietro.

"You once told me of a secret dream of yours," said

mad, he beat me, but he still was a good man. Once, at Easter, he gave me a kid goat."

Pietro stretched out inside the hut and Lamorra lay on the ground by the door. But the pallet was crawling with bugs and lice. Pietro tossed and turned, but he did not dare complain, for fear of offending Lamorra. But Lamorra knew what was bothering him.

"I have a few bugs in there," he said. "If you pretend not to pay any attention to them, they'll leave you alone."

"Good night," said Pietro.

The wine had brought out Lamorra's fondest memories.

"Once your father gave me a Tuscan cigar," he said. "What a cigar it was! He gave it to me on a Saturday night and I smoked it Sunday morning on the square in front of the church, while the women were coming from Mass. They don't make cigars like that any more!"

Pietro fell asleep, while Lamorra continued to remember all he had been through in his long life.

"In Buenos Aires, there's a little river called Riachuelo. The Italians live around there and they're called gringos or tanos. Once there was this big fat Negro woman . . ."

The following morning Pietro went very early to station himself at one side of the Porta San Giovanni. Romeo was not late, but since some other workers were with him, Pietro did not go to him but followed at a distance. The workers were coming from all sides. There was a beauty in the air which moved Pietro—the beauty of Rome at dawn, when the streets are full of people going to work. They have little to say and they go rapidly. Romeo took the Via delle Mure Aureliane. At the Porta Metronia he separated himself from the group and took the Via della Ferratella. Pietro went behind him and whistled a song which Romeo used to sing on the Island of Ustica, where they had both once been deported:

> Never a rose without a thorn
> Never a woman without a kiss.

Romeo turned, pretended he did not recognize Pietro and walked to the yard where he was the foreman. The building had barely been started; the wall was at the level

Uliva. "You spoke in terms of your home town: to make a soviet of the Fucino Valley and to nominate Jesus president of the soviet. Certainly it wouldn't be a bad idea, if that carpenter's son from Nazareth were alive and could do the job personally. But, once He'd been nominated and had accepted the nomination, wouldn't you have to name Him a deputy? Well, in this country we know how Jesus' representatives began and what they finally became. We know all about that. The poor Negroes and the Indians the missionaries have just converted don't know it; but we know it and we can't pretend we don't. Where's your historical point of view now, Pietro?"

"Among the nettles," said Spina. "If Christ ever was alive, He still is."

Uliva smiled.

"You're incurable," he said. "You have a fateful capacity for fooling yourself. I can't do it."

Then he added, "My father died at Pescara at the age of forty, an alcoholic. All he left me were some debts to pay. A few weeks before he died, he called for me one evening and told me the story of his life, the story of his failures. He began with the death of his father—that is, my grandfather. 'I die poor and disillusioned,' his father had told him, 'but I rest all my hopes in you—that you'll have what I lacked.' When he felt his end was near, my father confided in me that all he could do was to repeat my grandfather's words to me. 'I'll die poor and disillusioned too, son, but I have hopes for an artist like you, and I wish you in life what I hoped for in vain.' In that way, from generation to generation, along with the debts, the illusions are handed down. I'm thirty-five years old now and I'm already where my father and grandfather were. I'm already a conspicuous failure, and my wife's expecting a child. But I'm not enough of an imbecile to think that he'll get from life what I didn't. He'll die of hunger, or a slave—which is worse."

Pietro got up to go.

"I don't know if I'll be back," he said. "But if you or your wife ever need me . . ."

"It's not worth it," said Uliva. "We don't need anyone."

Via Panisperna resounded with the roar of about fifty boys in student hats, carrying a three-colored flag and a sign reading "Three Cheers for the War!" Some policemen were with them. They were yelling and screaming and stopping every passer-by, and singing a song: "We'll make a shoe brush of the Emperor's Beard." The people were looking in curiosity from the doors of the shops, but they didn't make any comments. In the Via dei Serpenti, Pietro came upon another group of students with the same flag and the same sign. They were singing the same song about the shoe brush, and they had the same sort of police escort. Among the crowd of loafers and among those who were going straight to work or straight home Pietro recognized the uncertain steps of the unemployed, of those who had nothing to do and who ended up following the crowd of students.

Near the Colosseum, Pietro stopped to watch an exercise performed by a vanguard of young machine gunners and artillery men. They were boys of from fifteen to seventeen, and they were learning the operations of the pieces and how to take them apart and put them back together, and how to transform them from the transport to the action position. They were like little men, most serious and attentive; and they executed the motions with the greatest rapidity. Pietro's expression attracted the attention of a woman.

"Why are you crying?" she said to him. "Are you sick?" Pietro nodded and fled. He wandered about aimlessly all afternoon.

His appointment with Romeo was in an inn in the Tibertine Quarter, in the Via degli Erinici, beside the Acqua Marcia aqueduct and not far from the railroad. The rust from the railroad and the smoke from the locomotives gave the street its color. The smell of coal and heavy oil impregnated walls. When Pietro came to the inn, it was almost deserted. In one corner, a policeman was eating spaghetti with sauce with a ferocious and lugubrious air as if he were eating the entrails of an anarchist. Sawdust was scattered on the floor to collect the spit. The only picture on the wall represented a great transatlantic steamer at night, with the cabins lighted up, on a moonlit ocean. Some porters and laborers came in later, ordered half a liter of wine, drank and looked at the steamer guardedly so the policeman wouldn't notice, and set out for America in their minds. Then they paid for their wine and embarked, spat on the floor, and went home in a bad mood.

Romeo came late, drank a quarter liter at the bar, coughed and left, without coming close to Pietro, who left behind him and followed at a distance. This was difficult because Romeo took a different street at every corner, evidently to make sure the police weren't following him. At the Vicolo della Ranocchia he slowed down and allowed Pietro to catch up.

"Did you hear about the explosion in Via Panisperna?" said Romeo.

Pietro did not know anything about it.

"Uliva's apartment was blown into the air, burying him with his wife, and the tenants on the floor below. They told the papers not to mention it. But it happened in the middle of the city and everybody knew about it right away. It seems Uliva was planning an attempt on the Santa Maria degli Angeli Church, when there was going to be a ceremony with everyone in the government there. A friend of ours, a fireman who worked on the ruins, told us they found a plan of the church with a lot of technical notes in Uliva's apartment."

"I saw him this morning," said Pietro. "I got the impression he was getting ready for a funeral, too."

"If the janitor at the house saw you, he's sure to remember you," said Romeo. "People don't forget your face easily. That's another reason for you to go abroad."

At the Piazzale Tiburtino there was a large crowd with some militiamen, policemen and soldiers.

"What's happening?" asked Pietro here and there.

Someone answered him, "We mobilize tomorrow. The new war in Africa begins tomorrow."

Tomorrow! It had been discussed for so long; but just for that reason war had become something incredible and strange. But the incredible was about to happen, was already there, behind the scenes, and tomorrow it was to be a fact.

"I forgot to tell you that the boy in courier work has been arrested," said Romeo. "They'll surely torture him to get something from him. In these cases the best thing is to count on the worst. So watch out. Here's the money which came for you a month ago, and here's your passport. We'll have to avoid each other for some weeks."

"I haven't any more time to lose," said Pietro. "I came back to Italy six months ago and I still haven't accomplished anything. Now I'm tired of waiting. I need someone I can trust in the Marsica region."

"An illegal organization is like a cloth which is woven and unwoven continuously," said Romeo. "You know this better than I. The cloth costs much patience and some blood. The organization in Rome has been destroyed again and again, and built up again each time. How much trouble it is to get in touch! And these contacts often don't last very long. I've seen many of my friends go to prison. And I've seen others disappear without a trace. There are still others we have to avoid because we think they're police spies. But we have to carry on."

"All right," said Pietro. "I'll arrange things myself."

"There's more," said Romeo, obviously embarrassed.

"What's that?"

"I saw Battipaglia, the regional coordinator."

"What did he tell you?"

"He warned me you might be thrown out of the party."

"That's not up to him."

"I'd be very sorry if it happened," said Romeo. "Try and avoid it. Don't be headstrong."

"Let 'em leave me alone!" said Pietro. "They can't expect the impossible from me. I can't sacrifice to the party the reasons which led me to join it."

Romeo insisted. "Leaving the party means abandoning the idea," he said.

"That's false thinking," said Pietro. "It'd be like putting the Church before Christ."

"All right," said Romeo. "But don't be headstrong."

They shook hands warmly, and went off in opposite directions.

## 19

Before he went back to Marsica, Pietro wanted to make another attempt to find an experienced comrade whom he could take along as his assistant. He wanted to provide for the danger that his arrest might leave Pompeo's young friends without leadership. Therefore he told Lamorra that he would stay in his hut for another couple of days. The old peasant took advantage of this to make him a proposition.

"I can't go back to Orta," he said. "I've already told you why. It's the only place in the world where I refuse to set foot. And you're not going to Orta either. Why don't you take me with you? I'm tired of working in the lime pit."

"What would you do with me?" Pietro asked him.

"Everything. Even the lowest services," said Lamorra. "I'd carry your bags. Do you shave yourself? I'd carry letters to your girl friend. It wouldn't cost you much. I'd eat your table scraps."

"You're mad," said Pietro. "I hate servants."

Lamorra was very sad at this.

"Don't think I could say that to anyone else," he said. "But you're the son of my old master. And—no offense— you really haven't grown up."

"Look for the person you know," said Pietro. "Don't waste time chattering."

Lamorra didn't find Murica, but Annina, his friend. She had moved to Via della Lungaretta in the Trastevere Quarter, into a large popular apartment building which exuded misery and filth. Pietro went there right away.

Pietro found a girl bent over a sewing machine in a room which served as both bedroom and workroom.

"Romeo will have told you about me," said Pietro. "I've come for news about Murica."

The girl was obviously disappointed. She was still

very young and had a peaked face, but a fine, well-formed
one, with two beautiful but hostile eyes. Pietro stayed at
the door, embarrassed, until the girl offered him a chair.
When he was close to her, Annina looked at him with a
smile veiled in sadness.

"You know, you have a funny resemblance to the man
you're looking for," she said. "Even your aggressive way
of visiting is like his. And he was born at Rocca dei Marsi,
not far from your home town, I believe. He told me about
it once."

"It's about ten kilometers away," said Pietro. "Where
is he now? I have to see him. It's urgent."

"He told me about you often," said Annina. "He
regretted that he didn't know you personally. But life
in the groups was very isolated. It was hard for the
companions to know each other."

"How long has it been since you've seen him?"

"It's been almost a year. Several people have come
to ask about him."

"Couldn't he be in jail?"

"No," said the girl with certainty. "Last year he was
taken, along with some others in the first-of-May raid,
and he spent a couple of months in jail. When he came
out he swore to me that he'd kill himself rather than go
back."

Footsteps sounded on the stairs. A little girl opened the
door, left some clothes to be repaired and went away.

"Had you known him long?" asked Pietro.

"Why open old wounds?" asked Annina.

"I'm sorry," said Pietro. "I don't ask just out of curiosity. If you knew me better, you'd know you can trust
me."

"I know it," said Annina.

She straightened up the table and her sewing machine.

"We met in the group about three years ago and fell
in love at once," said the girl with a blush. "It was more
than a casual affair. It was a passionate one. I was living
with my family then and my mother scolded me all the
time because I forgot everything else and had time only
for him. He was my first friend, and for me he was son,
brother and lover all at once. And he was very much in
love with me."

The girl got up and turned her back on her guest to hide her tears. When she came back to sit down her eyes were red.

"I didn't want to bring up these sad memories," said Pietro.

"I'm afraid the whole business hasn't been forgotten," said Annina. "It's a sad fact I always have before me. I have nothing else to live for."

"A conspirator's life is hard," said Pietro. "We have to be heartless to resist without total despair."

"But our friendship hadn't affected our participation in the group's work at all," said the girl. "On the contrary, we were the more active for it. We got up trips and reading groups; we dug up Socialist novels to study. We gave up getting married, having children, a home of our own, so we could give more time to the party."

"What was it that broke up this idyllic relationship?" said Pietro. "I'm sorry to ask that, but what interests me most of all right now is to know whether the break has been total, personal and political."

Annina was a bit undecided.

"Some things are hard to tell," she said. "But maybe I should do it and maybe you're the one I should tell it to. You're from his part of the country, you look like him, you think the way he does and you probably have all his faults."

The girl had another outburst of tears, after which she continued her story.

"When he was arrested last year," she said, "he was beaten. But more than the beating, he was humiliated; they slapped him and spat on him. He came out of Regina Coeli Prison confused and depressed. I thought it was on account of his physical weakness. But as the weeks went by, his nightmare of the police and of being arrested again didn't diminish. 'I'll kill myself before I go back to jail,' he told me over and over. The police had warned him to break off his old friendships and not to see me again, since I was politically suspect too. He was always nervous when he was with me. He would turn pale when he heard a car coming. We didn't know where to meet any more. He was still in love with me; he wanted to be with me often; he got very jealous if he spent two days without seeing me; but when he was with me he felt in danger, and he almost hated me for it. The old thoughtless gaiety was gone. Every meeting was an agony. 'The police could catch me at any moment,' he would say. And he got sick all the time: his heart was bad, his digestion was irregular, and he had attacks of asthma. A policeman came often to my place to look for him. He was from Puglia and he had red hair. He was awful. He came at the oddest hours, usually during the night, when I was in bed. I soon realized that he was looking for me more than for Luigi. Several times I had to defend myself. Finally, just to be safer, I invited a girl cousin of mine to stay with me.

"Last Christmas I had dinner with Luigi in a restaurant outside the Porta San Paolo. He was unusually calm that day, in a good mood, almost gay, as he used to be. We hadn't been alone together for a long time, so I invited him to my place, in a little apartment I had in the Via del Governo Vecchio, to spend the afternoon. On the way we bought some flowers, some fruit, some pastry and a bottle of Marsala. He was helping me to arrange the flowers in a vase, when there was a knock on the door, which we had locked. 'Who's there?' I asked. 'The police,' someone answered. Luigi started to tremble. He sat on the sofa so as not to fall. He made a sign to me not to open; but the knocking on the door got more and more violent. 'I'm not going back to jail,' he murmured. 'I'll jump out the window, but I won't go back to jail.' Meanwhile the police were almost beating down the door. Now this apartment had a little terrace, from which it was easy to get to the roof. So I told Luigi to escape to the roof. As soon as he was gone, I opened the door. Two policemen came in, the man from Puglia and another young man whom I didn't know. It was no use denying anything. They knew my friend was at my place because they'd seen us come there together. They looked under the bed and in the closet. The man from Puglia said, 'If he's not in the room, he must be on the roof.' I blocked their way to the balcony. 'You're not going to arrest him,' I said. 'Arrest me but not him.' The policemen tried to force

their way; but I bit and kicked them. 'You're not going
to arrest him,' I repeated. 'All right, but on one condition,' the policeman from Puglia answered. 'Any condition,' I said. I would have willingly given my life to
save my friend from jail; but the policemen took a bit
more than that. I don't know how long they stayed.
All I know is that it was much later when I heard my
friend's voice behind the half-closed doors of the balcony. 'Have they gone?' he asked me. He came to the
window and leaned out to see if the house were watched.
'There's no one in the street,' he said, satisfied. He took
a biscuit from the table and ate it. He went to the door
and listened to see if there were anyone on the stairs.
Then he came to me. 'Are you sleeping?' he asked again. I
was covered with a sheet, and he took the sheet off. He
saw that I was naked; and he saw traces of the two men
on the sheets. He sneered in disgust. 'Whore!' he shouted.
He spat on the bed, he dumped all the things we had
bought to celebrate Christmas on the floor, knocked
over the sewing machine, smashed the bottle of Marsala
against the mirror and left, slamming the door. I didn't
lift a finger or say a word. What had happened had happened."

The woman was silent. Her story was over. There
was a man's step outside the door.

Pietro suddenly got up.

"If it's that cop from Puglia," he said, "you'll go on the
roof this time and I'll deal with him."

But it was a messenger, who left a package and departed right away.

"The man from Puglia was prudent enough not to
come here again, and so was his colleague. I thought I
saw them a couple of times on the street at a distance;
but they went away."

"Where do you think Murica ended up?" asked Pietro.

"He probably went back home, to Rocca dei Marsi,"
said Annina.

"Did you ever think of talking to him?"

"What good would it do? What's happened has happened."

"I'll go speak to him," said Pietro.

"I couldn't live with him any more," said Annina resolutely. "Nor with anyone else. Everything disgusts me."

"Annina, thank you for the trust you've shown in me," said Pietro. "Maybe it won't be wasted."

## 20

In the railway carriage full of young men called back to the army two men with the party's emblem were talking about the war. The other travelers were silent and listened.

"With the new invention our army has, you'll see, the new war in Africa will be over in a few days," one of them was saying. "The 'death ray' will burn up the enemy."

He blew on the palm of one hand with all his might, as if to get rid of some dust, meaning that the enemy would be routed as easily.

"Did you read that the boys from Avezzano will be blessed today by the bishop?" said the other. "I guess that thing's going to pave the way for the missionaries too."

Among the young soldiers there was an old farmer with his organ. His son had his head on his father's shoulder and he was asleep. "Play something," said the people around him. But the old man shook his head. Maybe he didn't want to miss what the two men were saying about the war, which was about to break out, and about the mysterious "death ray." The two men were armed with hunting rifles and they had full cartridge belts. They were going to Fucino to hunt quail.

"The quail are late this year," said one of them. "But they're better than they were last year."

"There's always something to make up for it," said the other, and he laughed.

The laugh meant that the other man had said something witty, so the people sitting nearby laughed, a little later, not wanting to seem stupid.

More young men called to the war got on at every station. Almost all of them stank of the stall and of *grappa.* The ones who couldn't find seats lay on their packs. Others took black bread from their knapsacks and ate. The old man with the organ handed around a bottle of wine. "Play something," the people around him kept asking. But he shook his head. He did not feel like it.

Don Paolo was crumpled up in a corner. His wornout hat and his old cassock made him look like a poor priest from the mountains. He recognized the inhabitants of the villages from many small signs, and the ones from the valleys and from the mountains, the ones who came down from the sheepfolds, poor people whose capacity for suffering and resignation was truly without limit. They were used to living in isolation, ignorance, diffidence and the sterile hatred of one family for another.

Every time Don Paolo thought he recognized someone from Orta among the travelers, he covered his face with his breviary and brought his cap down over his eyes. Even the countryside was in uniform.

On the train, in the stations, on the telegraph poles, on the walls, on the trees, on the latrines, on the church towers, along the garden walls and along the parapets of the bridges were inscriptions in praise of the war.

He got to Fossa without any trouble. The place was almost unrecognizable under the many colored decorations, with the festoons, flags and inscriptions on all the walls, in paint, chalk and coal. The Girasole inn seemed to have become a mobilization center.

Berenice ran here and there in great agitation, with her hair and her clothes in a mess. But she did have time to kiss Don Paolo's hands over and over and to welcome him.

"What a stroke of luck that you're here on this glorious day!"

"Where's Bianchina?" said the priest. "Where can I find Pompeo, the druggist's son?"

But Berenice was already far away.

Boys and young men were running up and down the stairs and through the dining room. A group of men with the party emblem, already hoarse from talking too much, were seated at a table, discussing the details of a spontaneous demonstration which was scheduled to take place that afternoon. The whole population of Fossa and the surrounding area was to be there, with the most rigid and severe security precautions. Fossa was not to be forgotten.

"Do we have to send the trucks all the way to Pietrasecca?" one of them asked.

"I think so, even to Pietrasecca," answered another. "But we'll have to have some policemen on the trucks, so the people will know that they have to come spontaneously."

Around another table was a group of landowners and merchants under the direction of Zabaglia. They were fat, greasy men with shriveled faces. For hours and with dogged persistence they had been discussing the menu for the banquet that night. Zabaglione was so wrapped up in the job that he did not see Don Paolo coming. There was a grave disagreement on a question of principle, and as usual Zabaglione had ended by making it a matter of his own personal prestige. The question was: which wine should be served first, white or red?

On the second floor, in Berenice's bedroom, there was a meeting of the local recruiting office. Those who had not found chairs were sitting or lying on her bed. A gracious wish was embroidered on the cushions of the bed "Pleasant Dreams." At the head of the bed was a colored picture representing the Guardian Angel caressing a dove. The merchant who had a shop in the city-hall square, in front of the Girasole inn, which had had to close for bankruptcy, had opened that morning. His wife Gelsomina was seated on the bench and there was a sign on the door to the effect that "Creditors are informed that the proprietor of this shop has volunteered for the war." The clerk in the registry office, Don Genesio, after having looked over the list of those who had applied to volunteer had exclaimed, "This'll be a debtors' war!"

This felicitous remark was repeated to all who came by. Don Luigi the pharmacist was looking everywhere for his son and could not find him. He was desperate. Other men's sons were volunteering and his was staying?

He, too, was a businessman with some notes due soon.

"Have you seen Pompeo?" he asked everyone he met anxiously. "If I find him and if he doesn't volunteer for the war spontaneously I'll shoot him, by God."

With a different anxiety, but none the less anxious, Don Paolo was looking for Pompeo, too. Without saying anything to his father, he went to look for Pompeo in the Villa delle Stagioni. The villa was silent and deserted. The priest found Bianchina near the water trough, alone, singing, and playing with a rubber ball. The girl embraced him with great joy.

"Where's Pompeo?" he asked.

"He went to Rome," said Bianchina. "He was called."

"Who called him?"

The girl did not know for sure.

"It must be for the second revolution," she said.

"Where's Alberto?"

"At Pietrasecca. He's gone back to the fold. His father died. He left me because he was jealous of Pompeo, of you, of everyone."

"What's the cowherd doing?"

"I don't know; he's engaged. He wants to get married."

"I have an urgent request for you," said Don Paolo.

Bianchina curtsied and answered, *"Ecce ancilla Domini."*

"I want you to go to Rocca dei Marsi to find one Luigi Murica. Tell him just this: A friend of his from Rome would like to look him up. Can he come here? Even if he insists, you mustn't tell him anything else."

"I'll go on my bike," said the girl.

The bicycle was in a part of the villa devoted to sporting equipment. Don Paolo saw her on her way to Rocca and went back to the Girasole inn.

As the hour approached when the proclamation of the war was to be announced on the radio the crowd, which already filled the streets, got thicker and thicker. Motorcycles, automobiles, trucks full of policemen, carabinieri and militiamen and functionaries of the party and of the corporations were coming from every direction. The donkeys, carts, bicycles and trucks transporting peasants were coming along the country roads. Two bands were marching through the streets of the town, playing the same march over and over again. The players were dressed like lion tamers, or doormen in luxury hotels, with sumptuous braid and a double row of brass buttons down the front. In front of the barber shop there was a poster showing some Abyssinian women with huge breasts reaching almost to their knees. A tight group of boys had stopped in front of the poster, laughing and looking at it with avid eyes.

In back of the square, between the party headquarters and the city hall, a radio had been set up crowned with a garland of flags. The voice of the war was to come from there. Under this magic object, on which everyone's fate depended, the poor people were slowly gathering. The women squatted on the ground, as if they were at church or at the market. And the men sat on their knapsacks or on the rumps of their donkeys. They knew only in a general way why they were there and were looking at the radio's metal box with suspicion. Finding themselves gathered there, they were disoriented, sad and diffident.

The square and the nearby streets were already filled with people, but the flow continued uninterrupted. The lame men from the stone pits were coming, as well as the wall-eyed from the furnaces, the bent-over plow boys, the wine growers from the hills with their hands reddened by sulphur and lime, and the dwellers on the mountains with their legs bowed by mowing. Since one's neighbor was disposed to come, absolutely everyone felt like coming. If the war will bring misfortune, it will be a misfortune for everyone—in other words, not quite that much of a misfortune; but if it is to bring anything good at all, we'll have to try to get some of it. And that was why everyone bestirred himself. They had left the mashing of the grapes, the cleaning of the casks, the preparation of the seed, and they had come to the local capital on orders. Finally even the people of Pietrasecca got there and were crowded up by the Girasole inn. "Don't stir from this spot!" the local policemen ordered the newcomers.

The schoolteacher of Pietrasecca, Signorina Patrignani, was explaining to her group how to behave, when to cheer and when to sing, over and over. But her voice was lost in the general confusion. Grascia got angry.

"Leave us alone!" he yelled. "We're not children."

Don Paolo was talking with Magascià and old Gerametta about what had happened in Pietrasecca since he left. Magascià told him of the sad death of Don Pasquale Colamartini.

"That day he came down to Fossa with you," said Magascià, "he came back dead that night. The horse brought the body in the cart right up to the threshold. Several people met him and said hello during that return trip, but no one realized that he was dead or dying. His body was at an angle on the driver's seat, and his head was on his chest, as if he were asleep; but his hands still held the reins firmly."

"Poor Cristina," said Don Paolo. "Now she'll never get out from under her family."

"Donna Cristina has asked about you several times," said Magascià. "She wanted to know when you were coming back. Alberto's up there now, but he's no good at all."

The peasants of Pietrasecca were waiting in silence for the ceremony to begin, while the women were more curious and impatient. Cesira proposed that the women go to the church "before the machine starts talking." Filomena and Teresa were against it because they might lose their places. But since the others were going, they went, too. Meanwhile the men were passing around a flask of wine, pouring it directly down their throats without the flask's touching their lips.

"When is it going to talk?" Giacinto asked Don Paolo, pointing to the magic machine.

"Any time now, I think," he said.

This news passed from man to man and increased anxiety.

"It might talk any minute now," the people repeated among themselves.

Only Cassarola the wise woman had not wanted to get off Magascià's cart. The women were coming back from the church and were trying to drag her off.

"Come with us," they said to her. "Come and sit next to us."

The wise woman did not answer.

"What do you see?" asked Don Paolo of her.

The old woman looked at him with diffidence.

"There's a yellow comet in the air," she said. "First there'll be a war, and then the plague."

The other women did not see the yellow comet, but they crossed themselves all the same.

"Which saint should we pray to?" asked Cesira.

"There's no use praying," said the wise woman. "God reigns on the earth, the waters, and the sky; but the yellow comet comes from beyond the sky."

Sciatàp handed her the wine so she could drink. She drank and spat on the ground. Magascià got on his cart and whispered in her ear, "Tell me the truth. What do you really see?"

"A yellow comet," she answered, "with a long yellow tail."

In the midst of the frightened and anxious crowd some pale girls went about with a deep basket full of three-colored emblems. Don Paolo recognized Zabaglione's daughters. They came up to him and pinned an emblem on his chest. They were excited, confused and completely out of breath.

"Oh, Father," they said. "What a wonderful day! What an unforgettable day!"

The priest gave back the emblem.

"I'm sorry," he said. "I cannot."

Part of the crowd, pushed by some newcomers who wanted a place where they could see the radio, separated Don Paolo from the girls.

The noise of a motorcycle was heard above the buzzing of the crowd. It was Don Concettino Ragù in the uniform of an officer of the militia. To avoid meeting him, Don Paolo took refuge in his room. He stood by the shutters on his windows on the third floor of the hotel. From his observation post the assemblage of the crowd around the radio looked like a group of pilgrims in the presence of an idol. Above the roofs he could see two or three church towers crowded with boys, like pigeon cotes full of doves. Suddenly the church bells began to ring. The crowd was furrowed by the party's nobility, who were coming to put the patriotic fetishes around the fateful machine—the three-colored flags, the banners and a picture of the chief, with the exaggerated protuberance of his lower jaw. Cries of "Eja

Eja" and other cries equally devoid of intelligible meaning were launched by the group of notables, while the masses were silent.

Space under the radio had been reserved for the "mothers of the fallen." They could not do without them. They were poor little women who had worn mourning for fifteen years, who had been professional mourners all that time, decorated with medals, and in exchange for a small pension they were at the disposal of the Marshal of the Carabinieri every time a public ceremony made their presence necessary. Near the "mothers" and around the curate of Fossa, Don Angelo Girasole, were grouped the priests of nearby parishes—old priests, good-hearted but timid, gloomy priests, athletic and imposing priests and a white-and-red canon who looked like a well-nourished bird.

"What a great day," said the canon. "What a success it's all been!"

Under the main gallery the fat landowners were lined up; they were Bourbon versions of woodsmen, with diabolical eyebrows and clothes of hunting velvet. The church bells continued to sound at length, with the boys taking turns pulling the ropes. At one point a sign was made to the boys to stop ringing the bells, since the radio broadcast was coming any minute; but they did not understand, or pretended they did not understand. There were about ten church towers, with all their bells ringing as loudly as they could, making an intolerable noise on the square. Some militiamen appeared at the top of the nearest church tower and made the boys stop ringing the bells. But the sound of the others continued, so that the first raucous sounds of the radio passed unnoticed. A loud yell rose up from the group of notables and militiamen, a rhythmic noise, a passionate invocation to the chief: "CHAY DOO CHAY DOO CHAY DOO CHAY DOO!"

The invocation spread slowly and was taken up by the women and the boys; it was picked up and repeated by all the crowd, even by those the farthest away, and even by the people in the windows, in a measured and religious rhythm: "CHAY DOO CHAY DOO CHAY DOO CHAY DOO CHAY DOO CHAY DOO CHAY DOO CHAY DOO!" From the vicinity of the radio signs were made to the crowd to be quiet in order to hear the speech, but the crowd gathered in the nearby streets continued to shout the saving invocation, continued to call on the chief, the magician, the wizard who was in charge of their blood and of the future of all of them. The cries of the crowd, mixed with the persistent ringing of the church bells, made most of the speech on the radio incomprehensible. The two syllables themselves ended up by losing all meaning, they were scanned like a formula of exorcism, and they were lost in the air and mixed with the sound of the church bells.

At a certain moment the people nearest the radio made a sign that the broadcast was over.

"War has been declared!" shouted Zabaglione.

He made a sign that he wanted to speak, but his voice was drowned in the clamor of the crowd, which continued to invoke salvation and grace. The cars and motorcycles of the authorities made their way through the mob and left in all directions. When Don Paolo saw that Don Concettino had gone, he left his refuge and went down into the street. Zabaglione greeted him with open arms.

"Have you seen my daughters?" he said with pride. "Have you seen them distributing emblems? Patriotic sentiments have certainly transfigured them."

"They were beautiful as angels," said Don Paolo.

Zabaglione was moved by this compliment. Don Paolo added, "I spoke to the bishop about you. I hope I did you some good." Zabaglione wanted to kiss him. Although the priest tried to avoid it, Zabaglione succeeded.

"My dear man," he said. "I've already heard them saying you're a saint; but I didn't know the Church had such benevolent saints."

The lawyer took the priest by the arm and took him home, through streets covered by flags. "Viva! Viva!" he cried to every group he met. His wife opened the door. She was pale and trembling.

"Kiss the priest's hand and leave us alone," said Zabaglione.

The woman curtsied and kissed Don Paolo's hands,

but before she went, she said to her husband, "The girls haven't come back yet."

The man raised his eyebrows.

"Send the maid after them right away," he said.

In the dining room Zabaglione offered some refreshment.

"The Lord has wanted to punish me," he said. "Why has he given me daughters and not sons? By now they'd be in Africa. For the lack of sons, I've made all my clients awaiting trial volunteer for the war. Most of them won't be accepted; but it's a nice gesture."

The priest looked at him benevolently, as if to say: Among friends we can be franker and say things in greater confidence; why after all did I come home with you?

"The war will be hard," said Don Paolo.

"That's all right," said the lawyer. "Even at worst we're bound to get something. Don't you agree? After every war, especially after every defeat, our country has expanded."

"You were going to make a speech after the broadcast," said the priest.

"It was scheduled, but the crowd's enthusiasm didn't permit it," said the lawyer. "On the other hand, all I was supposed to do was to introduce the speaker of the day, one Concettino Ragù, who was to speak on the theme, 'The Rural Masses and the Roman Tradition.'"

"This 'Roman' business is a farce," said the priest with unusual frankness. "If the peasants let themselves get mobilized for the war, it certainly isn't for the sake of a 'Roman tradition' of which they are completely ignorant."

The lawyer was still irritated at not having been chosen as the official orator. He was glad to have someone with whom he could get it off his chest.

"You're right," he said. "It's nonsense to talk of Roman tradition these days. Our tradition goes no further back than the Bourbons and the Spaniards, erected on a cloud of Christian legends. Furthermore, there was no Roman influence here even during the days of the Romans. The religion, the language, the alphabet, the customs and the people were all different from the Latins."

"Do you think there are any elements against the war among the peasants?" asked Don Paolo.

"The peasants haven't enough to eat. How can you expect them to worry about politics?" said Zabaglione. "Politics is a luxury reserved for the well-fed. But there are some malcontents among the young people."

Don Paolo left in a hurry and went to the Villa delle Stagioni. After he got beyond the park, he thought he saw a girl stretched out on the straw, behind the pigeon cage. He walked up slowly. Too late, he realized that it was not Bianchina but one of Zabaglione's daughters, with a soldier. Having learned by experience, Don Paolo had no need to draw closer to realize that it was not Bianchina but the lawyer's other two daughters when he saw two girls in tender conversation with soldiers, at opposite sides of the temple of Venus. But the Villa delle Stagioni was deserted. In the wide, vacant courtyard some swallows cruised erratically about. Even the swallows were getting ready to leave for a winter in Africa.

Don Paolo went back to town, discouraged and impatient.

There was great activity in the streets of Fossa, especially around the inns.

Berenice had set up a roast pig in front of the hotel; a long pole had been stuck through it from the rump to the neck. A filling of rosemary, sage, thyme, and fennel had been stuck in a gash in the belly. There weren't many who were buying, only some militiamen who had received their first pay. Some young peasants were looking fixedly at the pig, showing their teeth like hungry wolves. A sergeant in the militia had a large piece of pork on a slice of white bread and was cutting it with a new knife, one of those instruments with a blade, corkscrew, scissors and punch all in one, which gained the admiration of everyone around him.

Under the gallery a shed had been set up with enlarged posters of Abyssinia. It cost ten centesimi to see it. Who doesn't have ten centesimi? Don Paolo paid, too, got in line with the other spectators, and passed by a series of holes with magnifying glasses in them. Putting his eye up to one of the glasses, he saw a series of Abyssinian women with hairy bare legs and protuberant breasts. The last picture represented the Empress. The passage of the line of spectators was much slower than Don Paolo would have wished; but the great crowd kept him there. Some of the ones in front of him stood absorbed in front of every picture. His timid request to hurry up caused screams of protest from all the line. When he was finally able to get away from the artistic renditions, his patience was almost at an end. He went here and there, tired and discouraged. He went back twice to the Villa delle Stagioni. Both times he saw the white clothes of Zabaglione's daughters between the straw and the grass but no trace of the cowherd or any of the other young people. It should be time for Bianchina to get back from her errand to Murica.

In this way the afternoon passed. The high society gathered in Berenice's inn for the banquet; while the artisans, the petit bourgeoisie, the peasants of Fossa, together with those from the villages who had stayed, camped in the meadow near the Cantina Buonumore, on the bank of the river. For the occasion the host had set up many benches outdoors and was selling dark-red wine from Puglia at reduced prices. Under a poplar tree near a path which went along the river reigned a great vat from which he drew the wine, filling the half bottles which a group of servants were bringing to the tables. Among others, Don Paolo recognized some from Pietrasecca—Magascià, Sciatàp, and others, partially drunk. Finally there was someone to talk to. He was almost from their village.

"Did you understand something of what's happening?" asked the priest of one of the people he knew.

"That's all we need," said Sciatàp. "No one told us we have to understand."

"Things go by themselves," said Magascià, "like water into a river. What good is it to understand?"

"If you fall into the river, are you going to let yourself get drowned?" said the priest.

Magascià shrugged his shoulders.

A certain Pasquandrea claimed that it would soon be possible to emigrate again and that was the important thing. Another, one Campobasso, added that there would certainly be requisitioning of horses and mules. "But if you have just a donkey, there's nothing to worry about," so he was all right. Sciatàp wanted to know from the priest if the "death ray" could destroy seed under ground. The others listened and drank, stupefied, deafened and silent. Magascià said to the priest, "You'd be better off drinking and not asking us things we don't understand. Look, at Pietrasecca a joke or a pun lasts many years, it passes from father to son and is repeated over and over again, always in the same way. But here, in just one day you hear so many new things it gives you a headache. What's there to understand?"

"Things always go their own way," said Sciatàp, "whether you understand them or not."

Don Paolo saw Zabaglione coming up the path along the river. He took Don Paolo aside and, pale and stricken, asked him, "Have you seen my daughters by any chance? I'm afraid something awful has happened."

The lawyer was soon recognized by many of the drinkers, who surrounded him, offered him something to drink and began shouting, "Speech! Speech! We want a speech!"

The crowd asked for a speech as if they were asking for music, a story or a dance tune, according to the player's whim. Zabaglione was against it; he resisted, but finally he had to give in. Some young men lifted him almost by force onto a table, near the wine vat. He twirled his mustache, ran his hand through his hair, looked over the crowd and smiled. His face was transfigured. He raised his hands to the starry skies and with his warm baritone voice began, "O descendants of The Eternal City! O my people!"

The orator greeted this group of artisans and drunken peasants as if they were a gathering of exiled monarchs. He erected a tissue of past glories on an alcoholic mist.

"Tell me: Who brought civilization and culture unto the Mediterranean and unto Afric shores?"

"We did!" answered some voices.

"But other hands have gathered all the fruits!" yelled the orator. "Tell me once more: Who carried civilization throughout Europe, even unto the foggy shores of England, there to erect villages and cities, while nearby the rude inhabitants grazed, among the wild boars and stags?"

"We did!" some voices answered.

"But other hands have taken all the fruits. And again: Tell me who discovered America?"

This time everybody got on his feet and shouted, "We did! We did! We did!"

"But others profit from it. And once again: Who was it who invented electricity, wireless telegraphy and all the other wonders of modern civilization?"

"We did!" some voices answered.

"But others profit from it. And, last of all, who was it who emigrated to every land on earth to dig mines, build bridges, construct roads and drain swamps?"

This time, too, everybody got on his feet and yelled, "We did! We did! We did!"

"This, then, is the reason for our noble poverty. But after centuries of humiliation and injustice, Divine Providence has sent to our land The Man who will recover all that is due to us and which the others have usurped."

"Tunis! Malta! Nice!" some of them cried.

"At New York! In America! In California!" cried others.

"At Sao Paolo! Along the Avenida Paulista! Along the Avenida Angelica!" shouted an old man.

"At Buenos Aires!" some others shouted.

Near Don Paolo, Sciatàp was seized with excitement, and although he was so drunk he could hardly stand on his feet, he wanted to get onto a table. He imposed silence on everyone around him and started shouting, "At New York, at Forty-second Street . . . at Forty-second Street . . . Listen! . . . Please! . . ."

People gathered around Zabaglione, urging him to continue; but from a distance, along the path which paralleled the river, he saw three girls walking arm in arm with some soldiers. He jumped down from the table and with great effort ran off after his daughters. After the speaker left, it was as if some pleasant music had stopped and everyone repeated to himself the tunes he liked best.

"At New York," Sciatàp was saying to those around him, "at Mulberry Street, there's this crook who calls himself Mr. Charles Little-Bell, Ice and Coal. He should be punished first. My idea would be—of course everyone's free to think up something better—my idea would be . . ."

Campobasso took him aside and asked, "What is there on Forty-second Street?"

"Fun, rich men's fun," said Sciatàp. "Beautiful women walk along there, women with perfume."

He half closed his eyes and breathed that far-away smell of those women. He did not say anything more because his son came up, wearing an ill-fitting soldier's uniform, with the sleeves tucked up at the wrists and the trousers barely reaching below the knees.

"Drink," said the father. The son drank. "Drink some more," ordered the father. The son drank some more. "Now listen. Don't forget what I'm going to tell you, here in front of everybody," advised the father. "If the government decides to send soldiers with the 'death ray' to New York too, volunteer for it right away. Tell the government that your father was there and has told you where things are. Now, as soon as you get off the boat at the Battery, you go to your right . . ."

The son was laughing openly, looking knowingly at his father and nodding at every sentence.

A group of drunken peasants had assembled around the wine vat to sing some old emigrant songs:

> We were thirty days on a ship
> And we came twa Merica . . .

There was a fracas because some soldiers were leaving without paying. The waitresses were howling and the innkeeper was threatening them with a kitchen knife.

"Make the government pay for it!" the soldiers shouted from a distance.

Around the almost empty vat there were about ten

peasants who continued to sing emigrant songs. Some of them had climbed up onto it and were holding on as if it were a ship in a storm at sea, and they were singing:

> We found neither straw nor sand
> We slept on the naked land
> Like the cattle going to rest . . .

Their voices were toneless, loud and drunken and the cadences were prolonged until they were out of breath. The whole thing was done with the grotesque gestures of travelers getting on ships and leaving.

## 21

Magascià was the only one who was aware that Don Paolo was weeping.

The priest got up with difficulty and with slow steps went back to town. It was already dark. He wanted to go back to the inn and his room and lie on his bed. But there was a group at the door in a complete uproar. He stood to one side, confused and undecided, until he attracted the attention of someone who called Berenice.

"Why don't you join the banquet? Come in!" she said to him. "Several of the gentlemen want to meet you."

"Thank you, I've eaten already," said Don Paolo. "Is Bianchina home?"

"She hasn't come back yet," answered Berenice. "I don't know where she is."

Don Paolo went off without knowing where to go, and he ended up once more on the path which led to the Villa delle Stagioni. As soon as he was beyond the houses, darkness was complete. He walked, then paused, not knowing what to do. He went beyond the bridge over the river and came into a narrow path flanked by gardens. Some bit of the emigrant songs arrived even down there:

> And America is long and wide
> Surrounded by rivers and mountains . . .

Near the city walls, Don Paolo was attacked by a large dog which leaped out of a hedge. Luckily a peasant came to his aid. It was the cowherd, Pompeo's friend.

"What are you doing around here at this time?" he asked surprised.

"I'm looking for Pompeo," said Don Paolo.

"He was called to Rome," said the cowherd. "He hasn't come back yet."

"And Bianchina?" asked Don Paolo.

"I haven't seen her," answered the cowherd. "Good night; I have to go."

"Haven't you a moment for me?" said Don Paolo. "I'd like to talk a bit with you."

"I'm sorry," the cowherd excused himself, "my fiancée's waiting for me."

Slowly and unwilling the priest went back to town. The streets of Fossa were almost deserted and scantily illuminated. The flags, trophies and arches and banners made the place look like a carnival evening. Don Paolo could only walk; he dragged his feet along, clothed in his dirty, dusty gown. But at the entrance to the inn he stopped once again. Voices and singing still came from the dining room. It was the last of the patriotic banquet. And he could not go to his room without crossing the dining room. To avoid the greetings and questions of those horrible people, the priest went around the inn and tried the kitchen door. He found it at the end of a little courtyard filled with chests, stacks of vine branches and piles of coal. Noises of dishwashing were coming from the kitchen.

The coal made the priest curious. It was soft wood coal. He took a few pieces and filled one of his pockets. On tiptoe he went back, forgetting all about his exhaustion, and began a little walk through the neighboring streets. The street leading to the station was deserted and the station itself was silent. A beggar with his dog was asleep in the waiting room. The last train had already gone. Above the ticket window Don Paolo wrote with the charcoal: "Down with the War!" "Long live Liberty!" He crossed the square by the station and went to the old part of the town, along a dark and tortuous street which led to the church of San Giuseppe. The walls of the church were crumbling and were not the right place for epigraphs in charcoal. But the three wide stairways which led to the main door were smooth and polished. "Wonderful!" said Don Paolo. It was as

if generations of Christians had polished these steps
every day for centuries in the expectation of Don Paolo
and his piece of charcoal. Don Paolo wrote in fine printed
letters: "Long live Liberty!" "Long live Peace!" When
he finished, he went off and looked at his handiwork
from two or three points. He was satisfied. The slogans
really looked well at the foot of the church. In the lunette
of the large door there was a fresco of San Giuseppe with
his flowering stick. Don Paolo smiled at him, tipped his hat
and continued his walk. On a corner he ran into a drunk
proceeding on a zigzag course. The drunk was bewildered
at the appearance of the priest. Then he laughed in an ape-
like fashion and began walking behind him, whispering,
"Hey, girlie, stop for a moment."

The priest walked faster, but inasmuch as the drunk
insisted, he stopped under a street lamp and let the
drunk catch up, ready to hit him. The drunk realized
the mistake he had made, made a funny gesture of surprise, and stammered an excuse. "Oh no! What a sacrilege
I was about to commit!"

Don Paolo continued his walk and arrived at the
post office. The office had an official sign on the door
and solid bars on the windows. Costly and useless ornaments. But the façade had recently been whitewashed. Had
they known what they were doing when they whitewashed
it? At any rate, Don Paolo wrote on the white wall in
large accurate letters: "Long live the Peoples of Africa!"
"Long live the International!"

Some drunken voices came from the nearby streets.
To avoid any more meetings, he went back to the hotel,
coming in through the kitchen, which was deserted by
then. He was surprised to find Pompeo waiting for him
in his room.

"I came back on the last train last night," he said.
"As soon as I found out you were here, I came to find
you. I've been waiting for you here because I have to
talk with you."

"And I've been looking and waiting for you all day,"
said Don Paolo. And he added, "Pompeo, this horrible
war has begun; the war of the bank against the poor
people. And what are we to do?"

Pompeo became pale.

"No, you're wrong, Don Paolo," he said. "This is a war of the people and for Socialism."

"Are you mad? How can you believe that?"

Pompeo told of the ups and downs of his trip to Rome, with a friend of his who was also a partisan of the second revolution. They had spent that evening with some rich friends of theirs, and of course the war had been discussed. Pompeo had been much surprised to hear from a banker who had been there that he had some reservations on the new war in Africa, which he considered rather a costly political undertaking. Several of those present had agreed with him. "Why is there this war, anyway?" several of the young men there had asked. The banker's first answers had been vague and uncertain. No one dared pronounce his name, much less criticize him. But at the end, and with much hedging, he had finally stated his views with frankness. In modern times, he had said, every war leads to state socialism and destroys private property. That's enough for me, Pompeo had said. If that's the way it is, he would volunteer for the Social Empire.

Don Paolo was about to answer something, but he hesitated. He was still holding his charcoal-stained hand in his pocket.

"The war will serve to get fertile land for our unemployed," Pompeo insisted. "They will all become independent landowners."

He took a piece of paper from a portfolio and showed it to the priest.

"I volunteered for the war this very day," he said.

In a strained voice Don Paolo told him, "In that case, we have nothing more to say to each other."

But Pompeo, with some uncertainty still, had an important favor to ask of the priest.

"Promise me," he said, "that you won't make anything of what has been established between us."

Don Paolo did not reply right away. Perhaps he did not want to lie.

"Promise!" insisted Pompeo.

"I promise you," said Don Paolo. And he added,

"Bon voyage. I sincerely hope that you'll come back from this war. When you do, we can discuss things further."

Pompeo embraced the priest affectionately.

"I'll write you from Africa," he said and left.

Don Paolo washed his carbon-stained hands. The sink stank of urine in a disgusting fashion. He looked at his wet and dirty countenance in the mirror. He had grown much older that day; and his black clothes made him look all the gloomier. While he was undressing, he was seized with a violent attack of coughing. Suddenly a light bit of bloody foam appeared between his lips. He spat in the sink. There was no doubt about it—it was blood. Slowly he lay down on the bed.

He was still lying down and still awake when he heard someone tiptoe up to the door to listen. "Come in!" he said. Bianchina came in.

"I saw the light and here I am," she said.

The girl was quite high and smelled of *grappa* wine.

"They were celebrating the war at Rocca, too," she said with a laugh. "Of course some of my friends there were happy to see me. But your friend Murica is dumb. After I'd looked for him everywhere, I finally found him in a garden, cultivating something or other. I gave him your little message. A friend of yours from Rome, I told him, has sent me here just to let you know that he'd like to talk with you. He'll come here if that's all right with you. He didn't even thank me—he didn't even offer me a glass of water. He answered rudely that he didn't want to see anyone."

Don Paolo had trouble breathing and was afraid of another attack of coughing.

"Why don't you say something?" Bianchina asked. "How come you're not in bed? You haven't even taken off your shoes yet! What's the matter with you? Are you unhappy?"

The priest nodded.

"Why are you unhappy? Are you in debt? Are you in love?"

He had another attack of coughing. He reclined his head on one shoulder and a thin streak of blood flowed out of the side of his mouth, onto his chin. He saw

Bianchina grow pale. She was about to run for help, but Don Paolo was in time to grab her by the hand. He smiled and said, "Don't worry about it. It's nothing. It'll go away by itself."

Bianchina washed some handkerchiefs in cold water and put them on his chest and forehead.

"Don't be afraid," she told him. "The important thing is for you to take it easy."

She took off a veil and wrapped it around the electric light to soften the glare. Every once in a while she renewed the cold compresses.

"I was with an aunt who had this," said Bianchina. "I know what to do. Leave it all to me."

Slowly, without his having to move a muscle, she covered him with a sheet. She delicately washed the traces of blood from his mouth and chin.

"Everything will be all right, dear," she said.

Bianchina forbade the sick man to talk. She gave him a pencil and some paper in case he wanted anything.

"Now it's time to go to sleep," the girl finally said. "Good night."

Bianchina stretched out on a pad on the floor near his bed. But neither of them could go to sleep.

At one point the sick man asked her, "Did you celebrate the war too?"

"Me too!"

"Why?"

"I did what everybody else did. Don't you like it?"

"No!"

"Go to sleep, don't think about it," said Bianchina.

The next morning the girl told her mother that Don Paolo was sick; but she was soon back in his room to tell him of the great to-do there was in town about certain infamous writings against the war on various public buildings. The inscriptions had been done in charcoal, during the night. While Bianchina was cleaning the room, she found large black stains on the towel, as if a collier had washed his hands there.

"What's this?" she asked him.

But instead of waiting for him to answer she hurried to wash the towel.

Then she went to Don Paolo and told him in a reproving tone, "You're still a child, an incorrigible child but a bold one." But she was moved by Don Paolo's expression and added at once, "But an awfully nice person."

"Bianchina," he said, "what a lucky thing it is that in this world of horrible calculating men there are women, too."

Bianchina thought about this.

"Maybe you're saying that for your own calculations."

"Of course."

"And how do you know I'm not calculating, too?"

Don Paolo looked at the girl as she washed the floor. Her legs were perfect. Her breast was like a well-filled bread basket. When he had first seen her, her breasts had seemed like bitter lemons. Now they looked like ripe apples.

## 22

"As soon as I'm well enough to travel, I'm going abroad," said Don Paolo to Bianchina. "I can't stand living in this horrible country."

"Find me a job and I'll come with you," said the girl.

The idea of finding himself abroad with Bianchina was amusing to Don Paolo.

"If you come abroad, I'll tell you a secret that'll make you laugh," said Don Paolo.

"Can't you tell me now?"

But Don Paolo would not let himself be persuaded.

Berenice took care of the priest according to the prescriptions of the doctor who had come from Fossa. He had particularly recommended that the sick man be distracted from gloomy thoughts. And Bianchina had taken particular charge of this part of the program. It was understandable that since the man was sick, the girl was somewhat restricted in her choice of means. There were all kinds of games and jokes which surely would have amused Don Paolo, but because of his illness she could not use them. But being an imaginative girl, she went over her memories of the harmless ways of killing time she had used in school to distract her from her gloomy moods, such as fly racing. In school fly racing was carried out above all during class hours. The game consisted in catching them in midflight, without hurting them and without the nun's noticing what was going on. A pin was put in the back of the captured flies and they were put on the bench and encouraged to run along a track called the "harness-racing run." Bianchina had made a certain name for herself in this sport. But now when she caught them in flight she wounded them every once in a while.

"I'm out of practice," she said by way of excuse.

"There are so many things you learn in a sisters' school, but later, when you need them in life, you've forgotten them."

The "harness-racing run" was set up on Don Paolo's bed. The black leather cover of his breviary was the track. Some of the flies started at once and went straight, while others went at an angle and went off the track or stopped after the first few steps.

"The ones who don't want to race are the wives," Bianchina explained. "They're slowing down so their husbands can win. How stupid they are!"

Don Paolo discovered that, except for its size, a fly race, when seen from up close was as full of surprises and amusements as an ordinary horse or automobile race. In spite of Bianchina's precautions, frequent echoes of the uproar in town about the charcoal writings against the war came to the sick man.

"We've never seen so many policemen at Fossa before," Berenice said. "It's as if we were a town of criminals."

Bianchina was silent. She was trying to change the subject.

Gelsomina, the peddler's wife, who had taken her husband's place (he had volunteered for the war), stood at the door of the shop and stopped the passers-by.

"Is there any news?" she asked. "It must have been someone from out of town," she would say.

In front of the inn door was a group of people who spoke of nothing else. The words of the prominent citizens were repeated from house to house and commented on.

"It was such a nice celebration; everyone was happy and everyone was in agreement," Berenice was saying. "Who could have thought of writing those stupid things on the walls?"

"After all, there's no lack of envy here," said Don Luigi the pharmacist. "Someone who couldn't volunteer for the war or who didn't have any sons to send has taken it out in that way."

"There's never a funeral procession without a joke, and never a marriage without some tears," said Zabaglione. "Let's not exaggerate."

"A night bird is one of evil omen," pontificated Don Genesio. "You mustn't put any trust in appearances."

"That's just how it is," said Berenice. "Among the peasants the fire is hidden. Watch out; you can't see the fire during the day, but it shines at night."

"Peasants, what do you mean peasants?" said the pharmacist. "The peasants can't read or write. And the things about the war were in block letters. It can't have been a peasant."

"You must recognize that some of the boys have lost their heads," said Zabaglione. "Of course I don't want to allude to anyone in particular."

But Don Luigi understood the insinuation and replied in anger, "For your information, my son has volunteered for the war! The honor of a volunteer is above everything else. And as for that, as long as we're on the subject, neither I nor my son have ever been Socialists."

Zabaglione was hurt to the quick. This was his Achilles heel.

"You're not going to get my goat with an allusion like that," he said, pale with anger. "Everybody knows that I sacrificed my ideas a long time ago. And who hasn't been a Socialist? Even the head of the government was."

"But why is there all this chatter," said Bianchina, "just for a little charcoal on the wall? Aren't you over-doing it?"

In this case the girl's ingenuousness was authentic.

"I really don't understand," said Bianchina, to Don Paolo as well, "why there's all this discussion about some charcoal on the wall."

Don Paolo appeared satisfied and tried to explain to her the real cause of the emotion which would not die out.

"Dictatorships are based on unanimity," he said. "If just one person says NO, the whole thing breaks into pieces."

"Even if it's just one poor, sick man?" the girl asked.

"Certainly."

"Even if it's a peaceful man who thinks in his own way but doesn't do anything bad?"

"Certainly."

This made the girl sad, but it was comforting to Don Paolo.

"In every dictatorship," he said to Bianchina, "just one man, even any little man at all, who continues to think with his own head puts the whole public order in danger. Tons of printed paper propagate the regime's order of the day, thousands of loudspeakers, hundreds of thousands of posters and handbills distributed free, and stables of orators in the squares and crossroads, thousands of priests from the pulpit, all repeat to the point of obsession, to the point of collective stupefaction, these orders of the day. But it's enough that a little man, just one little man says NO for that formidable granite order to be in danger."

The girl was afraid, while the priest was in a good mood once more.

"Suppose they take him and kill him," said the girl.

"Killing a man who says NO is a dangerous undertaking," said the priest. "Even his body continues to repeat in a whisper NO NO NO with the tenaciousness and stubbornness of certain cadavers. How can you make a cadaver shut up? Did you ever hear about Giacomo Matteotti?"

"I don't remember," said Bianchina. "Who's that?"

"A corpse whom no one can force to shut up," said Don Paolo.

Berenice burst into the room in an excited state.

"Finally, finally," she was saying.

"Did you win the lottery?" asked Bianchina.

"Pompeo knows who wrote on the wall with that charcoal," said Berenice. "Now he's going to Avezzano to tell the authorities."

"How do you know this?" said the priest.

"He told me himself, just now, at the shop."

Bianchina looked for her hat and ran off to the station.

"Don't get mixed up in things that don't concern you," her mother yelled after her. "Don't continue to be our ruin."

But Bianchina was already far away.

Don Paolo jumped out of bed to pack his bags and flee. He had not had a fever for several days, and his cough had diminished. But he could hardly stand. And then, where could he go? There was only one railway; if he were to get on the train, they would surely arrest him. Could he go and hide in the mountains for a few days? It would be silly to do that in his condition. So he unpacked his bag and went back to bed. All in all, an arrest at Fossa, in a town already in an uproar, could be "more useful" than an arrest at the station in Rome. Orta, his home town, was just a few kilometers away. Just a few kilometers away was Don Benedetto. There were school friends of his in all the neighboring villages. The news of his arrest would come even to the peasants. In the long winter evenings, near the hearth, the poor people would mull over his gesture.

Once again Bianchina's return was delayed.

After a hurried examination of his luggage and books, and the disposal of every trace which might incriminate someone else, Don Paolo had time to repeat the operation several times. With the arrival of every carriage he ran to the window, but his anxiety was not calmed. Such a delay was incomprehensible. Avezzano was hardly an hour's train ride away. Why were the police so late?

Bianchina and Pompeo did not get back until late that evening. Don Paolo was worn out by the long wait.

"We had something to eat and drink," Bianchina said to him with a laugh. "When we were about to come back, we passed by a movie house. Mickey Mouse was on the program, so we went right in."

"Nothing else?"

"No."

"Didn't Pompeo want to go to Avezzano to make a certain report to the police?" asked the priest.

Bianchina smiled.

"What a wonderful memory you have," said the girl. "I'd already forgotten about that."

"Well?"

"When we were getting on the train," she said, "Pompeo assured me that he knew with certainty who wrote the inscriptions. We talked about it on the train and we almost had a quarrel. At Avezzano, when we were getting off the train, there was the chief of police waiting for the report. But meanwhile Pompeo had changed his mind."

"Whom did he finally report?"

"There was a man on a bicycle from Orta," said Bianchina. "Pompeo assured them that he saw him from a distance and that he wouldn't recognize the man again. I confirmed the report. I saw a man coming from Orta that night on a bicycle too."

Bianchina had to tell all that to her mother.

"From Orta?" exclaimed Berenice. "Gelsomina was right. It was a stranger."

Berenice ran off to Gelsomina's house.

"Gelsomí!" she yelled. "We were right. It's just like we said. A stranger, a man from Orta, wanted to make the people from Fossa look bad."

The news spread through the shops and inns like lightning. And of course several other people had seen a man coming on a bicycle from Orta that night. But it wasn't one of the ones who usually go to the market; it was a stranger.

"The Solitary Stranger!" exclaimed the Marshal of the Carabinieri.

Safely out of danger, Don Paolo became merry. His adventurous spirit revived.

"I'll take you abroad with me," he said to Bianchina, "and I'll tell you some stories."

"Abroad? Where?" the girl wanted to know. "As a missionary among the unbelievers, in the colonies?"

"Yes, among the unbelievers, but in Paris or Zurich," said Don Paolo.

## 23

The next day the curate of Fossa, Don Angelo Girasole, came to his sister's inn to renew his invitation to Don Paolo to visit the parish church. The priest from out of town could no longer avoid this courtesy which was expected of him and which he had evaded up to now on various pretexts.

Don Angelo was just about sixty, but he looked much older; his hair was entirely white, his face was lean and yellowed and he walked with a stoop. On the way he told Don Paolo that he was the firstborn of ten children, of whom only he and Berenice survived. His religious ministry kept him busy from dawn to late evening without interruption. He was alone and his parish was large. Aside from Mass, confessions, funerals, novenas, tridua, rosaries and devotions of every description, over which he had to preside or at which he had at least to be present, there were tasks of a more secular nature: baptisms, marriages, and reading for the illiterate mothers who came to him with their letters from America. And there were the Daughters of Mary, the young people's club of San Luigi, the catechism to be taught in the elementary schools, the boys to prepare for confirmation, and others to prepare for their first communion, the Congregation of Charity, the Confraternity and the tertiaries of San Francesco.

"I have to take advantage of every spare moment," he said, "if I am to recite my breviary and have some privacy to prepare for death, which I feel is near for me, and which creeps up so slowly."

Every evening he felt so tired he could hardly stand up; but how many times, even in the worst of weather, he had had to get up in the middle of the night to at-

tend to some dying person. But he did not complain.
Quite the contrary.

"The man of God should always be tired," he said.
"Useless thoughts come in idleness, and the Devil will
follow soon after."

In the square in front of the church, a group of boys
were playing soccer. They stopped their game to let
the two priests pass.

"Catechism is due to begin in a quarter of an hour,"
the curate reminded them.

Don Angelo stopped a moment on the church stairs
to take a breath.

"You probably will have heard of the profanation
which happened here," he said to Don Paolo. "One
night a stranger with a mask on his face came here to
write nonsense on the threshold of the church."

"By the way," said Don Paolo, "what do you think of
the new war?"

A woman was waiting for the curate at the church
door to make an appointment to baptize her child.

"A poor country curate," said Don Angelo, "has a
lot to do and little time to think. For the rest," he
added, "there's the Old and New Testament and the
Pastor of the Church to guide us."

"I don't think I made myself clear," said Don Paolo.

The interior of the church seemed dark when one
first entered it, but one's eyes soon got used to the dim
light. The sunken pavement was partially covered by
women in black who were praying and whispering
among themselves in the oriental manner of humility
and familiarity with the house of God. One old woman
was sliding along on her knees toward the chapel of the
sacrament, with her face on the floor, touching it with
her tongue and leaving an irregular trail of saliva like
that of a snail behind her. A young man in uniform was
walking beside her, taking small steps, awkward and
ashamed.

Don Angelo kneeled a moment in front of the tabernacle, and Don Paolo imitated him. A corpselike figure
of Christ was on the altar, on the knees of the Virgin
who was in mourning. Christ looked like a peasant
who had been killed in a fight, whose corpse was al-

ready decaying; the wounds on his hands and feet and
the hole in his side seemed in an advanced state of
putrefaction; his red hair was probably full of dust and
insects. But the Virgin looked like the widow of a rich
merchant who had fallen on ill times; two paraffin tears
shone on her pallid cheeks; her black eyes looked up-
ward, as if not to see the son on whom she had placed
so many hopes and who couldn't have ended up worse;
a finely embroidered veil covered her wavy hair and
came halfway down her forehead; an elegant lace ker-
chief was tied to the little finger of her right hand, on
the pedestal at her feet were these words carved in
letters of gold: *Videte si dolor vester est sicut dolor
meus*.

The nearby altar of San Rocco was adorned with the
usual variety of votive gifts of chrome from the faithful
who had received miracles, according to the grace ob-
tained—hands, feet, noses, ears and breasts and other
parts of the body, some of natural size.

"Look," said the mother of the soldier who had
finished her progress on her knees. "If this allotment
doesn't come right away, how can I live?"

"What allotment?"

"Four lire a day," said the soldier, "is to go to the
mother of every man called up. It's in today's papers."

"Where do you go for the allotment?" another woman
asked the curate. "To the post office? To the city hall?
To the police?"

Another woman was waiting for him in the sacristy.
Her son suffered from erysipelas. She wanted permission
to bathe a piece of cloth in the oil of the lamp which
was burning near the tabernacle, to put on the heart of
the dying child. Don Angelo gave his permission.

"See? A country curate has little time to think of the
war," he said to Don Paolo. "Now we have to start on
pensions, then we'll have the search for prisoners of
war and the missing, then the leaves for harvest time,
then the widows' pensions, then the orphans."

"Aren't there government offices?"

"Yes, but the poor people distrust them and generally
they're not well received there. So they come to the
sacristy to complain of it."

"Several years ago, at some jubilee," said Don Paolo, "I met one Don Benedetto de Merulis, who came from around here. If I'm not mistaken, he taught Greek and Latin in some diocesan school. Is he still alive? Do you ever see him?"

"Come," said Don Angelo.

He wanted to show Don Paolo the treasures of the church. He came to a great chest which covered most of one wall and with great difficulty opened two huge wooden doors covered with inlaid work. He pointed to the crucifixes and the plaque and the golden ware in the center; in the opposite niche was the silver bust of a martyred saint; below, hanging like clothes in a closet, was a great number of richly embroidered chasubles, dalmatics and stoles.

The sacristan came in and served two glasses of wine.

"You were asking about Benedetto," said the curate. "Yes, he's still alive. He's a saintly man but a bold one. He has long lived in an exemplary fashion, having been for all of us an example of culture and virtue. But now, on the threshold of eternity, his scorn for the opinions of men and his excessive faith in God have led him to absurdities which border on heresy."

"A risk which the saints have often accepted," said Don Paolo.

"It's not my place to distinguish virtue from lack of discipline," said Don Angelo. "I can't tell you how much I suffer for him. He was consecrated while I was still a cleric, and I was full of admiration for his calmness, sobriety and dignity, and the stainless purity of his private life. He wanted to say his first Mass in a prison chapel and his second in a hospital. You can imagine how his relatives felt about that, since they usually take advantage of such an occasion for a worldly festival."

"I hope you don't agree with the relatives," said Don Paolo.

"No," said Don Angelo. "But his brusque manner of contradicting public opinion worried his superiors from that point on. For that reason they were afraid to give him his own parish and they put him into teaching. In fact, it seems that the study of the classics and the company of the boys had softened his character. But he didn't get on any better with his superiors. He was completely bereft of any social conventions."

"I don't know which of the Ten Commandments you're referring to now," said Don Paolo, but Don Angelo pretended not to understand.

"Finally he was taken from teaching. I have always tried to keep up my friendship with him in his solitude, but now I'm really not allowed to."

"Is it as dangerous as all that?" said Don Paolo.

"Judge for yourself," said Don Angelo. "I'll tell you the most recent episode. A man from Fossa, one of my parishioners who worked some days in his garden, told me Don Benedetto told him that the present pope is really Pontius XI. At Rocca dei Marsi, where he lives now, this has been spread all over. In their naïve ignorance and respect for him, many have taken this literally and believed it. This parishioner of mine, seized with doubt, came to me here in the sacristy to ask me if it were really true that the Church has fallen into the hands of a descendant of Pontius Pilate, the one who liked to wash his hands of the whole thing."

"And what did you tell him?" replied Don Paolo. "That would be interesting."

The priest looked at his guest in surprise.

"I'm sorry," said Don Paolo. "I expressed myself poorly. You of course told him that the Church doesn't wash its hands of the whole thing."

The sacristan came in to warn Don Angelo that the women were waiting for the rosary and the boys in the first catechism class were already coming.

"There's already an inquiry at the provincial level about exiling Don Benedetto," said Don Angelo. "That's where he's gotten himself now. One of his former pupils who is not without influence in the governing party and myself have been attempting to save him. We went to call on him. We wanted him to sign a short declaration of submission to the present government and the present policies of the Church. That would have been enough. He received us courteously; but as soon as I started to tell him that the Church must sometimes do as well as it can in a bad situation, he interrupted me. 'The theory of the lesser evil might be good enough for a party or a government, but not for a church.' I tried not to discuss it in the abstract, because the worst heresies are quite attractive in the abstract. So I replied, 'But can you imagine what would happen if the Church were openly to condemn the present war? What persecutions it would undergo? What material and moral damage would be done?' You have no idea of what Don Benedetto dared to answer me. 'My dear Don Angelo,' he answered, 'can you imagine John the Baptist offering a concordat to Herod to escape decapitation? Can you imagine Jesus offering a concordat to Pontius Pilate to avoid being crucified?' "

"That doesn't seem to me to be an anti-Christian answer," said Don Paolo.

"But the Church is not a society in the abstract," said Don Angelo, raising his voice. "It is what it is. It's almost two thousand years old. It's not like a little girl who can permit herself all kinds of headstrong caprices. It's like an old, a very old lady, full of dignity, prestige, traditions, and rights tied to duties. Of course there was Jesus Who was crucified and Who founded her; but after Him there were the apostles and generations upon generations of saints and popes. The Church is no longer a clandestine sect in the catacombs. It has millions and millions of souls in its following who need her protection."

"A fine way to protect them, sending them off to war," cried Don Paolo.

For an instant he seemed about to throw caution to the winds.

"The synagogue in Jesus' time was also an old, a very old lady with a great tradition of prophets, kings, lawgivers, priests and a great crowd of people to protect. But Jesus hadn't much respect for all that."

Don Angelo was seated in front of his glass of wine which he had not touched. He closed his eyes as if he were dizzy and kept them closed for a while. His deepset turquoise eyelids had a light nervous tremor. "Oh, my God, why are you trying to frighten me?" he murmured.

The sacristan came back to tell Don Angelo that the women were waiting for the rosary and the boys in the catechism class were making a devil of a noise. The curate got up.

"Excuse me," he said and followed the sacristan.

Don Paolo went back to the inn.

He found a noisy crowd in front of the city hall. Two peasants who had come to the city hall on business had been recognized as natives of Orta and had been attacked by the crowd which had gathered from all sides with all kinds of weapons. The two unlucky sacrificial victims, ignorant of the cause of all that hate, had barely been saved from lynching by some carabinieri and locked up in the police station. But the crowd continued to make the most violent threats against them. In vain did Zabaglione at the request of the carabinieri attempt to calm them down. The agitation was allayed only when it was announced that both the unfortunate peasants from Orta would be booked as presumed accomplices in the seditious writing on the walls of Fossa and would be transferred to jail.

"Why are they only accomplices and not the guilty parties?" someone protested.

"I appeal to your common sense," said the Marshal of the Carabinieri. "They're both illiterate."

To tell the truth, the appeal to common sense was not without its effect. The crowd quieted down and split up to discuss what had happened. To get back into the hotel, Don Paolo had to open up a path in a group of men and young mothers with their babies on their arms who were talking with Berenice.

"I'm leaving tomorrow," said Don Paolo to Berenice. "Where's your daughter? I want to ask a favor of her."

Pietro sent Bianchina straight to Rocca dei Marsi, to Don Benedetto, with a note signed with his own initials, asking his permission to visit him.

"This time," the priest told the girl, "I beg of you not to keep me waiting twenty-four hours."

"How old is this Don Benedetto?"

"Seventy-five."

"I'll come back right away, don't worry," said Bianchina.

She got onto her bicycle and left in a hurry.

The girl was back within an hour with a note written

in small clear, regular, but slightly rambling letters.

An unturned vat awaits with ancient wine,
Within my house. Come quickly! Lose no time!
                    (Horace, Book III, Ode 29)

Since the far-off years of school it was the first time
Don Paolo had seen his teacher's handwriting. It
looked like a homework assignment, but it was easy
and the invitation was cordial.

## 24

"Maybe he'll come later, when it's dark," said Don Benedetto to his sister.

"Don't you think it's dangerous for him to come here?" said Martha.

But he looked at her in such a way that she instantly corrected herself.

"I meant it might be imprudent for him, too."

"He must be somewhat used to these complications by now," said Don Benedetto. "He has been doing nothing but hiding and escaping for many years. At any rate, leave us alone," he added. "He might feel the need of confiding in me things which it would be preferable for no more than two to hear."

"I won't disturb you," said Martha. "But he can't live like a wild bird all his life. Don't you think we should tell his grandmother? His grandmother and his aunts and uncles are rich, maybe they could get him a lawyer and get a pardon from the government."

"I don't think Pietro would like to be pardoned."

"Why would he refuse a pardon? There's nothing to be ashamed of."

"I do not think that he feels that he has done anything wrong, that is the point. They only give pardons to people who are sorry for what they have done."

"But he can't spend all his life in hiding," Martha repeated. "He must still be a young man. How old is he?"

"He's Nunzio's age, thirty-four or -five."

"It's not right to ruin your whole life for a political opinion. It's not right. You've been his teacher. You must tell him that."

"I don't think he's doing it just for politics," said Don

Benedetto. "From the time he was a boy he seemed to me to be cut out for a hard life."

"But if they persecute him, it's for his political opinions."

"Do you remember when he came to us after his school examinations? That was the summer after the earthquake."

"He was wearing mourning, he had just become an orphan. Yes, I remember."

"Well, I remembered that meeting just now," said Don Benedetto. "At that time he confided something to me which must have had some influence on his future development. Of course he had been deeply affected by the death of his parents; but there was something else which happened in those terrible days after the earthquake, when we were all living between the ruins and temporary dwelling places, and which profoundly disturbed him. I don't think I ever spoke of this, since Pietro himself begged me not to tell anyone else. But that was so long ago.

"Now then," continued Don Benedetto, "he had had the misfortune to be present, without being seen, at a demonstration of bestiality which had filled him with dismay. He had been the only witness and he had kept the secret. He did not even tell me exactly what it was all about. But I could tell from the way Pietro acted and the way he related the story that it must have been a relative of his, or someone close to his family."

"There have always been crimes," said Martha.

"But in the one Pietro told me about," said Don Benedetto, "it was a case of someone whom everyone esteemed, who after the crime, which remained a secret, continued to live as before, honestly as it were, respected by all. That was what was monstrous about it."

"Couldn't you tell me what sort of crime this person was stained with?" said Martha.

"It was a robbery and murder against someone who was wounded or dying and still half buried in the ruins," said Don Benedetto. "The criminal was not in need. The crime took place at night, and Pietro, I repeat, was there by chance. He was fifteen years old at the time. Terror made him take leave of his senses. He was still shaking when he told me about it several months later. The murderer lived in the same neighborhood. He had acted in the certainty that he wouldn't be caught. He was a 'respectable' person, as they say. On thinking it over, I believe Pietro's flight began at that point. Earlier I had thought that he would end up in a monastery."

"Didn't you hear something?" said Martha. "Someone's knocking at the door."

Martha went quickly into her room. The awaited guest was on the threshold. He was in civilian clothes, with no hat, but the black garment which he was carrying under his arm like a mantle could be the soutane from which he had recently freed himself. Pietro and Don Benedetto greeted each other and shook hands, both of them quite moved.

"Did you come on foot?" asked Don Benedetto.

"I left the carriage in the village below," said Pietro.

Don Benedetto showed him to a large armchair and sat next to him on a slightly lower stool. Since old age had bent him, he looked smaller than his former pupil. Pietro tried to act casually, to appear self-possessed. He said, "Behold, the lost lamb has come back to his shepherd of his own accord."

Don Benedetto, who was looking with astonishment at the precociously aged face of the young man, did not understand the joke and shook his head.

"It would be hard to tell which of us here is the lost lamb," he said sadly.

"They talk of you a lot in the villages around here," said Pietro. "From what I have heard with my own ears, I am convinced that you're the only one in this part of the world who can save the honor of the Church."

"That's not my opinion at all," said Don Benedetto in a bitter tone. "And I assure you that it is not false modesty. Really, I'm not good for much of anything. I have lost my teaching position, I have no souls to care for. As you say, I have a certain reputation; but if someone comes to me to denounce some injustice he has suffered, I do not know what to tell him. That is the way it is. I am not good for anything. My friend, it is sad to make certain discoveries at my age."

Pietro's eyes were full of tears. He turned his back on Don Benedetto to hide his emotion. This dear old man, the mere memory of whom had been enough to bring him serenity in the wasted hours of imprisonment and exile, was himself in such anguish. But what could Pietro tell him that wouldn't seem inspired by pity?

"For the rest," added Don Benedetto, "those who say Mass and call themselves ministers of God are not necessarily those closest to Him in spirit."

Hearing the old man talk of God as he had once done, Pietro suspected that there was a serious misunderstanding which might give him the wrong idea of this meeting.

"I lost my faith many years ago," he said in a clear but submissive voice.

The old man smiled and shook his head.

"In cases similar to yours, it is just a silly mistake," he said. "This would not be the first time that the Eternal Father felt obligated to hide Himself and take a pseudonym. As you know, He has never taken the first name and last name men have fastened on Him very seriously; quite to the contrary, He has warned men not to name Him in vain as His first commandment. And then, the Scriptures are full of clandestine life. Have you ever considered the real meaning of the flight into Egypt? And later, when He was an adult, was not Jesus forced several times to hide Himself and flee from the Judeans?"

This religious apologia for the clandestine life made Pietro more serene and illuminated his face with childlike joy.

"I had always felt the lack of that chapter in the *Imitation of Christ*," he said laughing.

Don Benedetto took up the conversation in the same sad tone in which he had begun it.

"I live here with my sister among my books and the garden," he said. "For some time my mail has been obviously tampered with, the books and newspapers come late or get lost on the way. I visit no one and few people visit me. The few who do are unpleasant. However, I am in touch with a lot of things, and these are demoralizing. In other words, those things which are

God's are given unto Caesar and those things which are Caesar's are given unto God. It was to just such a crew that John the Baptist said, 'O generation of vipers, who hath taught you to flee the wrath to come?' "

Martha came into the room to say good evening to Pietro. She did this with a tiny little voice and a fearful smile which looked as if it had been prepared behind the door and held in place with some pins. She put a couple of glasses on the table and a flask of red wine. Then she quickly went back to her room.

The old man continued, "Every time faith in God is in question, you must remember an old story. Perhaps you remember that it is written somewhere that in a moment of great discomfort Elijah asked God for death and God sent for him on a mountain. He kept the appointment; but would he recognize Him? There arose a great wind which split the mountain and the rocks. But it wasn't God. After the wind, the earth shook; but that wasn't God. After the earthquake, there was a great fire; but that wasn't God. Later, in silence, Elijah felt a light sound, like a rustling in the bushes, moved by the evening breeze. That rustling, it is written, was God."

A slight wind had arisen in the garden. The trees began to rustle. The door leading to the living room creaked and opened.

"What's happening?" said Martha from the next room. Pietro shivered. The old man put his hand on his shoulder and said with a laugh, "Don't be afraid. You have nothing to be afraid of."

He got up and closed the door which the evening breeze had opened.

After a little while he continued, "I, too, in the dregs of my afflictions, have asked myself: where is God and why has He abandoned us? Certainly the loudspeakers and bells announcing the new slaughter were not God. Nor were the cannon shots and the bombing of the Ethiopian villages, of which we read every day in the newspapers. But if one poor man gets up in the middle of the night and writes on the walls of the village with a piece of charcoal or varnish, 'Down with the War,' the presence of God is undoubtedly behind that man. How can one not recognize the divine light in his scorn of danger and in his love for the so-called enemies? Thus, if some simple workmen are condemned for these reasons by a special tribunal, there's no need to hesitate to know where God stands."

Don Benedetto poured some wine in a glass and raised it to the light to test its clearness; then he touched it to his lips, since it had come from a new vat; then he filled the two glasses.

"I do not know if you are able to imagine what it is like to come to certain conclusions at my age," he continued. "On the edge of the tomb. At seventy-five one can change one's ideas, but not one's habits. A retired existence is the only one which suits my character. Even when I was a young man I lived apart. I have always kept myself far from public life because of my repugnance for vulgarity. Good taste has always kept me from action. But now passivity weighs on me. I look around me and I do not see what I can do. Among the parishioners? Nothing. The ones who know me personally avoid me because they are afraid of meeting me. In the diocese of Marsi, the few cases of priests who have left the Church in the last fifty years have all been due to scandalous infractions of the rule of celibacy. That is enough to give you an idea of the spiritual conditions of our clergy. If it got around in the diocese that another priest had thrown off his robes, the first explanation which would occur to the faithful, in a perfectly natural way, would be, 'Another priest has run off with his housekeeper!' "

"This afternoon I had to visit Don Angelo Girasole," said Pietro. "He impressed me as a most honest man—a good clerk in the administration."

"Precisely," said Don Benedetto. "But Christianity is not an administration."

"But the others, the ones who think they see a historic vision, are worse," said Pietro. "They believe, or pretend to believe, in the Man of Providence."

"If they deceive themselves, it is their own fault," interrupted Don Benedetto. "They have been warned for about two thousand years. They were told that many will come in the name of Providence and will seduce the people. We will hear of wars and threats of wars. All this must happen; but this will not be the end. Nation will rise against nation and kingdom against kingdom. There will be famine, pestilence and earthquakes in several places. Many will behave terribly and many will become traitors. If someone, no matter who he is, is to say, 'Here is someone sent by Providence; there is a man sent by Providence,' we must not believe him. We have been warned. False saviors and false prophets will present themselves, they will make great signs and prodigious things and they will seduce many people. We could not have asked for a clearer warning. If many have forgotten it, this does not affect what is to happen. The destiny of their 'Man of Providence' has already been written: *Intrabit ut vulpis, regnabit ut leo, morietur ut canis.*"

"What a beautiful language Latin is," said Pietro. "And what a difference between the honest old Latin of the Church and the modern sibilant Latin of the encyclicals."

"What this country lacks, as you know, is not the critical spirit," said Don Benedetto. "What it does lack is faith. Critics are dissatisfied; they often complain, sometimes are violent and in certain circumstances are even heroic. But they are not believers. What good would it do to teach some new ways of speaking and gesturing to a population of skeptics? Perhaps the horrible sufferings now being prepared will make the Italian people more serious. Meanwhile, when I am most depressed, I repeat to myself: You are good for nothing, you have failed; but there is Pietro, there are his friends, there are the strangers in the clandestine groups. I must confess, I have nothing else to console me."

Pietro was shaken by the alarmed tone in his old teacher's voice.

"Dear Don Benedetto," he said. "We haven't seen each other in fifteen years and perhaps we won't see each other again after this meeting. You're old and my health is uncertain; the times are hard. The few minutes of this visit would be wasted for me if we were to do nothing but exchange banalities. I am terrified of the faith you have in me. I am sincerely convinced that I'm

no better than my old schoolmates. I have been luckier
than they because, at the right time, and with the aid
of a series of accidents, I have severed the umbilical
cord. As for the rest, excuse me if I do not share the
optimism of your only consolation."

"There is no safety but in risking everything," said
Don Benedetto. "And it is not given to many. After
that first meeting with you at Acquafredda, that poor
soul Nunzio came to me and told me everything. He
told me of your case, with which he was already familiar. He asked me how one can live on a profession
which depends on government offices in a dictatorial
regime and still remain free. It is lucky that at least
Pietro has been saved."

"Saved?" said Pietro. "Is there a past participle of
save? Unfortunately I have been obliged to reflect
many times in these last few days on what is certainly
the saddest aspect of decadence because it concerns
the future. Dear Don Benedetto, perhaps tomorrow will
be like today. One might say that we are planting rotten
seeds."

Don Benedetto made a sign to him to be silent.

"Someone's at the door," he said in a low tone. "Let's
go in here."

They got up and went into Martha's room. At the
same moment there was a knock at the door.

"See who is at the door," said Don Benedetto to his
sister. "Do not let anyone in. Whoever it is, tell him
you do not know if I can see him. And before you open
the door please take the wine and the two glasses away."

There was another knock. Martha opened the door.
It was Don Piccirilli.

"Good evening," he said. "Am I disturbing you?
They told me Don Angelo Girasole is visiting Don
Benedetto. I would very much like to say hello to him."

"You have been misinformed," said Martha. "The
curate of Fossa is not here."

"Didn't a priest come here in a carriage from Fossa
just now?" said Don Piccirilli.

"There has been no carriage and no priest," said
Martha. "You have been misinformed."

This conversation was carried on on the threshold. Martha showed no intention of inviting him in.

"Since I've come all the way here," said Don Piccirilli, "I would at least like to say hello to Don Benedetto. I hope I haven't come at the wrong moment."

"I don't know. He may be resting. I'll go and see."

She found her brother alone in the next room. With a nod of his head at the window facing the garden, he gave her to understand that Pietro had already gone.

"Now we must try to keep Don Piccirilli here as long as possible," said Don Benedetto in a whisper to his sister. "Bring us something to drink as quickly as possible."

Don Benedetto went to greet his new guest.

"What are you doing there on the threshold?" he said in a reproving tone. "Come in! Come in! Don't stand on ceremony. You must tell me what you think of the wine from this new vat."

## 25

Matalena was preparing the flour for the bread on the first floor of the inn and Don Paolo was keeping her company. At Pietrasecca the bread was baked every fifteen days in a collective oven. The baking of the bread was a rite with its own strict rules. The women kept their hair wrapped up in a cloth like a nun's veil and passed the flour through a sieve into an open bin. This was how they separated the white flour from the chaff and the fine flour from the ordinary flour. The chaff was for the chickens and pigs, ordinary flour was for bread and fine flour was for the pasta. Matalena's face and hands were powdered with the flour which was rising from the sieve. On her knees in front of the fire Chiarina the goat keeper was weeping from the smoke coming from the green wood under the pot where the potatoes were being cooked. They were to be added to the bread to make it heavier and longer-lasting.

At one point the sieve stopped because a young stranger who looked halfway between a student and a workman had entered the inn and asked for Don Paolo, giving him a note. These few words were written in Don Benedetto's fine and trembling hand: *"Ecce homo,* my friend. Here is a poor man who has need of you; and perhaps you have need of him. Listen to him, I beg of you, to the end."

The young man was surprised and embarrassed at the presence of Don Paolo. He was about to excuse himself and retire.

"Don Benedetto told me: I'm sending you to a man you can trust. To tell you the truth, I didn't expect to find a priest."

"Come," the priest said to him, "Don Benedetto will have had his reasons."

Don Paolo brought the young man up to his room and had him sit near him.

"If you had come here as to a priest," he told him, "I would undoubtedly have asked you to go somewhere else. How long have you known Don Benedetto?"

"We're from the same village," said the young man. "Every family at Rocca knows everyone else. Everybody knows everything, or just about everything, about everyone else. When you see someone leave his house, you know where he's going, and when he comes back, you know where he's been. My family has a vineyard near Don Benedetto's garden, up the mountain beyond the village. For the spraying of the vines, we take the water from his well, and he takes from us the poles to hold up the tomatoes, beans and peas in his garden. My mother has always gone to him for advice about my education. Perhaps his advice hasn't always been good, but his intentions have been. He has always liked me, from the time I was a baby."

As the young man talked, Don Paolo got a clearer idea of him. On first sight, in fact, he looked somewhat like a cross between a worker and a peasant, mostly from the sloppy and patched-up way he dressed, from the numerous cracks in his face and hands, and from his messy hair. But on closer inspection his eyes seemed extraordinarily alert and intelligent; and his manners were calm and courteous. After some hesitation, the young man began to tell the story of his life.

"I was very delicate as a boy, and besides that, I was the only son," he said. "For this reason my mother thought I shouldn't cultivate the land. 'Our ancestors have cultivated the land and here we are at the same point,' my mother would say. 'We've been plowing, digging, sowing and fertilizing the land for all these generations and we're still poor. We'll send this son to school. He's weak and needs to lead an easier life.' My father was against it. 'The land is hard,' he said, 'but it's secure. School is for the sons of rich men. And we haven't any protectors.' Don Benedetto was our protector. 'Since the boy likes to study, send him to school,' he said. His advice helped my mother. As long as I was in the gymnasium, my family could be considered fairly well off. As well as the vineyard, my father had two fields planted to grain and vegetables and a stall with four cows. To tell the truth, my mother's checks for my expenses arrived not at all regularly, but they did arrive. During the three years I was at the *liceo*, the family situation went from bad to worse because of two bad harvests and my father's illness. And my expenses went up. We had to sell one of the fields to pay the debts. Two of the cows died in an epidemic, the two remaining ones were sold at the fair and the stall was rented. 'That's all right,' said my mother. 'When our son has graduated, he'll help us.' Three years ago I passed the state examination, and in October I went to Rome, where I enrolled at the faculty of letters. My mother really didn't know where the money was going to come from to support me until I could earn my degree."

"Why did you enroll at the faculty of letters?" asked Don Paolo. "That's not the best way to earn a living."

"Don Benedetto thought I was best at literary studies. A very hard life began for me in Rome. I lived in a room with no lights. At noon all I ate was some milky coffee and a roll, and some soup in the evening. I was always hungry. I dressed awkwardly. I had no friends. At the university, because of my provincial appearance, the first time I tried to make friends with the other students, I was the object of laughter and stupid jokes. Two or three episodes like that were enough to make me antisocial. I often cried with anger in my little room. I resigned myself to being alone. Being used to living in a family, I was lost in the noisy, vulgar, cynical world of the students. Most of the students spent their time on sports and politics, because they are both noisy affairs. One day, I saw one of the usual brawls from a trolley. A dozen or so students from my faculty were beating a young worker in the middle of the street. I can see it now. The worker was lying on the pavement, with his bleeding head leaning on the wheel of the trolley, while the students who

surrounded him continued to beat him and kick him.
'He didn't salute the flag!' the students were shouting.
Some policemen came up and congratulated the
aggressors for their patriotic action and arrested the
worker. There was a great crowd on the scene, but
nobody said a word. I was alone on the trolley, which
had stopped. 'Cowards!' I said to myself. 'Yes, it's
shameful!' said someone behind me in a low voice. It
was the ticket taker on the trolley. We said hello that
day, but we didn't say anything else. But since he often
worked on the line which came by my street, we met
every once in a while and took up the habit of saying
hello whenever we met, as if we had known each other
for a long time."

The boy paused for a while, as if he had lost the
thread of what he was saying. Then he continued. "One
day we met on the street when he was off duty. We
shook hands and went into a bar to have a glass of
wine. Each told the other something of himself, and
we made friends. He invited me up to his place and I
met other people, almost all of them young. These
persons, five in all, constituted a 'group,' and these
gatherings were 'group meetings.' This was strange and
new to me. Being introduced by the trolley ticket taker,
I was admitted to the group and went regularly to the
meetings every week. This was the first human contact
I made in the city. My being a student attracted the
sympathy of the others in the group, who were workers
and artisans. I was happy too. The purely human
pleasure I took in it prevented me from reflecting at
first on the importance of what I was doing. In the
group we read poorly printed newspapers and pamphlets
preaching hate of tyranny and announcing as a certainty,
as inevitable and not far off, the advent of the revolution which was to establish fraternity and justice among
men. It was sort of a weekly dream, secret and for-
bidden, in which we communicated and which made
us forget our daily misery. It was like the rites of a
hidden religion. Beyond these weekly meetings, there
was no other tie between us. If we chanced to meet
on the street, we pretended we didn't know each other.

"One morning as I left the house I was arrested by

two policemen, taken to the central police station and shut in a room full of other policemen. After some formalities I was slapped and spat upon for an hour. I probably would have preferred to be violently beaten rather than slapped and spat on like that. When the door opened and the functionary who was to question me appeared, my face and chest were literally flowing with spit. The functionary reprimanded his subordinates, or at least pretended to, had me washed and dried and taken into his office. He assured me that he was looking benevolently and understandingly at my case. He knew that I lived in a small room, he knew the place where I took coffee and milk at noon and where I had my soup in the evening. He had minute details about my family and on the troubles which made it doubtful that I could continue my studies. On the impulse which had pushed me to the revolutionary groups he could only guess. '. . . of and by itself that impulse can't be deemed entirely reprehensible, on the contrary. . . . Youth is dreamy and generous by nature. It would be too bad if that were not the case,' he said. 'But the police has the perhaps unpleasant but socially necessary role of closely controlling the generous and dreamy instincts of youth . . .' "

"In other words," interrupted Don Paolo, "that functionary proposed that you work for the police. What did you answer?"

"I accepted," he answered.

Matalena appeared at the door and asked, "Supper's ready. Should I set the table for two?"

"I'm not hungry tonight," said the priest.

He got up from his chair because he was tired and stretched out on the bed.

The young man continued in a tired voice. "I got a hundred lire for my room and in exchange I wrote a school composition on 'How a group functions, what is read and what is discussed there.' 'It's really quite good,' he told me. I was proud that he was satisfied with my work. I committed myself to remain in touch with him, for a hundred and fifty lire a month. In this way I could have soup at noon, too, and I could go to the movies every Saturday night. One day he presented me with a pack of cigarettes. I really had never smoked before, but I learned to, so as not to offend him."

"What did you write in your successive reports?" Don Paolo asked.

"I continued to write in general terms, but he began to protest," said the young man. "I always gave him a copy of the handouts distributed in the group, but he found that this wasn't enough, because he probably got the same stuff from other people. Finally he advised me to go to a different group, a more interesting one. It wasn't hard. As soon as I told my friends I wanted to be transferred to another group with some other intellectuals, they did it for me. In the new group I met a girl, a dressmaker. Immediately we fell in love. When I was with her, I felt the first regrets. With her I began to realize the possibility of a pure and honest way of living, completely unknown to me before. At the same time there opened an unbridgeable gulf between my real and my secret life. I worked hard and sincerely for the group; I translated whole chapters into Italian from revolutionary novels we got from abroad and wrote them out on the typewriter; I put up posters during the night; but I was just deceiving myself in that way. If my comrades in the new group admired me for my courage and activity, they only reminded my conscience that I was really betraying them. Then I tried to avoid them. Anyway, I thought, I have a right to live, too. I wasn't getting any more money from home. When I was hungry and the rent was due, I lost all scruples. I had nothing else. I realized that politics was absurd. What did I have to do with all that? I certainly would have preferred to live in peace, eat two or three times a day, and to hell with both the 'necessity for imperial expansion' and 'economic democracy.' But that was impossible. By myself I couldn't even afford the room or my meals. This cynical reasoning went to pieces whenever I was with my girl friend. We were very much in love. She didn't represent a certain way of thinking to me. On the contrary, she said very little but listened to the others. She represented a way of living, of existing, of giving oneself in an unequaled humane manner. I couldn't conceive my life without that woman, because she was more than a woman, she was a flame and a light; she was proof to me of the possibility of living on this earth honestly and cleanly, without interests, trying with all one's soul to find harmony with people like oneself. I thought that I was spiritually alive only from the time I knew her. I don't mean to criticize my parents. They were good and honest, but in a traditional way. That girl didn't follow the rules; she followed her heart. I thought she invented her life. But in her presence and in front of her naïve faith in me, how could I forget that I was deceiving and betraying her? Our love was poisoned at the source. Being with her, though I loved her so much, was a torment, an insupportable pretense . . ."

"Why didn't you break off with the police from the moment that you found the spying morally insupportable?" asked Don Paolo.

"I tried several times to cover my tracks," said the young man. "Once I moved, but I was easily retraced. For a while I tried to quiet my conscience by writing innocuous, false and reticent reports to the police. At that time I was beginning to get a little something from my mother every month. I tried to deceive the police, telling them I'd been thrown out of the group because my comrades didn't trust me any more. But they had other informers who could prove the contrary. Finally I was obsessed with the idea that I couldn't get out of it. I felt condemned. There was nothing to do. That was my fate."

The young man had trouble talking; he was almost panting. Don Paolo hesitated to look him in the face.

"No, no, I don't want to make myself less bad than I was," the boy continued. "I don't want to make my case sound more piteous. This is a confession in which I want to present myself in all my repugnant nakedness. Well, the truth was this: Fear of discovery in me was then stronger than remorse. 'What will Annina say if she finds out? What will my friends say?' This was what obsessed me. I was afraid for my own reputation, as well as for the evil I was doing. I saw the image of my own fear around me."

He paused. His throat was parched. There was a

flask of water and two glasses on the table. But Don Paolo did not think to invite him to take some.

"I knew that the police didn't trust me any more and that they were shadowing me," he continued. "So I avoided my friends, to avoid having to report them. The police threatened me with arrest for being in suspicious company without reporting it to them. I was in terror of being arrested again. I tried to live without seeing anyone. For this reason every meeting with my girl friend was a torment. But in spite of this, she was always as patient, gentle and affectionate with me as she had always been. We celebrated last Christmas together in a restaurant outside the gates."

Don Paolo was listening to a story which he already knew and whose every detail he heard again: The unusually gay dinner; the invitation to her house; the purchase of the flowers, fruit, sweets, and the Marsala; the arrival of the police; the flight onto the roof; the long wait on the roof. But the young man did not finish the story. He hid his face with his hands and began to weep. After a while he took up his story again.

"I came back to Rocca dei Marsi. I told my parents that the doctors had ordered me to go back to my native climate. I passed the winter at home, without seeing anyone. From time to time I visited Don Benedetto, who gave me books to read. In the spring I began to go with my father to the fields for the weeding of the grain, for the pruning of the vines, for the sapping and for the harvest. I worked until I could hardly stand on my feet, to the point of physical exhaustion. I went straight to bed after supper. At dawn I woke up my father. He would say, 'I can tell you come from a race of farmers; if you come from the land, you can't get free of the land.' But if you come from the land and then live in the city, you're neither a city man nor a farmer. The memories of the city, of my girl friend, of the group and of the police was an open wound which was still bleeding and which was beginning to fester and threatened to poison the rest of my life. My mother would say, 'The city air has ruined you and put sadness in your blood.' 'Let me work,' I answered. 'Maybe work will cure me.' But I often saw a mental picture of my girl friend before me while I was in the fields. How could I forget her? After I had seen the possibility of that other clean, honest, hardworking life, that frank communication and that dream of a better humanity, how could I resign myself to life in a village? But on the other hand, how could I destroy the irremediable? In that hard and solitary work, which didn't leave me a moment of peace, I passed from fear of punishment to fear of impunity. The idea that I remembered the evil I had done only because there was always the danger of being caught began to make me afraid. I therefore began to ask myself: If a better technique might make it possible to betray one's friends without running the risk of being unmasked one day, would the evil situation become more supportable for that reason?"

Don Paolo looked him in the eye.

"I must confess," the boy continued, "that my religious faith has never been very deep. I never believed very strongly. I was baptized, confirmed, took communion like the others. But my faith in the reality of God was very vague and intermittent. For this reason I did not oppose the so-called scientific theories which were propagated in the groups. These theories began to seem too comfortable to me. That everything was matter, that the idea of good was inseparable from utility (albeit social utility) and was sustained only by punishment became insupportable to me. Who was to do the punishing? The state, the group, or public opinion? And what if the state, the group, or public opinion are immoral? And then, if favorable circumstances or the appropriate technique make it possible to do wrong with certain impunity, what is morality based upon? I asked myself whether technique by eliminating every danger of sanctions could destroy the distinction between good and evil. I was afraid of such a hypothesis. I really began to be afraid of the absurd. I don't want to bore you with these digressions, which might seem abstract to you; nor would I want you to think I am trying to justify myself with moralistic chatter. No, these reflections had become the substance of my life. I didn't believe in God any more, but I began to want God to exist with all my being. I had need of Him to escape the fear of chaos. One night I couldn't stand it any more and I went out to knock at the door of a Capuchin monastery near our village. I met a brother I knew, a certain Brother Gioacchino. I told him, 'I would so much like to believe in God and I can't do it. Can you tell me how?' 'You mustn't be proud,' he told me. 'You mustn't claim to want to know everything, you mustn't force yourself, you must be resigned, close your eyes, and pray. Faith is a grace.' But I couldn't abandon myself. I wanted to understand. I couldn't not force myself to understand. My whole being was in a state of frightful tension. I couldn't resign myself. I wanted God through necessity. I had need of Him."

He stopped talking, exhausted.

"Maybe you're thirsty," Don Paolo told him. "Drink a little water."

"Finally I went to Don Benedetto," the young man continued. "I went to him not because he was a priest but because in my eyes he had always been the symbol of the just man. He had known me since I was a baby, as I have told you. When I went to him, I told him he didn't really know me because he had no idea of what I was hiding inside. I made a great effort and told him everything in a confession which lasted five hours and ended with me almost lying on the ground. I really thought I would die. That first time the words came from my mouth as if I were vomiting blood. At the end I had only a slight glimmer of consciousness. I felt like an empty bag. Don Benedetto sent his sister Martha to tell my mother that I would spend that night at his house and that I was going to work in his garden for the next few days. He would interrupt the work every once in a while to talk to me. He taught me that as long as you're alive nothing is unredeemable. No condemnation is ever definitive. He explained that one should not, of course, come to like evil, but that good derives many times from evil and that probably I would never have become a man without passing through those infamous moments and errors. When he finally sent me back home, I wasn't afraid any more. I seemed to have been reborn. I was struck by the air which came from the mountain. I had never breathed such pure fresh air in my village before. Not being afraid any more, I stopped thinking about myself so much and began to rediscover the world. I began to see the trees, the children in the streets, the poor people working so hard in the fields, the donkeys with their loads, and the oxen pulling their plows. I continued to see Don Benedetto from time to time. Yesterday he called for me and told me, 'I would wish to spare you the suffering, but there is a man near Rocca dei Marsi to whom I would like you to repeat your confession. He is a man whom you can trust completely.' He gave me the necessary indications, gave me some recommendations; and I came."

It was dark. The young man's tired voice faded out in the shadow. After a while the other voice rose out of the darkness.

"If I were the head of a party, or of a political group," said Don Paolo, "I would have to judge you according to the party's rules. Every party has its morality, codified in rules. These rules are often very close to those which moral sentiment inspires in every man; but they are sometimes the precise opposite. But I am not—or I am no longer—a political leader. But here and now I am just an ordinary man, and if I must judge another man I can be guided only by my conscience, within the strict limits within which one man may judge another."

"I didn't come here for pardon, or for absolution," said the young man.

"Luigi Murica," said the other in a low voice, "I want to tell you something which will show you how much faith I have in you. I am not a priest. I'm not really Don Paolo Spada. My real name is Pietro Spina."

On her own, Matalena had prepared supper for two and wanted the two men to come and eat.

"When you're a convalescent, you mustn't skip your meals," she said. "If you have guests, the least you can do is invite them."

She had put a bottle of wine and a clean tablecloth on the table. The two men ate in silence. The wine was from the previous year and the bread was fifteen days old. They soaked the bread in the wine. After the meal Murica wanted to go back to Rocca dei Marsi that same night, and Don Paolo went to his room to get a cape so he could walk some of the way with him. Matalena did not hide a certain jealousy for the sudden friendship between this stranger and "her" priest.

"You talked all this time," she said to Murica. "Do you still have something to say?"

"I was making a confession," said Murica.

When the two men parted on the little path which led to the valley, Murica said, "Now I'm ready for anything."

"Good, we'll see each other soon," Don Paolo promised him.

The priest walked very slowly back to the inn. He sat on the grassy side of the road, oppressed by many thoughts. Unseen voices murmured in the distance— shepherds' calls, the barking of dogs and the subdued lowing of the cattle. Mothers called their children from the windows. It was a good time for humility. Man went back to the animal, the animal to the plant, and the plant into the earth. The brook at the bottom of the valley sparkled with stars. All that could be seen of Pietrasecca in the dark was the cow's head with the two large horns on the roof of the inn.

## 26

Don Paolo had met Cristina at the cemetery. She had
been moved by his desire to put flowers on her father's
grave. After they left, he accompanied her to the gate of
her house. The girl's face was worn and showed suffering.
She was in a long black gown designed as simply as a
night dress, gathered at the waist with a cloth belt.

"I must apologize for what I said at our last meeting,"
said Don Paolo. "I regretted those words very much. I
was rude and presumptuous."

"No, it was my fault alone," said Cristina.

The two parted with the promise to see each other
soon.

With the end of the excitement caused by the announce-
ment of the war, Pietrasecca had taken up its usual habits.
On the thresholds of the huts, the women and old men
were eating their soup in silence without looking about
them. Some of the mothers were getting a small allotment
for their sons in the war and were praying that it would
last. The schoolboys, divided into Africans and Italians,
threw stones at each other in front of the inn. To the
horror and indignation of the schoolteacher, it sometimes
happened that the Africans beat the Italians.

For the rest of it, there was nothing to worry about,
since what was to happen would undoubtedly happen. The
war was going to happen and it did. If the plague were
really supposed to break out there was no way of avoiding
that either.

Magascià's wife had heard from Matalena, in great confidence, that Don Paolo had heard the confession of a
young man from the plain. That must mean that he was
finally allowed to hear confessions. The woman therefore
came to beg him to confess her husband, who had not
been reconciled with God for twenty-five years.

"He doesn't trust the priests around here," she said. "If you won't do this for him, he'll die in sin and go to hell."

The priest had undergone a bad relapse. The previous day he had had a bad cold and a splitting headache. He had not slept all night. He answered the woman with a distracted no. He did not think of it further until old Magascià himself came into his room, a tall, massive bearded man with his hat in his hand. He took up almost all the door frame with his bulk. The left sleeve of his jacket hung empty from the shoulder, the end tucked into a pocket. Don Paolo was sitting in a chair close by the bed; he would have liked to speak to him, but the old man fell on his knees at the priest's feet, crossed himself, kissed the floor and, holding his face there, he struck his chest three times.

*"Mea culpa, mea culpa, mea culpa,"* he murmured.

Without raising his head, and lowering his voice even more, he continued to mutter incomprehensibly for some minutes, so that all that was audible was a low hissing sound and a sigh or two. When even this petered out, the man stayed on the floor, taking up half the room with his gigantic body. His huge bones reminded one of a geological element, like a fossilized prehistoric animal; his hair and beard were like wild vegetation; only the fear he expressed showed him a man.

He lay there in silence for some time, then he raised his head and asked in a normal voice, "Have you given me your blessing? Can I go?"

"You can go," said the priest.

Magascià got up and kissed his hand.

"By the way," he said in a low tone before he went. "I'd like some advice I couldn't ask anyone else for. Is there any pardon for a murder after twenty-five years? If it's found out, does the murderer still have to be tried?"

"What murder?"

Magascià did not understand why the priest demonstrated ignorance on this matter, but since he needed the information badly, he murmured in his ear, "The murder of Don Giulio, the notary from Lama."

"Ah," said the priest, "I understand. That's right. I had

already forgotten. But I'm not a lawyer and I wouldn't know what to tell you."

The rumor that Don Paolo had gotten permission to hear confessions spread like lightning. "He understands and forgives everything," was all Magascià would say. "Matalena is right. He's a saint."

"He's a saint who reads the hearts of sinners," said Matalena.

The people rushed up to find out. Don Paolo's room belonged to everyone, and there was constant coming and going. Everybody wanted to make an appointment for his own confession. The children climbed the stairs and waited outside, not daring to come near the priest who was by now defenseless. He got up, went to the window and the door, like an animal struggling in a snare.

In spite of his fever, Don Paolo was about to leave, but he was stopped at the door. Mastrangelo came, supported by his wife Lidovina and by Marietta, his sister-in-law, since he had a bad leg and could hardly walk. Since he could not kneel, the two women helped him to sit in a chair next to the confessor. They kissed the priest's hand and went off. Mastrangelo began to talk, bringing his mouth right up to the priest's ear, so no one else could hear. His breath smelled of wine for several years back, and it made Don Paolo dizzy.

"My wife has had eighteen children, but God has already taken back sixteen," said Mastrangelo. "Two are left. Some flesh is already chastised when it is born. There's nothing to do about that. My wife's sister, Marietta, has been chastised in a different way. She was poor but in good health. Before she was married, everything was ready and the banns had been announced. Nicola, her man, came to me alone and told me, 'I have to tell you a secret; the war has chastised my body.' He showed me his misfortune. He wasn't a man any more. They had had to cut off his penis to save his life. That unfortunate man was alone, he had neither mother nor sisters, no one to wash his shirt, to make his bed or to cook his soup. It was natural that he wanted to get married. He had a vineyard and a medal. If Magascià were to die, his medal would get him the salt and tobacco sales. Magascià was already old then and we thought he would die soon. It's not my brother-in-law's fault that he's still alive. So Nicola and Marietta were married. Marietta found out about him only after the wedding feast. Nicola told her, 'Your brother-in-law Mastrangelo knows all about it.' Marietta sent for me at once and began to cry. 'You've ruined me,' she repeated. 'I'll kill myself for shame.' Nicola left us alone. Before he went he said, 'Since God has wanted to chastise me, I have no right to be jealous; but on the condition that honor is saved and that no one knows about it.' Marietta has had six children, and four of them are alive. Making children, as you probably don't know, is like drinking. You can swear, 'This glass will be the last'; then you get thirsty again and drink still another glass. 'Just this one more and then I'll stop,' you say; but who can command his own thirst? At one time the man is thirsty, then the woman, then both of them. At first the sisters didn't get on well. With time things got better. We have accepted with resignation all that God has sent us. Honor has been saved.

"There hasn't been any scandal; and nobody knew anything about it. But one day Nicola went to confess to Don Cipriano, and Don Cipriano made him change his mind. He told him that the chastisements received from God are nothing in comparison with what we deserve and which we will receive. What we don't pay, he told him, our children will pay, the ones who are the fruit of sin; and what our children won't pay, our grandchildren will, on to the seventh generation. But if God knows the truth, how can He punish us more? Haven't we already suffered enough?"

The penitent stopped and looked at the confessor with bloodshot eyes, waiting for an answer. From the stairs came the arguing voices of some drinkers who were playing games on the ground floor. On the glass of the window the confessor saw two dusty flies, one on top of the other, immobile, surprised by death in the act of love. It was raining outside. Don Paolo shivered. Mastrangelo shook his arm; he wanted an answer.

"Was Don Cipriano right?" he asked. "Are Marietta's children and grandchildren already damned?"

"Damned by whom?" said Don Paolo.

"Haven't they been damned by God?"

"God can't damn," said Don Paolo. "He has never damned a living soul."

"Aren't they going to have misfortunes?"

"Maybe they will," said Don Paolo. "But just like everybody else, neither more nor less."

Lidovina and Marietta, having been called by Mastrangelo, came back up the stairs, helped their man to leave the room, holding him up by the armpits and questioning him with their eyes to guess the result of the confession.

Other penitents, men and women, were seated on the steps waiting their turn to confess. A strong odor rose from the stairs, as if the people never washed. But there was a new odor, too, which wasn't often to be found in an inn—the odor of incense. Matalena had run to get the keys of the church from Cristina and had taken some incense from the sacristy. Don Paolo put on his coat and fled out into the street. The penitents watched him from the inn door, humiliated and disillusioned.

"Wait! Wait!" Matalena told them. "He's just getting a breath of fresh air. He can't go far in this rain."

After about an hour he was seen coming back, but instead of going into the inn, he set out for the Colamartini house.

Cristina opened the door for him. The girl looked much thinner and seemed to have suffered more.

"We were talking about you," she said to the priest.

The whole family, grandmother, aunt and mother, were gathered in the large room into which he was taken.

"But you're dripping wet," exclaimed Cristina as soon as she saw him in the light of the room. "And your teeth are chattering with the cold."

She made him give up his coat to be put out to dry and insisted that he sit by the fire.

"Stretch out your feet by the fire," she advised.

The room felt closed up as usual, but it was lightened by the odor of preserves and aromatic wine. The three old women weren't saying anything. Don Paolo avoided their glances. Through the windows of the room he saw the garden running with rain. The flowers had gone to seed and the seed had fallen to earth. Cristina's mother and aunt got up and went into the next room. Cristina murmured something in her grandmother's ear and followed them.

"Were you the last person to talk to my son before he left Fossa?" the old woman asked the priest. "What did he tell you?"

"He told me, 'This is the end.' He didn't want company. In fact, it was the end. He didn't tell me anything else," answered Don Paolo.

The old woman was dressed in black and seated in an armchair covered with red velvet, near the garden window. She was small, wrinkled and shriveled, and she looked at the priest with her glassy, inscrutable and abstracted eyes. When she talked she bared her toothless gums. The rain was beating on the streaming windows.

"They've left us alone," said the old woman, "because they want me to confess. But I don't want to confess. Shall I tell you the truth? To confess, you need to repent. And why should I repent?"

She kept her hands crossed on her chest, and these hands seemed old utensils used for a long and painful job. Her arms looked like two dried-up sticks, ready to be broken off and thrown in the fire.

"Why should I repent?" the old woman asked. "For eighty years I have wanted only one thing, a just thing and the only just thing, the honor of my family. I have thought of nothing else. I have wanted nothing else and I have worked for nothing else. For eighty years. And now why should I repent?"

Deep within her eyes, which had suddenly dilated, there appeared such a hopeless anguish, so long repressed a fear, so fixed and irreparable an alarm, and such an expression of primitive desperation that Don Paolo was quite shaken.

"Is it the end?" she asked. "Is it the end of everyone, or just of the Colamartinis?"

"I believe it's the end of all the landowners," said Don Paolo.

When the old woman realized that the priest was looking at her eyes, she closed them. Her worn-out, almost bald head reminded him of a sparrow's. It was a fragile object, but it had been so resistant, so obstinate, so tenacious, so pitiless, and so hard for eighty years! Cristina had told her grandmother that if she did not repent and confess, she would go to hell; and the old woman had answered her granddaughter, "Very well then, I'll go to hell." But since she had the chance to consult a priest, she wanted very much to inform herself on one detail which was close to her heart.

"The ones who don't repent and go to hell, how long do they have to stay before the Almighty Judge? Do they have at least the time to be able to tell Him the truth to His face?"

Don Paolo was forced to admit that he did not know for sure, but plain common sense induced him to give an affirmative answer. "That's how they'd do it in any decent court," he said. That was enough for the old woman.

Cristina returned to accompany Don Paolo to the door, but first she wanted to show him a little room next to the kitchen where there was a loom where she worked in the rare moments of the day she had to herself and late in the evening.

"We don't know where the next meal is coming from," said the girl. "You've heard that we've lost all our savings in the failure of the bank? The land we have left is not at all profitable. And the tenants aren't paying."

Cristina had hoped to make some money with her loom, but she soon found out she could not.

"Wool is expensive," she said. "Nobody buys hand-made cloth any more. It's a luxury. The few orders I've gotten up to now are from friends of mine, who've done it, I believe, to help me out."

"You're not thinking of the convent any more?" asked Don Paolo.

"How could I now?" she answered. "I'm the mistress and servant in this house, with three nonpaying guests. The most energetic of the three, my grandmother, even has to be helped into her clothes."

"I'm mortified that I can't help you," said Don Paolo. "You can't imagine how depressed I am by your situation."

"Thank you," said Cristina with a light smile veiled with sadness. "You'll help me a lot if you're not angry with me any more. Will you promise? On the other hand, believe me, the material difficulties are the least of our troubles. The spiritual anguish is much worse. Some of our family affairs, of which I'd never heard before, are now the object of continued arguments and discussions."

"And Alberto?" said Don Paolo.

"He enlisted in the militia," said Cristina. "He's not cut out for the military life, but there was nothing else for him. If he can make a go of it, he'll at least be able to provide for himself."

Cristina showed the priest some cloth she had finished the previous day, a little white-and-red carpet with quite pleasant geometric designs, copied from an old blanket.

"Did you know that my brother Alberto admires you very much?" said Cristina. "He also told me about your plot for the second revolution. Isn't that dangerous? Hasn't the Church condemned it?"

"There are many ways of serving God in our times," said Don Paolo with an evasive gesture.

"Don Benedetto thinks that way too," said Cristina. "Did you know that he was here with Martha for the funeral? Alberto and I had a long conversation with him. We asked his advice about our family affairs, and finally, I don't remember how, the conversation got around to obedience to civil authorities and onto Pietro Spina. 'No one should think evil of him,' he told us. 'I know him; he was my best pupil. Socialism is his way of serving God.' "

"Was that what he said?"

"I remember it exactly. He also said about Spina, 'This is a man who from the time he was a boy was touched by God, and God Himself sent him into the shadows, in search of Him. I am sure that he is obeying His voice.' In other words, Don Benedetto talked as if he knew Spina very well. I was very confused by all this."

"I can understand that," said Don Paolo. "But perhaps you shouldn't take it literally."

When the priest took his leave, Cristina expressed her desire to confess, wherever and whenever was convenient to him.

"Oh, no," answered Don Paolo, struck with surprise. Then he added in embarrassment, "Please don't be offended, but above all, I lack the proper detachment required between confessor and penitent."

Cristina blushed. "You're right," she said. "Perhaps it would have been hard for me as well."

"I like being with you," added Don Paolo. "But just as a man. I'm going through a hard time of life too, and seeing you more often would do me a lot of good."

"It's hard during the day," said Cristina. "I haven't a moment's rest."

"I'll come tonight, after supper," said Don Paolo. "I'll keep you company while you weave."

"All right," said Cristina, hesitating slightly.

That evening the priest ate with a good appetite and great pleasure. Matalena was radiant, on account of the confessions in the afternoon. Her inn had become a sacred place. She had lit two lamps in front of the Madonna of the Rosary.

"The carpenter is coming later to take the measurements," she said to "her" priest. "Of course the work will be at my expense."

"What measurements?" asked Don Paolo, crossing his fingers.

"The measurements for the confessional. Dioclegiano is a good carpenter, but he's never built a confessional. I'll have a confessional put up in your room, where the table is now. What do you think of that?"

"I think you're going mad!"

"Are you against confessionals? That's too bad, but your wishes will be respected. I'll tell you, it's for the girls most of all. I told them to wait until the confessional was ready. But if you'd prefer to do it without a confessional . . ."

Matalena put an apple and a handful of nuts on the table.

"The ones who were lined up this afternoon will come back later," she said. "Just to let you know."

"What do they want?"

"You know already. They want to confess. After all, you've begun to hear confessions."

"I don't want to hear any more confessions."

"Shall I tell the people to come back tomorrow? Most of them work during the day, you know."

"Just tell them not to come any more."

"Impossible. They would protest to me."

"You're not my boss."

"They'll say, Why did he confess them and not us? They'll say, It's Matalena's fault. They'll never forgive me."

"Let 'em say what they will. I won't confess them; that's for sure."

"If it's like that, they'll talk to you when they come. And they'll be persuaded that it's not my fault."

"When they come, I won't be here."

"I'll have them wait until you come back."

"Listen, Matalena," said the priest, raising his voice. "I won't set foot in this house again until they're gone."

The innkeeper got frightened.

"If you don't want to," she said, "no one can force you. I'll tell them you're tired tonight, and maybe you'll change your mind tomorrow."

The priest did not answer. But when she saw that he had taken his cap and really was about to go out, she was seized with remorse.

"It's raining outside," she said. "You'll catch cold going out in this weather. Stay here. I'll protect you. No one will bother you. And we can talk about it tomorrow. Where are you going in this weather?"

"Wherever I feel like," said the priest.

But when Matalena saw that he was going to the Colamartini house, all her fears were calmed. Evidently Cassarola's magic was having its effect.

Don Paolo found the door half closed and Cristina already at work on her loom, trying to untangle some threads.

"Can I help you?" said Don Paolo.

"Do you understand it?"

"Just try me."

Just for fun, the girl made room for him on the bench.

"The obstacle is in the register," said the priest with confidence after he had tried the threads.

Cristina was open-mouthed.

"Can you weave?" she asked.

"I used to help my mother, as a boy," he answered with a smile. "She was quite a good weaver. She worked at it more for pleasure than to make money. It was an amusement to me also, though I worked hard at it."

"Was it a loom like this one?"

"In her last years my mother got one just like this one, but she had an older type before, a massive and complicated affair. Have you ever seen one like that?"

"We have one in the attic."

"Then you'll know that on the old type of loom the weaver needed a helper who would point out the order and the time of the drawings, according to the changes in the design which he had. I was my mother's helper. While I was working, my mother would tell me the parables of the gospel, like fables. On thinking it over, I guess it was because of those fables that I'm more or less of a Christian now."

"What are you saying?" interrupted Cristina, amused and scandalized at the same time.

"Every once in a while the truth comes out," said Don Paolo in a serious tone.

"And were you diligent on the new loom, even though she didn't need your help?"

"My mother gave weaving lessons on the new loom to a girl who was a friend of the family. I liked the girl and took lessons myself just to keep her company."

"If I may say so, you're a recidivist," exclaimed Cristina, laughing.

Don Paolo laughed heartily too. Something in his face and his expression had cleared, as if he had taken off a mask. One memory led to another, and he continued to speak of his childhood. While Cristina went on with her work, he told of the discoveries and surprises in his first reading, of his first friendships and of his first trips. It seemed that there were no gaps in his memory. In this way passed an evening of peaceful friendship, which neither of them had had for a long time.

"It's time for me to go," Don Paolo said at one point. "You've worked all day and you'll need some rest."

"Yes, you'd better go," said Cristina. "Matalena might get jealous."

He took her hand at the door and added, "I hope I'll see you again soon."

## 27

"After all we have suffered, we can no longer talk of politics the way other people do," said Don Paolo to Murica. "Come to think of it, it has become entirely different for us."

"Hasn't it always been?" said Murica. "Could one of us have joined a clandestine movement without any possibility of immediate success, for political ends and calculations?"

Murica was walking ahead of the priest to push a way for him through the briars on a steep path which went down to the bottom of the valley.

"I'd like to tell you something which concerns you," said Murica at a certain point. "In a little pamphlet you wrote about two years ago, you spoke of the man who came painfully to an awareness of his own humanity. I got a copy of it from Romeo. It set me to thinking then; but perhaps only now do I feel capable of understanding what you meant."

"That can happen to its author, too," said Don Paolo. "Awareness has infinite gradations, like light."

The path soon came to the brook's stony bed. A rivulet of limpid water wound its way around the pebbles and boulders. The two were walking in single file, and every once in a while they had to stop where the path was interrupted by holes. In one of them shone the white of an ass's jawbone still armed with molars.

"Thinking of it now," said Murica, "it's clear to me that when I was in the movement I was from the beginning in the false situation of a gambler who bets much more than he owns. But maybe these cases are more frequent than I am aware of."

"If you felt unprepared to face the risks," said Don

Paolo, "why didn't you leave the group after the first meetings?"

"Actually, I wasn't capable of taking that into account then," said Murica. "Now, however, I think about it often and I would like to explain my thoughts to you so you can tell me if you agree. I think you can rebel against the existing order for two different reasons—if you're weak, or if you're strong. By a strong man I mean one superior to the bourgeois order, who refuses to have anything to do with it, holds it in contempt and fights against it and desires other values in its place, a just society. My case wasn't like that. I felt rejected by bourgeois society, I was on its fringes, I was a provincial student, poor, timid and awkward, alone in a big city; I felt incapable of facing the thousand and one petty difficulties of life and the daily humiliations."

"In such cases," said Don Paolo, "contact with a revolutionary movement can be a source of strength."

"No," said Murica. "Since the movement is clandestine, it offers the deceptive advantage of secrecy. The humiliated and offended man satisfies his resentments there, but in secret. His external conduct is unchanged. His negation of the law is intimate, as in a dream, and just for that reason it takes on very daring forms. Such a one conspires against the state in the same way as he might, in a dream, strangle his father, toward whom he would be respectful and obedient during the day."

"Until something happens to reveal his double life," said Don Paolo. "Then there is panic and terror."

After some minutes of silence, Don Paolo asked Murica, "Were you beaten after they arrested you?"

"They spat in my face and slapped me," said Murica. "But I was terrorized from the first instant. Just think; I couldn't remember what date I was born, or my mother's maiden name, when I filled out the police form. In other words, the challenge I had given to the law was out of proportion to my strengths. I had bet more than I owned."

The two went on in silence along the path which flanked the stream and came to where the valley widened and the wagon road crossed the path.

"Let's stop here," said Murica. "Someone might recognize us further on."

"Do you think they're following you at Rocca dei Marsi?" said Don Paolo.

"I don't know," said Murica. "It's not important, now that I feel myself strong. I was worried about you."

"Don't worry about me," said Don Paolo. "But you're right; after all that's happened to us, we have no reason to be afraid. It's the police who should be afraid of us."

Between the cart road and the stream there was a meadow with a sheepfold. This was the season when the herds came down from the mountains and went to the plain to pass the winter.

"When's Annina coming?" asked Don Paolo.

"Maybe tomorrow," said Murica. "She writes to me every day."

"She's a wonderful girl," said Don Paolo. "I really envy you."

"My father was in favor of our getting married," said Murica.

Near his herd an old shepherd was burning a stump. A young man was blowing on the fire; and a boy was looking around for some dry wood. The old man was called Bonifazio, and he told Don Paolo he had dreamed of St. Francis.

"He was smiling," he said, "and he wanted to give me a lira."

"Did he give it to you?"

"No. He looked in his pockets, but he didn't have it."

Don Paolo laughed and gave him a lira.

"Do you know the old story of the lake of Fucino?" asked Bonifazio. "It's not a story you find in books."

He thought of telling him the story to thank him for the money, since Don Paolo did not know that story.

"Jesus was looking for a job as a carpenter," said Bonifazio. "He went from village to village and even came here. 'Have you some work for a poor carpenter?' he asked everywhere. 'What's your name? Have you any references?' the bosses asked Him. So He said to all the unemployed without references whom He met in the streets, 'Come with me,' and they all followed Him. 'Don't turn around,' He warned them. No one turned around. When they had all gathered on the mountain, Jesus said, 'You can turn around.' Instead of the land and the villages,

there was a lake. Now they've drained it," added Bonifazio, "but if the bosses keep it up, the land will be flooded
again."

"Your story is well worth a lira," said Don Paolo,
laughing.

"The next time we meet, I'll tell you another," said
Bonifazio.

Don Paolo said good-bye to Murica and hurried back to
Pietrasecca. In the middle of the road he met a woman
doing the *strascino*—that is, she was walking on her
knees along one side of the road. She looked like a bag
of ashes and dust, a bag that staggered. At first Don Paolo
thought her mad. But, as the poor woman explained, she
was a mother whose son was in the war, and in a moment
of religious fervor, to calm a dark presentiment, she had
made a vow to come on her knees from Pietrasecca to
Lama, to obtain from the Virgin her son's safe return.
The miserable woman had been on the road since morning; her voice was hoarse, her face unrecognizable, her
eyes sore and prone to hallucinations and covered with
dust and tears. She looked as if she would collapse from
one moment to the next. Not being convinced that the
vow was permanent or inevitable, Don Paolo tried to
persuade her to get up, to walk on her feet, and he was
even about to pick her up by force. It was in vain. The
woman defended herself with bites and scratches. Since
she had made her vow, she had to fulfill it. If she did not,
the son would certainly die in the war. The woman was
astounded that a priest would not understand so simple
and well-known a thing.

"What kind of a priest are you?" she cried.

Don Paolo left the woman to her fate and went on his
way. It had gotten colder. The top of the mountain behind Pietrasecca seemed already white with snow. The
village had been invaded by shadows rising from the
valley. Only the Colamartini house, which was a little
higher than the rest of them, was still lit by the sun. Cristina showed her face at a window on the top floor and her
face was like a crystal on which the rays of the setting sun
struck. He saw nothing else in all the village but that
radiant countenance.

As soon as the sun had gone down, the air got colder. Matalena awaited the return of "her" priest at the inn door. She was passing a spindle through her fingers. "It's going to snow soon," said the woman, looking at the sky.

The snow came two days later. When Don Paolo got up in the morning, he found the countryside much different. Snow had fallen all night and it was still coming down evenly, in huge flakes, like something which had long been awaited, something fixed and inevitable, but very quiet.

Some people came into Matalena's inn that night to celebrate the first day of snow. Cristina came, too, a little later. Her eyes had swollen from her suffering. But her beauty had not changed. She was still enchanting to look at.

Don Paolo was seated next to the fireplace. Around him in a large circle were some peasants, women and children. Near the fire, on the floor, there was a dog on one side and on the other Teresa's child, the one who was supposed to have been born blind and who was saved in time. The child was in a small wicker hamper on the floor like a cauliflower; and his face had been heated to the shade of a red apple by the fire. The people asked Don Paolo to tell some stories. Cristina specified that they be sacred stories. Finally he could refuse no longer and he opened his breviary and looked in the "Index Festorum." He began to tell the story of the martyrs in his own way, from the material in the breviary.

The story of the martyrs was always different and always the same. It was a time of beatings and persecutions. There was a dictatorship with a deified leader. There was a moldy old church which lived on handouts, and an army of mercenaries to guarantee a peaceful digestion to the rich people. A population of slaves. Incessant preparations of new wars of loot to bolster the prestige of the dictatorship. Meanwhile mysterious travelers were coming from the east. They whispered of miracles which had happened in the orient. They announced the good news: Liberation is at hand. The boldest, the poor, the hungry, met underground to hear of this. The news spread. Some left the old temples and embraced the new faith. Some of

the nobles left their palaces. Some centurions deserted.
The police raided some of the clandestine meetings and
made some arrests. The prisoners were tortured and sent
to a special tribunal. There were some who refused to
burn incense in front of the state's fetishes. They recognized no God but their own. They confronted the tortures
with a smile on their lips. The young men were thrown
to the wild beasts. The survivors kept faith with the dead
and constructed a secret cult to them. Times change and
clothes change, along with food and work; languages
change; but at bottom, it's the same story all over again.

The heat of the fire made people sleepy. The ones who
weren't asleep listened and looked into the fire. Cristina
said, "In every period and in whatever society, the supreme
act is to give one's self, to lose one's self to find one's
self. You only have what you give."

The fire went out, the guests said good night and Don
Paolo went up to his room. He took up the notebooks of
his "Dialogues with Cristina," which he had begun in his
first days at Pietrasecca. He reread the first pages, full of
tender affection for the girl; he reread and tore out the
successive pages written in disillusion and scorn. Several
months had passed and not in vain, whether for him or
for Cristina. Before going to bed he added a few more
lines to the "Dialogues."

"Cristina," he wrote. "It's true that you have what you
give; but what and to whom should be given?

"Our love and our disposition to sacrifice and abnegation of ourselves are of value only if brought into the
relationship between people like ourselves. Morality
can live and flourish only in practical life. We are responsible for others as well.

"If we look sensibly at the evil which reigns around us,
we cannot remain inactive and console ourselves with
waiting for another life. The evil to be fought is not that
sad abstraction which is called the devil; the evil is everything which prevents millions of men from acting like
human beings. We too are directly responsible.

"I do not think there is any way of saving one's soul in
these times. He is saved who conquers his own individual
egoism, and his caste and family egoism, and who frees

his soul from the idea of resigning himself to the wickedness around him.

"Dear Cristina. We must not become obsessed with the idea of security, not even the security of one's own virtues. Spiritual life does not go with a secure life. You have to take risks to save yourself."

During the night the huge flakes of snow fell without interruption. The priest was still asleep when Matalena called him. There was a group of peasants and some boys in front of the inn, gathered about Garibaldi, Sciatàp's donkey. The body of a wolf which had been killed that morning behind Pietrasecca was on the back of the donkey. The wolf's skin was hairy gray, matted with blood and dirt; his teeth were white and strong. There were holes in his shoulder and on the side, where he had been shot. According to custom, the dead wolf was shown from house to house to gather contributions for the one who shot it.

Luigi Banduccia still had his rifle on his shoulder and was explaining how it had happened. It was the fourth wolf he had shot. He showed the love bite on the back of the beast's neck, the deep bite of the female. Wolves take love seriously. Banduccia knew their howls—the howl for danger, which the wolf gives when he is attacked; the howl of the feast, which means that he has found some other beast to tear up and is calling his companions, because beasts do not like to eat alone; and the love howl, which means he would like a female and is not ashamed to let everybody know it.

Cristina's grandmother did not want to give anything for the dead wolf; but Cristina, who had had a special respect for wolves since she had been a child, insisted to her grandmother.

"A dead wolf doesn't bite any more," the old woman said.

That same day Magascià took to Don Paolo an urgent note which he told him he had gotten from Murica's father in Rocca dei Marsi. Annina had signed the note, which said that she had just arrived at the Murica household and that Luigi had been arrested. Don Paolo wanted to leave at once, but Magascià was evasive, he said he was tired, and that the donkey was no longer young.

"I'll go on foot," said the priest. "A little fresh air will do me good."

"Is it that urgent?" said Matalena.

"A case of conscience," said the priest.

"Is it someone from your diocese?"

"From my diocese and my parish."

Matalena had never seen him so agitated. He left as quickly as a boy would have. Perhaps Don Paolo himself was surprised at his own energy. Fortunately the way to the valley was downhill.

## 28

The crown of mountains around the hollow of Fucino was all white with snow. In some places the snow came down to the hills which formed the first step in the mountainous ladder. Don Paolo was wearing a black cape which came to his feet, and he had a black wool scarf about his neck. All he would have to do to rid himself of his ecclesiastic appearance would be to unbutton the cape and take off the scarf. His most clever expedient was his hat, a common felt one which could be either lay or ecclesiastic, according to how it was put on his head or dented.

The road went slowly downward, serving as the boundary between a rocky little hill planted in vines and an area of recently plowed fields. It was easier to walk where there was no snow. At a turn in the road Don Paolo came on a cart stopped by the roadside.

"Don Paolo?" asked the man seated on the cart. "Get on! Annina sent me."

The priest got on the cart, and the man set the horse to trotting.

"They told me about you," he said simply. "I've been waiting for you for two hours."

"I came here on foot," said Don Paolo.

The man had not shaved for some days; his shirt and his clothes were dirty and worn; and he had the usual expression of a sick man.

"Is there any news of Luigi Murica?" asked Don Paolo. "Is he still in prison?"

"He died yesterday."

*"Consummatum est,"* said Don Paolo.

The air was very calm, the prewinter calm of the country.

"Were you a friend of his?" said Don Paolo.

"We were together," answered the man. "It was very

pleasant to be with him. He was a good man, and he made other people want to be good. He also told us of the revolution. To be together without being afraid, that's the beginning, he would tell us."

"We must always be together," said Don Paolo. "We mustn't ever let them separate us."

"Luigi had written on a piece of paper: 'Truth and brotherhood will reign among men instead of lies and hate; labor will reign instead of money.' When they arrested him they found that paper on him, and he didn't repudiate it. In the courtyard of the militia barracks at Fossa they put a chamberpot on him instead of a crown. 'This is the truth,' they said to him. They put a broom in his right hand instead of a scepter. 'This is brotherhood,' they told him. Then they wrapped him up in a red rug from the floor, they bandaged him and the soldiers beat him and kicked him. 'This is the kingdom of labor.' When he fell, they walked on him, with their spiked shoes. After this interrogation he lasted one day more."

"If we live like him," said Don Paolo, "it'll be as if he'd never died. We must stay together and not be afraid."

The man nodded.

He showed the Murica house to Don Paolo as they came into Rocca dei Marsi. Don Paolo approached it on foot through a grassy path. In that brief time he changed his costume to a lay one. The Murica house was one storey high; it was wide and thick-set, half a dwelling place and half a stall. The windows of the house were all closed and barred, while the main door was wide open, according to the custom for mourning. People were coming and going from the house to pay their respects. Pietro came in, hesitating. No one paid any attention to him. As soon as he had come into the house he found himself in a large room paved with pebbles which must have served as a kitchen and a place to put the tools and which was now full of people. Some women in black and yellow were sitting on the floor near the fireplace. Some of the men, on their feet around the table, were talking about the land and the harvest. Pietro found Annina in back of the room, seated on a stool, alone, pale, bewildered, trembling with cold and fear, among all these strangers. She was not even crying, because she could cry only when she

was alone or among people she knew. As soon as she saw Pietro she could hold herself in no longer and began to sob. The parents of the dead man came in from a nearby room, dressed in mourning. Luigi's mother came up to Annina, dried her tears, wrapped her in a large black cape and made her sit beside her, near the fire, on the same stool.

"Who's that?" asked some of the other women among themselves.

"It's his girl friend," said one of them. "The girl friend from the city."

The father sat down at the head of the table, with some of the men. Some of the relatives came from a nearby village. Some boys came. As was the custom, the mother spoke a eulogy for her dead son. She said she had wanted to save him, had sent him far away, to school, to save him from the fate which his weakness, his delicate condition might have led one to foresee. She had not saved him. The city air had not been for him. The land had called him back. He had gone back to working the land, helping his father. One might think that he had gotten tired and disgusted, because working the land every day is a chastisement of God. He woke up his father in the morning. He harnessed the horse, he chose the seed, he filled the barrels and he took care of the garden.

Every once in a while the mother paused in her eulogy to stir the fire burning in the fireplace, adding a new dry log. Martha, Don Benedetto's sister, came. The peasants of the neighborhood came. Some left their places and departed. The elder Murica, standing at the head of the table, gave food and drink to the men around him.

"It was he," he said, "who helped to sow, to weed, to thresh, to mill the grain from which this bread was made. Take it and eat it; this is his bread."

Some others arrived. The father gave them something to drink and said, "It was he who helped me to prune, to spray, to weed and to harvest the grapes which went into this wine. Drink; this is his wine."

The men ate and drank. Some of them bathed the bread in the wine.

Some beggars arrived.

"Let them in," said the mother.

"Maybe they've been sent to spy on us," someone murmured.

"Let them in. We'll have to take this risk. Many have given food to Jesus without knowing it in feeding beggars and giving them to drink."

"Eat and drink," said the father.

Finding himself in front of Pietro, the father observed him and asked, "Where are you from?"

"From Orta," he said.

"What's your name?"

Annina came up to the old man and whispered a name into his ear. He looked pleased and embraced Pietro.

"I knew your father when I was young," he told Pietro. "He bought a horse from me at a fair. I heard about you from that son whom I have lost. Sit here between his mother and his bride and have something to drink yourself."

The men around the table were eating and drinking.

"The bread is made from many ears of grain," said Pietro. "Therefore it signifies unity. The wine is made from many grapes, and therefore it, too, signifies unity. A unity of similar things, equal and united. Therefore it means truth and brotherhood, too; these are things which go well together."

"The bread and wine of communion," said an old man. "The grain and the grape which has been trampled upon. The body and the blood."

"It takes nine months to make bread," said the elder Murica.

"Nine months?" asked the mother.

"The grain is sown in November and harvested in July." The old man counted the months: "November, December, January, February, March, April, May, June, July. Just nine months. It also takes nine months for the wine to mature; from March to November." He counted the months: "March, April, May, June, July, August, September, October, November. That makes nine months, too."

"Nine months?" asked the mother. She had never thought of it before. The same length of time it takes to make a man. Luigi was born in April. Under her breath, she counted the months backwards: "April, March, February, January, December, November, October, September,

August. There are nine months from August to April."

Some of the Muricas' friends were arriving and others were departing to make room. Martha said to the mother, "Do you remember when Luigi was a baby and you were still young and you were carrying him in your arms on the hill? Don Benedetto said then that you were like a vineyard and he a cluster of grapes. You were like a stalk of grain and he an ear."

Bianchina appeared at the door and Pietro went to her. The girl was so shaken that she could hardly speak.

"Pietro," she said.

"Why do you call me that?"

"Aren't you Pietro Spina?"

"Yes, I am he."

"You'll have to escape as soon as you can, you've been discovered!"

"How do you know?"

"Alberto Colamartini told me. He's in the militia now. They're coming for you at Pietrasecca tonight or tomorrow morning. You haven't a minute to lose!"

Pietro consulted Annina and on her advice asked the elder Murica to lend him a horse for an hour or so. The old man went into the stall and led out a young colt which had hardly been tamed.

"A little exercise will do him good," he said as he gave him to Pietro.

"What can I do?" asked Bianchina.

"Do what Annina tells you," said Pietro. "I'm going to Pietrasecca where I've left some papers I'd like to burn. If there's time, I'll come back down to Pescasseroli, Alfedena or Castel di Sangro. Don't worry and don't be afraid. I'll let you know my news as soon as I can."

## 29

The colt had neither saddle nor bridle, but a simple piece of rope around his head. As soon as he felt the weight of a man on his back, he neighed and galloped off across the fields. Pietro was taken by surprise. He had not been used to riding for several years. So as not to fall to the ground, he had to hang on to the horse's neck and mane. After the first rush the animal became more reasonable and let himself be guided to the valley of Pietrasecca, trotting along a path parallel to the cart road. The first part of the valley, although it sloped steeply, was traversed by the horse without his having to take a breath. He slowed down as soon as he saw the road covered with snow.

Pietro looked behind him from time to time, but he found no sign that anyone was following him. The further he went into the valley, the stranger it seemed to him. A great deal of snow had already fallen; and the gray sky boded for more. The horse was breathing heavily and foaming at the mouth, but he was keeping a rapid and regular pace. Pietro looked at the white walls of the ravine. They had never before looked so high and impenetrable.

When he was in sight of Pietrasecca, he adjusted his hat and buttoned his cape. His eyes were fixed on the mountains close by the village, with their two unequal peaks, like the back of a dromedary. Between them was a deep valley, which was called the Goat's Saddle. It was the only existing valley which led to the other side of the mountain. In the summer it took four or five hours to get to the first group of houses on the other side. But in the winter? Barring that, was there any other way to escape? If there wasn't, was there any possibility of concealment?

When he got to Pietrasecca, he tied the horse to a shackle fixed into the wall and was about to go in when

272

he heard someone coming up behind him. It was Cristina. The alarm he saw on her face made him afraid.

"Alberto told me," the girl was able to stammer.

"Are you perhaps ill?"

"Please tell me the truth; are you Pietro Spina?"

"Yes," he answered. "I'm he."

Matalena came from the inn and interpreted the emotion she saw on both their faces in her own way.

"Wait here a minute," said Pietro to the girl. "I have something for you."

He went up to his room in a rush and took his notebook from the drawer in the table. On the cover he wrote: "Dear Cristina, My justification will be found here, and something more, which concerns you personally; beyond the compulsory pretenses, the hidden truth, the heart's truth. Pietro Spina."

He came back down to the kitchen and gave the notebook to Cristina, who had remained outside the door, deathly pale and almost paralyzed. The girl went off, almost at a run, without saying a word. In front of the inn Pietro saw Sciatàp going by. He called him and proposed that he bring the horse to the elder Murica at Rocca dei Marsi. For this he would give Sciatàp a day's pay.

"Thank you," said Sciatàp.

This was an unexpected fortune in wintertime. Matalena was present and she saw the man whom she still thought of as Don Paolo go back up to his room. Nothing had yet happened to make the innkeeper suspicious. Cristina's passionate attitude was what Cassarola the wise woman had foreseen. Matalena left the inn with a smile, to buy some salt. She stopped for a while to converse with Magascià's wife and some other women, because she was in a good mood and was in no hurry.

"How's Don Paolo?"

"Very well. Now I'm sure he'll stay here all winter."

"When will he hear confessions again?"

"In a little while. As soon as he gets a definite answer from the Pope."

As soon as she got back to the inn, and she still had no idea of what was really happening, she prepared supper.

How long had it been in all since she had last seen "her" priest? Perhaps an hour, and perhaps an hour and a half. As soon as supper was ready, she went up to call the priest to the table. The room was dark and empty. Matalena turned on the light. There was some money and a few words of apology and thanks on the table. She couldn't believe her own eyes. What kind of a joke was this? With her heart in her mouth the woman went down to the garden. She recognized his tracks in the snow. She followed them until she came to the stream. From there the tracks did not lead to the valley, but to the mountain. Matalena encountered the deaf-mute and asked him in sign language if he had seen the priest. With other signs he answered her that he had seen him running toward the mountain. Magascià came and confirmed this incredible tale. The priest was running like a mad man. He must be far off by now.

"He's gone mad!" cried Matalena. "Why didn't you hold him back?"

Without waiting for an answer, she ran back and went to the Colamartini house. She knocked several times at the door; but no one showed himself from inside. She ran around the house and came in through a back door she found open.

"Donna Cristina!" she cried several times up the stairs. But no one answered.

Cristina was in her room, alone, in a state of utter terror. The papers of Pietro Spina's notebooks were trembling in her hands.

"Our priest has gone mad!" yelled Matalena, bursting into her room.

"Gone mad?" asked Cristina.

"He left all of a sudden, and he took the mountain road," she added. "It wasn't you by any chance who made him this way?"

Cristina ran to the window and looked toward the mountain. There was no trace of a man on the white slope leading to the Goat's Saddle. He must have taken the longer and easier way, the mule path which first went along the stream and then zigzagged up to the pass.

"If he'd only had supper," said Matalena weeping. "If

only he'd taken some warmer clothing. But he left them in the chest in his room."

The bed of the stream at the bottom of the valley was so hidden by the boulders and shrubs that Cristina couldn't see how the fugitive had gone. And the air was not very clear.

"It will be dark soon," Matalena wept. "Even if he gets to the Goat's Saddle, he'll be caught in a blizzard."

Cristina had stayed at the window, with her eyes fixed in the direction taken by the fleeing man. It was an adventure that might cost him his life, with his weak health and lack of knowledge of the region, and without warm clothes or food. Suddenly Cristina made a decision.

"Go!" she said to Matalena.

As soon as she was alone she hid the notebooks under the pillows on her bed. She took some warm clothes from a chest in the hall—an athletic sweat shirt, two scarves, a pair of warm socks and some gloves—and wrapped them up in a bundle. She went down to the kitchen, took a piece of bread, some cheese and some wine, and put them into the bundle. So as not to be seen or heard, she left with that big bundle from the back door where Matalena had just passed. She turned, passed behind the church and the cemetery and slid down a thirty-foot bank to the path which went along the stream and took it toward the spring. When Cristina was sure that no one from the village had seen her or followed her, she began running. She had no time to lose if she were to catch up with the fugitive. There were still some tracks in the snow, and she tried to guess which were his as she ran. They were getting sparse, but they did not depart from the bank of the stream. It was a sure sign that he had taken the longer way to the Goat's Saddle, the mule path, instead of the steep short cut which clambered up the slope for about a hundred yards.

Getting up there, even in summer, was something only the boldest of the boys, or the goats, would try. In winter it would be almost impossible. Cristina jumped the stream without hesitating and began climbing the slope. She climbed with her hands and feet, pulling herself up by stumps and clumps of bushes and bits of rock sticking

through the snow. Sometimes she stumbled so that she fell
on her face in the snow and slid back. Fortunately there
was less snow where the slope was steeper, on account of
the wind. But Cristina often fell deep into the snow between the rocks and had to struggle with all her might to
pull herself out. Her skirts and the bundle hindered her;
but these were two things which, for different reasons,
she could not get rid of. She fell on the ground, exhausted,
where an overhanging cliff made a sort of dry cave. Snow
was coming up from the valley. A gray pall filled the deep
ravine, hiding the houses, the fields, the bushes and the
walls. The land appeared unformed and empty, as if it
were deserted. Cristina got up and continued her climb.
The snow was harder above. It was easier to walk, but it
was also easier to slip. The girl was covered with sweat
and her hands were bleeding from the thorns which she
had to grab a couple of times so as not to fall. Her heart
was beating so hard that she had to hold her chest to keep
it in. When she came to the edge of the escarpment, Cristina found herself in a wide, almost rectangular space
called the Witches Meadow. Beyond the meadow, the
mountain continued on a slight slope. The snow was
untouched around her. There was no trace of a footstep.
To continue to the mountain top would be senseless, as
well as extremely tiring. It would be better to go around,
so as to cross Spina's path. She went in this direction. She
completely lost sight of the valley of Pietrasecca. In front
of her and around her nothing was to be seen but the slope
and the white peaks of other mountains. Visibility diminished rapidly. There was a cold, biting wind. Sunset was
near, and so was a squall. Cristina was coming to the point
where the valley splits the mountain in two and forms the
Goat's Saddle. There was no trace of the man in the
snow. The ground was strewn with boulders and rocks
loosened by the floods; the snow came to her waist, Cristina could not see far. She began climbing toward the
Saddle. Perhaps she thought that she would be able to
see Pietro from there, since both slopes were visible from
that point, or at least that he would be able to see her.
But at one point she couldn't stand it any longer and she
fell in the snow.

To avoid his going by without seeing her, she called his

name from time to time, with every ounce of strength in her lungs. She called him with his new name, his real name: "Pietro! Pietro!"

He certainly would have heard her if he had gone by there. She fixed her hair, dusted the snow from her face, eyebrows, and neck. And she kept calling him: "Pietro! Pietro!"

Finally a voice answered from far away; but it was no human voice. It sounded like the barking of a dog, but sharper and more prolonged. Cristina probably recognized it. It was a wolf howl. The call to the feast. A call to the other wolves on the mountain. An invitation to a common banquet. Through the snow and the darkness of the coming night Cristina saw a beast coming toward her, appearing and disappearing in and out of the snow drifts. She saw others coming from further away. Then she fell on her knees, closed her eyes, and crossed herself.

# Afterword

*Bread and Wine* was written in 1936, but it appears today as fresh and moving as it did a quarter of a century ago. This is not because the author revised it in the mid-fifties and the reader is now offered a new version of the novel; the main reasons that compelled Silone to make a literary "facelifting" of his work were mainly technical. He wanted to eliminate passages that were too topical and belonged therefore to a bygone era. He also felt that in the thirties, deeply affected by the Fascist occupation of Ethiopia and by Moscow purge trials under Stalin, he could not help being too emotional and sentimental. And finally, he wished to prune and lighten his narrative, cut secondary incidents and make the story more streamlined, presenting it in twenty-nine short chapters instead of the twelve long ones into which it was initially divided. But all these changes have not touched the very essence of the novel; it remains the best Silone has ever written and the most representative of European fiction between the two world wars. Some critics see it as a book of a whole generation and recommend it to those who wish to explore the ethical and social problems of our century. But *Bread and Wine* is not a moralizing sermon or a philosophical treatise in fictional form. As a true artistic creation, it gives a vision of life through the temperament of the writer, and like any fiction of high quality, it can be enjoyed and interpreted on many levels. The most obvious of these is formed by the realistic narrative, which unfolds a panorama of Italy ruled by Fascism. Silone chose a particular moment in his country's history, the year 1935, when war was declared against Abyssinia in order to enlarge the Italian colonial empire and bolster national morale by spectacular victories over the Ethiopians. Mussolini is never named in the novel, and its various characters only hint at him as a secret and formidable power, but his regime is depicted by Silone in all its live and often horrifying details. *Bread and Wine* made a great impression at the end of the thirties in Europe and America as the first honest and truthful revelation of what was going on "inside Italy" behind the flashy banners of a boastful and threatening state. For Silone it was a modern tyranny based on fear, maintained by violence, enhanced by propaganda, and provoking corruption and abuse in the rulers and passivity and weakness in the masses. Although Fascism has been defeated and belongs to history, the passages of *Bread and Wine* depicting its use of brute force for the body and lies for the mind have a ring of actuality even today because they define the very essence of a totalitarian regime, whatever its labels.

Don Benedetto, one of the best drawn characters of the novel, says (in the first version of the novel) that under a dictatorship "truth is found expensive, primitive and crude while hypocrisy is smooth, always up to date and not only cheap but profitable." At the age of seventy-five, Don Benedetto, a priest and a retired schoolmaster, admires classics, poetry, and plants, everything that beautifies the world. He is not interested in politics but can't help despising what goes on around him; and his liberty of spirit, his warmth of heart, and his bluntness of speech become tragically dangerous in a country ridden with secret police and general cowardice at a time when "honest work is useless without influence and wire pulling." "I live here with my sister among my books and the garden," he tells his former pupil. "For some time my mail has been obviously tampered with, the books and newspapers come late or get lost on the way. I visit no one and few people visit me. The few who do are unpleasant." Don Benedetto's indictment of the regime derives from high Christian ideals combined with humanism in the manner of the ancient Stoics. He rejects sham and evil and has the courage to expose them. But the poor peasants with whom he sympathizes are deprived even of that satisfaction. Silone depicts in masterful strokes the mountainous, poverty-stricken Abruzzi, his native region in southern Italy, where destitute inhabitants constantly struggle for food and shelter. A large part of *Bread and Wine* deals with *cafoni*, indigent and often illiterate peasants, and presents an extraordinary analysis of their psychology. The *cafoni* are the first victims of Fascism, but their attitude toward it borders on complete indifference. They believe that all the trouble comes from the city and that there is an eternal conflict between the monotonous, miserable, but peaceful existence of those who till the soil and breed cattle according to the rhythm of the seasons, among olive trees and orchards smelling of thyme and basil, and the inhuman metropolis, which sends over troopers, policemen, tax collectors, and prison wardens and fattens on war, politics, and other Devil's tricks. The Italian peasant is hit by nature and oppressed by the state, which he endures like any other calamity. Earthquakes demolish his house, storms destroy his crops, epidemics kill his children and his sheep, and the government bleeds him white and the police beat him up and throw him in jail. There is no way out, and what is left to wretched humanity is animal resignation, blind acceptance of fate or of a wrathful and incomprehensible God. A whole gallery of *cafoni* and other pathetic or comic figures give *Bread and Wine* the width and diversity of a social panorama. There is no need to deny the social impact of this book as a document of an era and as a picture of the Italian countryside with all its ills and sufferings. But it would be wrong to call it a "social novel" in the same sense that we apply this term to American novels of the thirties, for example *The Grapes of Wrath*. In Silone's work the central theme is ethical, not social, and descriptions of the environment serve only as a vast background to the main drama, which revolves around the individual and goes beyond the boundaries of a mere social message. Silone's attention is focused on biography and not on history. Conditions of material existence and political ordeals are brought in to explain and intensify the inner crisis of the main hero, and the latter is the bearer of what could be called the basic, intimate truth of the novel.

*Bread and Wine* is built around an extraordinary figure, that of Pietro Spina, a revolutionary saint. A member of the Communist party, Spina sneaks back from exile abroad into his native country with the purpose of engaging in anti-Fascist activities. In order to elude spies and police, he assumes the name of Paolo Spada, and disguised as a priest, takes refuge in a forlorn hamlet, where illness immobilizes him for many weeks. Spina is a former pupil of Don Benedetto. In his adolescent school years he dreamed of becoming a saint; later he lost his faith and turned to socialism and revolution. However, he brought into his affiliation with a political party the same impulse and passion he put into his early denial of worldly goods and his yearning for sacrifice. The same Christian fervor that pushed him toward virtue and goodness made him fight for justice on earth and the regeneration of society. In him again the ethical preceded and determined the social. But after his clandestine return to Italy, Spina, confined to his sickbed, begins wondering whether one can remain sincere and upright while following the tenets of a party, obeying its discipline and accepting its intransigence combined with cynical opportunism in periods of dire necessity. Spina left the Church because he found an abyss between its preaching of love and spiritual freedom and its practice of submission to tyranny and to society ruled by greed, lust, and money. But politics—any politics—now strikes him as abstract and false, just like the Church that advertised excellent principles but signed compromises with inhuman governments and kept silent when confronted with wars, executions, and corruption. "Is it possible," asks Spina, "to take part in politics, to serve one party, and to remain sincere? Hasn't truth become for me the party's truth? and justice, party justice? Has not the organization ended up by extinguishing in me all moral values . . . and has not the organization itself become the supreme value? Have I then not fled the opportunism of a decadent church to fall into the Machiavellianism of a sect?"

The reality of existence that Spina discovers in Italy does not correspond to abstractions of political theory. He came home to organize underground cells and a revolutionary movement, but he finds his former friends discouraged, submissive, or broken by prison and torture, and peasants and workmen inert and dull like beasts of burden. Moreover, he questions his former tactics and ideas. He gradually comes to the conclusion that good relationships between human beings and not good principles and dialectics constitute the highest and most precious values. Each encounter with men and women in villages and in Rome, where he goes to reestablish contacts with old comrades, confirms this revelation. He belongs to the generation that wanted to change the social order by upheaval and violence and believed in ideologies. Now he is not so sure that the revolution is the right answer and that it would bring freedom. Uliva, a disappointed workman, warns him: "If you people win, and probably you'll be unlucky enough to win, we'll just go from one tyranny to another . . . a totalitarian orthodoxy which will use all means, from the movies to terrorism, to stamp out any heresy and tyrannize individual thought. The present black inquisition will be followed by a red inquisition."

Spina examines those very ideas that, until recently, determined all his activities. Is not Marxian bureaucracy as obnoxious as any other? Is a concentration camp any better because it is located in Russia and run by Communists? And does not the rigidity of an imposed dogma always sterilize and impoverish life? How can man's potentialities and creativity be reconciled with any form of moral and political coercion? If the new order for which Spina immolated his youth and suffered exile, arrests, expulsion from various countries, privations, and sickness might turn into a new oppression and degenerate into a dictatorship with its inevitable escort of deceit, intrigues, mendacity, and propaganda, then something must have gone wrong, and no casuistry and verbiage can hide the ugly truth from those who are not afraid of it.

Spina has enough courage and integrity to draw a new outlook on things from his daily experiences and the incessant probing of his mind. More than ever before, he is wary of words: they have become false, equivocal, hackneyed: they are instruments of double dealing and serve to disguise facts under loud slogans and empty phraseology. Who cares if leaders talk of justice, freedom, interests of the country, or supreme goals of peace and class emancipation? Life teaches that only acts really count. "Freedom is not something you get as a present," says Spina. "You can live in a dictatorship and be free— on one condition: that you fight the dictatorship. The man who thinks with his own mind and keeps it uncorrupted is free. The man who fights for what he thinks is right is free. But you can live in the most democratic country on earth, and if you're lazy, obtuse or servile within yourself, you're not free. Even without any violent coercion, you're a slave."

Spina meets all sorts of people, cowherds and noblemen, journeymen and lawyers, illiterate farmers and priests, future nuns and prostitutes, and all these encounters strengthen his faith in simplicity, sincerity, and friendship. Spina understands the anxieties, worries, hopes, and sufferings of all these human beings; he shares with them bread and wine, man's basic nourishment, and he finally comes to accepting the principles practiced by Martha, the sister of Don Benedetto. Her actions seem to proclaim: "The gifts that life has given to us are truly precious. But he who forgets them and forgets himself and gives himself entirely and devotedly to somebody or something receives a thousand times more than he gives." Spina makes a substantial addition to this statement of Christian faith. He writes to Cristina: "Our love and our disposition to sacrifice and abnegation of ourselves are of value only if brought into the relationship between people like ourselves. Morality can live and flourish only in practical life. We are responsible for others as well." Otherwise all our best inclinations become barren and serve abstract and inhuman symbols. Spina understands that the impulses he wished to eradicate in himself when he exchanged the Church for the party are still alive in him. He identifies them with his strivings for justice and faith and with his dream of a Christianity denuded of all mythology and theology, of all Church controls. "Christianity is not an administration," says Don Benedetto, "and it should not abdicate to the face of Mammon, should not support a wicked and cruel society, or offer easy careers for the ambitious. It should rather lead to prison, since crucifixion is now out of fashion." Thus Spina recognizes that he wants to serve man in the wake of Christ, but he translates evangelical precepts of love and brotherhood into secular terms of social justice and companionship. These values, together with common decency, are as necessary as bread and wine, those symbols of spiritual communion and of physical sustenance.

It is perfectly clear that *Bread and Wine* reflects the moral crisis of its author and contains many autobiographical inferences. Silone, a former student in a Jesuit school and himself a member of the Communist party from 1921 to 1931, had been leading the adventurous life of an underground political organizer similar to that he described in his novel. He risked his life, was smuggled by friends into Switzerland, and went through a painful "reevaluation of all values" that resulted in his definite break with Communism. Like Spina, he put life experience above theory and charity above discipline. He rejected dogma and asserted brotherhood, companionship, and genuine freedom as supreme objectives for himself and his fellowmen. There are other personal touches in the novel. Silone's own brother, not unlike Murica, a character in *Bread and Wine*, was tortured and beaten to death by the Fascists. And Silone had known since childhood the landscape of the Abruzzi, as well as the peasants and the artisans who move within it.

But, of course, *Bread and Wine* transcends the narrow limits of a confession or of a therapeutical self-projection. The spiritual odyssey of Pietro Spina is typical of a whole generation, and the problems he raises are as burning today as they were twenty-five years ago: What is man? What is human life? What must we do? What are truth and justice? And since rebellion and negation are as insufficient as abstractions and words, a new way should be found for those who aspire to honesty and genuine life and are to break bread and drink wine with all "men of good will."

The artistic achievement of Silone's novel lies in the organic merging of all its levels. The hero lives his ideas—they are not an intellectual appendix to a series of life adventures as is often the case today in contemporary fiction, but constitute his life and his adventures. The moral peregrinations of the man who is attracted to sainthood and to revolution take place within the framework of his travels. It is, as an American critic called it, a "peripatetic narrative," and the reader follows Spina along the country roads and in the streets of Rome and feels the pulse and color of Italian life. Yet, despite many episodes and the lively portrayal of various secondary characters, the novel never deviates and has form and unity of plot and of inner structure. Its chief unifying force is the intellectual and spiritual development of Spina. In a way one can compare *Bread and Wine* with those German novels, from Goethe's *Wilhelm Meister* to Mann's *The Magic Mountain,* that are called in German *Bildungsromane*, or novels of education and instruction. The evolution of Spina or his education by life experience brings him to wisdom, which should be the aim of any formative process. And it takes place in nine months, from April to December. In a conversation with Murica's father, Spina is reminded that this is the natural cycle of birth. Nine months elapse from the time the grain is sown in November till it is reaped and threshed in July, ready for making bread; grapes ripen from March to November before wine can be made; and a woman bears a child for nine months—the time it takes to make a man. Thus Spina was born to a new life after the natural period of gestation. But the symbolic analogy with food goes further. Bread is made from many grains, wine is made of many clusters of grapes; therefore each stands for unity. In Spina's mind, conditioned by the image of sacramental flesh and blood, bread and wine become emblems of brotherhood and love. It is easy to detect a whole series of other symbolic images throughout the novel. A careful reader will find them for himself, and he will certainly not miss the fact that Spina disguises himself in the vestments of a priest, or that Cristina is devoured by wolves. Silone's subtle art, however, never insists on allusions and hints; it remains vigorous and full-blooded in characterization, and concrete descriptions are made with a delightful mixture of humor and sharp observation. Even those who are not stirred up by the main themes of *Bread and Wine* or remain insensitive to Silone's moral search will always remember Sciatàp, who brought from America only one English word, "shut up," widely used by his boss in Mulberry Street, or the tragic Uliva, who is blown up with his clandestine laboratory of explosives, or Cristina, the victim of abstract spirituality, and her counterpart Bianchina, the lively victim of sensuality. All the protagonists that Silone brings onto the broad stage of his narrative are real; they exist in their own right, animated by the love and imagination of their creator. Not less alive and convincing is Pietro Spina himself. This "picaresque saint," as R. W. Lewis called him in his essay on Silone, has defects and failures; he is not an embodiment of virtue but an ordinary though highly sensitive and intelligent human being, animated by his thirst for truth. And truth is, in a way, the main protagonist of the novel; and the truthfulness of the characters, the sincerity of their ideas, and the authenticity of Silone's vision of existence and morality are precisely what make *Bread and Wine* such a genuine and ardent book. We trust it and we are deeply affected by it. No wonder that its artistry, depth, and veracity have gained it a lasting place among the outstanding specimens of modern European literature.

MARC SLONIM

# Selected Bibliography

## Other Works by Ignazio Silone

Fontamara, 1934    *Novel*
Mr. Aristotle, 1935    *Stories*
The School for Dictators, 1938    *Study*
The Living Thoughts of Mazzini, 1939    *Study*
The Seed Beneath the Snow, 1942    *Novel*
And He Hid Himself, 1945    *Play*
A Handful of Blackberries, 1953    *Novel*
The Secret of Luca, 1958    *Novel*
The Fox and the Camellias, 1961    *Novel*

# SIGNET CLASSICS from Around the World

☐ **THE MARK OF THE BEAST and Other Stories by Rudyard Kipling.** Fifteen of the finest of Kipling's timeless, vividly realistic tales, set in India, England, America, and Europe. Foreword by Roger Burlingame.
(#CD246—50¢)

☐ **THE TRAVELS OF MARCO POLO.** The enduring record of Marco Polo's thirty-five years of fabulous Eastern travel. Edited with an Introduction by Milton Rugoff.
(#CD97—50¢)

☐ **CANDIDE, ZADIG and Selected Stories by Voltaire.** Voltaire satirizes with ruthless wit the social, religious, and human vanities of his day in sixteen biting stories. A new translation with an Introduction by Donald Frame.
(#CP420—60¢)

☐ **RESURRECTION by Leo Tolstoy.** The Russian master's final work tells the story of a young man who seeks salvation by following into exile the girl for whose career in crime he was responsible. Translated by Vera Traill with a Foreword by Alan Hodge.
(#CQ403—95¢)

☐ **THE GOLDEN SERPENT by Ciro Alegria.** The lyric story of the Indian farmers of the Peruvian Andes, whose livelihood depends on the turbulent Maranon River. Translated with Afterword by Harriet de Onis.
(#CP114—60¢)

☐ **BOULE DE SUIF and Selected Stories by Guy de Maupassant.** A new collection of twenty-three short stories by the 19th century French master of this form. New translation by Andrew R. MacAndrew. Foreword by Edward D. Sullivan.
(#CD240—50¢)

**THE NEW AMERICAN LIBRARY, INC., P.O. Box 1478, Church Street Station, New York, New York 10008**

Please send me the SIGNET CLASSICS I have checked above. I am enclosing $_____(check or money order—no currency or C.O.D.'s). Please include the list price plus 10¢ a copy to cover mailing costs. (New York City residents add 5% Sales Tax. Other New York State residents add 2% plus any local sales or use taxes).

Name_____

Address_____

City_____State_____Zip Code_____
Allow at least 3 weeks for delivery